T0301113

Praise for *The House on Vesper Sands*

'A gloriously unorthodox confection, part Wilkie Collins, part Conan Doyle, with a generous handful of police procedural and a splash of Stella Gibbons's *Cold Comfort Farm*. Both disquietingly eerie and impossible to read without laughing out loud'   *Guardian*

'Tremendously good – and tremendously good fun'   *Observer*

'Brilliantly written, compelling and satisfying in so many ways. It demands to be read by a fire on a cold winter evening (but make sure the doors are locked before you begin). I only wish it had been twice as long'   *Irish Times*

'Some of the funniest lines of dialogue I've read in ages ... I liked *Vesper Sands* a lot. It's a clever Gothic mystery, evocative and meticulously faithful to its time and setting'   *Sunday Independent*

'A lush, shape-shifting Victorian mystery, full of ghostliness, humour and chiaroscuro with satisfying detective and romance flavours added to the batter'   *Irish Independent*

'A hugely entertaining read, spry of pace, funny, beautifully descriptive and satisfyingly sinister. A perfect book to read by winter candlelight'   *Sunday Express*

'O'Donnell writes wittily and well'   *Sunday Times*

'A compelling, darkly funny portrait of late Victorian London, and focuses on crimes with a supernatural flavour'
Observer, '50 Biggest Books of Autumn 2018'

'Engrossing ... The narrative canters from high-society soirees to East End tenements, infused with menace both earthly and supernatural'
Irish Mail on Sunday

'O'Donnell's talent truly shines ... his style can be likened to Charles Dickens on steroids and *The House on Vesper Sands* ... An expertly crafted and uproariously entertaining novel, spun by a writer approaching his peak'
Irish Examiner

'An immersive and darkly entertaining story of love, loss and lies set in a vividly realised Victorian London'
iNews, 'Best 19 Books for Autumn 2018'

'Not since Sarah Waters has a modern novelist played with Victorian language and mores with such wit and skill ... This mastery of voice wouldn't be half as satisfying, of course, if the story were not a properly ripping yarn'
Sunday Business Post

'A rollicking romp through the dark alleys and gaslit streets of Victorian London ... Spine-tinglingly spooky with a touch of Dickens and also properly funny'
Red Magazine

'Reading this terrific Victorian-set mystery was the most fun I've had in ages. It unfolds so thrillingly and cleverly. Do not miss'
The Bookseller, Editor's Choice

'A vivid and enjoyable romp'
Heat

'Moves effortlessly as the story needs between pacy dialogue, gripping drama and an elegiac, other-worldly mournfulness ... creates a deeply satisfying world, where tone and language and character combine to provide a rich, credible texture. A comic delight'
Associated Press

The Naming of the Birds

Paraic O'Donnell

WEIDENFELD & NICOLSON

First published in Great Britain in 2025 by Weidenfeld & Nicolson,
an imprint of The Orion Publishing Group Ltd
Carmelite House, 50 Victoria Embankment
London EC4Y 0DZ

An Hachette UK Company

The authorised representative in the EEA is Hachette Ireland, 8 Castlecourt
Centre, Dublin 15, D15 XTP3, Ireland (email: info@hbgi.ie)

1 3 5 7 9 10 8 6 4 2

A CIP catalogue record for this book is
available from the British Library.

ISBN (Hardback) 978 1 4746 1486 3
ISBN (Export Trade Paperback) 978 1 4746 1487 0
ISBN (Ebook) 978 1 4746 1489 4
ISBN (Audio) 978 1 4746 1499 3

Typeset by Input Data Services Ltd, Bridgwater, Somerset

Printed in Great Britain by Clays Ltd, Elcograf, S.p.A.

MIX
Paper | Supporting
responsible forestry
FSC® C104740

www.weidenfeldandnicolson.co.uk
www.orionbooks.co.uk

'As arrows are in the hand of a warrior; so are children'

Psalm 127:4

'Assuredly we bring not innocence into the world, we bring impurity much rather: that which purifies us is trial'

John Milton, *Areopagitica*

'Not one girl, I think, will ever look on the sunlight
of another time who has such gifts as this one does'

Sappho fragment 56 (trans. Anne Carson)

I

WHEN THE
BLOSSOMS CAME

February, 1872

One

The children are taken far away, after the fire, and they are given new names. One morning they are led from their dormitories and made to line up in the passageway. Maybe it is the first morning or maybe it is later. Everything is strange here and they have no hold on the days yet.

The girls stand on one side and the boys on the other. The nurse tells them to stand up straight, even those swaying on crutches. Stand up straight for the master, she says, though the lean man in the dark robes is bent over a book and seems to take no notice. The light is hung with dust, and the children are hushed when they cough. Some cannot stop. Their breathing is still bad.

When the children have taken their places, the master opens his book. When he speaks, he is looking out above their heads. This is a great day, he says, a momentous day.

He carries on, using other words they do not know. The children take no special notice yet. They twitch and shiver in their thin gowns. Their hands wander from their sides to worry at bandages, to puzzle over skin that has turned raw and unfamiliar. The places where they hurt.

They are to have new names, the master says. They are to be called after birds. He has dropped his eyes to look at them now, and he says this as if it is ordinary. He says it as if such names would come to them easily. The Asylum stood near a great forest – the Asylum was the place from before, the place they were taken from – but they knew no more of that forest than they knew of the sky. Most could not tell a sparrow from a thrush.

When one of the girls lets out a throttled sob, the nurse seizes her hand and slaps it smartly. The child goes white and rigid. She blinks into the air as if she cannot tell where this new pain has come from.

The master begins with the boys. He stands before each of them in turn and reads aloud from his heavy book. The words are slow and strange, like vows or last blessings. The boys keep their heads bowed, not raising them until they think they are meant to answer. Some are too dazed for that, so the nurse must take hold of their chins and point to show them what is wanted.

Of all the children, only one is paying close attention. She stands near the end in the line of girls. She is not the tallest of them, or the sturdiest. Her wounds are not the worst or the least. Her left hand is bandaged, and those burns are still blistered and weeping. Some of her cuts are bad, too – the ones from the glass – but she has peeled the rest of the dressings off. She wants to see the marks.

She is paying attention because that is what she does. It is easily overlooked, her way of watching and listening. She hardly recognised it herself, before the fire, but now she knows how much it matters. She keeps still, but not too still, letting her eyes rest nowhere. When a thought comes to her, she keeps it from her face.

The thought that comes to her now is that something here is waiting to happen.

The master has reached the last boy but one, a moon-faced creature whose mouth hangs open like a hinge. This time the master pauses before he begins. He thumbs the corner of a page, then he looks up from it as if in distraction. He turns his head a little and makes a sound with his tongue tip. A slow *tack, tack, tack*, like the dripping of a cistern.

The girl sees and hears these things slantwise, keeping her eyes unfixed. Outside the morning is changing, and the light from the high windows sharpens and pales. When she parts her lips, her breath shows and vanishes.

The master begins again. The words are the same as before, but now a quietness opens around them. When he comes to the end, it is a moment before the moon-faced boy looks up. His expression is all but empty.

'From this day,' the master says, 'your name is Magpie.'

The boy's mouth works, but he makes no answer. The nurse jabs him with a finger. 'Now you. Say your new name.'

The boy flinches, and a twitching starts up in his cheek. Half of his face is mottled with burns, and sheeny with some ointment that will do him no good. That skin will never mend right. At last he begins to speak, and as soon as he does, the girl knows the moment is now. She feels its parts snicking together like the workings of a clock.

The boy saying, *But sir.* The master closing the book, freeing a hand that curls behind a fold of black cloth.

The boy saying, *But sir, my name is Dan.*

The master taking a backward step, the movement almost dainty, then loosing his arm. The fierce snap of his sleeve, scything the quiet, then the next sound. Like a lead pipe against tender meat.

The moon-faced boy bucks on his heels. He draws a quick, hitched breath, disbelieving. Then he slumps to the floor like a dropped flour sack.

For a moment the master seems not to notice. He smooths out the pages of his book. Then he speaks quietly, as if to himself. 'I took a new name myself, when I came here.'

On the floor, the boy makes a thick snuffling sound. His hand is clamped to his face. The master's backhanded slap was to the unburned side, but the girl doubts it was meant as a mercy. His right hand was free, for turning the pages. It was less effort.

'I was something else once,' the master says, 'but now I am the Chaplain. The change was no great hardship.'

The Chaplain. It is another new word. The girl keeps her lips together. In secret, her tongue makes the ghost of its shape.

'Now,' the master says – the Chaplain says. '*Up. Again.*'

When he moves on to the girls, they try to be quicker with their answers. It doesn't come easily. Some are hoarse still, from the smoke. Some are just senseless with fright. One of the smaller girls loses hold of her bladder, but she is made to keep her place. She stands in her own spreading water until the words come out right. Then the nurse hauls her away.

The watchful girl is next in line. Near her left foot, the bright seam of piss creeps between the boards, but she is careful not to stir. She keeps herself straight, lowering her eyes but not her head as the Chaplain's black shape settles before her. The little girl's water smells of nothing, but the air about this man is laced with scent. It is a fine and shimmering fragrance, of the kind that comes from crystal bottles, but beneath it there is old sweat, musted cloth, male flesh. That butchery tang.

He fusses with the pages, but she knows he is studying her. He is watchful too, she thinks, in a way that suits his purposes. He is seeking out some weakness, but he has not sighted it yet. He is curious, or impatient, or something she cannot name. After a time, he gives an unsated grunt – like a man refusing thin broth – then he licks a fingertip and turns over a page.

The girl knows the words by heart now, though sometimes she must guess at their meaning. She lifts her eyes a moment before it is time, and at this he looks over her face, his lips gone tight. Either he finds no fault, or he finds one he means to store away.

He reads out her new name, and the sound of it is both strange and familiar. She has heard it before, surely, though she has never had cause to speak it aloud.

She says the word now, and her voice sounds new in her own ears. Sure and cold. Again the Chaplain gives her a look, and this time there is an edge of menace in it. She does not shrink from him. It is not that she feels no fear, only that the feeling does not seem her own. She is growing used to it, this gathering otherness in her nature.

On the night of the fire, while she was still trapped, her terror was like a living creature. Some writhing and eyeless thing that had squirmed from her gut to her throat, meaning to choke her from within.

But that was not what happened. That was not what the fierce creature did.

Her bandaged hand twitches. She masks the slip, stilling the movement in the folds of her smock. The Chaplain's eyes flicker to her side, too late to catch it. When they return to her face, there is something in them that she cannot read. He thrusts out his chin and turns away.

The girl keeps steady in her place, but now she lets her gaze drift just a little. The view from the high windows is empty save for one corner pane, where she can see a stark lattice of bare branches. She cannot tell what kind of tree it is, but on the road here she heard talk of a thaw. Perhaps it will soon be in leaf.

And birds. It will be filled with birds, she supposes. When the children pass by this window – the boy who is now called Finch, or the girl who is now Starling – will they look out and wonder which is which?

She will not catch sight of hers, she thinks. It is an uncommon sort of name, and it must be for an uncommon sort of bird. It would make no difference anyway. It belongs to her now, this name, not to a handful of glimpsed colours in some faraway wood.

She repeats the word inwardly, to practise it. She finds she has taken to it, though she is not quick to bestow fondness. She likes how its three parts slip and clink together. The beads and slivers of it touching, bright against dark.

It is hers now, this name. The others cling to their shreds of remembrance, but when she reaches back, there is nothing milky, nothing warm. Maybe there was once, but all of that is burned and blackened now. It is gone.

She was meeker before. She primped her coverlet and sang her hymns. She chirruped her prayers.

But then she crawled on her belly from a furnace. She drowned in black air, heaved up blood and cinders. She battered and bled herself free, on the night of the fire, and afterwards she fell into the deep and sharded dark. She took a secret with her, from the time before, but she took nothing else.

She needs nothing else because now she is something else. Now her name is Nightingale.

The place they have been brought to is called the Chapel, though they cannot tell why. It is not like any church they have seen. The masters dress in black, but Nightingale does not think they are clergymen.

There were clergymen who came to the Asylum, and they carried on as such men do. They talked of how the Lord looked kindly on children who accepted their lot, as if any child could do otherwise. The masters at the Chapel do not talk in that way, or if they do, they make it sound like a secret joke. Like words that might mean something else.

Their rooms at the Chapel are high up, like the lodgings of servants in great houses, but they look out on almost nothing. From the dormitories, part of another wing can be seen. Its windows are blind with dust, its gutters slack and broken.

From the schoolroom, the view is of a blank yard surrounded by walls of streaked grey stone. It holds shuttered outbuildings and a mossy trough. Scattered around it are ancient tools and lengths of chain. A barrow with a broken knee is slumped in the weeds.

They see no one come or go outside the Chapel, and they hear no clatter of work, no carried scraps of ordinary talk.

Out past the walls a lane twists away between pitted and scrubby fields. Beyond a distant rise there is a huddle of rooftops, the stump of a mean church tower. None of the children know the look of this country, but how would they? The Asylum took in no children above the age of seven, and most were no more than babes in arms. Between them they hardly remember a lane with a name. Only an inn with a black sign or a flower market, a run of cracked steps.

Nightingale does not recognise this country either, but she knows what it means. It is no one's remembered home, and it is grey and signless for a reason. They are nothing now, and they are nowhere.

Nightingale is not the only one who takes note of such things. Most of the others are still sunk in themselves. They crouch whimpering on their cots, or shuffle empty-faced from room to room. But the boy called Finch is different. She sees him slip away from the rest when he can. She sees him linger by the windows when he thinks no one is watching.

He is careful, but he is not careful enough.

She finds him in the schoolroom one afternoon. It is often empty, since they are not made to go to lessons yet. None of the masters have come today, and the nurse is in the musty, dog-legged room she calls the infirmary. She changes dressings there, and doles out bitter spoonfuls of tonic. She does it grudgingly, and she is content to be left alone.

Nightingale crosses the floor almost noiselessly – she goes about barefoot when she can – but at the last moment the boy turns and starts.

'Blast you for a sly little cat,' he says. His whisper is sharp but not spiteful. 'I near shit my breeches.'

The girl hesitates. Until now, she has kept a wary silence amongst the others. Amongst the boys, especially. They were kept apart at the Asylum, except for the tests and the strange games. She is not yet sure of their ways. When she can think of nothing else, she says, 'You're not wearing breeches.'

The boy glances down at himself. Like her, he wears a coarse linen gown. No doubt his underclothes are the same too: a thin, discoloured vest, drawers of scratchy wool. He looks at her, a wry twist to his chin. 'And you ain't wearing your boots. They'll clout you for that.'

The masters strike them all the time. Nightingale does not fear it especially – the fire left her scornful of lesser pains – but she will not say so. She will not show anything of herself without good cause. 'They'd have to see me. And they didn't say it was forbidden.'

His lips quirk. 'You wouldn't be sneaking about if it wasn't. And I might tell.'

'You won't,' she says. Her new voice has hard edges, and her hold on it is not yet sure. The boy, Finch, lifts one eyebrow. The other has been scorched away. His coppery hair is all patches and tufts.

'That right?' he says. He means, *And what would you do about it?*

She says nothing. She keeps her eyes level with his. Her altered nature is simple, in some ways. There is nothing she would not do.

'Well, you're a ready one,' he says. He looks away again, out beyond the walls. 'Dan reckons— Magpie, I mean to say. He reckons they've fetched us away to the highlands. Ain't never been up that way myself, but I don't know. You'd think there'd be more in the way of hills.'

She sees the joke, but it stirs nothing in her. Maybe that's gone too.

The boy lets it pass. 'I didn't say nothing,' he says. 'About the highlands, I mean. He ain't come right yet, old Magpie. Or maybe he weren't right before.'

This kind of talk comes easily to him. She wonders if she could learn the trick of it. She says, 'Not far enough.'

'Eh?' He turns again, this time in puzzlement.

'When they put us on the carts,' she says. 'After the . . . afterwards. We didn't come far enough. Eight hours, maybe ten. There was talk and noise on the roads, for half the night. That means we went south, through town. Then it was quiet again.'

Finch looks her over again, his face doubting. 'You was awake?' he says. 'The whole time? Most of us was dead to the world.'

Her eyes slide away. 'I couldn't sleep. I was thinking of—' From the dark of her, the images screech and skitter.

A ring of black keys. A plump face leeched pale with fright. *Unlock it.*

She waits, takes a careful breath. 'I was just remembering.'

He draws back by a fraction, as if wary of what he might have touched. His nod is hesitant. 'Aye, well. Eight or ten hours, then. That tells us something, don't it? And across town, for all to see? Queerish, that. I'd have struck out through the woods, up Essex way.'

She shakes her head. 'Walthamstow. Someone said to head for Walthamstow first. They followed a canal. Then I don't know. Someone said, *Less of that free talk.* Someone else said, *Yes, sir.*

She sees him wondering all she has wondered. The same who, what and why. Coming to the same nothing. 'So where does that leave us?' Finch says. 'You know your counties? No? Well, I suppose it don't make much odds.'

No, it doesn't. But like him, she cannot let it lie. She looks about the schoolroom, as it is now called. It was plainly put to some other use before. And until recently, she thinks. The air here remembers tobacco and boot polish. She has studied the scraps that cling to the paintwork, the remnants of maps, maybe, or duty rosters. Notices useful to men of the world.

Men who might say, *Less of that free talk.*

The picture of the Queen was not taken down, or the five brass clocks fixed in a neat row. Their faces are shadowed with dust now, and their hands are stopped at odd hours. On their plaques are words she does not know. Names or places, maybe. They make her think of salt air and summerhouses, of inkstands and beeswax.

HUDSON, WINDWARD, GOLD, DELHI, CAPE.

Scraps, nothing more, and her untutored guesses. *I was something else once.* She understands so very little. She chafes at it, as she does now at all disadvantages, all hindrances. There are things she must do. Things she must *know.*

'You all right?' says Finch. 'Got to be off somewhere?'

Something must have shown in her face. 'They said there would be lessons soon,' she says. 'That we would have to learn things. New things.'

'Aye, right. Can't wait to get back to your times tables, is it?'

She stares at him. 'You don't understand. These masters, they're not like the ones from before. The things they say, sometimes – we have to listen, when these lessons start.'

'Why?' he says. 'You reckon they'll say where we are?'

Nightingale presses her lips together. Perhaps it was a mistake, talking to this boy. 'I need—' She checks herself. 'We need to find things out, about this place, these people. And about—'

'About what happened?' He casts a glance at the door. 'And why we're here?'

She considers this quickly. What happened no longer interests her, or not in a way he could grasp. Those memories are sacred now, and she keeps them locked away. But why they are here – that interests her very much. He would not understand that either, or she could not explain it. 'Everything,' she says. 'We have to pay attention to everything.'

She watches him closely. It makes her uneasy, saying this much. If he shows reluctance or scorn, she will not speak to him again. But the look he gives her is solemn. He pushes away from the window and dusts himself down.

'Fair enough,' he says with a curt nod. 'I ain't much of a hand at the kings and queens, or them poems about villages. I'm good at nosing about, though. Might be able to work out the doors. And the stairs.'

At this she wavers.

'The doors the masters use,' he says, as if she were not following. 'They're crafty about it, but they ain't creeping in and out through mouseholes.'

'I knew what you meant,' she says. She hesitated for another reason. For Finch, it is simple. This place is dangerous. Find the doors. Find a way out.

For Nightingale, it is different. This place is dangerous, yes, but it does not frighten her. She understands now that this is simply the true nature of the world. Maybe it is her nature too that now lies bare. Maybe black threads always coursed through the tissues of her being.

If the danger runs deeper here, in the Chapel, it is because secrets do too. The masters here were something else once, or they are still. Men of the world. Ordering its doings, shaping the fates of its creatures.

But Nightingale is a creature of her own shaping, or she could be. She wants to pass through the masters' doors, just as Finch does, but she wants more than that. She wants to hold the keys.

She sees that Finch is waiting. 'So?' he says. 'You with me, then? We look for the doors, and while we're about it we try to work out where we are.'

With me. Her spine hardens. She is only with herself. But maybe that, too, is something she can learn. 'Yes,' she says at last. 'We'll look. We'll try.'

'Right,' Finch says. He moves to leave, taking care not to pass too close. 'I best slip off.'

'In a minute,' she says. It comes out unblunted again, but she ignores his look. This is important. 'If you do find something out, or if I do, we should be careful. They can't know what we know.'

His face twitches. 'Don't go telling old Magpie, you mean? Yeah, don't worry. I know how to keep it buttoned.'

She studies his face while she considers this. Maybe she looks for too long.

'What?' he says. 'Bad, is it? I don't look in the mirror that much.'

'No,' she says. It is true enough, though it is not what she was thinking of. He is not badly marked, compared to some, and he is not witless. She is glad of that, she realises, and not only for her own sake. She has seen how the masters look at some of the children. She has considered what it might mean. For some, she thinks, there will be dangers of a special kind. 'No, it's not bad. Thank you, Finch.'

He only shakes his head in amusement. 'Nightingale now, isn't it? Not Gale, for short?' His good eyebrow juts up. 'Or Nighty, maybe.'

She keeps her face still. These jokes are not something she wants to learn. After a moment he gives a complicated cough. 'Right, then,' he says. 'I'll be getting on.'

Nightingale has turned away already. She means to stay a little while, looking out into the oncoming dark. There are things she wants to think about. She hears Finch shift on his feet and, after he leaves, hears the small noises he makes on the way back to the dormitory. Quiet, but not quiet enough.

There are things she could teach him too.

Their lessons begin three days later, but there are no books in sight when they are called to the schoolroom. A blackboard has been propped in one corner. On a table beneath the picture of the Queen, a collection of oddments has been laid out.

A knife, jewelled and needle-like. A bulb of glass enclosing intricate workings. Some unknowable fruit, whose reds gleam like sealing wax or finger blood. Nightingale must scatter her glances carefully, filing with the others to the benches. She cannot take everything in.

A new master stands by the table, humming softly as he polishes a pocket watch. He is balding and plumpish, and his black clothing has a rumpled look. He appears absent-minded, but it is an appearance that Nightingale does not trust.

She is proven right when the last of the children enters. It is the girl they named Lark, a nervy and twitching creature who clutches her side as she scurries to her place. She was burned about her middle and the flesh there is still oozing. It shows sometimes, even through the dressing and her undershirt.

'Door.' It is the new master. His voice is low and rich.

The girl, Lark, seems not to hear. She winces as she folds herself into her seat, where she sits hunched and tense.

The master slips the watch into his gown with a sigh. He raps on the table with his knuckles, measuring the beats to his words. 'Child. The door.'

Two more beats. 'Close. It.'

Lark stares in confusion until the boy in the next seat nudges her. When she has crept to the door and fumbled it closed, she slinks back to her place like a whipped pup.

'Dear me,' says the master. He comes to the front of the table and rests his haunches on its edge. 'It is as well I didn't bid her wind the clocks. We might be here until Easter.'

He waits, as if he expected laughter. As if that were possible here.

'I am the Choirmaster,' he says, adjusting himself. 'Or that is the name I have taken. I am not here to tutor you in scales and cantatas. No ear for such things, sad to say. The other masters will give you lessons of a practical kind, since the day will come when you are called upon to do practical work. But my lessons will be . . . well, let us say that they will be of a miscellaneous character.'

He gives a satisfied sigh, his hands joined above his belly. Then he reaches behind him and takes up the strange-looking fruit. It is a deep, burnished red, topped with a ragged little crown.

'Yes,' he says. 'Miscellaneous subjects. Exotic subjects, sometimes. Like this fine specimen. Who can tell me what it is called?'

The room falls silent. Children lower their heads and shift in their seats. At the Asylum, in the weeks after Michaelmas, they were given slices of apple on Sundays. Once, after a garden party given by the governor, a girl called Kitty Fellowes claimed that she had stuffed half a dozen strawberries up her sleeve and eaten them in secret. She turned out her sleeve to show the pink stain.

Nightingale remembers staring. She wanted to tear away that sleeve and hide it. She wanted to suck it white.

'No one?' says the Choirmaster. 'Well, never mind. It is a pomegranate, or a wine-apple to those who know no better. It is perfectly wholesome, but to the Greeks it was the fruit of death. The goddess Persephone had a fondness for its seeds. She would gorge herself on them, though she knew it was forbidden, and she was made to pay the price. For each seed she ate, she was obliged to pass a month in the underworld. In hell, that is to say.'

He weighs the fruit in his palm, plumping up his lips in a show of thoughtfulness.

'Whereas we Christians – you are all good Christian children, yes? Well, speak up.'

Sensing surer ground, three or four of those nearest the front answer in dutiful murmurs.

'There you are,' he says. 'Very commendable, I'm sure. But wouldn't you rather be pagans, like the Greeks of old? Think of it. For our sins, we are packed off to hell for good. But for theirs, a reasonable bargain could be struck. Three pomegranate seeds, their gods would say. Shame on you, you greedy scamp. But you might have done worse. Call it three months down below, then back in time for the fine weather. That seems a reasonable sort of arrangement, wouldn't you say?'

He spreads his hands and scans the children's faces. Some look uncertain, fearing that they are being tested. And they are, Nightingale is sure. She just doesn't know how yet.

She watches and listens. She isn't trying to grasp everything, isn't straining after every difficult word. She lets the master's talk sink through her, feels it settle like silt.

The Choirmaster sighs and returns the pomegranate to the table. 'The sin of gluttony,' he says. 'One of the seven deadly sins, the churchmen tell us. Wrath, that's another one. Drives men to acts of violence. Not that it takes much, mind you.'

He picks up the glittering knife, holding it out for them to see. The handle is threaded with silver and studded with pale blue stones. The blade is perhaps eighteen inches long, and oddly narrow. It looks precious, but more than anything it looks dangerous. Some of the children squirm and look away. They are carrying hurts, all of them, and some of those hurts are fresh.

'You may rest easy,' the master says, not quite kindly. 'I told you – you will not get your practical lessons from me. Now, this dagger – it is prettily made, is it not? It is also very sharp indeed. However—'

Shifting abruptly, he slams the edge of the blade into the fruit. Benches rattle as children jump in their seats, but the blow does little damage. The fruit is still whole, though the knife has bitten into the rind. The Choirmaster frees it and holds it upright.

'What's this?' he says. 'The old fool boasts of his sharp dagger, yet it is hardly fit for tableware. Ah, but wait.'

With his free hand he picks up the fruit again. He tosses it into the air and, with the deftness of a conjurer, guides the point of the blade into its path. They connect with an exact little thump, and when the Choirmaster holds out the knife again, the pomegranate rests halfway down the blade, pierced clean through.

'A dagger,' the master says. 'But a dagger of a particular kind. A stiletto, to be exact, which is used for stabbing and not slashing. Not for wounding, that is to say, but for killing.'

He whips his wrist back to the table. This time, breached from within, the fruit splits neatly in two. Its glistening halves are chambered, and each chamber brims with dainty garnet beads.

'*Killing*, mark you,' says the Choirmaster, stepping out again from behind the table. 'Killing, not murder. Murder is a sin too, of course, but killing? That's just a job, surely. Ask any soldier. Now, then. Let me see if I can tempt you.'

He approaches the nearest bench, where the boy called Wren is cowering. 'Here, boy. Pluck out a few of these seeds.'

Wren looks doubtful, but he scrabbles at the innards of the fruit. The seeds are slippery and clinging, but with effort he gouges out a jewelled clump and captures it in his fist.

'Very good,' the Choirmaster says. 'Don't gobble them up just yet. Hold onto them for now.'

He shuffles about the schoolroom, pausing before each bench to repeat the exercise. Many of the children fumble just as Wren did, but the master does not scold them. If anything, their struggling seems to please him.

When Nightingale's turn comes, she has learned from the others. She works a single seed from its chamber with her thumbnail, sliding it delicately onto her upturned palm.

The Choirmaster lingers over her. He has taken up his soft humming again. 'You are the last but one,' he says. 'You might help yourself to more.'

Her eyes graze his face. He has the lips of a fat man, lush as innards, and at odd moments his glazed jowls twitch. Something has inflamed his interest, or his appetites.

Nightingale shakes her head. A simple *no*, not insolent. She thinks she has guessed how this game will play out. She has given thought to her part in it.

The Choirmaster sighs pertly, like the governor's daughter used to do when she was exasperated with her kitten. He moves on to the last bench.

When he returns to the front, he tosses aside the empty husks and sets out another of his curiosities. It is some intricate machine, with clockwork wheels set between flutes of milky glass. He begins explaining its purpose, just as if the last twenty minutes had been forgotten.

Some of the children show their confusion, glancing from the master to the seeds cupped in their palms, but Nightingale is unconcerned. She follows along, just closely enough. The machine is called an electrotome, the Choirmaster says, and it produces a spark quite as bright as lightning. He cannot induce it to do so today, so he fills the time with preening talk.

Conductivity, unlike charges, resistance. Nightingale examines the words only lightly before stowing them away.

What she must do, she thinks, is learn to pay two kinds of attention at once. There are glimmers on the rippling surface, but underneath there is a current. It is gentle, for now, but it is insistent. She thinks of the day they were given their new names, of how everything – the straying dust, the seeping piss, the silence – seemed drawn taut towards a gathering moment.

That was only a week ago, and she knows there is much more to come. There is a shape to all this that she has caught in glimpses, which swells and coils in search of its end. Today, another moment is approaching, but it will not be as coarse and unmistakable as the first. The Choirmaster will not knock some dazed and drooling boy to the floor. He is hungry, this man, but he is patient.

She must be more patient still, whatever her yearnings. There are many currents here, braiding and writhing in the depths. They could suck her under, down to the soundless dark, or they could carry her away.

She fingers the tiny capsule in her palm, learning its shape. The act feels intimate and sacramental. *A single moment.*

An hour passes, and outside, long shadows lean across the barren yard, yet still the Choirmaster talks. He talks because his own voice pleases him, Nightingale thinks, but that is not the only reason. He wants them lulled and unready.

He will have to try harder.

He holds up a blue bottle, and makes a dainty pantomime of drawing the stopper. It is laudanum, he says, which is at least a word they know.

Laudanum and *cholera*. *Childbed* and *penury*. The words that make orphans.

He takes a draught, then turns to tip the bottle at the Queen's portrait. 'Your health, ma'am.'

The girl called Robin gasps at this, which he notes with satisfaction. 'Laudanum, yes,' he continues. 'No doubt you have heard fearful tales. Great men reduced to squalor, virtuous brides stooping to depravity and what not. But think of the wounded midshipman, thrashing beneath the surgeon's saw in the whole of his senses. It is no transgression, surely, to grant him an hour's bliss. For you see, there is no sin so black that it is a sin in all cases.'

Robin's hand is still clamped to her mouth, but Nightingale lets nothing stir in her own face. This little performance needs no more of her attention. It is the stray words that she fixes on. For all the Choirmaster's high talk, he speaks just as readily of soldiers and midshipmen.

She glances at the clocks, and at the names that puzzled her before.

Hudson, Windward, Delhi.

Yes, there is a shape to all this. There are locked doors and there are keys.

'The blackest of sins,' the Choirmaster says. 'That reminds me. You are still clutching your pomegranate seeds, yes? You haven't forgotten poor old Persephone? Splendid, splendid. Well, I believe we shall conclude today's lesson with an exercise. Listen carefully, please. First, take up your seeds like so.'

He mimes the action, dipping his fingertips into his empty palm and raising them to his lips. Nightingale lifts the plump bead from her own hand. She turns it against the light, noticing its delicately scalloped surface.

'Don't they look delicious?' the master says. 'But before you taste them, I want you to imagine something.'

The moment is near now. It is coming.

'I want you to think of a sin, or perhaps more than one. As many sins as you have seeds, if you like. But whether it is one or half a dozen, you must *choose* your sins. They must be your own true desires, for which you would go willingly to the underworld.'

The children shift and murmur. They are doubtful and unsettled, and by now they are weary too. For once Nightingale lets her surroundings fade. She no longer needs to follow.

'And remember, a trifling sin will not do. You will not be consigned to eternal agony for stealing a hairpin. Your sins must be wicked and forbidden, or they are not sins at all. You must be truthful with yourself. You must say to yourself, yes, it would be vile and despicable, but if the chance came and I could be sure of escaping judgement in this life, then law and scripture be damned. In my heart of hearts, I know that I would do it.'

The Choirmaster draws out these last words, beating another slow measure on the table as he speaks. A colour has risen in his cheeks, and he licks his lips as he looks about the room. He pats himself down and brings out his watch.

'You will be given one minute to contemplate your choices in silence. When that minute has passed, you will swallow your seeds to seal your little covenant. Ready? Begin.'

In the hush that follows, Nightingale takes a moment to steady herself. It is not that she has put the night of the fire out of her mind. She escaped lightly compared to some, but her wounds are far from healed. The pain is so fierce sometimes that she wants to hurl herself from these high windows.

She knows that to the others she must seem cold and unnatural. She does not wake up screaming like they do. She does not clutch at the nurse's skirts while her dressings are changed, does not sob and plead for her mama. But she is not untouched, however she might appear. She lived through that night just as they did, and she saw things they did not.

She did things they could not. She did very bad things.

The black ring of keys, the clutching pink-white fingers.

She had no choice when the moment came, but that does not lessen the sin.

Unlock it.

She had no choice because she wanted to live, needed to live. She *burned* to live.

And it showed her how, the black creature. It was terrifying, the thing that burst from her in a torrent of inky vomit, but it meant her no harm. It caressed her burned flesh, bound her bleeding hand in its coils. It held her, soothed her, guided her.

She touches the palm of her bandaged hand, lets her fingertips graze the seed.

She knows the creature is not real. The fire left her changed, but it did not take her wits. It is not real, but it is true. The fire taught her things about the world's secret nature and her own. It is wound about her wrist still, unseen and unsleeping. It will never let her go.

Her sin is a dreadful secret too, but it is true and it is her nature. That is why she was ready when this moment came. When the Choirmaster told them to choose a sin, she had already chosen.

The moment has come.

The Choirmaster calls time, and afterwards he goes about the room, clapping his hands and cajoling the stragglers. Nightingale isn't listening. She cradles the seed on her tongue, taking care not to burst it. The taste is curious, a slanted kind of sweetness. She closes her eyes and swallows.

In my heart of hearts.

Her seed, her sin, her secret jewel. She carries it inside her now. She nurtures it in secret.

The boy called Finch proves as good as his word. He finds one of the masters' secret doors, though it does not come about in the way he imagined.

It begins when one of the children is taken to the oubliette. It is a place they have heard the masters talk of, and in a way that is meant to fill them with dread. The nurse has been known to mention it, when someone soils a bedsheet or pukes up a dose, but the nurse often repeats the masters' words and sometimes she gets them wrong.

It is different when the masters talk about the oubliette. The word itself is strange and unfamiliar, and these men know the uses of mystery. The masters here are not like the men who ruled over them at the Asylum, whose fine talk was meant to set them an example. They were taught to say 'lavatory' for 'jakes', because coarse speech told of a coarse nature.

But at the Chapel no one talks of their betterment. When the masters speak to them, it is often in a sly and shadowy language of their own, using words that cannot be unfolded in the ordinary way. 'Oubliette' is one of those words. When you say it to yourself, it makes you think at times of satin or ash, and at other times of swollen berries or rusted blades.

If the Chaplain has already taken his strop to a boy's legs, and if the boy commits some fresh offence, then the Chaplain might hiss it out: *Curse you for an imbecile and a whelp. If you cannot be improved by the lash, you will be cured by other means. You will learn your manners in the oubliette, do you hear me?*

They hear it at other times from the Dean, a greying man with a scooped-out face who is fond of humiliations but fonder still of beatings. He will call a boy to the front of the schoolroom if he gives an unsatisfactory answer, and he will mock the boy for his fidgeting, for his stammer, for his unwashed face, then he will send him to his fate.

Out of my sight with you, and wait at the lectern in the hall.

The lectern is where the Dean whips them. It is a word they know, and it is frightening enough on its own. But then the other word comes.

I will take my time over your strapping, and when that is done, I will send you to the oubliette, where the sun never rises. I will send you to the shadow chamber.

The shadow chamber. That is the Dean's own name for it, and no doubt he chose it for its fearsome sound. That is how words work at the Chapel, and how secrets work. A door is unlocked, and it opens into a deeper darkness.

The oubliette must be a dark place, then, but until Robin is taken away, it is a place no more real to the children than the belly of Jonah's whale or the Choirmaster's underworld. They have no notion of where it might be, though a boy named Dunnock says it is a prison, and a worse one even than Coldbath Fields.

It happens on a bright morning, the first since they arrived that seems touched with colour and gentleness. The nurse says it is a day for airing, and when she hauls up the sashes in the dormitory, they catch threads of birdsong and a surge of grassy sweetness.

After the bell is rung for breakfast, Nightingale lingers for a moment in the passage outside the dormitory. The lone tree is no longer bare, or not quite. It is softened about its fringes by smudges of pinkish white. It is a wild cherry, she is almost sure. She finds it consoling to look at, though she does not know why.

She stirs herself. The others have all gone ahead, and she doesn't like arriving last. It draws notice, even if it is only in passing. But it is not only that. From around the corner at the end of the passage, she has caught a glancing echo of raised voices.

The room where they take their meals is not like the refectory at the Asylum. It is called the wardroom, and like many parts of the Chapel it has the look of a place long occupied and hastily abandoned. Its panelled walls are hung with gentlemanly oddments: a painting of a stag; a case of medals couched in velvet; a ship in a bottle, bedded in merry waves of putty.

There is even a broad hearth, and on the nights when the fire was lit, the wardroom must have seemed a cheery place. Nightingale has pictured men standing about it in soft breeches and scarlet coats, tipping their tankards and whooping at bawdy stories. There is no laughter now, and the raised voices that she heard have subsided. Children are hunched over their tin plates, or crouched as if about to rise. Their eyes are fixed on Robin, who stands with her back to the chimney breast. Her cap is awry, spilling tangles of hair. Her pale cheek is streaked with ash.

She is clutching a poker.

At the head of the trestle table is the master known as the Proctor, a smallish man with spectacles who watches over them at mealtimes. He gives no lessons and is rarely heard to speak. He has risen from his place, but if he is shocked by Robin's conduct, he does not show it. His hands are clasped loosely at his back and his expression is weary.

Robin catches sight of Nightingale in the doorway. She stares, knuckles whitening as she tightens her grip on the fire iron. '*You*,' she says, her voice thick with desperation. 'You never talk to anyone. But you remember, don't you?'

Nightingale says nothing, only tilting her head to show that she is listening. And that she is curious. The Proctor sends her a quick glance, then turns away with a sorrowful shrug. 'Miss Robin,' he says. He is the only master who addresses them in this way. 'Miss Robin, you need only hand that to me and take your seat again. We will say that you became light-headed. The nurse will take you to lie down.'

But Robin is still glaring at Nightingale. 'I only said—' Her voice catches, and she makes a wet, retching sound. 'I only said it still comes up when I cough. It's been weeks now since the fire, and I'm still hacking up soot.'

She has been coughing into her sleeve, and she lifts it now to display a shadowy smear. So, that was how it began. Talking of the fire. It is a worse offence even than saying their old names.

'You see?' says Robin, her eyes going wide and accusing. They flick back to the Proctor. 'There it is, plain as day. And he says, dear me, no. You must say it some other way, child. You must call it by some other name.'

'So I did,' the Proctor answers mildly. 'We do not speak of that night, out of kindness to those who would sooner forget it. Or if we must, we call it by some gentler name. We talk of when the barley was brought in, or—'

'When the *barley* was brought in?' Robin stiffens, the poker jerking and swaying in her grip. 'You want me to lift this smock up and show you my back? You want to see where the skin still comes away in tatters? You think that happened when—when the fucking *barley* was brought in?'

Her agitation brings on a fresh fit of coughing. She bends her head to her shoulder, fighting to keep the poker upright in her hands.

'Indeed,' says the Proctor, seeming not to notice the foul word. He has edged away from the table, and he follows her movements as if puzzling out a conjuring trick. 'Or when the blossoms came, since we see the softer weather returning.'

Robin can no longer answer. Her coughing has eased, but she is breathing in quick and ragged gulps. She folds against the wall, a strand of discoloured drool clinging to her chin. The Proctor steps forward lightly, and she hardly resists when he wrests the poker from her shaking hands. He deposits it neatly into an empty scuttle.

He stoops, spreading his hands on his knees, to study her streaked and haunted face. He shakes his head gently. 'Such a spirited creature,' he says. 'And all to the good, but it is not yet the time. Perhaps you will come to see it, though. It is not what we are taking away. It is what we are offering.'

He hooks an arm under her and braces her at his side. Robin is limp, and can take only shuffling and uneven steps, but she does not resist as he guides her towards the door. Nightingale moves aside quietly, but she keeps close enough to miss nothing. It is just as well, for the Proctor's voice drops to a whisper as they pass.

'Better it happened here,' he says. 'For if the Dean had heard, well, I should not like to think. All the same, it will not do. You will think it a cruelty, but the falconer does not hood his hawk out of malice. No, there is really no other course. The oubliette, my dear. We must show you to the oubliette.'

It is the afternoon of the next day when Robin returns. She is brought to the schoolroom during one of the Chaplain's lessons. The Proctor is with her, shepherding her with murmurs and nudges to her seat. She does as she is bid, but she is ashen and speechless, her limbs as slack as a doll's. When she has taken her place, the Proctor watches her for a time, making delicate adjustments to his spectacles. His expression is regretful, or that is how he chooses to appear. Nightingale thinks he is satisfied.

Robin is not called on during the lessons that follow, and at supper time she is missing from the wardroom. Nightingale finds her in the dormitory, slumped and vacant on the edge of her cot. Robin is facing the wall, her gaze unfixed, but when Nightingale comes in, she looks away to the windows. The days are getting longer, and outside the evening sky is washed with colour. Lemon and milky rose, deepening to iodine.

But Robin isn't looking at the sunset, just looking somewhere else. Now Nightingale faces a difficulty of her own making. She does not shun the other girls, but she talks to them only when she must. It seemed the best course until now. They so rarely say anything useful. Was she to spend hours as they did, pinning up each other's hair and whimpering about their mamas and their market days and their cats that could near enough sit up and talk?

But in keeping apart, she has placed herself at a disadvantage. Robin has been to the shadow chamber, to the oubliette. Whatever she suffered, she is party to a secret, and there is nothing Nightingale now prizes above secrets.

'Would you—' Nightingale says, but it is all she says. She sees it is useless even before she speaks. Robin flinches at her first indrawn breath. There is no rancour in it, no malice. She flinches like a child who has not yet woken from the dream, like a child who still sees the monster.

Nightingale falls silent. Perhaps the girl she once was would have found a way. Would have known how to draw the other girl close, how to lay a hand over hers or stroke her neck just so. How to uncover her own hurt just enough, her own heart.

She drifts from the room. It is later, lying awake, when she sees her mistake. She could not comfort Robin because now she is the monster from the other girl's dreams. She is a creature sprung from some other shadow chamber, and she has no heart to uncover.

*

When sleep will not come, Nightingale walks the halls. At night there is only the nurse to keep watch, and the nurse has a fondness for gin. Passing the schoolroom, she goes still. A shape at the window.

'All right.'

Finch. His voice light and indolent. His voice natural.

She edges into the room, keeping her back pressed to the near wall. He is slouched against a window frame, watching her idly.

'What?' he says. 'I ain't going to bite. Who'd you think I was waiting for?'

She threads her way between the benches, halting when she is near enough for whispering. They have met here three times in as many weeks, but it hasn't altered her habits. She takes a moment to look him over. His hair is coming back, and his marks are now settling into scars.

'Getting handsomer, ain't I?' He tips up his chin. 'And look at you, full of the joys of spring.'

Nightingale says nothing as she goes on with her examination. She notices his bare feet.

'Yeah,' he says. 'Took your advice there. Reckoned it might come in handy. Specially now.'

She looks up, and this makes him smirk. He wants her to ask. 'Why now?' she says.

'Because now we got some idea where it is.'

'Where what is?'

He gives her a skewed look. 'Like you ain't got no idea. The *ooblet*, or however you're supposed to say it.'

'The oubliette. And how do you—how do we know?'

'Because that's where they took our Robin. And she weren't took far, was she? Got marched off yesterday and comes straight back today, no coat or nothing. So, it's down below somewhere. We just got to find out where.'

'But Robin isn't—'

'Isn't talking? Tried your charms on her, did you? Yeah, I know she isn't. Not to anyone. And you could hardly get her to button it before. So, we've got to find out for ourselves, ain't we?'

She is distracted for a moment. *Your charms.* Then her left hand clenches. It doesn't matter. None of that matters. 'One of us has to go too. Has to be sent there.'

'Yeah,' he says. 'One of us.'

She waits. It is always a kind of game, talking to Finch.

'Yeah, don't worry,' he says. 'I meant me. Be something to see, though, you swinging a poker. Effing and blinding about the barley.'

She thinks of saying something. She has done more than just clutch a fire iron. Why does she feel this with him, the urge to give up her secrets? 'It wouldn't work, doing the same thing again. They would know.'

'Course they would. So, I'll have to go one better, won't I.'

Nightingale thinks about this. 'They might not send you, even if you're clever. They might just give you a whipping.'

He gives her a testing look. 'What, you worried about me getting hurt?'

'No,' she says, and it comes out harder than she wanted. 'We get hurt all the time, all of us. But if they do send you, you might come back like Robin. You might stop talking.'

He looks down, thumbs the ripple of scars above his knuckles. 'You worried about that? Me not talking anymore?'

But she leaves without replying. It is easier, sometimes, when there is only one answer, and when it is true.

*

31

What Finch does is clever. First, he waits. He is quick in his talk and his gestures, but in this he shows patience. He waits nine whole days, which in this place seems an interminable age. Nightingale has counted the days since they arrived, and sometimes she doubts her tally.

At the Chapel, time thins out and stalls. They can hear no church bells here. No baker's boy clatters up on his bicycle at daybreak, and no lamplighter sways up a ladder at dusk. After a week, the other girls are talking of how Robin is like her old self. Her cough has eased, they say, and look at her sitting cross-legged with Lark, tying off hair bows or playing at cat's cradle. Nightingale thinks the other girls are mistaken. She thinks something is broken in Robin that can never be mended.

Then Magpie is taken away. The whispering begins on a Wednesday afternoon, after he has missed a whole day's lessons. He was in his cot that morning, the boys say, and nothing seemed amiss. But what sign might Magpie have given? He rarely spoke, having been so often jeered at or beaten for his clumsy words. The nurse no longer tended to his ruined face, and he wandered the halls trailing filthy rags of bandage.

By supper time everyone has heard the story, though no one can say where it came from. The masters took pity on him, someone swears, and he was fetched away to town to be set right by proper doctors. He might be gone for weeks, being in such a bad way, and wasn't that a turn of luck? Proper doctors meant mutton dinners and featherbeds and taking your ease out of doors. It is empty-headed nonsense, all of it, and maybe the children do not even believe it. Maybe something is broken in all of them.

If Finch is biding his time through all of this, he gives no sign of it. He is not distracted during lessons, and at mealtimes he still wrinkles his nose at the soup, still rolls his bread into pellets and flicks them into his mouth. He hides by showing himself. It is a skill that Nightingale studies closely.

He chooses a moment late in the afternoon, when the children grow restless and the masters are waspish and quick to find fault. Today it is the Dean who gives the last lesson, and for nearly an hour he has been talking about a war that lasted a hundred years. Afterwards, to show the others that he is still himself, Finch will say that he talked for a hundred years about a war that went on for an hour.

'So, what did King Edward forget?' the Dean is saying. 'What did he forget, while he was trailing his banner nearly to Paris itself, thinking himself the finest sovereign who ever sat a horse in a field? To be sure, he won us Calais, but what did he fail to do, hmm? Where should he— you, boy, what is that?'

Finch is half out of his seat, scrabbling desperately at the floor-boards, but he gives it up when he sees the Dean coming. He straightens, thrusting his hands into his lap. He looks stricken with dread. Perhaps he really is.

The Dean stands over him. 'Pick it up,' he says. 'Show me.'

Nightingale sees Finch's shoulder twitch, sees his jaw work as he contemplates what is coming. He bends and scoops something from the floor. The Dean snatches it away and turns it to the light. The master's sneer is almost joyous.

'A medal,' the Dean says. 'Some Romish charm. Is that what you were so anxious to hide, boy? Have we nurtured a papist viper in our bosom?'

'No, sir,' says Finch faintly. 'It ain't that.'

'Well, you were not hiding it for its worth, a shabby little trinket like this. Answer me now, why did you wish to hide it?'

'Sir, please, I can't—'

'You will *answer*, damn you.'

'Sir, it's just . . . it's just something I saved from the fire.'

The fire. The unsayable. Now Nightingale understands.

The Dean's face hardens. 'From the *what*?'

'Nothing, sir. I didn't mean nothing.'

'You may as well say it all, boy. Fire or no, you kept it for a reason. Speak up now.'

When Finch answers, he sounds near to tears. Perhaps he is. Perhaps some of this is true, or all of it. That would be clever too. 'My ma gave it me,' he says quietly. 'It were my father's, from when he was at sea. Saint John of something. Supposed to keep sailors safe. Didn't do much for Pa, though.'

'I am saddened to hear it. So, why give it to you, then? Surely she did not mean you to follow your father to sea?'

'No, sir. It weren't that. It was just . . .'

The Dean lowers himself carefully to his haunches, the better to examine Finch's face. 'It was just what?'

'That was my name, sir. From before, I mean. My name was John.'

It is late that night when Finch returns from the oubliette. He finds Nightingale in the schoolroom, where she has waited in silence since lights out.

'Oy, oy,' he says, catching sight of her. 'Couldn't sleep for worrying?'

'Worrying?' The thought had not occurred to her, but she thinks better of saying so. 'Yes, I was terribly worried.'

Finch looks tired and drawn, but this seems to amuse him. 'Christ,' he says with a quick shudder. 'Don't do that again. It ain't natural.'

She folds her arms about herself. 'So, pretending is natural?'

Finch shakes his head in weariness. 'Look, it don't matter,' he says. 'I got a lot to tell you. Had my work cut out, mind you. 'Cos the first thing they do is, they blindfold you.'

'The masters?'

'No, the Duke of Clarence and Mrs Flounce from down Garter Street. Yeah, the masters. Well, just the Proctor, really. He's the jailer, it seems like.'

'So, you couldn't see anything. You don't know where he took you.'

'Didn't say that, did I?' He settles back against one of the benches. 'You remember when you was little? Before you got took in, like?'

Nightingale takes a quick breath. The memories are almost nothing now. A scented heat, a flaring of colour, fingertips tracing a fine silver chain. She doesn't like to disturb them.

'I don't—' She breaks off. 'I was very young.'

Finch coughs into his knuckles. 'Right, yeah. Well, I was with my ma until I was coming up on seven. And round our way, you put the candles out as soon as the plates was scrubbed. You heard the cat scratching in the night, or you needed your pot? You had to just get on with it, didn't you? So, it comes natural, finding your way in the dark.'

Nightingale nods. 'I prefer the dark. It makes things simple.'

'There you are, then. So, yeah, I know where I was taken, or near enough. And the *oob-let*, or however you're supposed to say it?'

'The oubliette.'

'Right, yeah. Well, it ain't far. It's here, in the Chapel. There's a hidden door, right enough, and it ain't just the way to the oubliette. It's how they come and go, to their quarters or whatever. And to the outside.'

Nightingale feels herself stiffen. 'The outside.'

'Ha,' says Finch. 'I knew that'd perk you up. Don't get too excited, though. It ain't like I could draw us a map. Besides, you ain't heard the rest of the story.'

Nightingale doesn't answer. *The outside.* The thought flickers and dances, like a moth behind gauze. She doesn't want to let it out. She doesn't want to touch it.

Finch rubs his hands together. 'So, this secret door. Beyond that was just a corridor, far as I could tell, with another door at the far end. Felt the handle when I put my hand out, before the Proctor smacked it away. Not that way, boy, he says. Only I've already heard the voices from the other side. Sounded a bit rowdy and all. My brothers are at table, says the Proctor, and I fear some are already in their cups.'

'Their quarters,' Nightingale says.

'That's what I reckon,' says Finch. 'And they ain't exactly living like monks. Anyway, that was as near as I got. Come along, young man, says the Proctor, and we was off again. Down some steps, along another passageway, through another door, then down again. That's when I caught the change in the air. Mind how you go now, says the Proctor. This tower is old, and I'm afraid we must descend a little way.

'So, we start down these winding steps, me with one hand glued to the wall on account of the blindfold. And I tell you what, he weren't joking about the place being old. You know your bricks and stones? No? Well, there was a kiln down the end of our lane, and sometimes I'd get thruppence for helping out with the rubbing. Now, them bricks was your ordinary yellow stock, same as you see all over London. But the walls of that tower? Can't say what the stone was – granite, maybe – but I know it was old. It ain't the spalls so much, it's the places where it's worn smooth.'

Nightingale presses her lips together. 'Why are you telling me this? Is it important?'

He casts his eyes up. 'Boring you, am I? You're the one who said we had to find out whatever we could. And yeah, I reckon it's important. These fuckers carted us off to some big pile in the middle of nowhere, and it turns out bits of it have been standing since King Arthur was a lad? You don't think that might tell us something?'

She ponders this. 'It's England. Everything is ancient.'

Finch shakes his head, impatient. 'You ain't catching on. A big old place like this, out in the country – ain't everyone got the run of a place like this. Think about it.'

'The masters are men of a certain station,' she says. 'We already knew that.'

'Men of a certain station?' He stares at her. 'Nightingale, we been shut up in this place for nearly a month. You seen anyone poking about? You seen anyone even turn a cart up the lane? That takes more than men of station. It takes—'

In his agitation he makes to seize her by the shoulder. Too close, too sudden. In her next conscious moment, she has snatched his wrist from the air, is gripping it hard enough to leave pale and spreading marks.

When she releases him, he draws away, nursing the hand. 'Go easy, will you? I got burns there.'

'I'm sorry,' she says. 'I can't help it.'

He shakes his head, but his scowl is fleeting. 'You really can't, can you? Good job I didn't try for a kiss.'

She cannot think what to say, and in the next moment he is laughing. 'Christ, your face. It's all right, I ain't serious. I reckon I'd best get on with this story, eh? So, yeah, the winding steps. When we get to the bottom, the Proctor brings us up short again. Says I'm to stand where I am while he attends to something. Don't stir from that spot, he says, which means there's something he don't want me noticing. I don't want to waste my chance, so I stand stock-still like a good boy. Stock-still suits me fine anyway. I might have a blindfold on, but I can hear as good as any terrier.

'He must have fetched the key out nice and quiet, but I know what he's at as soon as he starts fidgeting with the lock. And with this door he ain't got a hope. Sounds like half a ton of solid oak, on hinges that ain't seen grease for a thousand years. Then I catch the change in the air. Good, honest fresh air, mind, with that lovely sweetish taste you get after rain.

'I had to catch hold of myself, I don't mind telling you. One whiff of that and I was itching to make a break for it, blindfold or no. But I told myself, I said, that Proctor ain't nobody's fool. He ain't gone and stood you right next to the front door. And sure enough, I start piecing it together. Worked it out from the sounds, mostly. Little echoes, see. Little splashes of noise like you get under arches or railway bridges. Reckoned we'd come out at the base of that tower, and that door must've opened onto a coachyard or some such. Anyway, the Proctor must have caught sight of someone out there, because soon enough I hear him giving some bloke a talking to.

'I couldn't make much of it at first. The Proctor was trying to keep it quiet, on account of I was nearby, but you could tell this other fellow was getting his dander up. The Proctor starts cursing him for a slovenly whelp and a shabby whoreson and worse besides. What do you make of that, then? Not the sort of language you'd expect from the Proctor, is it?'

Nightingale takes care over her words. 'Finch, this is— some of this is very interesting, but we haven't much time. The oubliette. Tell me about the oubliette.'

Finch cocks his head. 'Well, excuse me,' he says. 'Excuse me, I'm sure. Here I was thinking you might be pleased, seeing as how I put myself in harm's way to find all this out. Sorry for keeping you, Miss Nightingale.'

She tries again. 'I'm sorry,' she says. 'I say things the wrong way sometimes. I *am* the wrong way. Maybe I can learn not to be. But there isn't time now. It isn't safe. Do you understand?'

But something in his face has hardened. 'I'll tell you what I understand. I understand that there's things in this life I can figure, even if I have to work at it, and there's things I ain't meant to. I reckon maybe you're one of them other things. I'll tell you something else too, while we're about it. You're a rare sort, no question about that, but when you get right down to it? I don't think you can figure yourself any better than I can. Still, here I am talking to you. Come straight here to tell you everything even though I'm aching from arse to tit and all I want is my bed. You ever think about why that is?'

Nightingale looks away.

'Yes,' she says quietly. 'I have wondered why. I'm not very nice.'

She sees Finch's jaw working. 'No,' he says, 'you ain't. You ain't bad, exactly, but you ain't nice. Probably ain't quite right in the head neither. I swear, sometimes you scare me worse than the fucking masters. But you understand this place, even if you can't put it into words. You understand it, deep down. I talk to you because you're the only one who might be able to make sense of it all. Maybe not now, but some day. You'll remember what old Finch told you, and you'll know what to do about it.'

'I don't—' For a moment she cannot look at him. 'I don't know what you mean.'

He gives a bitter little laugh. 'I thought you didn't know how to pretend. You know what I mean, all right. You said it yourself. It's dangerous, this place. There's a smell I can catch sometimes, like in the schoolroom when someone's got a whipping coming. Couldn't place it for ages, but it came to me the other night. I had an uncle when I was little, used to breed up fighting dogs. Kept them in kennels that looked like the pits of hell, and I'd have to hold the bucket while he was blooding them with butcher's scraps. That's where I first smelled it, and I knew it weren't just the guts or the sweat or the dog shit. It's this ancient reek, and it catches you somewhere way down deep. It's *fear*, Nightingale. It's fucking *terror*. We ain't got a clue what they brought us here for, or not so we could put a name to it. But in our bones, in our blood? We know it like them dogs knew it.

'So, yeah, I get half a chance, I'm running and I ain't looking back. I ain't kidding myself about the odds, though. Not for me, not for any of us. You, though, you're another story. No, don't say nothing. Don't pretend it ain't true. Give me that much, all right?'

Nightingale cannot tell what she feels, only that for once she does not keep it from her face. 'Yes,' she says, after a hesitation. 'All right.'

Finch studies her for a long moment, then he clears his throat gruffly. 'Good,' he says. 'That's good. I'll tell you about the oubliette, then, though there ain't nothing much to tell. It's down in the foundations of that tower. The Proctor took the blindfold off for that part. Said I'd kill myself otherwise, the steps are that steep and narrow. At the bottom he lights a lantern, though it ain't like there's much to see. A bare stone cell with a hatch set into a pit in the floor. The Proctor hauls it up and says, "Climb into that hole like a good lad." Then he closes the hatch over your head and that's it. Night-night, sleep tight.'

'The shadow chamber,' Nightingale says.

'Bit of a dressed up name for it, if you ask me. I mean, it ain't a *nice* hole. It's pitch dark down there, right enough, and dripping with damp. Cramped, though. Can't hardly sit up without knocking your head. Little bones strewn about, from a rat most like. No live rats, though, 'cos what are they going to eat? You can see why poor old Robin didn't like it much. Me, I just curled up and went to sleep.'

The falconer does not hood his hawk out of malice. Oh, but this one does.

'Yourself,' she whispers. 'They lock you inside yourself.'

'You reckon? Well, maybe it's nice, being inside me. Anyhow, that's the oubliette. Ain't much of a laugh, but there ain't much else to say about it either. I still reckon the first bit was more interesting, when the Proctor was outside talking to that other bloke. Couldn't make much of it, mind, except that I wasn't supposed to hear it. At first I thought the lad was just a porter or some such, because the Proctor was on at him about dumping the oat sacks on the damp flags.

'But then he starts up about pouches, and it takes me a while to work out what pouches he's on about. Then he says something about the letters getting soaked, and I twig that it's mail pouches. They were to be entrusted to Mr Rickard alone, the Proctor says, so what's this chap doing with them in the first place? Well, now the other fellow gets his nerve up. Says Mr Rickard come off his horse and done his ankle in. Weren't no wonder, he says, with the roads down here no better than ditches.

'Well, the Proctor don't like that one bit. He says, "You listen to me, boy. If you wish to see the roads improved, I will gladly send you to split stones at Holloway. You walk abroad at our pleasure, and you would do well to remember it. The Chancellor's letters are for my hand or the Dean's, do you hear me? Handle them carelessly again and you will suffer a worse mishap than Mr Rickard." That's what he said, cool as you like. Put the fear of God in *me*, never mind the other fellow. And here I thought the Proctor was a mildish sort of cove.'

'He's not kind,' Nightingale says without hesitation. 'His cruelty takes longer, that's all. Did they say anything else?'

Finch yawns and stretches. 'Not much, no. Just something about getting rid of the kitchen scraps.'

Nightingale grips the cuffs of her nightgown. She holds herself carefully. 'What about the kitchen scraps?'

'Eh? I don't know, something about digging a proper pit for them. I was more interested in them oat sacks and letters. Means there's somebody coming and going that we ain't seen. Somebody with a cart, maybe. What do you reckon?'

A proper pit. 'Please, Finch. Try to remember.'

'Yeah, all right. Give me a minute. The Proctor says, "You disposed of the kitchen scraps, yes? From this morning?" And the other chap says he did, and then he starts on about how it near killed him, all that digging. So, the master cuts him straight off. Says he'll be out to inspect the work first thing, and if he finds any fault, he's putting this fellow straight in the same hole.'

'But why would they be burying kitchen scraps in the first place?'

'Well, I don't know, do I? Maybe the place is coming down with rats. But what do you reckon about them deliveries, eh? Because I was thinking, right. I reckon I could find that door again, some night when it's quiet. You game for that? Here, Nightingale – you asleep on your feet or what?'

She cannot think what to say. How does he not see it?

From this morning.

It was this morning when Magpie was last seen. And all those silly stories about doctors and featherbeds – hadn't they begun in the wardroom? No, the Proctor is not kind, and he lets the children prattle for a reason.

A sack of scraps.

She wants to be wrong about this. She sees him now, Magpie, slack-faced and aslant at his bench. She sees him wandering the hallways as if lost, sees him mumbling and plucking at his soup-stained sleeves. A boy of meagre gifts, and not made for any of this.

'Nightingale?'

'I'm all right. I'm thinking.' She can't tell him, not now. Maybe not ever. Finch is bright, and he has proved himself able and courageous. There is goodness in him, she thinks, though perhaps she is no judge of such things. But he is the same boy he must have been before the fire. He was not made new, was not made ready. 'We should go, I think. We've stayed too long.'

'But we'll talk again, won't we? We got plans to make now. Tomorrow night, maybe?'

'Plans to make, yes.' Finch is right. He should run from this place, from these men. But Nightingale cannot run, not now. She sees what she must do now. She has chosen her sin. She turns to leave. 'It's late. It's getting late.'

'Here, hang on a minute. Nightingale, wait.'

She pauses, not looking back. 'Finch, I . . .' She tries for the words, her fingertips skimming the door jamb. But the words are never right. 'I'll remember, like you said. I'll remember.'

Back in the dormitory, she slips noiselessly beneath the covers. Turning and settling, she bares her scarred arm to the elbow, cradles it close. It has soothed her, this little ritual, on the days when she is struck with a hazel rod or made to bathe in lye and freezing water.

It is no comfort now. She finds that she is weeping, and that is new and strange. She has no ritual for it. If only Finch were here to see it. For once, he might think her ordinary and natural.

But it doesn't matter. She will sleep soon, and in her dreams she is never sad or angry, never hurt or afraid. In her dreams, her transformation is complete. She is the black creature, burst glistening from its husk. Sometimes it has great shadowy wings, this creature, and sometimes a sleek pelt of charcoal fur. But it always has teeth and claws.

Tonight, she thinks, it will be in no hurry. It will scale the walls of the Chapel idly, and it will laze on the slates long enough to lick itself clean. But soon it will remember, just as it always does. It will remember what it is for, and it will rise and arch itself under the perfect cusp of that clouded moon. Then it will stalk away to hunt.

II

SPEAK THEIR NAMES

March, 1894

Two

Inspector *Henry Cutter* of Scotland Yard was in an unconvivial temper. The morning was bleak, and for well above a minute he had stood hammering at the gate of a gun merchant's yard. Whatever the exact interval, it was far in excess of his natural tolerance. When the gate was at last hauled back, he had just announced to Sergeant Gideon Bliss – who had at that moment stooped to retch – that he would shortly climb over it and scald some blackguard's arse.

'Quite right, sir,' said Sergeant Bliss, staggering a little as he tried to right himself. Gideon was keenly attentive to his superior's moods, since they regulated most aspects of his own existence. He had entered the Inspector's service only thirteen months before, and he feared he had done little since then to elevate himself in anyone's estimation. Inspector Cutter's opinion of him, certainly, remained unremittingly dismal.

'Quite right,' he said again, though it was a feeble sort of response. Thankfully, the Inspector took no notice, so Gideon turned his attention to the man at the gate.

The gun merchant was a squat and leering fellow with a piratical manner of dress. His thinning locks were in wild disorder and under a much-abused leather greatcoat he wore a pair of burnished pistols, each as long as a chair leg. The butt of a heavier firearm jutted from above his shoulder, and an assortment of hilts and scabbards protruded from other regions of his person. He appeared, indeed, to be carrying a considerable portion of his stock-in-trade, which perhaps accounted for his late appearance.

'There he is!' the gun merchant called out to Cutter in greeting. 'The only straight copper left in London. And I should know. It was me slung a bribe to the other cunt.'

But the Inspector had already shouldered past him, intent only on regaining his lost momentum. Even in his more pacific moments, of which there were not many, he was a man of notably vigorous gait. Gideon had rarely seen anyone match his pace who was not on horseback or a bicycle. And when he was agitated, as in the present case, he made his way much in the manner of a mail train crossing the moors, and with similar consideration for all that surrounded him.

'You must pardon us, sir,' said Gideon, straightening with some effort but keeping his handkerchief to his mouth against the foulness of the air. 'I fear the Inspector is preoccupied. You are expecting us, I believe. I am— *mluh!* Forgive me. I am Sergeant Gideon Bliss.'

'Sweet Virgin,' said the man at the gate, clamping a gnarled hand to his breast. 'There's a tender intonation for you. I haven't heard the likes of it since I sheltered one night at a convent in Tarragona. You ever been down that way?'

'No, sir,' said Gideon, who did not welcome the observation. Before becoming a policeman, he had been an unpromising student of divinity at Cambridge. The habits of speech he acquired there had by no means eased his passage in his new calling. 'No, sir, I have not.'

'No? Here, step in, Sergeant, so as I can bar this gate again. Prying eyes, and all that. Well, I'll say this to you, Sergeant Fish – Josiah Pruitt, by the by, formerly of Her Majesty's Navy, or the nearest thing. In an unofficial capacity, as you might say. I'll say this to you about nice soft-speaking voices. You can be no judge of them, sir, until you've heard the barefoot novices of Tarragona. You ain't supposed to hear them at all, mind you, on account of their vows, but there's such a thing as ways and means. And when you do, oh dear me. Like having your parts brushed, I swear to Christ, by the wingtips of a dove. You go along in, that's the lad, while I see about locking up.'

The yard of Mr Josiah Pruitt, gun merchant, occupied a narrow and dismal sector of the wharfside at Millwall, overshadowed to the north by the vast gable of a cordage works and to the south by a warehouse whose purpose was not advertised, but from which arose the potent stench of putrefaction that had assailed Gideon even a hundred yards from the gate. Now that he was alongside it, he could draw breath only in cautious doses, fearing not only that he might disgrace himself by vomiting but that his pulmonary apparatus might suffer some permanent injury.

'Dear *mluh!*' he said, bending again to retch. Pruitt had turned from the gate and paused now in appraisal, screwing up his leathery features in a pitying grimace. 'Dear me,' Gideon repeated, by way of clarification.

Pruitt worked a plug of chewing tobacco from his cheek and, having squinted to gauge the distance, ejected it with a violent plosion into a brazier fully fifteen feet from where he stood.

'Bat shit!' he exclaimed, smacking his hands together.

Gideon dabbed at his mouth as he rose. 'Forgive me, sir?'

'Bat shit,' Pruitt repeated, clapping Gideon's back to urge him onwards. 'That's what you can smell, since you seem to have took notice. Come on, there's your guvnor halfway up the yard already. Stride on him like the Queen's horse in the Gold Cup, bless him. Bat shit, aye. From Peru, don't you know? Off the coast of Spain.'

Gideon started forward a little unsteadily, Pruitt's arm slung now about his shoulder. It was a moment before he ventured to speak. 'Peru, if I remember correctly, is in the Americas. But perhaps I am mistaken. My training was not in cartography.'

Pruitt gave him a sidelong look. 'The Americas, that's right. Still off the coast of Spain, though, ain't it, or their lads wouldn't have found it with ships. You're a schoolmastery little fucker, ain't you, for a beanpole copper? What was it again, Sergeant Fizz?'

'Sergeant Bliss, sir,' said Gideon. 'It is an uncommon name, I fear, and quite often remarked upon.'

'So you reckoned you'd see about some shooting lessons, that it? Had it up to here with all that remarking?'

Pruitt seemed entirely in earnest, though Gideon was not always confident in such judgements. 'Ah,' he said. 'Not exactly, sir. The lessons were the Inspector's idea. He believes I must have a broader formation in policing. He is a strong advocate of practical forms of learning.'

'That right?' Pruitt glanced at the Inspector, who stood waiting now before a low barrier formed of planks and trestles. Beyond it the yard widened to a swathe of littered scrubland that stretched almost to the river's edge. 'Most coppers don't get barkers, though, do they? Even sergeants with uncommon names.'

'Forgive me, sir, I'm afraid I don't . . .'

'Barking-irons.' Pruitt indicated his own guns. 'The brass at the Yard don't exactly hand them out like pamphlets, far as I know.'

'No, sir,' Gideon agreed. 'There is a certain reluctance, on the grounds of public safety. However, they are issued to those officers whose duty might bring them into harm's way, and whose discretion can be relied up— *mluh!*'

Pruitt lifted his face and gave a great whoop of laughter, clapping Gideon's back again as he did so. 'Harm's way, he talks about, then one whiff of knock-off manure and he near enough needs a priest. Here, boy, what you're doing wrong, see, you're sipping it like a glass of Madeira. Never get a head for it that way. What you do, right, you haul in a lungful – through the nose, mind, like this. Then bottle it up and hold it.' Gideon attended as he demonstrated, though his eyes were now streaming.

'Go on, then,' Pruitt said, releasing his breath at last. 'Same as I did.'

Gideon readied himself without conviction, making loose fists at his sides.

'Big swalley through the nose, then stop her up.'

He forced himself to comply, though the fetor felt as thick in his throat as a curl of blood pudding.

'That's the way, boy, get it in you. Don't stop or you're done for. That's it, that's it. And then, when you're full to the gills—' Without warning, Pruitt clamped one scabbed and brownish hand over Gideon's mouth, reaching about him and pinching shut his nostrils with the other. Gideon bucked and struggled, but Pruitt had braced him hard against his chest. 'Hold it now, hold it. Got to give it a minute, see, or the pipes won't coat up.'

Gideon scrabbled at Pruitt's forearms, but he found them as unyielding as spars of oak. He scuffed his heels wildly, hoping to attract Cutter's attention, but the Inspector was hunched intently over a bench arrayed with pistols. He gave up the effort, his strength beginning to desert him.

'And out with it!' Pruitt exclaimed, releasing Gideon abruptly and stepping smartly away. 'All out, then puff up your bags again, quick as you like. Ten bob says it'll go down like honey.'

Gideon could hardly do otherwise, being perilously starved of breath, but he was amazed to find that Pruitt was right. He heaved in one grateful lungful after another, and without the least ill effects. He might have been Jonah himself, tasting sweet air after three days in the belly of a fish.

'I thank you, sir,' he said, when he was somewhat recovered. 'It seems there is method in your remedy after all.'

'Didn't I tell you?' Pruitt swung his hands together in mad delight. 'Bat shit, my boy! Finest Peruvian guano. Nothing like it for the roses, so I'm told. Now, then, let's see about picking you out a piece.'

Inspector Cutter, when they reached him, had selected a pistol for closer examination. Weighing it for a moment in his hand, he addressed Pruitt without turning around. 'The Bull Dog is a fine, sturdy article,' he said. 'It is what I carry myself, when it is called for. I have not found it wanting yet.'

'Nothing wrong with a Webley,' Pruitt allowed. 'All business, and none of your dandy notions about it. I took down an ape with the same piece in the Congo – that's off the coast of Belgium, Sergeant Whiz. I'd left the campfire to unburden myself, so to speak, and while I was in the thick of the business a gorilla came at me sidewise out of the trees. Nine foot tall if he was an inch, and murder in his heart. But he was given no satisfaction there. A single shot, sir, at a dozen yards out. Aye, a reliable item, indeed.'

Cutter raised the gun. A makeshift firing range had been laid out on the waste ground, and crudely sawn plyboard figures stood at intervals, their torsos starred with ragged punctures. Amongst these stood a peculiar gallows-like structure from which hung some obscure bulk, draped all about in sackcloth. The Inspector sighted this now and straightened his gun arm. But he did all this idly, and presently he returned the pistol to the bench.

When he turned to face them, his expression was remote. 'It is a sound sidearm,' he said at length. 'But with a kick to it. And there is the question of concealment. A man would want a bit of heft about him.'

Pruitt eyed the Inspector, a man of considerable stature who was capable when roused – and this Gideon had witnessed for himself – of rupturing the doors of a bonded warehouse with bodily force alone. Pruitt turned to Gideon then and squinted in deliberation.

'Which I believe I perceive your meaning, sir. Something in the lighter line, then, for the young gentleman?'

Gideon coughed and adjusted his stance, but he could not readily form an objection.

'Yes,' said Cutter, working with a knuckle at the underside of his jaw. It was a habit of his, when he was occupied with a problem. 'Yes, maybe that would suit. Something in the lighter line, Pruitt, but something dependable. This gun is not wanted for an ornament.'

'Very good, sir,' said Pruitt. 'I'm with you entirely. The Bull Dog itself is a four forty-two, as I needn't tell you, but a little brother to it can be had now, chambered for a thirty-two. Don't bark quite as fierce, of course, but the leaner gentleman will find it easier on the arm. One moment, my friends.'

He walked a few paces off and bellowed in the direction of a low tin shed that served as a smithy, to judge by the fierce glow from within. 'Milo! Milo there!'

From the doorway emerged a tall, dark-skinned man of easeful bearing and indeterminate age. He held a fearsome-looking knife, almost the length of his own forearm, and with it he was peeling an apple. He worked at this with great precision, so that the skin slipped free in a single graceful helix. 'Look at him,' Pruitt grumbled. 'Like the Prince of fucking Persia. He'll remind me in a minute that he don't exactly work for me, mind, and I'll remind him that there's such a thing as a senior partner. *Oy!* We got punters, in case you ain't noticed. Might I trouble your highness to seek out an item of stock?'

The scroll of glossy peel fell away, but Milo caught it with the tip of his knife, slinging it with a careless movement into a nearby bucket. He tipped up his chin by way of acknowledgement, but he did not seem inclined to strain himself beyond that.

'Have we the Webley thirty-two?' Pruitt called out.

53

The man cut a segment from the naked fruit, sucking its tip contemplatively before consuming it. 'For a lady?' he said, when he had swallowed. His voice was gently sonorous, and his accent was French. Neither observation gave Gideon much pleasure.

'Just fetch it out like a good fellow,' Pruitt growled. 'And then I'll trouble you to serve up that cut of bacon, if it ain't beneath your dignity.'

Gideon had no notion of how bacon might enter into these proceedings, but he did not risk further embarrassment by enquiring. Cutter and Pruitt were now discussing the virtues of the solid frame, and since he had no notion what that might be, he made a show of studying the armaments arrayed on the bench. This did not occupy him for long, since he could scarcely distinguish a rifle from a shotgun. Presently a vigorous little colony of sea holly caught his eye, and when he stooped to examine it he succeeded almost at once in lacerating the pad of his thumb. He lurched upright again and thrust his hands into his pockets.

When Milo returned he had shed his leather apron, revealing a handsome suit of mustard-coloured tweed.

'You have fallen in love?' said Milo, seeing himself observed. 'You are composing me a verse?'

'Forgive me, sir,' Gideon stammered, averting his gaze. 'I am feeling a little unwell, nothing more.'

But Milo was already busying himself. Setting down a leather pouch, he drew out a black pistol of rather stunted appearance. 'Your hand, sir,' he said.

Gideon hesitated before offering it. Milo's hands looked sure and supple, whereas his own were stiff and blotchy from the cold. If the gunsmith noticed this, he did not say so. He conducted his examination with the impassiveness of a surgeon.

'It may suit,' he said at length, then he took up the revolver and broke it. He thumbed home the cartridges with casual assurance, then raised the weapon to check its sights. He entrusted it to Gideon with a solemn nod, pressing his hands about it as if to ensure that he grasped its nature.

'Show us your grip,' he said, stepping back.

The Inspector and Mr Pruitt had likewise retreated by a pace, and Gideon felt the eyes of all three upon him as he sought to recall what he had been taught. The Inspector was not a man of abundant patience, and he was by no means marked out as a natural educator. In most matters of police work he had given his sergeant no instruction at all, beyond pointing out his shortcomings at all opportunities. In this matter, though, he had made an exception.

It had begun only recently, and in a manner that struck Gideon as peculiar from the outset. He had served alongside Cutter since the winter before last, and in that time they had confronted all manner of hazards, yet he had seen the Inspector draw his own revolver only twice. He had never appeared to relish its use. Indeed, he was so little attached to it that he had more than once found himself without it at inopportune moments. On one occasion, when an escaped lunatic had armed himself with a pickaxe and commandeered an omnibus, the Inspector had been obliged to subdue the offender by swinging a feed bag at his head.

In recent weeks, however, a change had come over Inspector Cutter. It was not that he had grown fearful – that would have been an unthinkable transformation – but he had come to seem wary of dangers other than those that confronted him at a particular moment. He had become punctilious in keeping his weapon about him, and he had begun ruminating in a vague and sombre way on Gideon's future and his own.

'I'm past my prime,' he had remarked more than once, and much to Gideon's puzzlement. The Inspector was surely well below fifty, and he was constructed along the lines of a municipal monument. 'I'm past my prime and I may not always be with you.'

It was on a Sunday morning in January when Cutter, having given no notice of his intentions, led Gideon down the steps by Southwark Bridge. Striding in silence over the deserted foreshore, he selected a wharf post and on it he chalked out a neatly circled cross. Having stood for a time as if in deliberation, he tramped back over the frosted shingle. Then he drew out his pistol and, as if it were the most ordinary thing in the world, pressed it into Gideon's hands. 'Here,' he said stepping back. 'Aim at that. Try not to maim one of us.'

Gideon's training in firearms had begun.

Since then, they had returned to the same spot perhaps half a dozen times. Although the wharf post was fully five feet in girth, it was not until their third visit that Gideon succeeded in striking it, a triumph that impaired both his hearing and his penmanship for several days. The Inspector might well have chafed at this, since Gideon's notetaking was among his very few undisputedly useful abilities, but in the event he showed remarkable forbearance. And while he continued to berate Gideon for all manner of unrelated faults, on his halting progress in marksmanship he offered no view whatsoever.

Only now, as he weighed the unfamiliar pistol in his grip, did Gideon feel the weight of Cutter's expectations. He kept the weapon low, as he had been taught, and he laced his hands so that the trigger finger rested on the guard. Milo studied him. 'How does it sit?'

Gideon hesitated.

'It should fill your grip,' Milo explained. 'Fill it, but not stretch it. Like shaking the hand of a man your own size.'

Gideon nodded, appreciating the aptness of this. 'It sits well, I believe. I fear that is no guarantee, however.'

Milo shook his head curtly, dismissing the distraction. 'It is double action, so you need not cock it. Your thumb should reach the striker without straining. With the trigger finger it is the same, though you must put that one to work.' He turned and gestured towards the firing range, stepping aside as he did so. '*Voilà*. In your own time.'

Gideon raised his head, catching sight of the Inspector away to his right. Even without turning he could tell, by his upthrust chin and the set of his folded arms, that he was looking on with wary attention. He approached the bench, scanning the ground for fear that some tussock would foul his footing and cause him to trip. It would surprise no one, he knew, but today it would not do.

'The first target stands at five yards,' said Milo, indicating the nearest of the timber figures. 'The next is at ten, the next again fifteen. It is within range for your thirty-two, but do not hope for too much.' He gave an elegant shrug, then spread his hands as if concluding an argument.

'No, no, no! No, sir! Ach!' It was Pruitt who had raised his voice. He had stepped away to relieve himself, but emerged now from behind a rank of barrels, shaking himself with considerable agitation. 'No, Milo, for shame! Did you not hear me? The woodwork is for the sailors and the tinkers. For the Inspector and his friend, we must show a bit of pink, what?'

Milo regarded him silently for a moment. 'It is inexact, Pruitt. The elevation is wrong, and it shows the strike poorly.'

'Inexact be damned!' Pruitt exclaimed. 'To hell with you, then, for a cock-lapping cur. I will rig it up myself. Where is the sweet mark, did you say?'

The gunsmith picked at a tooth with a splinter. 'Fifteen yards,' he said.

'Fifteen yards, very well.' Pruitt rounded the bench and strode off. 'Hold your fire there, Sergeant. You might as well enjoy the full effect, since I've took the trouble.'

Reaching the gallows-like structure, he took hold of its sides and braced himself. It stood on four great iron casters, but hauling it over such rough ground was a laborious business. Like some monstrous pendulum, the shrouded bulk swayed above him, but a counterweight in its base kept the whole apparatus from toppling. It was heavy work, plainly, but Pruitt was animated now by a fierce delight.

'Fuck me!' he cried out. 'Must have given me an elephant by mistake.'

'Ha,' said Gideon weakly. 'Indeed.' A new reek drifted from under the sackcloth, tainted and carnal. His throat worked drily, a dread rising from his gut.

'Now, then!' Pruitt began slashing at the sacking, disclosing glimpses of coarse flesh. When only a few clinging rags remained, he struck a theatrical pose.

'Right, gentlemen! Fresh from – well, maybe fresh ain't quite the word. Directly from Her Majesty's own Victualling Yard—'

'Pruitt,' Inspector Cutter interrupted, taking a tone that Gideon knew to be ominous. 'It was a gun we wanted, not a penny show. Take your bow, like a good man, before I sprout roots.'

'Right you are, Inspector. Point taken entirely. Well, without further ado.'

Gideon looked away as Pruitt swung his cutlass. He heard the frame shudder, in the silence that followed. He heard the rope creak as the carcass listed and settled.

Milo coughed. It was a discreet cough, but it carried a distinct implication.

Gideon straightened and assessed his grip. He mastered his breathing. He found that if he kept from blinking, his vision clouded just enough that—

The carcass lurched and pivoted, bringing the pig's eye into view. Caught by the breeze, its frill of lashes stirred and lifted.

Christ.

He had fired before catching sight of it, that roiling knot of maggots, and perhaps it was for the best. The shot had gone wide, but the recoil had jolted him only a little and he had managed not to exclaim aloud. Still, a miss was a miss, and if he was to emerge from this with any semblance of dignity, he had only one course open to him. Though it was far from natural to him, he tried to summon something of the Inspector's self-possession, of his towering disregard for the opinions of those around him.

Cutter would not have missed in the first place, but if he had, he would not dwell upon it for long. If he were to reproach himself at all, it would be in a simple and unvarnished fashion.

Fuck it, thought Gideon and emptied the barrel.

Three

It was some hours later when Gideon arrived at Leggett's Fine Wines and Viands, the favoured eating house of Inspector Cutter. It was some hours later because Leggett's was in Soho, fully seven miles from Millwall, and because he had been obliged to walk all the way.

It was an eventuality that Gideon might have anticipated. Although the Inspector was required to present himself from time to time at Scotland Yard, his strictly reserved nook at the eating house in Warwick Street was the nearest thing he had to a regular place of business. It was at Leggett's, too, that Cutter took most of his meals, since it was within easy reach of his rooms in Frith Street.

It was an establishment, in short, to which Inspector Cutter was considerably attached. When he had announced, on leaving Pruitt's yard, that he was in want of a pair of chops, Gideon had experienced a chill of foreboding. His head ached, as did his arms and shoulders, and his lungs were still congested with cordite and Peruvian dung. There were chops to be had, surely, in the vicinity of Millwall. Her Majesty's Navy, as they had just learned, had its victualling yard only over the river. But this was a vain hope, Gideon knew. The Inspector was a man of fixed habits and – this was of more proximate concern to Gideon – of near-inhuman stamina. It would not weigh with him if beefsteaks were a penny each on every corner from Millwall to Limehouse, and it certainly would not enter his calculations that Warwick Street lay half a day's march from their present position. Cutter took cabs only when he was on pressing business, and trains only when he was called out of town. Otherwise he walked.

And when the Inspector walked, Gideon was expected to do likewise. Notionally, too, he was expected to keep up, but that was a strenuous business and could not be sustained for long. So it was that Gideon had trudged and hobbled in Cutter's wake across Mill Meade and Stratford Marsh, through Limehouse and Whitechapel and the southern bounds of Spitalfields. He was wheezing badly as he skirted the City, and by the time he stumbled into Holborn, his calf muscles had all but seized up. He was obliged to conduct a series of stretching exercises while propped against a public urinal. This attracted a good deal of open mockery, but at that point Gideon had surrendered his small quotient of official dignity.

In fact, although he was exhausted almost to the point of stupor, he felt oddly elated. The journey had been gruelling, but it had given him time to reflect. He had done a good deal of ruminating – indeed he had startled himself by settling upon a course of action. He was by no means persuaded of its wisdom, but he had resolved to see it through before his better judgement could intervene.

He found the Inspector at his accustomed table, set apart in its own shadowy parlour at the rear of the establishment. Cutter occupied the armchair to the left of the fireplace, where a whippet of uncertain colouring was curled up in slumber. The whippet was lacking a hind leg, and in its place was a neatly rigged wooden peg with a brass shell case for a ferrule. It seemed otherwise replete and at peace. Its twitching and crooning suggested easeful dreams.

Cutter did not look up. A brown paper package lay before him on the table, whose contents he kept hidden as he examined them. He extended the toe of his boot, and with it he nudged back the armchair opposite his own. Taking this for an invitation, Gideon made to seat himself.

'There's presumption,' said the Inspector.

Gideon arrested himself, his hindquarters poised above the seat of the chair. 'Sir?' he said.

'I might have pushed out that chair for Spider.'

'For Spider, sir?' He looked about the sepulchral little room, but no one else seemed to be present. Still, Leggett's attracted a somewhat miscellaneous clientele, and this was just the sort of name one encountered there. It was conceivable that the Inspector expected a visitor.

'The whippet,' Cutter said. 'Can you guess how he came by that name?'

Gideon deliberated, still awkwardly poised. He knew very little of dogs, having spent much of his life in austere scholarly lodgings, but he recalled that their diets were highly various. 'Might he be partial to flies, sir?'

Cutter still did not look up, but he closed his eyes briefly. 'Partial to flies,' he said quietly. 'Sweet Jesus. Sit down, will you, before your scrawny shanks seize up altogether.'

Gideon sank down gratefully, though he was conscious of having made a poor start. The matter he hoped to discuss with the Inspector might prove delicate, and missteps of this kind would not help his case. He would be obliged to proceed with the utmost care.

'Remind me, Bliss,' said the Inspector. 'How long have you been in London?'

'Thirteen months, sir. Since February of last year.'

'Thirteen months, is it? It might be thirteen minutes, to hear you talk.'

Gideon lowered his head. He despaired sometimes of ever rising in the Inspector's estimation.

'He's called Spider,' the Inspector said, 'because he has only three legs. Any infant could explain it to you. Any infant born between here and West Ham, at least.'

'Only three legs,' said Gideon meekly. 'Ah, yes. Most apt.'

Cutter studied his bundle for a moment longer – Gideon glimpsed something hard and gleaming – then he folded over the paper and sat back with a weary air. 'Only three legs, bless him,' he said. 'Yet he leapt up as lively as you like when he saw me come in. Whereas you—' He broke off, fixing Gideon with a severe look. 'Whereas you have lolloped in fully twenty minutes behind time. And look at you. You look like a savaged hen. Did you topple into a stock cellar again?'

Gideon looked himself over. He had paused before a haberdasher's window to put himself in order after his exertions, but he saw now that he had been remiss. He had gone awry in his buttoning, and one shirt tail had spilled into his lap. It might do more harm than good, he felt, to correct these oversights now.

'Yes, sir. I'm afraid I could not quite keep to your pace. We came a considerable way, you might allow, and I was not feeling quite myself to begin with.' He shifted discreetly in his place, so as to work his hands a little nearer the fire. They had stiffened alarmingly, and he found that he had limited command over his fingers. He noticed a plate on the floor by the sleeping dog's head. It had been licked wholly clean, save for a smeared arc of what might once have been gravy. 'Spider's had your chops,' said Cutter, by way of explanation. 'I didn't want to see them go to waste. That's what dogs eat, by the way. You've learned that much today, if nothing else.'

'Yes, sir,' Gideon replied. His mood was veering again towards dejection. He had not taken a morsel since bringing up his breakfast in Mr Pruitt's yard.

'Oh, for the love of God,' said Cutter, rising abruptly and striding to the doorway. 'Barney!' he called out in a thunderous voice.

'Barney there! Another plate of chops, like a good lad, and two more cups of cordial.'

He returned to his seat, shaking his head. 'Yes, sir, he says, with a face like a haunted bedsheet. I would do as well with Spider there for a sergeant. At least he has sense enough to eat when he is hungry.'

Gideon said nothing. He watched the whippet twitch and start in its sleep. Presently it gave vent to a solemnly emphatic fart. Perhaps, Gideon reflected, he might indeed profit from the animal's example.

Then the Inspector surprised him. 'Still,' he said. 'You did well enough this morning.'

Gideon stole a wary glance at Cutter's face. He saw no trace of mockery there. 'I am afraid I did not, sir. It took me three tries to hit the mark, and after that I suffered a dizzy spell.'

'True enough,' the Inspector answered. 'But I've seen others take six tries, and that has a worse outcome than a dizzy spell. A week-old pig is not a blackguard with murder in his heart, but it's not a pier post either. It was enough to put the fear of God in you, certainly, yet you kept your feet long enough to put a bullet into it.'

Gideon pondered this. He found that it heartened him, and his spirits rose further when he saw Barney appear with a grimy platter. 'Chops and hash for the young miss,' the boy said, setting down a plate. Gideon glared at him, but he could summon no ready answer. The youngster was perhaps ten years old, and a lighted scrap of cigarette was lodged in the corner of his mouth. 'And two mugs of the usual. What you want drinking that for, guvnor? Ain't it for washing down steps?'

'Mind your manners, boy,' said Cutter. 'I'll warrant *you* never shot a pig in the face.'

The boy gave him a skewed look. 'What would I do that for? A pig, you just cut its throat.'

'Get on with you, Barney. And remember what I told you. Keep your eyes open and your wits about you. There's a bob in it for you if you're sharp.'

'Right you are, guv. Ain't seen nothing yet, though.'

Gideon puzzled over this exchange after the boy had left them, but he was soon taken up with his meal. The chops were pliant enough, and the hash tasted as much of onions as sawdust. He had lived on very little during his time at Cambridge and he had no high notions in the culinary line.

Having cleared his plate – and since it had proved safe enough ground – he ventured to return to the subject of his marksmanship. 'Did I really shoot it in the face, sir? That animal?'

The Inspector looked up, having fallen into private reflection. 'So you did, Bliss. Well, there or thereabouts. Hard to say, with a pig. A man is another matter. You can tell where his face begins, but putting a bullet in it – yes, another matter entirely.'

'Well, naturally,' said Gideon. 'It is a question of the sanctity of life. It is the sternest of prohibitions, after all. And even if the cause were just, the text of Romans leaves us in no doubt as to the—'

Cutter held up a hand. 'You mistake my meaning, Bliss. It's easier to miss, shooting at a man's head. Aim at his chest, where he is widest. That way, even if you're off the mark – and most shots are – you may still put a stop to his gallop.'

'Yes,' said Gideon, without conviction. He was staring at his plate, where a pool of pinkish juices still glistened. 'Yes, I see.'

'And as for the sanctity of life,' the Inspector continued, 'it's a fine notion, to be sure, but it won't keep the other fellow in check. You have seen proof of that for yourself, as I recall.'

Gideon stirred uneasily. The Inspector was speaking of events they seldom discussed, which had taken place the winter before on a bleak Kentish beach. He had seen a great deal that day. He had suffered a loss that still seemed beyond accounting.

Even so, he was obliged to acknowledge the weight of Cutter's words. Gideon had been wounded himself that day. He might have suffered a worse fate if the Inspector had not intervened.

'I have,' he said quietly. 'Yes, I have.'

'Well,' said the Inspector after a pause, 'we'll say no more about that. And I fancy there'll be no more target practice, if that eases your mind. There isn't time.'

'Indeed, sir?' Gideon felt a moment's relief, but it gave way almost at once to fresh misgivings. 'But my training is far from complete, surely? Certainly, Mr Pruitt gave me the impression that I still had much to learn.'

'Never mind Mr Pruitt. Mr Pruitt has nothing to teach you, unless it is how to talk a man to death.'

Gideon was perplexed. 'But did you not seek him out specially, sir? Did you not say that we had urgent business with Mr Pruitt?'

'I said that I had urgent business at Mr Pruitt's *yard*. That bit of business is concluded now, or maybe it's only just begun. Either way, nothing to my liking has come out of it yet.'

'I am at a loss, sir. Did you not find the pistols satisfactory?'

'The pistols will serve well enough. Pruitt will send them over in the morning, and then we must see about fitting you with a holster. But that isn't the business I meant, Bliss.' Cutter took a draught of cordial and set down his cup with crisp finality. Plainly he considered the matter closed.

Gideon fell silent himself, having much to consider. It was Cutter's mysterious behaviour and cryptic pronouncements that had preoccupied him on the way here. Since he could not account for any of it, he had turned to the question of when it all began. And he had, or so he persuaded himself, hit upon the answer.

The Inspector had received a letter, nothing more, and in what seemed the most ordinary of circumstances. Some weeks before, Gideon had been with him as he passed one night through the duty office at Scotland Yard. In keeping with Cutter's habits, they had called there late in the evening and stayed no longer than they must. Gideon had been making a hasty amendment to a report, and the Inspector was badgering him to finish when he was drawn aside by the Duty Sergeant.

The two must have discussed nothing remarkable at first, for Gideon had gone on with his annotations. Five or six minutes might have passed before something made him look up. What had it been, exactly? Even now, he could not single it out in his mind.

In any case, he raised his head just as the Inspector was slipping the letter into his coat. He glimpsed the ornate black seal, and that detail struck him as curious. Whatever the nature of the letter, it was enclosed not in an ordinary envelope but in a leaf of some rich stock, folded over in the antiquated style.

And all the while Cutter was haranguing the Duty Sergeant about where this letter had come from. Mattingley, the man's name was, a lumpen and timid fellow who stammered over and over that there weren't no one seen about the place, that he had done no more than come upon the said dockerment sitting apart from the pile and fetch the said dockerment straight up to the party in question, which here was the thanks he got and that was him told good and proper.

Cutter berated him then, though he did so in a strained undertone. 'We are six flights above the public office, Mattingley,' he said. 'Was it left by a conjurer, then, or dropped by a raven?'

But what marked out the incident, more than any detail of what had occurred that evening, was its insidious effect on the Inspector. On their arrival at the Yard, he had appeared as untroubled as his nature permitted. Indeed, when he had first entered the duty office

– having learned that the superintendent was away on other business –
he had clapped his broad palms together and announced that he
might celebrate by battering a whoremaster. After his own fashion,
in other words, he had been in a light-hearted and whimsical mood.

Then he had been shown the letter, and in the next moment all
that passed for gaiety in him had vanished. It had not returned
since. And now? Now, it seemed, Gideon was to be equipped with a
revolver he did not trust himself to use, and all because they faced
some enemy that Cutter refused to name. He could go along with
this madness no longer. He was determined to speak his mind.

'What is it, Bliss? Since you came out of your daydream, you've
been twitching like a mouse in a coat pocket.'

'Have I, sir? I had been striving not to disturb your thoughts.'

'That would explain the twitching. Spit it out, will you, before you
choke on it.'

'Yes, sir.' Gideon shuffled to the edge of his chair. He took his hat
from his lap and tucked it behind him. Then, fearing that he might
crumple it in a forgetful moment, he restored it to his lap. 'I was
wondering, sir, if I might put a question to you.'

The Inspector thrust out his chin and rasped at it with his knuckles. 'Is that the question?' he said. 'Or is it a lady's maid sent down
to say that the question is getting dressed?'

'Your pardon, sir.' Gideon took a fortifying breath. 'I will try to
come to the point. I do indeed have a question, but I should like
to make a brief observation first.'

Cutter lifted his eyes at this, but Gideon felt he must press on or
risk squandering his chance entirely. 'The fact is, sir, that I have been
growing concerned. I have not served with you long, and no doubt I
have a great deal to learn. You have been good enough to persevere
in my instruction, but I am under no illusions. If ever there was an
unlikely policeman, it is the one sitting before you.

'I was an indifferent scholar, too, but at least I was a diligent one. And having little else to recommend me, I have tried to apply the same diligence to our profession. I have tried to learn a little of the law, though I know I might read every law book in Lincoln's Inn and still be no nearer to a real policeman. For that I must rely on your example, and in that too I have done my utmost. I have studied you closely, sir.'

'Have you now?'

'Yes, sir, I have. And I do not pretend to know your mind, but I have spent long enough in your company to become accustomed to your ways. I know that if you are sometimes— well, if you are curt in your manner, it is only because you dislike finding obstacles stand-ing between you and your duty. I did not understand that at first, and I was often discouraged when you rebuked me. But in time, I came to see that I myself was often the obstacle. In my ignorance, I have sometimes been more of a hindrance to you than a help.'

'Bliss.' The Inspector's tone was foreboding, and no doubt his expression was darker still. But Gideon kept his eyes fixed on his own knees. If he faltered now, he would never find the resolve to begin again.

'I have not much more to say, sir. I know you are opposed to speeches, and that you like long and earnest speeches least of all, but I must ask you to make an exception. I am nearly at the end of my observation, and I promise that my question will be brief. Being accustomed to your ways, I never minded when you checked me or found fault. If I did not see the reason at the time I would find it out later and see that it had been needful, that it was meant for my own good. But lately, sir, I have begun to doubt what I thought I knew. Lately a change has come over you, and whatever it is that has troubled you in these last weeks, I fear I will not discover it without your aid. A blackness has descended upon you, sir, and I cannot begin to guess at the cause. It grieves me to see it, yet until today I said nothing.

'I said nothing because it was not my place, but it was not only that. I said nothing because I did not know what to say. How could I, when I could scarcely put words to my own misgivings? I still know next to nothing, sir, I will not deny it. But I remembered something today, on the way back from Millwall. It had eluded me for a long time, but it came to me clearly on the Tottenham Court Road. I remembered the moment when all of this began, or so I now imagine. And that brings me to my question, sir.'

'Well, now,' said Cutter. 'At least it has brought you to something.'

Gideon raised his eyes at last. The Inspector was still watching the window, as if he might recognise some shape among those indistinct shadows. His jaw was set, but not in the forbidding scowl that Gideon had seen so often. Indeed, nothing in his look or manner seemed familiar.

Gideon found himself fidgeting with the brim of his cap, so he set it on the table. He gripped the arms of his chair.

'Sir,' he said. 'Five or six weeks ago, we went one evening to the duty office at the Yard. You were given a letter that night, which had been left for you by some unknown person. My question is not about the contents of the letter, since they may well be private, but I must ask you this much. Am I right in thinking, sir, that something in that letter continues to trouble you? That it gave you reason to believe we are in some kind of danger? And if we are in danger, sir, ought I not to know of it? I may not be of much aid, since I was scarcely able to fend off a deceased farm animal, but haven't I some right to know what peril we might face?'

A long silence followed. Indeed, the Inspector was silent for so long that Gideon feared he would not answer at all. And as the silence stretched out, his earlier resolve began to desert him. What had he been thinking, jabbering on in that way? And how had he dared to ask such a presumptuous question? Surely his only course now was to make his apologies and tender his resignation.

He was on the point of doing just that when the Inspector raised a hand. 'You're right about this much, Bliss. I don't like long speeches. So, I'll give you a piece of advice before I say any more. If you ever feel the urge to unburden yourself like that again, will you do me a kindness and write it down instead.' He paused for a moment to scratch a smudge from his cuff with a thumbnail. 'And then cross out at least two-thirds of it.'

'Yes, sir,' said Gideon meekly.

'You're right about something else, too,' the Inspector went on. 'What was in that letter was a private matter.'

Gideon hung his head.

'It was a private matter, and I hoped it would stay that way. I hoped that for many years.'

At this Gideon stirred, but he did not dare to speak.

'But I fear that it will not stay private for much longer. As for your question, all I'll say for now is that there is more to this than a letter. I'm not about to make a long speech of my own, and not only because I have neither the time nor the inclination. As for the nature of the danger, well . . . if I'm right, you will soon have your answer, and the answers to a great many questions you never thought to ask. I can set your mind at rest on one point, however. You may not have the leisure to study my moods for much longer. Will I tell you why?'

The Inspector turned to him at last. He had put the question almost lightly, but his face was utterly grave. Gideon only nodded.

'Because within the next hour, Bliss, perhaps in the next few minutes, someone of our acquaintance will come through that door. He'll be coming to give me the name of a dead man, and that name might well be my own.'

Four

It was Milo who came, the elegant young man from Mr Pruitt's
yard. Gideon might have been astonished at this if he were not so
riven with anxiety. The Inspector had twice reminded Gideon to stop
fidgeting and keep his seat, but otherwise he had scarcely spoken
since making his chilling pronouncement. In consequence, Gideon
leapt to his feet the moment the gunsmith appeared in the doorway,
having formed no clear notion of his own intentions. In the next
moment he found that he had planted himself athwart the Inspector's
chair, his arms flung out rigidly before him. Quite what this posture
was intended to convey he could not have readily explained.

'*Bon soir*,' said Milo, surveying him with mild curiosity. 'You were
taking exercise, perhaps?'

'Bliss,' said Cutter from behind him. 'Sit down, will you, before
you do yourself an injury.'

Gideon complied, lowering himself haltingly into his chair. He
lurched briefly to his feet again to murmur a belated greeting, but
Milo appeared not to notice. He sauntered to the table, inspecting
it fastidiously before setting down his hat. He had shed his earlier
clothing – which had seemed to Gideon smart enough for any setting – and was dressed now in a suit of pale grey wool. His waistcoat
was of satin, in some bewitching shade of violet. He looked as if he
belonged in one of the more turbulent epistolary novels.

'Well?' said the Inspector.

In answer, Milo merely nodded. He made this simple gesture seem both courteous and deeply solemn.

'And?'

Milo looked about him with what might have been faint disdain. 'Not here,' he said. He took up his hat again, flicking a speck from it before restoring it to his head. 'I have engaged a cab, having much to do in little time. I regret that you must pay.'

'You're not the first to say so,' answered the Inspector. His tone was bleak, but he got to his feet swiftly, as if relieved at the chance. He swept his coat and hat from their pegs. 'If you mean to join us, Bliss, you might stop gawking and show a leg.'

Gideon brought himself awkwardly upright, knocking his hat to the floor as he sought out his own coat. Milo, meanwhile, had taken notice of Spider, stooping to scratch the whippet behind the ears. 'A good boy,' he said. 'A very good boy.'

'His name is Spider,' said Gideon. 'It is on account of—'

'Only three legs,' said Milo promptly. 'Yes, the English and their amusing customs. *Alors*, we are ready?'

'We're ready,' said the Inspector, who stood waiting already in the doorway. Again, the words seemed freighted with meaning, but whatever weighed on his mind, the prospect of movement had restored his vitality. He held himself erect, and his entire frame was taut with purpose.

Milo slipped past him to lead the way.

The cab let them out in Haymarket, where Milo bade the driver wait, but Gideon had no notion yet of their precise destination. Neither Milo nor the Inspector spoke until they had turned into Pall Mall, and even then they kept their voices low. Following one murmured exchange, Milo passed Cutter a scrap of paper. The Inspector folded it away after the briefest of glances.

'A Whitehall man, then,' he said, eyeing the dour bulk of the War Office. 'Though the name means nothing to me.'

'Once, maybe,' Milo answered in a murmur. Threading with feline purpose through the late afternoon crowds, he turned into a side street. 'He is old, it seems. Was old.'

Cutter gave a subdued grunt. 'They're Whitehall men to the end.'

He and Milo began speaking more freely only when they had crossed into a secluded little park to the rear of the ministry. Whatever great matters of state were discussed behind the windows above, these gardens were silent save for the delicate clamour of birdsong.

Coming to a cobbled circle ringed with cherry trees, Milo turned about and halted. 'So,' he said, when he had made a wary survey of their surroundings. 'It is not much, what I know. I might have thought it was nothing, if you had not spoken earlier. This morning at Pruitt's yard, you said someone dangerous had been seen about town, and that—'

'Not seen,' Cutter interrupted. 'This person has not been seen for some time. I've had intelligence, however, and yesterday – well, yesterday I received a certain token.'

'Pardon me, sir,' said Gideon. 'You received a—'

But Gideon's dazed interjection came too late, for Milo had passed on with no more than a diffident nod. 'My mistake,' the Frenchman said. 'In any case, you said that this person may already be at work, and would be seeking out individuals of a certain kind. Make urgent enquiries, you said, and I have done all I could in such a short time. Well, this much I can tell you. No one has been out buying tools, or not in the usual places. And no one in the profession has heard of someone new. And *that* I do not like.'

Cutter lifted his chin. 'Why? What does that matter?'

'In this business, there is no one I don't know,' Milo said. He paused for a moment, then spread his hands in equivocation. 'Well, there is no one good. And if this person is as dangerous as you say, well – our profession, it is a business, yes? I like to know of the competition. So, I begin wondering, why must it be a hired man? This man who was killed today, he was some *vieillard* from the army. Maybe he got medals once for killing a hundred Khartoum boys with spears, but maybe he had enemies closer to home. The army cleans its own house, no? So, maybe you are looking for a soldier. They know how to kill, yes?'

'Not this kind of killing,' the Inspector said. 'And not these people. It's not their way.'

Gideon could not tell what people the Inspector might be referring to, but for his part Milo appeared indifferent. 'If you say so. We will know more when we see the body. But if it was clean work, and if it was a stranger, that would be a curious thing.'

'You'd better get used to it,' said Cutter. 'This is only the first. How did you come by your information, then, if there was no talk of this among your acquaintances? I'm about to pay a call in an official capacity, so I must have something resembling a straight story.'

'*Bien entendu*,' said Milo. 'I understand. No, there was no talk, so I began looking in other places. I spoke to some of your friends at the Yard, to men I have had dealings with before. I see that you are surprised, so I will try to explain. Pruitt, most of what he says is shit talk – this is the phrase, yes? – but it is true that many can be bought. When you do the work I do, there are certain expenses. Sometimes you wish a policeman to tell you something, or you wish him to forget something. Sometimes it is a high-up policeman, and he asks a high price.'

The Inspector's lip curled. 'Such men are no friends of mine, and I would sooner do without their help. I hope you chose your words very carefully.'

'Do you not know me by now, Henri?' Milo touched three fingers to his breast. 'I do everything very carefully. I said very little. That some harm might come to a person today, and that this person might have some high-up office. I said that if he heard of such an unfortunate thing, he would want to send a man who was used to such delicate matters, yes? I assured him that I knew such an officer, and that I would get word to him. Everything would be correct, but also quick and quiet, which such men like to hear. I did not say your name even once.'

'For all the good that will do,' the Inspector said. 'He'll know my name within the hour, if he's that well placed. And he agreed to all that, did he? He must be paid handsomely, to let the likes of you tell him his business.'

'Let us say that he is paid enough to make it my business too. In any case, it seems I was very lucky in choosing my moment. The unfortunate thing had already happened, you see, and he had not yet given any orders. Perhaps he has not many men with your skills. On that question I put his mind at ease. Do not trouble yourself, I said. The officer I spoke of, this matter will be in his hands before you are sitting down to dine at your club. And look, here you are, before he has even put on his white tie.'

Gideon had kept himself in check throughout this bewildering exchange, but he could do so no longer. Inspector Cutter, if he had understood correctly, had just calmly received intelligence resulting from a bribe to a senior officer. And as if his mysterious letter were not enough, there was now talk of an unspecified 'token'. 'If I may, sir—'

The Inspector only held up a hand. 'Not now, Bliss. Here I am, yes, for better or worse. I'm no stickler for protocol, Milo, but this is far from tidy. Still, you did what you must, I suppose. Now, then, we've stood long enough in the open. Is there anything else I should know, before we begin?'

'We?' Milo cocked an eyebrow. 'It would not appear irregular, if I were with you?'

'Irregular?' Cutter cast a sour look in the direction of the War Office. 'Nothing in this nest of vipers is ever regular. But have you anything else to tell me? Your crooked friend at the Yard must have let something slip, since he was being so obliging.'

Milo stroked his cheek as he considered this. 'More interesting, I think, was what he did not say, or did not know. He could not say what post this man held, only that it must have been something important. He was one of these *chevaliers*, yes? A something of the order of the something? You said the name was nothing to you – well, it was nothing to my man at the Yard either, and this is a person who likes to know such things.'

The Inspector was silent for a moment, and Gideon's attention was caught once more by the birdsong. It seemed to crowd about them more closely now, and in its liquid notes he sensed a gathering urgency. Perhaps it was only that the birds resented their presence.

'Well,' said Cutter. 'That tells its own tale. Come along, Bliss, unless you're staying here to question the blackbirds. We have work to do.'

The dead man was one Aneurin Considine, a Commander of the British Empire whose home stood at the end of a splendid terrace faced with snowy stucco. It was a grand and dignified place overlooking a lush swathe of St James's Park, but the Inspector had never been greatly moved by the trappings of high station. Having appraised its façade with a grudging snort, he turned to take in the view.

'Convenient for the park,' he said, pointing ahead. From the carriage circle at the end of the terrace, a broad flight of steps led down to The Mall. A late mist was settling over its stately plane trees, and beyond them the darkening parkland seemed deserted, its paths leading away into nothingness. 'Milo, would you oblige me?'

Milo nodded, as if the same thought had occurred to him, and trotted lightly to the foot of the steps. From there he made a brief survey of the townhouse's side elevation, and when he returned, his expression was appreciative. '*Agréable*,' he said. 'Like a gift, tied with a pretty bow.'

The Inspector grunted again. 'Maybe too pretty. And my birthday is some way off. We must get on with it. Now, listen, both of you. Leave the talking to me, if you can help it. If you have observations to make, make them quietly. Bliss, have you your notebook about you?'

Gideon straightened, eager to have some useful part in the proceedings. He tapped his breast pocket with a modest flourish. 'Of course, sir.'

'Well, write in it as much as you can, even if it is only to record the colour of the drapes. I want them wondering.' With that he swept into the portico, squared his shoulders and tugged smartly on the bell-pull. 'Better yet,' he murmured, 'I want them fucking terrified.'

The door was opened not by a servant but by a composed and keen-eyed lady who was perhaps in her middle thirties. She was dressed as if for dinner, in a gown of sumptuous burgundy velvet, and she clutched what Gideon took to be an ornate dagger. Noting his expression, she held up a neatly transected envelope. 'A letter opener,' she said, in a tone of distant amusement. 'I do hope I haven't alarmed a policeman. You *are* policemen, I take it?'

The Inspector stepped forward, obscuring Gideon from the lady's view. 'Inspector Henry Cutter, madam. I am not easily alarmed, I assure you. I might be concerned, however, depending on who that letter is addressed to.'

'Goodness, might you?' She fanned herself with the letter. 'How upsetting. And these other gentlemen?'

'Sergeant Gideon Bliss and Mr Milo, a trusted associate.'

'Trusted, you say? Yes, he rather has that look. Well, do come in, all of you. I am Mrs Sylvia Lytton, the niece of the deceased. And a trusted associate also, I suppose one might say.'

She stepped back, allowing them to pass into the lofty vestibule. Closing the door behind them, she crossed to a table topped with gleaming white stone. She tossed the opened letter onto an untidy pile and discarded the opener with a heedless clatter. 'It was for Sir Aneurin, since you mention it, but you'll find I was doing you a service. He was rather behind on his correspondence, as you can see, and most of it concerns orchids. He used to go on expeditions, you know, to Borneo and such places. He had one named after him. An orchid, I mean. It looked like a little dishevelled slipper.'

Recalling the Inspector's wishes, Gideon drew out his notebook discreetly and began jotting down these details. It struck him that he might fill several pages at this rate, without ever mentioning the drapes. 'How delightful,' said Mrs Lytton. 'Just like in the stories. You really ought to have licked your pencil first, though.'

Cutter gathered up the spilled pile of letters, squaring them briskly against the tabletop before tucking them away beneath his coat. 'These will be returned in due course,' he said. 'Now, if we might begin with some questions, Mrs Lytton. Did you live here, with Sir Aneurin? Was it you who sent for us?'

'Live with him?' she said. 'Dear me, no. My uncle disliked company. Disliked most things, really, other than his little frilly flowers. He kept only a few servants, and I imagine even they scarcely saw him. Apart from Coulton, of course. He was always somewhere about. It was me who sent for you, though.'

'Coulton?' said the Inspector.

'Sorry, yes.' Mrs Lytton had addressed herself to an ornate mirror. She turned, having corrected some indiscernible fault in the arrangement of her hair. 'Coulton was . . . I suppose you'd call him my uncle's manservant, though he didn't seem at all the right type. Touch of the ruffian about him, I always thought. Whereas your Mr Milo here—'

Cutter held up a hand. 'Mrs Lytton, do not take it amiss, but I must ask you to keep nearer the point. This Coulton, was he the one who found your uncle? And where might we find him now?'

'Gosh,' said Mrs Lytton, touching the pale skin below her clavicles. 'How severe you are. He wasn't, no. It was Mrs Carr who found him, poor thing. She's the housekeeper, and horribly ancient herself. I'm quite surprised she even noticed. I expect she's downstairs somewhere now, being infused with something restorative.'

'We'll need a word with her. And this Coulton?'

'You'll find him in the orchid house. That's just upstairs, two rooms away from the library. The library is where my uncle was found. Did I mention that? I did say that Coulton was always to be found lurking somewhere in my uncle's orbit.'

The Inspector allowed a moment to pass. 'In the orchid house?'

'Just so.'

'And what might he be doing there, madam? Seeing to some urgent watering, is it?'

'I rather doubt it. He's dead too, I'm afraid. Perhaps I ought to have mentioned it.'

At this, Gideon looked up from his notebook. Milo's posture was easeful, though it was clear that he was paying close attention. The Inspector's expression, however, was singularly baleful. 'Unless I'm mistaken, Mrs Lytton, we were informed of only one death.'

'Well, really,' said Mrs Lytton, with a careless flourish of her fingertips. 'A man like Coulton ... well, it's hardly the same, is it? And after all, you were going to be coming anyway.'

'You'll find it is exactly the same, madam. We do not leave murdered servants for the streetsweepers. We treat all witnesses alike, too, in case you had any expectations to the contrary. We find them helpful or otherwise, and those are the only classes we recognise. So, Mrs Lytton, have you any other revelations for me? Have any other dead men slipped your mind?'

Mrs Lytton raised her finely sculpted chin. 'No. No, I think that's everything.'

'I will take you at your word for now, though I suspect we will return to this subject. It is getting on for eight o'clock at night and I have the impression that you have been about the place for much of the day. A fellow might be forgiven for wondering how you occupied yourself for all that time, but for now I have more pressing concerns. Has anything been touched up there, madam? Have you been busying yourself with anything other than Sir Aneurin's letters?'

Mrs Lytton took a step towards him, her head canted in an attitude of cool appraisal. 'What a delightfully commanding tone you have, Inspector Cutter. In my circles, one meets any number of military men, but in the moments when it matters, so few seem to have the requisite . . . stiffness.'

'Mrs Lytton,' said Cutter. 'Did you touch anything?'

'No, Inspector. I couldn't bring myself to, if you want to know.'

He kept his voice even. 'In your distressed state, you mean?'

'Do I seem distressed, Inspector? No, I simply meant that it was all so neatly done. You'll see what I mean, I'm sure. And so little blood. Remarkable, really. I thought it made quite the tableau. But what would I know of such things? In any case, do feel free to go up. I shall be drifting about down here, if you should need me again.'

'I cannot rule it out. Be kind enough not to drift too far.'

He swept past her to the staircase. Milo made to follow, pausing before Mrs Lytton and offering her a nod. '*Madame*,' he said simply.

'Such exquisite manners,' she said, studying him in turn. 'I should quite like to retain *your* services myself.'

'You are kind,' Milo replied, turning fluidly away. 'But you have not seen my work.'

Gideon fumbled his notebook shut and hastened after him, shuffling around Mrs Lytton with what he hoped was a polite smile. As he was passing, she took hold of his elbow. Her grip was surprisingly sure. Leaning close to him, she spoke in an undertone that seemed at once humid and icy. 'Have you written my description yet, in your little book?'

Gideon coughed. 'I'm afraid it wouldn't be proper to—'

'Good,' she said, tightening her hold. 'Better to wait. Because you haven't seen me yet, my darling. You haven't even glimpsed me.'

The orchid house proved to be a grand conservatory whose glass cupola must have risen twenty-five feet above the floor. By day it would have commanded an enviable view of the park, but with the settling of dusk the glass vault had become a sombre hall of mirrors. When Gideon entered, he confronted the arrayed slivers of his own lamplit form, gliding through several darknesses at once.

'The dead man is on the floor, Bliss.' The Inspector was at the far end of the room, obscured by a profusion of glossy foliage. 'When you have finished marvelling, you might bring me those lamps. It's like wandering through the botanical gardens at midnight.'

Gideon located the lamps in question, but it was the work of some moments to free them from their stands. They were elaborate items, made to resemble intricate bird cages, and the tendrils of some creeping plant had insinuated themselves throughout the frames.

When he had tugged them clear, he turned to find that the Inspector had dragged Coulton's body into the central aisle. Gideon approached cautiously, holding the lamps out before him.

The Inspector had dropped to one knee and was hunched intently over the awkwardly splayed corpse. Milo hovered decorously behind him, but his attention was wholly absorbed.

Cutter gestured absently, not looking up. 'Set them down on the shelves there, on either side. Dr Carmody wouldn't thank us for hauling him about like this, but it's better than peering through half a jungle. And Carmody will have to examine him somewhere else, I think. The less that woman sees, the better. In the meantime, I want to see this for myself.'

He reached into his coat and drew out a pocket knife. Unfolding it, he extended the blunt side and used it to gently lift aside the left flap of Coulton's jacket. The white shirt beneath was plainly bloodied, but it was by no means soaked. The stain originated high up on the man's left side, where a patch of cloth of about a hand's breadth was thickly sodden, and from there it spread in a darkly glistening delta across his ribs.

Gideon had disgraced himself in the first days of his service by fainting at a post-mortem examination, but those had been different circumstances. What he saw before him now put him in mind of a scene in a threepenny melodrama, of a player lying with a hand clasped to his breast, his mortal wound no more than a plucked-out scarlet handkerchief. He said nothing, fearful of betraying his ignorance, but he could not fathom it – there was hardly any blood.

The Inspector scratched his chin, but the look on his face was not one of puzzlement. He nodded and gave a low, bitter grunt. He undid Coulton's tie and folded it carefully before setting it aside. Then, with sure and practised strokes, he began cutting open the man's remaining clothing.

'The location of the wound.' He glanced up at Milo. 'Would you care to hazard a guess?'

Milo's answer was prompt. 'Between the fourth rib and the fifth, about halfway across.' He moved closer to the body, making a scrupulous examination of the floor tiles before sinking to his haunches. 'And very small, if I am not wrong. An inch or two, no more.'

'See, Bliss?' said Cutter. 'You're not the only scholar among us.'

Gideon eyed Milo with renewed uncertainty. He had seemed an enigmatic figure from the start, with his assured manner and his enviably stylish attire. This morning he had been a gunsmith and now, without a word of explanation, he was a trusted associate, pronouncing with the easy confidence of a surgeon on the characteristics of fatal wounds.

The Inspector laid bare the dead man's torso. 'Bliss,' he said, his voice low and solemn. 'More light.'

Gideon's answering look was sullen, but once he had returned with the lamp he found himself absorbed. There was very little blood, though what blood there was looked as inky and viscous as pitch. More puzzling still was the wound itself. Most murders, in Gideon's small experience, were acts of inexpert savagery, and most fatal wounds gave a lurid accounting of the victim's fate.

Coulton's injury was not of that kind. Scarcely an inch from end to end, the incision had begun to pucker and swell, but even now it appeared impossibly neat. Gideon could not imagine how such a wound could kill a man, or even how it might have been inflicted. However stealthy the murderer had been, the killing stroke must have come at close quarters. And this Coulson could not have been easily overpowered. His exposed flanks were thickly muscled, and in life he must have stood a little over six feet, taller even than the inspector. He had a brutish look, even in death. His whitened jaw was nicked and ill-shaven, and beneath the loosened flap of his shirt collar Gideon could make out crude scrawls of ink.

'Sir,' he said, gesturing towards the marks.

'A tattoo,' said Cutter. 'Of a crow, or something like it.'

'Ah,' said Gideon. He hesitated, still wary of appearing foolish. 'And the blood, sir? Will Dr Carmody be able to account for it, do you think? For why there is so little, I mean.'

'Account for it?' The Inspector gave a bleak chuckle. 'He'll likely write a monograph about it. It's not a thing you see every day. Is it, Milo?'

Milo did not answer at once. His gaze was still held by the wound, and for once his face did not appear impassive. It betrayed what might have been wonderment. Reaching out, he held his flexed wrist above the man's rib cage, extending two fingertips in approximation of a blade. His head cocked to one side, he made a sequence of minute adjustments to their attitude and elevation. Seeming satisfied at last, he withdrew his hand with a reverent sigh.

'Not every day,' he said quietly. 'And like this, so perfect? Truthfully, I have never seen it. I have heard it spoken of, but only – what is the expression? *En principe?*'

'In theory,' Gideon said.

'Just so, in theory. And perhaps it will be plain enough to your Dr Carmody, when he has opened him up. Then it looks simple, perhaps. There is little blood because the knife did not strike an artery.' He touched his own chest. 'It struck the left chamber of the heart.'

The lamp shuddered in Gideon's grip. He had inured himself to a good deal, in the last year, but he nurtured a peculiar horror of such injuries. Nothing was inviolate, it seemed. Not even the heart. 'Sorry,' he said. 'It's just rather . . .'

'Yes,' said Milo, not unkindly. 'Yes, it is. It is very difficult also. First, you must reach the heart, which nature does not want.'

Steadying himself, Milo reached out again, this time with both hands. 'The heart is here,' he said, his left index finger poised above the breastbone. 'But it is no good stabbing a man there. That bone is hard and thick for a reason. So, you must go in here.'

With the opposite finger, he measured out the distance to the wound. 'Between the fourth rib and the fifth, just as I said. And you see, in a man this size, that is nine or ten inches. But that is not all. Let us say your knife is long enough. The right weapon would be a *poignard*, maybe. It is long, yes, but at the tip it is like a needle. You know what happens if you stick a needle in a man's heart?'

Gideon shook his head. He was disinclined to contemplate it.

'Nothing,' said Milo with a casual shrug. 'It does not pop like a balloon. It is made of strong muscle, and it is filled with blood. You make a little prick, and the pressure from within closes it up again. You have not killed the man, but you have made his temper very fierce. And now your good hand is nowhere useful.'

'Yes,' said Gideon faintly. 'Yes, I see.'

'*Alors*,' said Milo. 'It is not enough to make a little hole. And you cannot twist, since your blade is trapped between the ribs. You must slice, and yet still it is not so easy. The tip is a long way from your hand, so the force is weak. You remember cutting your chops, in the eating house? Well, imagine you are trying to do it through a keyhole.'

Milo rose from his place and stepped back, perching on the rim of a great stone pot and assuming a meditative air. 'It is not only difficult,' he said, 'it is close to impossible. But if you do it right, then this is what you get. The heart is stopped at once, and the man drops like a stone at your feet. There is not much blood because now there is nothing to pump it out. There is only gravity, and soon the blood is too thick. Henri, may I give you my professional opinion?'

The Inspector rose in his turn, though his eyes lingered on the body. 'Milo,' he said wearily. 'You are a charming fellow, I'm sure, but it has been some years since I felt any romantic longings. It was for your professional opinion that I brought you here.'

Milo accepted this with an equable nod. 'Very well,' he said. 'I will tell you. This here, it is a nice trick, *hein*? It shows talent. But doing this work, it is not performing on a stage, and those who pay you do not want to be entertained. What they want is to be sure. You yourself want to be sure, since otherwise you may not live to spend the money. So, you cut the man's throat like a normal person and it is done. You go home, you take a bath and a cognac, you go to bed. But the man who did this – I can admire him, maybe, but I cannot respect him.'

Gideon had been staring as Milo delivered this summation – the nature of the Frenchman's true occupation was becoming increasingly evident – but something in the Inspector's expression caught his attention. Something fleeting and sorrowful. 'The man who did this,' he repeated.

Milo spread his hands, as if he failed to see the point, but Cutter's attention was already elsewhere. 'No doubt that's all very reasonable,' he said, 'but we have no time to ponder the matter any longer. We have more than one murder to investigate, and I fancy we've spent far longer over the first than Mrs Lytton would like.'

The Inspector skirted about Coulton's still form, but he paused halfway to the doors and stooped to examine an orchid.

'Listen to me now, both of you,' he said. 'It may be too early yet for giving opinions. Remember that this fellow here was no more than an obstacle, and we have yet to see the main event. As for theatrics, I like them no more than Milo, but I'm sorry to tell you that we've done more tonight than make a house call. We've walked onto a stage, and we must be mindful from now on that we have an audience of our own. Our murderer knows it, you may be sure, but do not let that fool you – our murderer has precious little interest in entertaining anyone. But if I'm right about this person's intentions, then God help us all, for we are going to see more than mere trickery. We're going to see the performance of a lifetime.'

Five

S ir *Aneurin Considine* might have been sleeping.
The doors to his library had been left standing open, and
when Gideon entered, he was struck by the homely serenity of the
scene before him. Gentle lamplight spilled from sconces fixed to the
bookcases, and a scattering of lesser lights burned beneath tasselled
shades.

Sir Aneurin himself was seated in a winged armchair before
the fireplace. The chair stood with its back to the doors, and when
they entered nothing could be seen of its elderly occupant but his
mottled scalp. A book was splayed face down on the hearth rug,
yet at a glance even that might have been easily dismissed. Gideon
had encountered any number of octogenarians at Cambridge, and
they were apt to doze off, letting their books slip from their grasp.
Indeed, he had known them to do so during tutorials.

But if Sir Aneurin had fallen into a doze, he had been roused from
it. Taking his place at the Inspector's side, Gideon saw that there
was nothing tranquil in the dead man's posture. His head had come
to rest where it did only after someone had wrenched it forward
and stabbed him in the back of the neck, leaving his fawn-coloured
smoking jacket drenched almost to its cuffs with blood.

The old man's eyes were wide open and had rolled back in their
sockets so that only the whites showed, ghastly and lustreless. His
jaw had locked half askew, leaving his mouth plaintively agape. For

a moment Gideon stared, then he twisted away, his hand clamped to his face. 'His tongue, sir. His tongue is gone.'

The Inspector sighed dolefully. 'No, it isn't, Bliss. Look again.'

Gideon forced himself to comply, though he kept one eye closed and his face half averted. At first he could make out nothing but Sir Aneurin's teeth, a bracelet of pitted ochre bathed in a sickly pink-ish foam. Then something resolved itself deep in the cavity of the mouth, something taut and white amidst the dim bulges and the membranous hollows.

'Did he—' His throat constricted again. 'Oh, my. Did he swallow it?'

'Not on purpose,' the Inspector muttered. He had crossed to the fireplace, where he had found some cause for agitation. 'Look at this, will you,' he said, jerking the handle of the damper. 'Every lamp filled to the gills and the fire blazing fit to roast an ox. If that blasted Mrs Lytton wants a tour of the Yard, she is going the right way about it. Open a window, someone, or we will have to pour this fellow's body into a stockpot.'

Milo obliged him, casually hauling up the sash of the nearest window. Gideon was grateful for the resulting draught of crisp air, but he felt a surge of resentment too. Opening the window was a trifling task, to be sure, but it was a task that would normally have fallen to him. If not for such minor functions, he might have been left on many occasions with nothing to do.

He straightened and coughed. Remembering Cutter's earlier injunction, he fished out his notebook. Since nothing else came readily to mind, he jotted down the word *frenulum*, underlining it with a swift and resolute stroke of his pencil.

'Chartreuse,' said Milo, returning to the hearth and perching on the arm of a chair.

Gideon looked up warily. 'I beg your pardon?' he said.

'The colour of the drapes,' said Milo, flicking a hand towards the windows. 'Chartreuse, I think. But perhaps you wish to check. Colours and fabrics, these things are not my – what is it? – my *métier*?'

'Yes, thank you,' said Gideon with the faintest trace of asperity. 'The word is used in English also. But I was recording an anatomical detail, in point of fact.'

'Good man, Bliss,' said Cutter, who had quelled the fire and was now wiping the coal dust from his hands with the hem of a linen tablecloth. 'If it is the anatomical detail that caught my eye, there will be a prize in it for you.'

'Well, sir—'

'But never mind that for now,' the Inspector said, returning his attention to the body. 'I am getting ahead of myself, and we must give Sir Ovaltine here his due.'

With that the Inspector pulled on his gloves and took hold of Sir Aneurin's shoulders. Handling the frail corpse without ceremony, he wrested it free of the bloody upholstery and allowed the head and torso to slump over the arm of the chair.

'Hmph,' he said, considering. 'There, look, on the back of his neck. That's a nasty-looking nick.'

Releasing the body and stepping back, he surveyed the remainder of the dead man's person. Sir Aneurin's arms were left out-thrust and stiffly asplay, his fingers curled into puny fists.

'Do you see that, Bliss?' said Cutter. 'Make a note of it, like a good fellow, and be sure to put down the time. And have a stab – no, that's an unfortunate word to use. Have a guess at the temperature when we came in. I want some notion of whether this rigor is coming or going. Either way, we'll be obliged to tell poor Carmody that this specimen here was cooked like a Christmas goose.'

'Of course, sir,' said Bliss. It was not a matter of great consequence, but it was a step up from documenting the furnishings. 'I will give a precise account.'

'In the meantime,' said Cutter, stooping to peer at the victim's nape, 'we must make out what we can of the manner of death. What do you say this time, Milo? Enough blood for your liking?'

Milo sauntered to the Inspector's side. He affected an idle interest as he examined the wound. 'Well, what do you wish me to say? Again, it was prettily done, but why not just cut his throat?' It would be nothing, like killing a little *poussin* for the table. But now you will tell me again that I am speaking too soon, and that I am ignorant of some great mystery.'

'Did I hurt your feelings, Milo? If I did you must get over it, I'm afraid. We have an arrangement, as you might recall, so don't start mooning like a girl with an empty dance card. Now, tell me: What was prettily done? And *how* was it done, more to the point? Show me the moves.'

Milo made a prim adjustment to his cuffs, then he stepped briskly to the rear of the chair. 'Very well,' he said. 'He comes up behind.' He paced forward, beginning a demonstration. 'He takes hold of the head, perhaps by the hair. He jerks it forward, like so, then he brings the knife hand down. And then . . .'

But here Milo hesitated. Leaning over the back of the armchair, he altered the set of his arm. Seeming dissatisfied, he began again, curling his fingers about an imaginary hilt and sweeping his empty fist through a complicated sequence of arcs and flexions.

'*Merde*,' he said, letting his hand fall slack.

'*Merde*, indeed,' said the Inspector. 'It isn't so easy, is it? Not for such fine work as that. Your target is what, about the size of a fig? And to reach it, your knife must pass between the base of the skull

91

and the top of the spine. You have made space, wrenching the old boy's head forward, but not much of it. You need a sure hold for a thrust like that, and you couldn't find one. You were at the end of your reach, with your wrist twisted out of true.'

Milo raised a cautious fingertip. 'Perhaps ... perhaps if you pushed his head further; if you pressed his face to the arm of the chair.' He leaned over the chair again, his arm straining outwards as he tested some new hypothesis. But even as he did so, his face betrayed misgivings.

'You have your answer, I believe,' Cutter said. 'Your grip is better, but look at your reach. You're like a fellow picking a cabbage over a garden wall.'

The gunsmith gave a small grudging nod. 'It is true,' he said. 'But perhaps he was not so precise this time. There is no need, in this case. It is quicker, striking the— again, I do not have the word. We would say *la moelle*, like the pith of a fruit.'

Gideon looked up from his notebook. Again, he found that the word came to him unbidden. His late uncle had been a doctor of both medicine and divinity, and as a child Gideon had pored over his textbooks. He had hoped for his benefactor's favour. He had been hoping for someone's favour all his life.

'It is called the medulla, I think.'

'The medulla, yes. If you strike there, it is very quick. But my meaning was, what does it matter if you cut an inch too low? You are stabbing a man in the neck and he is two hundred years old, so what do you care? You are not making a lace cap for a baby.'

'You have the soul of a poet, Milo,' said Cutter. 'Dr Carmody will confirm it, I hope, but for now I will ask you to take it on trust. Our murderer did not miss by an inch, or even by an eighth of an inch. So, how was it done?'

Milo shook his head slowly. 'I confess, Henri, I do not understand this little game. But how was it done, or how could it be done? Honestly, I cannot see a way. Unless . . . but no, we are imagining stories for children now.'

'Unless what?'

'Unless you knelt before him in plain view, unless you were whispering to him like a lover. Ugh, *putain* – I will see that tonight before I sleep.'

Cutter snorted richly. 'Bless your innocence if that's all that troubles your dreams. You could do it kneeling, you said. So, show me.'

For once, Milo appeared at a loss. 'What? How can I show you?'

Seizing Sir Aneurin's shoulders once more, the Inspector levered his torso from the arm of the chair. Then, like a draper fussing over the posture of a mannequin, he brought the corpse halfway upright in its seat. Shifting his grip, he drew back to examine the effect.

'Bliss,' he said, 'will you oblige me by fetching up some cushions? Make them good and plump, mind. They are not for decoration.'

He made the request sound perfectly ordinary, as if he were merely sending to the stationers for stamps. After only a moment's hesitation, Gideon began hunting about the library and it was not long before he had gathered up a sizeable pile.

'Might these be acceptable, sir? They appear to be expensive items, I'm afraid.'

'All the better,' said the Inspector. 'With a bit of luck, we will find they were gifts from Mrs Lytton. Now, we want two on either side to keep him from toppling. Stuff them down against the chair arms there. Get them good and firm.'

Gideon complied as if in a trance. In some deep stratum of his being, he remained troubled – was he desecrating human remains, even if only very gently? – but he was once again providing practical assistance, while Milo looked on with patent disdain. The thought gave him some consolation.

'Good,' said Cutter. 'Now, that stiff bolster with the thistles on it – shove that down behind the small of his back.'

'I believe the pattern is of fleur-de-lys, sir.'

'I don't give a damn if it's the pattern of Her Majesty's drawers, Bliss. The small of his back, I said. We are propping him up, not tucking him into bed.'

When the cushions had been positioned to the Inspector's satisfaction, Gideon withdrew discreetly. Cutter himself made some final adjustments, then tentatively loosened his hold of Sir Aneurin's jacket. At last he stepped back, his face grimly creased as he scrutinised his handiwork.

'It will have to do,' he said finally. 'He looks more like a mummified juggler than an attentive listener, but it'll serve our purposes. Now then, Milo. Show me.'

Milo gave an elaborate sigh. '*Jesu Maria*. What is the purpose of this, Henri?'

'I could tell you that it is to serve justice, but now is not the time for such talk. For now, it's to keep me content, which should be reason enough. So, get on with it. Show me.'

Milo let out a *pfff* of distaste, but he saw that there was no more point in arguing. Composing himself, he approached the seated corpse and began a complicated dumb show of measurement and calculation. Coming to some reluctant conclusion, he lowered himself gracefully to one knee.

'You understand that this will not be exact,' he said.

'It goes without saying. Oh, and Milo – you were fairly near the mark, I believe, but forget the part about the whispering lovers. Whatever guise our murderer came in, it would have been

believable. Imagine instead that you are kneeling to offer him something. Show me.'

Milo seemed to accept this, since it no doubt came as a relief.
Shifting slightly, he positioned his left hand above Sir Aneurin's
right, gathering his fingers as if to display some trinket. The illusion
was not altogether convincing, since the old man's bony fingers remained tightly curled. If anything, it looked as if Milo were trying to
persuade him to surrender something precious.

Milo must have thought it a close enough approximation. He
brought his right hand – his knife hand – into play. As it snaked
about the dead man's right side, he leaned in closer, making a show
of disguising his movements. Bringing his lips within inches of Sir
Aneurin's left ear, he began murmuring.

'*Regardez-le, monsieur. N'est-ce pas joli? Prenez-le, prenez-le.* Take
it, please. It is so pretty, so very pretty.'

All the while, he was making tiny and stealthy refinements to
the position of the knife hand. He fell silent, his locked fist poised
between the dead man's shoulder blades. There was a moment of
utter stillness, then Milo gave a violent hiss and – with astonishing
swiftness and precision – his fist flashed through the empty air,
coming to a halt no more than half an inch from the base of Sir
Aneurin's skull.

'Check it please, Henri,' he said, taking care not to move a muscle.
'It feels right, but from here I am aiming blind.'

Cutter leaned in, intent as a hawk. Then his expression softened.
'Well, Milo,' he said. 'It's a good thing I know where you were
today.'

'It is good?'

'It is damn near perfect. I will let you get up now, before you strain
something.'

Milo rose with a discreet flourish, pausing with a sharp *tsk* to flick a shred of something from his trouser leg. 'Well,' he said. 'It seems you are happy at last, so perhaps you no longer need me.'

Cutter did not turn around. He had dismantled the nest of cushions and was endeavouring to restore Considine's remains to something approximating dignity. 'The word I used was "content". Happiness is another thing altogether. In any case, I must ask another favour of you. I've worked you to the bone today, I know, but it's a small thing. Well, two small things.'

Milo thumbed the bridge of his nose, which seemed to be his delicate way of signalling impatience.

'Good man,' said Cutter. He made some brisk final adjustments and stepped back to examine the results. 'Well, never mind. We're not putting him on the marriage market. Yes, two small things. First, you might seek out Mrs Lytton before you leave. Tell her I'm obliged to her for waiting, but given the lateness of the hour, I will not trouble her with further questions this evening. That housekeeper can get herself off to bed, too.'

Gideon felt compelled to interrupt. 'Forgive me, sir, but were you not most anxious to speak to Mrs Lytton? I made a note to that effect.'

At any other time, the Inspector might have issued some severe rebuke – he seldom welcomed interruptions, and nor was he fond of explaining himself – but the outcome of his grisly experiments seemed to have given him some obscure satisfaction. 'So I was, Bliss. At that time, I believed she might be withholding something of importance – and no doubt she would have, had it been in her power – but the case is now altered.'

'Of course, Inspector,' Gideon answered, though he had no notion of what Cutter meant. 'I quite understand.'

'The second thing, Milo,' the Inspector went on, as if Gideon had not spoken at all. 'On your way home, you must pay another call on your friend at the Yard— but no, it's getting on for ten, and by now he will be guzzling his walnuts and port. Never mind, our Duty Sergeant will do – third floor, last door on the left. Tell him I sent you, and that I have two guests needing immediate accommodation at Golden Lane. That is one of the better morgues, by the way. He'll give you an earful about City facilities and forms in triplicate and what have you, but you need pay him no mind. There will be more of these to come, and I will not have them slung in some falling-down shed for river rats. Have you got all that?'

'You know my business, Henri. My instructions are often specific. But listen, I want to ask something of you also.'

'Do not think me ungrateful, Milo, but I'm a little pressed just now.'

'It is only a question. It is the question I asked you before, but you did not seem to hear it.'

Having made the body presentable, Cutter turned his attention to a nearby bureau. Encountering a drawer that would not yield, he drew a cunning-looking implement from his coat pocket. The Inspector had nimble fingers, for a man of his stature. 'Well,' he said, selecting a toothed blade, 'I am fonder of asking questions than answering them, I'll grant you that. But since I do not recall what you wanted to know, you may try your luck again.'

'What was the point of all this, Henri? So, these were skilful jobs. You did not need me to tell you that. One look and you could see it. What difference does it make, if someone is stabbed from the front or the back? How will it help you to find this man?'

The Inspector seemed on the point of answering, then his gaze flickered away to the darkened windows. He let out a breath that might have been the shade of a laugh. 'Now, Milo. You know I cannot uncover all my methods. You are what you are, even if we are on cordial terms. But I have put you to a good deal of trouble today, so I will make a small concession. For a start, I will tell you that you have asked the wrong question. A murder is not always hiding something from you. Sometimes a murder is telling you a secret. Does that satisfy you?'

Milo's lips took on a sour quirk. 'Did you mean it to?'

But Cutter had already turned his back. The bureau's lock had not detained him for long, and he was now rifling assiduously through a cache of papers. 'Goodnight to you, Milo,' he said over his shoulder. 'You have earned your cognac and your rest.'

After Milo had taken his leave, the Inspector occupied himself for a while longer at Sir Aneurin's desk. While he did so, Gideon maintained a discreet distance and, since he could not very well record what was now taking place, made some inconsequential emendations to his earlier notes. At length, he heard the front door being closed. Milo had made his exit, having conveyed the Inspector's message. The Inspector himself seemed to take this as a cue. Returning the papers to their drawer, he slid it shut almost noise-lessly. When he had locked it again, he rose with sudden purpose and crossed swiftly to the hearth.

No sooner had he reached it than the doors to the library were wrenched open. Mrs Lytton did not enter the room, but her eyes swept over its entire expanse as if itemising every last speck of dust. Gideon allowed his fingers to creep to his waist, fearful that her devouring gaze would find his shirt tails untucked, but the Inspector did not stir. Keeping his back to the doors, he warmed his hands by the damped remnants of the fire.

'Mrs Lytton,' he said. 'You received my message, I take it.'

'I received it, yes.' Her poise was unaltered, but there was a new brittleness in her voice. 'I chose to ignore it. You wish to remove my uncle's remains, I gather. I'm afraid I cannot allow that.'

'I agree with you entirely, madam.' Cutter's demeanour was tranquil. 'You cannot allow it. I'm sorry to tell you, however, that you cannot forbid it either. We have Members of Parliament for that, and they have already ruled on the matter.'

The Inspector kept his back turned, and for a moment Mrs Lytton studied it with feline intensity. 'Oh, I *see*,' she said. 'You're one of those moderately educated policemen who can recite his acts and his sections. Does it impress people, usually? Perhaps it does, in certain quarters. But it won't do you any good here. Did you happen to look around you on your way here, Inspector? Do you have the slightest idea where you *are*?'

The Inspector agitated his shoulder, as if working a kink from a muscle. 'Well, madam,' he said mildly, 'as for my education, it's not even moderate. However, I do know that I'm not within the limits of a palace, which I'm heartily glad of. Did you know that the Queen's household has its own coroner? It's a thing I discovered as a young officer, and I will admit that it caused me some embarrassment. A fellow I had chased through Hyde Park leapt over a wall, you see, and managed to impale himself on the Duchess of Argyll's sundial. The Princess herself took it in good sport, as I recall, but I was sent packing all the same. In any case, the point of the story is this: if you meant to obstruct my business, you ought to have dragged your uncle a hundred yards down The Mall to the Palace. As it is, I'm afraid you must suffer me.'

'Inspector,' she said, advancing now into the room, 'I think perhaps I must make myself clearer—'

Cutter whirled about at this, shedding his placid guise, and in three strides he had crossed the floor to confront her. 'You're mistaken there, Mrs Lytton,' he said. 'For you have done more than make yourself clear; you have shown me more than you intended.

Now, let me be just as plain with you, so that I need endure no more of your hints and insinuations. I do not know you, madam, but I've known your like before. I've made myself unwelcome in finer houses than this one, and I have been threatened by better than you. Yet here I am, still walking abroad. Will I tell you why that is, Mrs Lytton?'

She raised an eyebrow by the merest fraction. 'Oh, do. You enthral me.'

'The reason is simple,' the Inspector said. 'It's not who I am that matters. It's what I know and what I can do with it. Do you not wonder why I did not speak up an hour ago, though you began in much the same way? You made sure to let us know that you were a person of influence, and you made a great show of being bored and discommoded by our presence. And then there was that business with your uncle's letters. That was a nice touch, I'll grant you. Oh, don't mind me, I'm just rooting through my murdered relative's affairs. Nothing you need to concern yourself with. Not the finest performance I've seen, but not the worst either. Which reminds me . . .'

Reaching into his coat, the Inspector produced the bundle of envelopes he had confiscated earlier. 'You may have these back,' he said, tossing them onto a side table. 'If they were of any value, you would have done your tampering in private. That much was obvious straight away, but I went along with your little charade all the same. And it was a bolder bit of misdirection than I thought. You weren't offering me the letters because you were holding back something else. You had nothing to hold back, but you wanted me to believe otherwise.'

If Mrs Lytton was discomfited, she did not show it. 'You seem remarkably sure of yourself,' she said, her tone still even and frigid. 'You realise that I'd been here for hours, don't you? That I had all the time in the world?'

'I believe I noted it,' Cutter answered. 'And yet you overlooked the one thing there was to be found. It would likely have meant nothing to you, if that's any comfort. I imagine there were some things your uncle kept close, even from you. But I found it all the same, and it tells me a good deal. I will not say much more than that, but I will offer you a word of advice.'

Mrs Lytton gave a vitreous laugh. '*You*? You think you are in a position to advise *me*?'

'If I were not, Mrs Lytton, you would not have scurried up here the minute you got my message. I had a feeling you might, though I can give you no satisfaction. Or at least, I cannot tell you what you want to know. I do not say that to spite you, Mrs Lytton. What happened here today was not some intrigue for you to untangle. It was part of a long and sad story that has not yet reached its end. So, my advice to you is simply this: you may complain to whoever will listen of my rough manners, but let it rest there. Believe me when I tell you that there are some secrets you should not discover.'

Mrs Lytton held the Inspector's gaze calmly as she considered her response. 'A long and sad story,' she said at last. 'Do you know, when you said that, you did look truly sad. Only fleetingly, but still. I wonder why that might be.'

The Inspector's face darkened at this. 'I must ask you to leave us now, madam,' he said. 'We're not yet finished here.'

'No, indeed,' said Mrs Lytton with a faint smile. 'We are not yet finished. We will see each other again.'

When Mrs Lytton had withdrawn, the Inspector closed the doors behind her and stood for a moment in thought. Gideon watched him furtively, hoping to divine something of his present mood, but that was an inexact science on the best of days. Cutter's expression was not especially forbidding, but nor did it betray any other signs that Gideon recognised. It was still and opaque, a face that might have been carved from marble.

Gideon had intended to choose his moment with care, but it had been a long and bewildering day. He had a great many questions, and he had spent hours standing meekly by while the Inspector took others into his confidence. He straightened his back and cleared his throat, but before he could begin, the Inspector held a finger to his lips.

'Wait, Bliss,' he said.

Gideon subsided into a grudging silence.

'There,' said Cutter. 'She is gone, finally, though she made a long and drawn-out production even of that.'

It was a moment before Gideon understood. 'Ah,' he said. 'You were listening for Mrs Lytton's departure.'

'What did you think I was doing? Observing a minute's silence? Of course I was listening, though she's as quiet as a famished cat. Your fidgeting didn't help either. Now then, we must stir ourselves. The wagon from the Yard will be here before long, and we have one more bit of business with our friend here.'

'Of course, sir,' said Gideon, though he could not imagine what the Inspector meant. 'Only, I had hoped—'

'Yes, Bliss,' said the Inspector, who had returned to the hearth. This time his attention seemed to be fixed on Sir Aneurin's arm. 'You had hoped for some answers. No doubt you have more questions than a census taker by now, but most of them will have to wait. All but one, in fact.'

Gideon felt his right eyelid twitch, as it was apt to do when he was exhausted. He rubbed at it with his knuckle. 'Only one, sir?'

'Only one, yes. There is only one question you *should* be asking, if you are any kind of detective. And come here, will you. I'm not tinkering with this fellow's arm for the good of my health.'

Gideon gave a discreet sigh. He had hoped never to look again at those avulsed and sightless eyes, at that desiccated and tongueless maw. Despondently, he returned to his place at the Inspector's side.

'Well?' said Cutter. He stepped back, and Gideon saw that he had contrived to loosen the cadaver's right arm. It remained unnaturally contorted, but the victim's tightly curled fist was no longer clamped to his breast. Instead it was extended outwards by perhaps eight or nine inches, as if Sir Aneurin were on the point of surrendering some cherished prize.

But Gideon remained mystified. When Cutter had directed Milo to re-enact the murder, he had at least hinted at his objectives, but the purpose of this exercise seemed wholly opaque.

'Forgive me, sir,' he said. 'I am rather tired, and it may be that there is some point I have failed to grasp.'

'Oh, for the love of suffering Christ,' said the Inspector. 'What must I do, lay out a trail of breadcrumbs? What did I say to Milo? What did I say to Mrs Lytton, come to that?'

Gideon's eyelid twitched again. He rubbed at it with the heel of his hand, and when he tried to focus again on the dead man his vision was smeared and lopsided. The buttermilk knurls of Sir Aneurin's knuckles whitened; the blotches on his skin darkened like ink on a blotter.

What had the inspector said? Or rather, since he had said a great many curious things, what had he said that ought to have seemed noteworthy? And what were those marks called again, those hideous blotches that formed on the skin in the hours after death? *Livor mortis*, wasn't it?

'Well?' said Cutter again. 'Are you deep in thought, Bliss, or are you having one of your apparitions?'

'A moment, sir.' Wait, wait. There was something. Whatever his shortcomings as a policeman, Gideon had a few paltry advantages. He had been a student of divinity once. He had spent thousands of hours attending to endless litanies of mystery. He had been a good student, though a failed one in the end. He had not always understood, but he had paid attention.

To Milo: *Imagine you are offering him something.*

And to Mrs Lytton: *Your uncle may have kept some things close.*

Gideon opened his eyes again. Craning his neck, he peered again at Sir Aneurin's bony fist. Not from the front this time, but from the side. For a moment he saw nothing, just the roseate whorl of shadows where the thumb encircled the bundled fingers.

In a low voice, he said, 'Sir, the thing you found. Is it in Sir Aneurin's hand?'

'Tell me what you see, Bliss.'

'Almost nothing, sir. Just the tiniest nub of something, I think. Something pale and chalky.'

'The tiniest nub, indeed. Very good, Bliss. I was near to despairing, but you got there in the end. Stand back a little now. I will need some room. Oh, and Bliss?'

'Sir?'

'I managed so far without breaking any bones, but I fear I must cut some corners now. Do not mind the noise.'

Gideon swallowed carefully. 'I understand, sir.'

'Good lad,' said Cutter, and with a grim snuffle he addressed himself once more to the body. His broad back obscured his actions from Gideon's view, but nothing could mask the sounds. Cutter shifted his position, his elbow jutting as he altered his grip. He muttered something, then grunted with effort. Gideon heard a sombre crunch, like the yielding of snow under a boot heel. A sourness blossomed in his throat.

At length the Inspector drew back. He had done his best to refold the brutalised hand, but the results were imperfect. He turned away with a curt shrug.

'Needs must,' he said. 'Now, then—'

Cutter broke off, hearing the timorous peal of a bell. He strode briskly to the window. 'The boys from the Yard,' he said. 'And they brought a respectable-looking carriage, at least. I had visions of a pair of shovel-handed lummoxes with an open cart. Right,' he said, returning, 'we must keep this brief, since we may be obliged to let them in ourselves. First, I will set your mind at rest. The item I have just prised from that poor fellow's hand is a piece of evidence. I've no intention of concealing it, or at least not for long. You may put it in your notes, but you need not go into detail. Call it an article found on the person of the deceased, but say no more than that for now. Ordinarily, I would be content to wait for Dr Carmody to come across it, though of course I would have to listen to him crowing over how I missed it. As it is, well . . . it's not that I don't trust Carmody, but there'll be all sorts flocking about a case like this. I must keep a tight hold on certain particulars.'

'Yes, sir,' said Gideon promptly. He had been party to such minor subterfuges before, and it was not matters of conscience that now preoccupied him. He glanced at the Inspector's gloved fist.

'Very well,' said Cutter, looking about him. He settled upon a table with a serviceable lamp that stood in a nearby alcove. Here they would be partly hidden if anyone were to enter unannounced. 'Come closer, then.'

Gideon realised that he had no idea of what he expected, beyond fanciful notions that he had most likely encountered in silly novels. In such books, the dead were most often found to be clutching some glinting heirloom, or the key to a hidden crypt. What he had glimpsed was not like that.

The Inspector regarded him gravely. 'Understand, Bliss, that there will be no time to explain. Not now. And what I am about to show you – you will not speak of it to anyone without my leave. Not Milo, not our superiors, not anyone. Understood?'

'Understood, sir.' Gideon tugged his coat closer. The window was still open, and he was newly conscious of the cold. The Inspector had wrapped the item he spoke of in a navy blue handkerchief. As he teased out the folds of cloth, Gideon was struck once more by the peculiar contradictions in the Inspector's nature. He was a man of lean but imposing build, and he had just cracked open a cadaver's fist as if it were a mussel shell. Yet he handled this little bundle as if it were the holiest of relics.

He held out the contents of the handkerchief, and Gideon went still. He knew what it was, of course. He had seen others like it. But none so fragile. None so small.

It looked paler now, against the dark cloth, but it was not perfectly white. It must have been bluish and pristine once, but it was yellowed now by age. It had been scoured clean, but even so it bore foul traces along its fissures, and at its minutely honeycombed terminus. Wherever it had come from, it had once lain in the ground.

'You know what it is?' The Inspector spoke so softly that Gideon might not have recognised his voice.

He lowered his head. 'A fingerbone. A phalanx. A child's?'

'A child's,' the Inspector said. 'Eight, ten, twelve. Hard to say. Poorly fed, as like as not. Well, now you know.'

He folded the bone away again, just as gently, and slipped it into his coat. 'Best get downstairs,' he said. 'Someone has to let those two charmers in, now that I've sent everyone packing.'

Gideon was still staring, his eyes fixed vaguely on an empty pool of lamplight. He blinked and turned away. He brought his cuff to his cheek.

'But how did it . . . what does it . . .'

The Inspector laid a hand on his shoulder, just for an instant. He moved away towards the doors. The bell had rung again, somewhere down below. 'Not now,' he said.

Gideon stirred himself, settling his disordered clothes and raking a hand through his hair. He did not look again at the corpse as he left, but searched the empty air that surrounded it, trying to imagine, trying to see. His vision was clouded still, and his limbs felt heavy and useless. He was deeply tired, he realised, but he did not want to sleep. He only wanted to close his eyes.

The Inspector paused at the doors, his head bent. 'It's a sad story,' he said again. 'It had a sad beginning, and I'll warrant it will come to a sad end. There will be time enough for tears, Bliss. There always is.'

Six

M iss Octavia Hillingdon was often a difficult person to find. Yet Gideon reflected, as he skirted the summit of Parliament Hill and struck out towards the ponds, that he had sought her out in much less attractive places than Hampstead Heath on a bright spring morning.

Gideon and the Inspector had made Miss Hillingdon's acquaintance while investigating another difficult case. She had been conducting enquiries of her own, in her capacity as a newspaper writer, and she had proven herself a formidable ally, possessing both enviable connections and a voracious appetite for research. It was Gideon's understanding that Miss Hillingdon remained a journalist of sorts. She had inherited her grandfather's newspaper in the early days of their acquaintance, and soon afterwards had established a periodical of her own. She was of a restless disposition, however, and she had acquired a good many competing interests in the same period.

Once, having need of Miss Hillingdon's advice while she was overseeing sanitation works for an artisanal commune, Gideon had been obliged to converse with her in a sewage tunnel. On another occasion, having promised to assist her in an investigation of industrial pollution, he had tracked her down on Peckham Rye Common. There he had been compelled to board a hot-air balloon, so as to officially witness her observations. Noxious clouds, she said, were being emitted in proximity to the public amenities of Nunhead. Gideon had vomited while hovering above a schoolyard.

Today he felt rather less apprehensive. For one thing, he had been freed of his usual duties, if only for a few hours. It had been three days since the murders, and throughout that time the Inspector had kept up a merciless pace. From seven in the morning until late at night, they had crossed and recrossed the streets between Victoria Embankment and St James's. They had ranged further afield, too, calling at records offices in Rolls House and Temple Chambers, and at obscure parish registry offices from Mortlake all the way to the eaves of Epping Forest.

Gideon had not uttered a word of protest throughout, for there had scarcely been time, nor had he once questioned why he was copying down hundreds of birth records or transcribing the testimony of some gin-addled reprobate who had once served as a quartermaster in the Household Cavalry. Though he could not tell how these obscure enquiries might be connected to the murders, Gideon had simply accepted their necessity. He had found them wearying, however, and he had grown more and more resentful that Cutter should demand so much of him while telling him so little.

It was evident by now that Cutter knew more than he admitted about this case. It was plain, too, that his enquiries were not as haphazard as they appeared, and that he was acting in accordance with some hidden method. Yet for all that the Inspector clung to his secrets, he could not hide his moods. Whatever he was looking for, he had not found it yet. All their scratching around in the archives had so far come to naught.

Yet as much as all this weighed on him, Gideon had felt a childlike elation when the Inspector announced that he was wanted at the Yard. Then the Inspector had come to the point, or as near to it as his pride would allow. He had suggested that Gideon pay a call on Miss Hillingdon.

'You might mention the records,' he said, as if the thought had just occurred to him. 'Tell her we've been doing a bit of digging. Only if the subject comes up, mind. She has a fondness for such things, as I recall.'

'She is a devoted archivist,' Gideon agreed. 'I will be sure to note it in passing.'

'In passing, yes. And you might throw out a few choice details, to give the thing a bit of colour. She'll have read about our friend Considine, since her newspaper friends have made so much of it. You might mention that he was given the rub of the sword twenty years ago, though on what account no one can say. Just in her line, that sort of thing. She might well take an interest. Give her the flavour of the thing, without saying too much.'

Gideon might have replied that there was no great danger of that, since he himself had been told almost nothing. He might have noted, too, that the details he was to mention in passing seemed highly specific. But he had the prospect of half a day's freedom before him, so he was not about to press the point. Instead he had simply stuffed his notebook into his coat and lunged for the hatstand. His high spirits had not dissipated in the intervening hours, and he had hardly minded when he called at Miss Hillingdon's offices to find her out. The weather had taken a pleasant turn, and as he started out downhill towards the South Meadow, he caught traces of sweetness in the newly warmed air.

If Gideon was troubled at all, it was by minor difficulties of navigation. He had come to know London tolerably well in the last year, but the nature of his duties made that knowledge selective. The borough of Hampstead had, presumably, endured its quotient of murders and other outrages, but none that he and the Inspector had looked into. He had been on the Heath only once before today, and he was relying on rather scant directions.

From a clerk at her offices, he had learned that Miss Hillingdon was leading some sort of youth group, which he had not thought unlikely. She was an energetic young woman, and committed to all manner of causes. She had planned an outing to some woods, it seemed, that would take her 'up Kenwood way'. That was the full extent of his knowledge.

He paused to take his bearings. Locating Kenwood had been a simple enough matter. He had consulted a map outside a tea room. The Kenwood estate had been clearly marked, near the north-ern edge of the map, nestled amidst a tidily demarcated patch of woodland. What lay before him now was certainly woodland, but it seemed far from tidily demarcated. He could just about make out its eastern bounds, off in the direction of Highgate, but otherwise it stretched far out of sight.

Hearing a strained cough, Gideon looked about him to find he was being glared at. He had wandered into the midst of a party of watercolourists, he noted, and was obstructing their vista. He touched his cap, muttered a haphazard apology and marched on, suddenly conscious of the impression he must be giving. He was a police sergeant, or nearly so, and presently in uniform. It would not do to give the appearance of dissolute loitering.

He plunged into the woods, settling out of necessity on the most rudimentary of navigation techniques. Since he lacked the skills of an outdoorsman – indeed, he had only a hazy notion of what skills an outdoorsman might possess – he would simply keep within sight of the woodland's border and carry on walking until he had circled its entire expanse. He was not tracking down a solitary fugitive, after all. Miss Hillingdon was here with a youth group, and children were bois-terous and uninhibited creatures. He need only keep half an ear open.

Gideon set out at a stroll, and he soon found his earlier lightness of mood returning. It grew warmer as midday approached, so he slung his jacket over his shoulder and carried his cap in his hand. He whistled, at first in an abstract and desultory way. Then he began mimicking snatches of birdsong, choosing a call from the delicate susurrus that filled the air – he really ought to learn to identify them – and shaping a tentative refrain.

It was as he tried to perfect one particular call, pausing mid-stride to correct its cadence – there, that was it: *tsiyu-tsaauu-tsit-tsit* – that he was shot in the chest with an arrow.

'Ow!' he cried out, staggering backwards and flapping at his chest. The arrowhead was not deeply lodged, but when he winkled it free it left a respectable splotch of blood on his shirtfront. 'Ow,' he said again, more in perplexity than in anguish. 'Honestly, what on—'

'Halt!' called a high, firm voice from somewhere in the surrounding trees. 'Not another step, or I'll shoot again.'

'What?' Gideon looked about him in bemusement. 'Who said that?'

'A *sister*,' said the sharp little voice. 'And I said *halt*. That includes sidling away. You're a prisoner now.'

'What? A sister? Whose sister?' Still searching the shifting foliage, Gideon caught sight of a pale and narrow face with dark streaks on its cheeks. It was a child's face, and its owner was perched high in the crook of a beech tree. She was a young girl, perhaps eight or nine years old.

'Oh, for goodness' sake.' He stooped to pick up his cap, then held it aloft. 'Look here, do you realise I'm a—'

The child had vanished, and it took him a moment to locate her again. She had leapt, it seemed, to a neighbouring tree.

'Do you realise that I'm a policeman? I'm sure you were just play-ing games and didn't mean any harm, but it's rather serious, you know, assaulting a policeman. I could arrest you.'

'No, you couldn't,' the little girl called out. 'You've no authority here. These woods belong to the sisters. Besides, you'd be much too embarrassed.'

'Yes, well . . .' said Gideon, in a less commanding tone. The point had been rather astutely made. 'Be that as it may. Look, you've had your fun, but that really did hurt quite a bit. And I've got police business to see to. I'm going to carry on now, if that's all right. I'd like you to lower your bow, please.'

He took a determined step forward, then hesitated. The girl had narrowed her eyes and drawn her bowstring taut. Her aim appeared disconcertingly steady. 'I warned you,' she said. 'Next time I'll shoot to kill. I am a Sister of Artemis. You ought to fear my wrath.'

'Oh, I do.' Gideon huffed and scratched his ear. 'Honestly, I do. But look, there's no need for wrath.' He looked about him again, alert to the preposterousness of his predicament. What if someone were to come along?

Yes, good day to you. Yes, I am an officer of the Metropolitan Police, and yes, you are correct. I am being held hostage by a small child with a homemade weapon. Now, please move along.

It was some moments before it occurred to him that there must be an adult in the vicinity. The girl's parents, perhaps, or at least a governess.

A second thought arrived in a slow and queasy trickle.

'I say,' he said. 'I say, you're not with Miss Hillingdon, are you?'

A short while later, Gideon was led into a clearing where Octavia stood amidst a ragged half-circle of cross-legged children. She was holding up a length of rope, the girls looking on intently as she held out a carefully formed loop, and so her attention was absorbed. This might have proved awkward, since he had been ordered not to speak without express permission, but presently his escort nudged him forward by a step.

'Sisters!' she called out in a ringing voice. 'I have apprehended an interloper. I have brought him here to answer to the company.'

Octavia looked around distractedly at first, then she let out a shriek of laughter. '*Gideon!*' she cried, rushing over to intervene. 'Oh, how dreadful. I really am sorry. Flora, do put down that bow, for heaven's sake. Gideon is a friend of mine.'

Flora lowered the bow reluctantly. She had kept her arrow tip trained on Gideon all the way here. 'But you posted me as a sentry, Elder Sister. And it's death for anyone who isn't a sister to enter the glade. And I'm Sister Hestia, not Flora.'

'What? All right, Sister Hestia, then. And no, it isn't. You've made that rule up. Oh, Gideon, you poor thing.' She embraced him fondly then stepped back to brush him down. 'Oh, good Lord! Flora, did you *shoot* him?'

Flora's chin jutted defiantly, but her martial fervour seemed to have dissipated a little. 'Well, yes. I *was* the sentry. And you *did* give us archery lessons.'

'Oh, Flora, really. Give that to me.' She disarmed the child with a gently despairing look, then briskly tousled her hair. 'I'm sure you did what you saw as your duty, but our bows are for ceremonial use only. You won't tell your mama, will you? That you shot a man? Because she mightn't let you come again, and we should hate to lose such a valiant sister. All right? Good. Go and sit with the others, then. We're learning how to tie clove hitches.'

After the lesson, the children were dispatched to a nearby camp-fire where lunch was being served. Octavia took Gideon aside, and when she had settled him on a canvas folding stool, she began packing away her ropes and rooting in a picnic backet.

'You will have some lunch, won't you?' she said. 'We could join the girls, but I expect you've had enough of them for one day. And Suki's roasting them a boar. Suki is my – well, she and I are close. You'll meet her in a bit. Anyway, she's roasting a boar, only it's just suckling pig, really. And I'm not sure she's cooked anything on a spit before. Or cooked *anything*, come to that. Comes from money, you see, which is why I'm trying to make a philanthropist of her. Are you hungry? I've got bread and cheese here, and some sort of tart.'

'Oh, you mustn't go to any trouble,' said Gideon, though he was gnawingly hungry. In his eagerness to get away, he had forgotten about breakfast.

'Same old Gideon,' said Octavia, shaking her head. 'You can see I'm not; I'm just plucking things out of baskets at random. And you're probably ravenous. Honestly, that man never remembers that people need to eat and sleep. How is he, by the way? The Inspector, I mean?'

'Hmm?' said Gideon. 'Oh, you know. Same as ever, I suppose. Well, mainly the same.'

Octavia cast him an incisive look. 'Mmm,' she said. 'And he sent you, I suppose? Nothing for months, and then another peremptory request. He has *heard* of visiting, hasn't he? And of writing letters? Here, I've made you up a plate. Well, I've put some things on a plate, at least. It's terribly higgledy-piggledy, I'm afraid.'

Gideon accepted a chipped plate and a sloshing tin mug. On the plate was an enormous slice of bread and butter, ringed with forlorn scraps of picnic food. He took a bite of the bread.

'Mmm, it's delicious. Awfully kind of you.'

'It must be three days old. Look at you, you can hardly chew it. Did he, then? Send you?' Octavia had seated herself opposite him. She gave him a prompting look.

'Well, yes,' said Gideon, managing to swallow his mouthful at last. 'He'd have come himself, I'm sure, if he weren't so taken up just now. Our present case is a murky sort of business, and it seems it might have something of a historical dimension. We've been doing a bit of poring over the records ourselves, but I'm afraid our amateurish efforts aren't proving—'

'Gideon,' said Octavia. 'Please don't do that. The flattery, I mean. You don't have the aptitude. It's disconcerting.'

'Oh, gosh.' Gideon upset his plate and dislodged a pickled onion. 'Oh, no, I wouldn't dream of – that is, naturally, I hold you in the highest esteem, but I only meant to convey that—'

'Oh, stop tying yourself in knots. It was his idea, wasn't it? It's not the sort of thing that occurs to you. What else did he tell you to do? To get me interested without saying too much?'

'Well, I don't know that I'd put it in quite those—'

'It's all right, I know what he's like. Impatient with everyone for not keeping up, and all the while he's got his revelations locked away like the good China.' Octavia dipped her finger in a jam pot and sucked at it. Rearranging herself, she nudged his thigh with the toe of one boot. 'Well?'

'Well, yes,' Gideon admitted, swirling the contents of his tin mug. 'It has been a bit like that. Even more so than usual, unless I'm imagining it. It's become quite trying.'

'Gideon, listen. It was trying a year ago, but now? It's intolerable. The man is a fanatic and a brute and he doesn't deserve you. And do you know what the worst thing is? He knows perfectly well that he could trust you with anything. He simply refuses to because he's besotted with the idea that the world is his to save – and because he can't be bothered to explain, half the time. Well, you tell him from me that whatever it is he wants, I won't lift a finger to help unless he starts treating his sergeant like, well, his sergeant. Gideon, are you listening?'

Gideon shook himself. 'Sorry, yes,' he said. 'I was just imagining saying that. Well, I was trying to. You're quite right, of course, about the principle of the thing. It's just that – well, I'm not very good at being forthright. And it's strange, this case. He knows things, things he's not telling me. He knows what he's looking for, maybe even *who* he's looking for, but he's reached some sort of dead end. And there are going to be more killings. He's said that much. It's awful of him to put you in this position, but I'm afraid he might really need your help.'

'Well, of course he does,' said Octavia. 'He wouldn't dream of giving me the satisfaction otherwise. And look, I'm not really refusing to help – it'll probably be something deliciously interesting. I'll gladly help *you*, since you've had the decency to come and ask. You needn't tell him that, though. It's only fair that you get to keep some secrets too.'

Gideon toyed with a meagre and brownish grape. 'There would be some justice in that. But I'm afraid I'm not very good at that either.'

'You might surprise yourself.' Octavia brushed off her plate and tossed it into the hamper. 'It wouldn't be the first time. Now, then, let's make a start. I want you to tell me everything you *do* know.'

Gideon found that he had a great deal to say. He began by explaining how little he knew, and how he'd pieced it together from the merest scraps. As he talked, though, he found there were details he had overlooked, recollections that had gone unexamined. And he had forgotten, too, how much easier talking was with Miss Hillingdon. It wasn't like Cambridge, where his every utterance was snatched up and held like soiled linen against the light. It certainly wasn't like his conversations with Cutter, which often felt like strewing daisy chains in the path of a charging warhorse. When he and Octavia spoke, it was as if they were wandering the same country lanes or contemplating the same painting. If only for a little while, it felt natural and ordinary.

He told Octavia of the Inspector's dark moods, and of his pre-occupation with nameless dangers, though he made no mention of the letter with the black seal. He told her about his shooting lessons, and they laughed together at those pained recollections, but he was more circumspect about Milo and the nature of his assistance.

He described Cutter's mounting wariness in the days before the murders, and his peculiar fervour once the investigation had begun in earnest. He hinted, too, at the Inspector's distrust of certain senior colleagues and at the unusual measures he was taking to preserve secrecy.

It was now all but impossible, Gideon said, to account for the Inspector's mood at any given moment. When he was not impenetrably silent, he was voicing undecipherable misgivings; when he was not excluding Gideon entirely from his deliberations, he was sending him on inexplicable errands. He was as much a mystery now as the murders he was investigating.

He presented the facts of the case then, giving as frank an account as he could without betraying any confidence. And where he could not speak plainly, he spoke in hints and intimations. The details seemed meagre by themselves, and though there was a great deal he did not know or understand, he had formed certain impressions.

'I don't know how to explain it,' he said. 'Cutter said that sometimes a murder is telling you a secret. He talks that way a lot these days, but this time I felt I understood what he meant. I don't know what that secret might be, but I feel there must be one. They were *exact*, the things that were done to those men, though I'm not sure that's quite the right word. They weren't just done skilfully or precisely. They were *measured*. I think ... but no, it would sound foolish.'

He fell silent for a time, and Octavia did not press him. She was skilled in that way. Her manner of listening was attentive yet seemingly weightless. With Octavia, he could voice thoughts that he had not yet articulated even to himself.

'I think,' he said at last, 'that we are uncovering other crimes, past crimes. I told you what he said, the Inspector, and I hope I did not do wrong in revealing it. He said that this was a long and sad story. And he's looking for traces of something, in the records. Something must have happened, long ago. I don't know what secret these murders were telling us, but they were speaking in a voice that Cutter knows.'

Again, she simply waited.

'And this is something that touches him personally, I think. Something he hoped had been put to rest.'

Octavia considered this for a time. Finding a berry stain on her skirts, she scrubbed at it absently with her sleeve. 'Well,' she said, 'I think I'm beginning to understand why he sent you. So, this Considine. I'd read about the case, naturally. The name rang a bell, too, though I can't think where I've encountered it before. Tell me about him.'

Gideon had allowed his attention to drift. It was pleasant here, in this undemarcated woodland. There was woodsmoke rising among the beeches. There were campfire songs and archery contests. There were fierce children, but no fatal wounds. 'Sorry, yes. Considine. The Inspector was hoping you could begin with him.'

Her face had taken on a familiar cast. Miss Hillingdon had many interests, it was true, but perhaps she had only a single ruling passion. She had scented a secret. Her bowstring had been drawn taut. 'I'm sure he was. I wonder why, though. Is that why he's trawling the records? Did this Considine have an interesting past?'

'But that's just it,' said Gideon. 'I don't know. We've been looking over all these deeds and contracts and registers, and he's never even explained why. And Considine never did anything notable, as far as I can tell. He seems to have been some sort of gentleman scientist. He liked orchids, not that that's of any use.'

Octavia flicked at a crumb. 'And you haven't formed any impressions?'

Gideon wavered. 'I don't . . . I mean, I suppose certain patterns emerged.'

'That does tend to happen,' she said. 'Tell me about these documents you've been scouring. It sounds like he knows *where* to look, but what about *when*?'

'Oh, gosh.' Gideon's plate wobbled again on his knees. 'That reminds me. I was supposed to mention that Sir Aneurin was knighted about twenty years ago, or whatever they call it when someone is made a CBE. And now that you mention it, that's the period we've been looking into. About twenty years ago, give or take.'

'You see?' said Octavia mildly. 'Certain patterns. Early 1870s, then. And what was Considine up to in the early 1870s?'

'Nothing. Or nothing that I've discovered. All I've come across are property deeds and articles of association, for charitable trusts and such like. Oh, and births and deaths. Hundreds and hundreds of them. I can't make anything of it.'

Octavia paused for a moment. 'Can't you, though? You notice much more than you realise, you know. It's where those feelings of yours come from. Don't worry, you'll get better at recognising them with practice. You'll get better at concealing them too.'

Gideon toyed with a radish. 'I'm not sure I altogether—'

'The Inspector isn't the only one who's troubled by this case. You're frightened, that much I can tell, but there's something else too. There was a look on your face, when you were talking about the crime scene. I've seen it before, that bewildered and heartbroken look, and I saw it again earlier when Flora was making her apologies.

You weren't even listening, and you seemed to have forgotten that she'd just shot you. You looked stricken, as if little Flora had reminded you of something unutterably sorrowful.'

Gideon was peering at his plate. A beetle had alighted on it, tiny and delicately coloured, and was struggling to surmount the rim. He lowered the plate to the grass, tipping it carefully so that the insect could find purchase on a stalk. Octavia waited. 'Her hands,' said Gideon eventually. 'I was looking at her hands, her fingers.'

Octavia looked at him in bewilderment. 'Her fingers? Flora's fingers? I don't understand.'

'I'm sorry, I can't ...' Gideon pressed his palms to his knees. 'I know I'm not making any sense. It's just that there are details I haven't mentioned, that I can't mention. There was a piece of evidence that ... but no, I shouldn't say. And it mightn't mean anything.'

Octavia leaned closer to him. 'I'm not going to ask what it was. But you don't believe that, do you? That it meant nothing?'

Gideon shifted on his stool. Even with Octavia, there were things he seldom spoke about. 'I don't— I worry sometimes that I see things differently because of what I was. What I *am*, I suppose.'

'What you are?' said Octavia, uncomprehending. Then her expression changed. 'What *we* are, is that what you mean?' Orphans, she meant. Octavia and her brother had been adopted by the man she had called her grandfather. Unlike Gideon, she was not reticent about her origins.

He offered her a watery smile. 'What we are, yes. And what we've seen. It makes me doubt myself sometimes, my judgement. I wonder if I don't imagine things.'

'Of course we imagine things,' she said brightly. She prodded him again with the tip of her boot. 'Otherwise we'd never learn anything new. Gideon, what is it that you think you know?'

Gideon looked away. Nearby, the girls had begun chanting in some ritual of call and response. In one moment, their voices were a bright and rushing torrent. In the next they were dissipating rain. 'Children,' he said finally. 'I think something happened, something awful. And I think it involved children.'

'Ah.' Octavia considered this. 'Well, that doesn't seem such a stretch. Awful things happen to children all the time. And it would explain Cutter's interest in birth registers and charitable trusts. It might explain why he's had no luck, too. Records like those can be a dreadful mess. Or missing altogether, as often as not. It takes skill and patience, finding the traces. It's a good thing you came to me.'

She laughed at his solemn nod. 'I'm joking, Gideon. If I ever do start talking like that, you must shoot *me* in the chest. Having practice will help, of course, but we'll have to be lucky too. Think of the Princes in the Tower.'

Gideon thought of pretending, but with Octavia that was seldom advisable. 'I'm sorry, I'm not sure I—'

'Oh, it's one of those undying stories. You know, bits of history for people who don't know any. They were the heirs apparent when the Duke of Gloucester was regent, or Richard III, as he came to be known. He had them declared illegitimate and locked in the Tower. They never came out again, needless to say, but that's not my point. My point is that their bones weren't found for almost two hundred years, and even then no one was quite certain. It's the Tower of London. That place is bones all the way down.'

'Yes,' said Gideon. 'Yes, I think I—'

'Sorry, I'm not explaining it very well. The point is that some things stay hidden, especially when it's in someone's interest. There's plenty of darkness to hide them in, and that's assuming anyone ever looks. Gideon? You are following, aren't you?'

'Hmm? Sorry, yes.' He had been thinking of bones. Of fragile things, and how long they endured. 'But you'll be looking, won't you?'

She gave him an astringent look. 'Oh God, there's that look again. Yes, I'll be looking. It's only been twenty years, not two hundred, and if something did happen, well, no one is ever quite as thorough as they like to think. Oh look, here's Suki. I'd forgotten all about the time. Suki, you must be seething, you poor thing. I'm afraid I deserted my post. Did I miss the mustering out?'

Gideon stood too, as a tall, strong-limbed woman crossed the clearing towards them. She wore what seemed to be mismatched riding clothes and a scarf of bright vermilion was twined loosely about her neck. 'Yes, you did, you wretched layabout. I was alone and forsaken, with no one to tell me that I'd forgotten to take my laurels out. Look what a fright I am. And I've just seen the girls off like this. Can you imagine? Come here, you slattern. I shall have to punish you soundly.'

Wrestling Octavia towards her, Suki gave a ravening growl. Gideon pivoted decorously away, rubbing urgently at his cheek.

'Suki!' Octavia protested, ducking free of her grip. 'Suki, this is my good friend, Gideon Bliss. Sergeant Gideon Bliss, I ought to say.'

Suki whirled about, her face vivid. 'It's who? Oh, bless me, what a ninny I am. I thought he was that park chap, you know, the one you tipped to help with the lugging. Do forgive me. Sergeant Bliss, was it? How do you do? Susannah Bryant. I'm Octavia's, well . . .' She flapped a hand, then let it drift to her side.

'Yes, of course,' Gideon said. He dipped his head, having mislaid his hat. 'Delightful. Delighted, I mean to say. Miss Hillingdon's been telling me about your exploits with the girls.' A further clarification seemed warranted. 'With the children, you know. Your wholesome woodland exploits. Just delightful.'

Miss Bryant had lodged an array of pins between her lips, which she was now dispersing about the riotous coils of her hair. Luckily, she didn't seem to be paying close attention. 'Mmm,' she said. 'Yes, jolly good. Good for you. I know the Murrays a bit, you see, whose land this is. They were good enough to let us tramp about the place. This spot used to be a duelling ground, you know. Positively drenched with blood, this entire clearing. Isn't it marvellous?'

'Yes, Gideon spilled some of his own,' said Octavia. 'Flora shot him in the chest, the poor lamb.'

'Did she really? How splendid. Of course, I oughtn't to say so, since we're mired in scandal as it is.' She paused, an accusatory hairpin out-thrust. 'Hang on, you're not *that* policeman, are you? The unpleasant one who's always badgering Octavia into going on ridiculous quests?'

'Suki, honestly. Stop being such a harridan. Here.' Octavia balled up a blanket and hurled it at her. 'Start folding these. Gideon does serve with Inspector Cutter, since you ask, but he himself is the soul of kindness. And I choose my own ridiculous quests, as you very well know.'

She shoved Suki away towards the hampers and took Gideon by the elbow, leading him to the edge of the clearing. 'Don't pay any attention, will you? She's very sweet, really, but she has no idea how to behave. It's all that money. They never have to *learn* anything. Anyway, you should probably slip away while you can. I'm sorry we didn't have more time.'

'Oh, not at all,' said Gideon, flapping a coat sleeve that was refusing to admit his arm. 'It was my fault entirely, appearing like this without any warning.'

'Don't be silly,' Octavia said. 'It was lovely to see you. And there never is any warning, is there? Not when it matters. Here, this way.'

Following her down a gentle decline, Gideon found himself on a shaded path beneath a vault of latticed boughs. Drifts of early wild-flowers caught the sifted light. 'Isn't it lovely?' she said. 'You oughtn't to rush back, you know, though I know you will. And when you do get back, you will be careful, won't you?'

Gideon tried for a hearty tone. 'Oh, I'm feeling quite dauntless now, after my little adventure. Not many men have angered a hand-maiden of Artemis and lived to tell the tale.'

Octavia gave him a measured look. 'I think you know what I mean. I know you haven't told me everything – no, it's all right, I understand why – but you've told me enough. Stop worrying about Cutter. He can look after himself. As for you, you must trust those feelings of yours. And leave the past to me for now. It sounds like there are plenty of awful things happening now, in the present.'

'Yes,' said Gideon. 'Yes, I know you're right.'

'And remember,' said Octavia, turning to climb back up the bank. 'I've agreed to help you, not Cutter. You'll have secrets of your own. Don't give them up, or not until he's done something to deserve it.'

'I'll try,' said Gideon. He attempted a resolute expression, but another thought had occurred to him. 'You'll be careful too, won't you? The Inspector, he won't say who, but . . . well, it seems people are watching.'

Octavia turned, already half hidden by brambles. She smiled, shaking her head gently. 'I do this for a living, you know, finding things out. Someone always gets upset. That's how you know it's working.'

And then she was gone, back to Suki, back to her ropes and tin cups and picnic baskets, to her endless plans and inexhaustible hopes. She seemed careless and unhurried. If anyone were watching, it would be easy to mistake her nature.

Soon, Gideon knew, she would take on another appearance. She would descend into the labyrinths, into the catacombs and ossuaries of England's secrets. She had drawn back her bow and she knew the way, even in those places, even where there was nothing but shadows.

Seven

G ideon expected to find the Inspector at Leggett's. Cutter had left no instructions to that effect, but that omission could not be relied upon. Though he recognised no fixed bounds to the working day, he rarely stayed late at the Yard. It was nearing five o'clock by the time Gideon reached Soho, and by now the Inspector would be stationed in his private parlour. He would expect Gideon to join him as a matter of course, and, though he would never say so, he would anticipate a full account of his encounter with Miss Hillingdon.

Gideon was preparing his response as he turned into Warwick Street, having reflected on Octavia's advice. Miss Hillingdon had agreed to help, with certain stipulations, and perhaps that counted as a secret in itself. Naturally, he could not withhold that information altogether, but perhaps he could obscure it for a time using elliptical turns of phrase.

Halting before the window of a chemist's shop, he considered his appearance. He adjusted the set of his chin. Having looked about him, he addressed his reflection in a cautious undertone. 'Miss Hillingdon? Oh, yes, I found her in excellent spirits. We passed a most agreeable . . .' He paused to detach a scab of dried jam from his chin. 'We passed a thoroughly . . .'

Gideon trailed off, having grown conscious of a disturbance. That disturbance proved to be Inspector Cutter, who was hurdling cart handles and clattering aside bystanders as he charged southwards in the direction of Piccadilly. Gideon edged towards the safety of the kerb, his right arm tentatively raised, just as Cutter himself swerved into the road to avoid injuring a small child. The Inspector was gesticulating and shouting, though it was some moments before he came within earshot.

'Into the cab! Into the cab, you gawking halfwit!'

It became clear that the Inspector was bellowing at him.

Gideon turned, mildly dazed, and saw that a hansom was waiting before the public house opposite. The driver was standing on his bench, craning to follow Cutter's progress, and he had already nudged his horse out for the off. Gideon noted absently that it was Milo's driver, the same man who had been engaged on the day of Sir Aneurin's murder. Then the Inspector flew past him, sending a coal boy sprawling onto the bed of his cart.

Gideon pitched himself into the street and pelted towards the cab.

They had turned into Charing Cross before Gideon ventured to speak, and even then he was obliged to wait for an answer. It was a busy thoroughfare at almost any hour, and the afternoon rush meant that much of Cutter's attention was taken up by the traffic. He was continually springing up from his seat to bawl at dawdling drivers, and he had twice leapt from the cab altogether to threaten some carter or cabman with arrest.

'If I may, sir,' Gideon said. 'Where is it we are going?'

The Inspector got to his feet again, this time to heave himself clear of the canopy and address their own driver. 'Left here!' he cried. 'What are you about, damn you? Bad enough that you did not have the sense to take St Martin's Lane to start with, but you can at least make for it now.'

He subsided into his seat, but he remained watchful and restless. Even when they had gone a quarter mile at a nearly steady pace, his gaze scoured the street ahead as if every doorway and awning might conceal some new hindrance. Beside him, Gideon settled back in resignation. He had hoped to find the Inspector eager for news, and hence, perhaps, more willing to take Gideon into his confidence. How was he to force the Inspector into some momentous admission if he could not even wring an address from him?

But even as this thought formed, he saw that Cutter had turned abruptly in his seat and was eyeing him with murky displeasure. 'The Damask,' said the Inspector curtly.

Gideon knew what the word meant, but he was otherwise at a loss. 'Sir?'

'The Damask,' Cutter said again. He pulled out his watch, glowered at it, then stuffed it back into his coat. 'A private establishment in Maiden Street, just off the Strand. You asked where we were going.'

'I see,' said Gideon. It was an answer, at least, but it was hardly illuminating. 'But what I—'

Cutter was still haranguing the driver. He was half out of his seat, his right arm flung out to signal an upcoming turn. 'A private establishment,' he repeated, 'providing gentlemanly entertainments. *Here, you palsied monkey! This turn here!* Or that's the polite way of saying it. It's a house with certain notions of itself, since it caters for those who can afford notions, but under the frills it's no better than a hundred other such places. It's a rich man's dolly shop.'

'Ah,' said Gideon, who might once have been thoroughly mystified. He coughed discreetly, feeling pleased with his astuteness. 'An establishment for the procurement of young women.'

Cutter turned and fixed him with a bleak look. 'Young boys, Bliss. That's the gentlemanly part.'

'Ah, indeed,' said Gideon, but before he could reconfigure his expression, the Inspector sprang from his seat again. His agitation now seemed held in check, and as he jerked his head towards the kerb, he made a slowing motion with the flat of his hand. When the labouring horse had been soothed to a halt, he gave a grudging nod.

'That'll do,' he said to the driver. 'Do not mind my antics earlier, will you? I am an unruly passenger at times, but there was nothing in it. You are a gem of a fellow, really, and all the better for saying precious little. Keep your station now, just as we agreed. Bliss, shake a leg there.'

The Inspector had skipped lightly to the footway, and already he was striding away down Bedford Street. The bright afternoon was yielding to a chilly and sulphurous dusk, and a lamplighter had mounted his ladder outside a coachmaker's yard. The light flared about his hunched shoulders, quick and lemony at first, then sputtering to a feeble apricot. Coal smuts and kitchen smoke lazed about his haloed form. The evening smelled of kerosene and burnt sugar.

There were crowds that might have been late or early, and Gideon lost sight of Cutter almost at once. He fumbled through the press of bodies, aware of rough and furtive touches. He scented jasmine oil and untended flesh. He heard laboured breathing, skittish laughter, the drawl and scritch of a gramophone. Under an awning he was wrenched aside, and in an unlit doorway, broad hands braced his shoulders. Clean hands. The Inspector silenced him with a look.

'I cannot say much,' he said, 'so listen to what I do say.'

Gideon nodded.

'You know the Strand at this hour,' the Inspector said. 'Not too lively yet, but getting there. And you know the crowds here. Some respectable, for the matinees and what have you, but mostly otherwise. Keep your wits about you, such as they are. As for the evening's entertainment, well – have you eaten yet?'

Gideon hesitated, momentarily perplexed. 'Miss Hillingdon had prepared a light picnic lunch, but—' He noted the Inspector's dismal expression. 'No, sir. Almost nothing.'

Cutter pursed his lips. 'Just as well. Whatever this is, it won't be pretty. I have people out now. Errand boys, you might say, with ways of getting word to me. It was the proprietress of this place who found him, a Mrs Finucane. Seen a bit of the world, this Mrs Finucane has. Or she thought she had, before today. No name for the fellow yet, but he was something in the Home Office once. No doubt he was more besides. He was something to someone, anyway. Special treatment, by the sound of it.'

'To someone?' But Gideon was rebuking himself before he had the words out.

'Have a guess.'

It was a moment before Gideon took his meaning. 'The murderer, sir?'

'Sing it out again, why don't you? They didn't hear you in Clerkenwell. Anything else? Make it quick, mind.'

It was hardly the most pressing question, but perhaps it would show that he was paying attention. 'Was that not Milo's driver, sir? Will Milo himself be joining us?'

Something near to amusement stirred in the Inspector's face. 'Joining us? He has hardly left our side these last three days. Now, we must get on. This fellow won't be getting any fresher, and I have put off my own dinner. Let's see if we can work up an appetite.'

The Damask was an establishment that might easily have gone unnoticed. Opposite the rear of the Adelphi Theatre, the Inspector drew up by a costumier's shop and rapped on a door of undistinguished appearance. A small hatch was drawn back, then smartly clapped shut again. They heard discreet muttering from within, and a fussing over chains and locks.

The young man who opened the door was pale and thin. He seemed exhausted by the effort and disappointed by the results. He scanned the crowd behind them then lifted his chin, edging aside to let them pass. The vestibule they entered was small but richly decorated. The walls were hung with silk, pale jade and patterned with bamboo. A polished side table was crowded with exotic ornaments: a fan of peacock feathers, a brass elephant with sapphire eyes, a clockwork carousel. Roses and peonies spilled from a vast Chinese vase, lavish but unreal. Gideon had known a flower-maker once. He thought of her vanished face, her fondness for sweet peas.

'They're silk,' said the thin young man, noting his interest. 'Them flowers, I mean. By Monsieur Fouchier.'

'We'll be sure to look him up,' said the Inspector. 'And you are?'

'They call me Lysander,' said the young man.

'Not your name here, you painted stick of misery. Your real name.'

'She made a list.' The youth twitched a shoulder towards the stairs, indicating someone up above. 'Said you'd be asking.'

'Well, don't stir from this place before I do,' said Cutter. 'Were you here when it happened?'

He nodded warily, clutching his arms about his narrow frame.

'See the punter go in?'

Another wincing nod.

'See anyone else go in?'

The young man shook his head, this time with some vehemence.

'See or hear anything else?'

Lysander ventured something approaching a sneer. 'We never do. Not supposed to.'

Cutter took a slow step towards him. 'Today is different. Today, there's only one thing you're not supposed to do, and that's disappoint me. You wouldn't want that, would you?'

'No, guv,' the young man said, then shuddered at some recollection. 'But I didn't, I swear. Not until Mel woke up. Till she started screaming.'

The Inspector thumbed his jaw, his expression pained. 'Mel?'

'Mélisande. Stage name's all I know. Madam's made a list, like I said.'

'She's not the only one,' Cutter murmured, casting a dour look about the opulent vestibule. The thin young man made a weary show of puzzlement, at which the Inspector rolled his eyes. 'Just show us up, will you. You can faint when we're finished.'

Upstairs, they were led into what Lysander called the salon. It was a lounge of sorts, and even more richly furnished than the entrance hall, but it was a room meant to be couched in shadow and flattered by spreading chandeliers. Its thick velvet drapes were now drawn back and the ebbing light seeped from mirrors rimed with dust, over table linen fretted by years of boiling. On a low stage in one corner, a cheval glass leaned in its frame, staring at nothing. A discarded stocking trailed from an empty chair.

Three more pallid young men were gathered around the table nearest the stage, two in vestigial evening wear and the last wearing what seemed to be a wine-stained chemise. They looked up sullenly but made no move to rise. One of them gave a protracted sigh then reached behind his chair and tugged on a tasselled cord.

'Rung for her,' he said. 'Make yourselves at home, do.'

'Oh, do,' said the youth in the chemise. 'Welcome to the Damask. Let it enchant and enfold you. Ain't that what we say, Jules? Even when we've been kept on half the day, not even a cup of beef tea. Let it enchant and enfold you, only do try not to shoot your muck on the velvet. Half the day, after a night like that. You're lucky there ain't five fucking bodies.'

'Shut it, can't you. Bad enough without you giving lip to the charpers.'

'Be lucky for them if they did find my body, mind you. Only way they could afford it, unless I was feeling free. Which I might be for this nice cut of white meat.' This last was addressed to Gideon, though he had only an approximate sense of its import. 'What's your name, chicken? You going to show us your truncheon?'

Before Gideon was obliged to answer, a stout woman with a crimped expression emerged from a curtained-off annex. She wore a heavy black shawl over her cerise gown, perhaps to mark her patron's passing, and she carried what appeared to be a sceptre. She silenced the young men by rapping it three times against the floor.

'What did I fucking tell you?' Mrs Finucane demanded. 'I told you to keep your painted traps shut until I say different. You heard me say different yet?'

The young men fixed their gazes on the tablecloth.

'That's right, you ain't. You want to earn with them tongues again, you keep them in your fucking gobs. Now.' She turned to the Inspector. 'You're him, are you? Heard you might play nice if we're accommodating, so here I am, being accommodating. The whole lot's your oyster, within reason. I want to put a smile on your face, but not as much as I want to keep my wicks lit. How do we set about that, then?'

Mrs Finucane's tone struck Gideon as startlingly presumptuous, but the Inspector did not seem perturbed. 'Well,' he said, 'putting a smile on my face would be a high bar to reach, but you might help me keep my temper. As for keeping your wicks lit, all I can tell you is that I am not like some. As long as these fine fellows are all of age, it makes no odds to me how they earn their keep.'

'Ain't the boys I'm worried about,' said Mrs Finucane. 'Not these here, anyway, since they can't mind their manners. It's them as comes here to get their collars starched. They're a certain sort, as I expect you know. Not just quality. People who know people. People who ain't keen on seeing themselves in the picture papers.'

'Again, I am not like some,' said Cutter. 'I don't give a damn where Lord So-and-So gets his silver polished, and I tell no tales to those who do. What I do give a damn about is the truth of what happened here, and I mean to know every jot of it. So, here is how we set about it. First, where's the fellow who was in the room, this Mel?'

Mrs Finucane jerked her sceptre at the curtain. 'Back there, having a lie-down. And you won't get far calling Mel a fellow. I got the proper name wrote down, but it ain't stage with this one. It's through and through. Had a mind you'd want her kept separate.'

'That's what I like to hear. And I will call her the Princess Consort as long as she gives me straight answers. We'll have a word with her first, and if she is forthcoming, we will let her go. She won't be going home, mind. She'll be boarding with you.'

'Come again?' Mrs Finucane's face was strained.

'You have your own lodgings somewhere out of the way, I'm sure. Ladies in your line generally do. I don't want to know where. Keep her there for a few days. Call it a special favour.'

'How many days?' Mrs Finucane said sharply. 'She gets asked for special. She's worth a bob.'

'She'll be asked for now, right enough. Make up whatever story you like, just keep her out of harm's way for a bit. Think of it as protecting your investment. After we talk to her, we'll want a look at the scene. We'll want the dead man's name and everything else you and your boys might know about him. Everything, do you hear me. If he had a name he liked to call them, write it down. If he preferred pink drawers to white, write it down. Then write down an account of everything that happened last night. It might turn out to be the most tedious story ever set to paper, God help us, but it'll begin when you opened your doors yesterday evening and it will tell the tale of every single soul who came and went, accurate to the hour and the minute.'

Mrs Finucane compressed a cigarette between her lips. 'Anything else?'

'There is, yes. You needn't confine yourself to last night. If you took on a new kitchen porter last week, I want to know of it. If a cat wandered into your yard that wasn't familiar, I want a count of its paws and the colour of its coat. I want everything, down to pounds, shillings and pence, and when I have read it through I will quiz you on it. Witnesses are inclined to get the answers wrong when they make things up. And send out for a nice batch of meat pies, will you. These poor lads are half starved, and I want them kept upright.'

There was nothing troubling about Mélisande's appearance, beyond what was always troubling in such circumstances. Her loveliness was native and ordinary, and she carried her damage as if that were native and ordinary too. Cutter and Gideon found her hunched on a cot in a little garret room, plucking anxiously at the sleeves of her gown. It was of pale apricot satin, and no doubt it had been costly. It was now ripped at the bodice and marked with crazed spatters of blood. There were traces of blood, too, on the finely crafted blonde wig that rested on one of the bedposts.

She scrambled to her feet as soon as they entered. 'Can you look at it quick?' she said. 'I want it off me, but she said to leave it.'

Cutter shook his head. 'You're a witness, not a Persian rug. Take it off if you want. We'll wait outside.'

'Yeah, bless your heart, but I ain't your sister. Besides, someone's got to unlace me.'

The Inspector gave a rumbling cough and turned to inspect a cabinet lined with figurines. 'Bliss,' he said. 'Help the young lady.'

Gideon thrust his hands behind his back, as if hiding a deformity. 'I'm afraid I don't . . . I'm not sure I . . .'

'Please.' Mélisande turned her back to him, keeping her arms wide. She gestured, her wrists stiffly flexed. 'Please. The blood. I can't.'

Gideon worked as delicately as he could at the puzzle of laces, wincing when he touched her skin. It was coarse from the cold, and the corset left marks that were almost bruises. He saw a fading bite mark, low on her neck. 'Thank you,' she kept whispering. 'Thank you, thank you.'

When she had been released from the gown, Mélisande twisted eagerly away and began rooting in a hamper. She seemed more at ease now, though she wore nothing underneath but bloomers and a filmy camisole. Her scalp was shaved clean, for the wigs. She looked slight, shorn of her colours, and as vulnerable as a china saucer.

Perhaps Cutter had formed the same impression. When she had pulled on a simple tea dress and scrubbed her face, the look he gave her was grave.

'Miss Mélisande, I must ask you something before we begin.'

'Mel,' she said. 'It's just Mel, when I ain't working.'

'All right, then. Listen, Mel, I will make no trouble for you, but you must be straight with me. How old are you?'

She perched on the edge of the bed. 'Ain't like that,' she said. 'I'm just scrawny, is all. They like that, some of them.'

The Inspector looked away for a moment, passing a hand over his face. 'You need a bit of feeding, right enough. Are you ready to start?'

Mel settled on the cot again, shuffling back and drawing up her knees. She examined her arms before closing them about her. 'Ain't got any smokes, do you?'

'Sorry,' said Cutter. 'Will I ask someone?'

She shook her head, her narrow chin jutting. 'They wouldn't give you one. Not for me. That's what happens when the punters like you. All right, go on, then.'

'Bliss.' Keeping his hand by his side, Cutter made a scribbling motion. Gideon backed away towards the washstand and drew out his notebook without a sound. 'The man you were with – what time did he come in?'

'Late. He always comes late. Always came, I mean. Half-twelve, maybe.'

'And he spent time outside first? In the salon?'

She shook her head, made a sour face. 'Few minutes. One drink, to make it look right. He weren't here for the company. Weren't the sort.'

'Good,' the Inspector said. 'That is just the kind of thing I need to know. Anyone with him? Anyone speak to him?'

She made a scornful sound. 'Talk to *that*? Face like an undertaker? Nah. Finished his drink and he gave me the look. Not cheeky, not like some punters. Not even, you know, like he wanted it. This look, all it said was *now*.'

'Good. Very good. I'll tell you this, Mel, I wish I came across more witnesses like you. And then?'

'And then we come in the back room, the fancy one. The Bourbon Room, we're supposed to call it.'

'And? Did anything change in him then? Was he different in private?'

She considered this doubtfully. 'Why you asking me all this? About him, I mean. Ain't you looked yet, at what happened to him? Wait, you don't even know who he was, do you?'

Again, the Inspector nodded. 'You're a sharp one, all right. I could tell you I came to you first so that you could get yourself off to bed, but you wouldn't believe me, would you? You'll have to trust me, Mel. Is that all right? Now, did he change?'

Mel clutched her knees. She stared straight ahead. 'Not much. You ask me, it was like he didn't want to be there. Like he wanted to get it over with. He talked a bit, I suppose, but only because he had to say what he wanted.'

Cutter's eyes narrowed. He took a moment to weigh his next question. 'Do you want to tell us about that, Mel? About what he wanted? You need not give us chapter and verse, but it may tell us something about him.'

She gave a bitter little laugh. 'It might, yeah. It told me plenty.' Bending her head, she picked at a painted fingernail. 'First time he come here, he brought this bag with him. Started unpacking it like he was away at the seaside. Took out this black gown first, and I'm looking at him, thinking, what am I supposed to be tonight? Another nun, is it? Only it's for him, this gown. You know, like a priest or a schoolmaster. Had to keep my fan over my face, in case he saw me laughing. Then he got the whip out.'

Gideon looked up from his notebook. He kept very still.

Mel was staring at the wallpaper. Its pattern of blossoms was faded and peeling. She jerked her hand to her cheek, tipping her face away as she scrubbed at it. 'I only let him do it the once. I think Madam had a word with him after. But he still brought it every time. I'd show him my back, or my whatever, and he'd whip something else. You imagine that? I don't know what it was, 'cos I never turned around, but he brought something with him so he could pretend. Fucking men.'

The Inspector rarely fell silent during his dealings with witnesses, but he did so now. He lowered his head, his hand working wearily at the muscles of his neck. When he resumed, his voice was soft and deliberate.

'When he did these things,' he said, 'did he say anything out of the ordinary?'

'I told you,' said Mel. 'He weren't a talker.'

'He was careful, no doubt. But he had something he wanted to say to someone. What were all his antics for, otherwise? Did he never slip up, even once?'

Gideon began to understand why the inspector had sought this interview before seeing the body. Mel was toying with the lace on her cuff. She paused and looked away. 'Wait,' she said. 'Once, maybe. He sort of hissed something out, in a whisper, like.'

The Inspector waited.

Mel hesitated, and when she spoke, the distaste showed in her face. These words were not her own, and she did not want them near her.

'*This is how we made you, little bird. This is how we made you perfect.*'

They spent twenty minutes more with Miss Mélisande, before Cutter sent her away in a cab. Seeming satisfied at last with what she had told him of the victim, the Inspector turned again to the events of the night before. She was a good witness, but there were things she could not tell them.

'I'd just sat down at the dressing table, making like I was getting ready. It was just to have somewhere else to look, really, while he was getting out all his . . . it was just to look away. And maybe that's how I didn't see, 'cos I didn't. A shadow maybe, but too quick for— I swear, it was like it weren't even real. Then there was a hand over my mouth, and all I knew was it weren't his. It was strong, but not that kind of strong, just sort of exactly enough. I know it don't make any sense. And there was nothing else. Like someone's smell, someone's breathing. Just nothing. And then I was gone, out like a light.'

She fell silent then, in a way that made Gideon look up from his notebook. He saw that she was crying, and no longer troubling to scrub away the tears.

'And you know what? I woke up screaming later, and people came running. I don't even remember who. 'Cos it was so . . . what I saw when I looked up – and I've seen things, mate, I've fucking *seen* things. But I didn't realise until afterwards, why it was. It was so I wouldn't see any more than I had to. It was a kindness. And you're going to think this don't make sense either, but when I thought back on it, that hand, that touch. It was fierce, but with me it was gentle. It was . . .'

She took a gulping breath and looked up, her hand splayed under the hollow of her throat. 'It was the gentlest anyone's ever been with me.'

The Inspector told Mrs Finucane that it was time. He asked her to bring him whatever serviceable lamps she could lay her hands on. When she had led them to the Bourbon Room and unlocked the door, he put his hand out and waited for her to surrender the key.

'And your notes,' he said.

She passed him a single page that looked torn from a ledger. Hardly a quarter of it was filled. 'All I know about him, which is near enough to nothing. A few other names, from last night. No one new, and nothing happened except what's in there. Don't make nothing up, you said. Her ladyship any use to you?'

But Cutter had already turned away. 'Keep her safe,' he said. 'I'll be checking.'

When Mrs Finucane had left them, he folded the paper neatly and passed it to Gideon, who regarded it with open astonishment.

'You'll want to check the spellings,' the Inspector said. 'For your notes.'

Paraic O'Donnell

NOTES MADE BY SGT. G. BLISS CONCERNING:

AN INCIDENT OF VIOLENT DEATH IN THE VICINITY OF
THE STRAND AND CERTAIN RELATED MATTERS

The report that follows is preliminary and
serves as a memorandum of contemporary
observations by the attending officers. It omits
certain particulars, including the precise
location of the incident under investigation.

These omissions are judged to be necessary to
the preservation of official secrecy pending the
outcome of this investigation and enquiries into
certain other matters.

The necessity of these measures was determined
by Insp. H. Cutter, the senior officer attending
the scene, and the present officer concurs as
to their propriety and sound basis in moral
principle.

Signed,   Signed,

INSP. H. CUTTER,   SGT. G. BLISS
This 25th day of March, 1894.

CONTEMPORARY RECORD BEGINS

INTERVIEW WITH WITNESS "M."

At approx. 5.20 p.m. on the 25th inst. the
present officer, in company with Insp. H. Cutter,
attended premises in the vicinity of the Strand
pursuant to a report of violent death. On
arrival at the premises, Insp. Cutter conducted
an interview with a person we will refer to as M.

Insp. Cutter determined that M. had been in
the company of the deceased prior to his death
and had on previous occasions been engaged by
the deceased in a professional capacity at the
same premises.

He further determined that M. was present but
incapacitated at the time of the deceased's
death, having been rendered unconscious by an
unknown third party.

In the course of our interview, M. furnished
certain intelligence regarding the habits and
disposition of the deceased that we deemed
valuable to our investigation. We will reserve
further comment for the reasons set out in the
foregoing.

EXAMINATION OF SCENE OF INCIDENT

Following our interview with the witness "M.",
another person present at the premises (witness

Paraic O'Donnell

"F.") supplied a brief written statement
confirming the deceased to be one JOHN MEREDITH
ASPELL, understood by "F." to have been
"something in Whitehall" and "next thing to
a Duke".
[The present officer has since established
that, until his retirement in 1882, Mr Aspell
was an Under-Secretary at H.M. Home Office,
with oversight of such matters as adoption
and reformative institutions. Though himself a
commoner, Mr Aspell was second cousin to the
15th Earl of Cleveland (d. 1879).]
Having concluded these preliminaries, Insp.
Cutter asked to be shown to the scene of the
incident. "F." duly admitted us to a bedchamber
at the rear of the premises.
We made the following observations:
The bedchamber was well appointed and
comparatively large, with windows overlooking
St. Peter's Hospital in Henrietta Street. We
found the curtains drawn back, suggesting that
the incident and its aftermath might have been
observed by persons in the immediate vicinity.
However, Insp. Cutter expressed the view that
the curtains were drawn back by the perpetrator
subsequent to the victim's death.
The victim's body was in a kneeling position
at the foot of a large canopied bed.
The victim's wrists had been bound to the
bedposts. He had been stripped to the waist.
His knees and ankles had been bound tightly

together, permitting only the most limited
movement. The victim's mouth was stuffed with
cloth and this makeshift gag was held in place
with a buckled leather strap.

A horsewhip lay neatly arranged on the
bed, directly in front of the victim. The
bedclothes immediately beneath it had absorbed a
considerable qty. of blood.

In view of the nature of the injuries to the
deceased (vide infra), it is highly likely that
the said horsewhip was the murder weapon. Insp.
Cutter also speculates that the victim was still
alive when the whip was placed before him.

NATURE OF INJURIES AND MANNER OF DEATH

It is difficult to convey the extent and severity
of the injuries sustained by the deceased.
Although many distinct lacerations to the
shoulders and upper back were discernible, the
region from the shoulder blades to the waist had
sustained such grievous damage that almost no
intact tissue was visible.

In several places, repeated lacerations had
ruptured [illegible, notes obscured by soiling]
NOTES RESUME AFTER INTERRUPTION
[The present officer was indisposed for a short
time. Insp. Cutter maintained supervision of the
scene.]

In several places, repeated lacerations had
ruptured not only the superficial tissues but the

muscle beneath. We defer to Dr Carmody for more
competent observations, but we noted at least
one exposed vertebra in the dorsal region.

Fearing that injuries of comparable severity
had been obscured by congealing blood, Insp.
Cutter swabbed an area of interest with a pillow
slip, causing [illegible]

NOTES RESUME AFTER INTERRUPTION

[ctd.] causing the displacement of a sizeable
flap of muscle tissue. Two ribs were visible
in the resulting void, as was a wound [or
compound lacerations having the appearance of
a single wound; again, we defer to Dr Carmody]
sufficiently deep to have penetrated the
abdominal cavity.

As might be expected, the victim's remaining
clothing was saturated with blood, as was an
irregular area of the floor carpeting extending
outwards by two or three feet. The bedclothes
had likewise absorbed a considerable qty. of blood.

Blood had also been dispersed widely by the
perpetrator in the course of inflicting the
injuries described. The Inspector noted that
the murder weapon's physical characteristics
and mode of action had transmitted more blood
than was common with e.g. slashing knife wounds
and that further, the perpetrator had "gone at
it like someone decorating a [elided] Christmas
tree".

Whatever the case, we observed splattered blood
on almost every exposed surface in the room,

including the walls, the ceiling, the floor, the
window panes, the curtains and the door, as
well as on sundry items of furniture including
a wardrobe, a dressing table, a nightstand, a
number of lampshades, a sampler with a cross-
stitched verse (in praise of chastity and allied
virtues) and a large, gilt-framed oil painting
(depicting Ulysses beset by nude sirens).

The reporting officers have acknowledged the
limits of their medical knowledge and can make
only provisional determinations pending a
post-mortem examination. Moreover, we believe
that the particulars of the scene speak for
themselves.

However, Insp. Cutter wishes to enter into the
record a number of brief observations intended
to convey the singular nature of this offence and
the urgency of investigating both this crime and
certain related matters:

1. The perpetrator of this crime entered and
   exited the premises without detection, and
   without leaving any trace that was not
   plainly intended.

2. Before restraining and murdering the
   deceased, the perpetrator incapacitated a
   would-be witness, presumably by administering
   a soporific agent. This was accomplished
   swiftly and in plain view of the deceased,
   indicating both considerable skill and
   what can only be described as marked
   self-assurance.

3. The perpetrator whipped a man to the point of
    death and compelled him to spend his dying
    moments contemplating the murder weapon.
    Such an act requires more than brutality. It
    requires a singularity of purpose that should
    not be underestimated.
4. The perpetrator is still at large and likely
    intends harm to persons who cannot presently
    be named.

APPENDIX: CONCERNING CERTAIN OTHER PARTICULARS
OF THE SCENE

Note: The observations in this appendix were
made contemporaneously but will be withheld
from the record until Insp. Cutter is satisfied
that they can be disclosed without endangering
the integrity of the present investigation. The
Inspector wishes to be solely answerable for
these unusual measures, and is therefore the
sole signatory to this appendix.

Signed,

INSP. H. CUTTER
This 25th day of March, 1894.

We noted in the main body of our report that
the bloodied whip used in the fatal assault was
deposited on the bed and was positioned within
sight of the deceased.
The following items had also been arranged
immediately in front of the victim. Note
that these items were entirely free of blood,
indicating that they were laid out after the
assault had concluded.

i   A large sack of burlap cloth of the kind used by merchants of grain and similar. The sack had been laid out flat to form a makeshift backdrop that was free from blood.

ii Seventeen (17) human bones so arranged as to comprise a partial but painstaking reconstruction of a skeletal hand. Sgt. Bliss made a careful sketch for later examination by a suitably qualified person. Pending same, Insp. Cutter ventures the opinion that these are the bones of a child aged between nine (9) and thirteen (13) years, and that these remains had been interred for in excess of twenty years.

iii A human mandible (jawbone) arranged with respect to the hand such that it occupied its approximate relative position in a living person. Again, competent examination is required, but the dentition was substantially intact and presented features intelligible even to a layman, viz. unshed deciduous second molar, adult canines in early development, &c.

iv We naturally cannot determine whether the hand bones and jawbone belonged to the same individual, but the preserved dentition gives greater confidence to our estimation of age. These were the bones of a child aged between ten (10) and twelve (12) years.

v   A message had been daubed on the wall of the bedchamber using the blood of the deceased.

The wall chosen by the perpetrator was to the victim's rear, and it is therefore unlikely that he was intended to read it.

We have attempted to reproduce the message below. Note that the first two symbols are stricken through.

SPEAK THEIR NAMES

Eight

I nspector Cutter did not hold with umbrellas. Indeed, he was opposed except in dire necessity to any modern conveniences that might impair his view or impede his progress. Since the Inspector's convictions in such matters were understood to regulate Gideon's conduct as well as his own, his sergeant was prevented not only from carrying an umbrella in inclement weather but even – for fear that close questioning might unmask his betrayal – from owning one.

Gideon reflected on this prohibition with resentment as he stumbled along Regent Street in the Inspector's wake. The early spring weather had turned fitful and squally in the two days since the murder of John Aspell, at times giving rise to icy and vehement showers. Gideon would not have minded that, since they were often out in all weathers, but he was anxious today to keep an orderly appearance.

He had visited the barber this morning, and he had put on what his landlady termed a 'visiting coat'. The coat in question had belonged to her eldest son, who had succumbed last winter to pleurisy, but she had consented to rent it to Gideon for sixpence. In the hope of keeping it dry on one side at least, he adopted a crabwise attitude as he skittered from one awning to the next.

Arriving in this way before a tobacconist's shop, he looked up to find the Inspector had halted and was standing in his path, seemingly examining a selection of pipes. He came to an abrupt halt, still clutching the knot of his tie. His landlady had performed this service too, and he was not at all confident that he could reproduce her handiwork. 'Ah,' he said. 'Were you thinking of bringing a gift, sir?'

The Inspector's jaw hardened, but he kept his eyes on the shop window. 'No, Bliss.'

'No, sir.' Gideon coughed. He glanced down at his shoes and noticed a murky seepage where his soles met the paving. He had applied three coats of boot-black in an effort to disguise the more pronounced fissures. 'And you do not partake of tobacco yourself, sir.'

Cutter kept his eyes on the window. 'Bliss,' he said, in a terse undertone. 'Shut your squawk hole, like a good fellow.'

'Sir.' Gideon inched a little way to the left, meaning to rinse away some of the excess polish with the aid of a nearby downspout. As discreetly as he could manage, he dabbled the toe of one shoe in the outflow. The result was partly satisfactory, so he began manoeuvring the other foot into position. Tugging up the ends of his trousers, he stooped to appraise his efforts. As he rose again, he found that the Inspector had turned at last from the window. His expression was austere.

'Ah,' said Gideon. 'You've finished. I was just—'

Cutter held up a hand. 'Whatever it was, Bliss, I fear an explanation will not help. Come along, will you. And keep up. I want a word as we go.'

With that he turned and launched himself into the road, heedless as ever of such niceties as rights of way. By the time Gideon caught up to him, he had turned already into Pall Mall, and at such a clip that he might have outpaced a leisurely pony.

'In case you're wondering,' he said, 'we're being followed. Don't look back or I'll clout you.'

'I wasn't—' Already somewhat winded, Gideon was obliged to answer in brief snatches. '—about to, sir.'

'Caught sight of him as we were crossing the Circus,' Cutter went on, 'though I daresay he was with us from the off.'

'And did you – did you recognise him, sir?'

'The face, no. Your pardon, sir.' The Inspector had nudged a dithering churchman from his path. 'The type, either Special Branch or a close cousin. Not a fellow you would bring to tea with your mama, in any event.'

Intent as he was on simply keeping up, it was a moment before Gideon saw the implication. 'But isn't that—' He ducked around a newspaper vendor. 'Doesn't Sir Alastair Ma—'

'Yes, Bliss. Our appointment is with Assistant-Commissioner Massey, who oversees that pack of wolves, but I am not drawing any conclusions yet. However— here, this way.'

Gideon had been edging his way through a knot of bystanders – a minor fracas had broken out in front of the Army and Navy Club – but he now found himself jolted aside by his collar and hauled bodily into a richly carpeted foyer.

Cutter held up his card to a liveried attendant who had scurried from a nook to intercept them. 'Police business,' he said. 'Show us to the tradesman's entrance, and look lively about it.'

They were directed below stairs and passed through a humid labyrinth of kitchens and store rooms before emerging in a yard crowded with the carts of vintners, butchers and laundrymen. The Inspector hauled an unattended ladder to the gable of an outhouse. 'Up you go, Bliss,' he said, propelling Gideon before him with the flat of his hand. 'We'll make this blackguard work for a living.'

From the tin roof of the outhouse, Cutter leapt down into a neighbouring stable yard – Gideon lowered himself more cautiously, finding handholds in a thick swathe of ivy – and from there they crossed a mews lane and entered an alley that seemed scarcely wide enough to accommodate the Inspector's shoulders. They came out at last in St James's Square and, once Cutter was satisfied that their pursuer had not divined their course, they struck out across the park.

As they drew near the gates at its western edge, the Inspector drew Gideon into the shelter of a stand of horse chestnuts. 'Here,' he said, pulling out a handkerchief, 'I cannot stretch to a clothes brush or a comb, so you will have to make do with that. Swab your face first, then do your best with your clothes. How did you contrive to cover yourself with straw, in the name of God? It was St. James's we cut through, not a farmyard. And be sure to do your shoes last. What did you polish them with, boiling pitch?'

When Gideon had brought himself to some semblance of tidiness, Cutter stood back to look him over. 'Good enough,' he said. 'Or as near to it as you ever get. I don't want you spick and span in any case. Massey wants me ill at ease, summoning me to his club like this, and I mean to show him that it will take more than fine linen and claret jugs. However, he wants something else, too, or he would not have made a point of inviting us both. Do not take it amiss, Bliss, but to the likes of him a sergeant is something akin to a privy pot, to be kept out of sight except when it cannot be helped.'

Gideon adjusted his borrowed Sunday coat. 'I understand, sir. It did strike me as an unusual privilege.'

The Inspector scratched at his chin. 'It is not a privilege, Bliss. It's something I have not yet fathomed, which means I am assuming the worst. For now, here is what you must know about Massey. First, he runs the dirtiest crew this side of a pirate ship, though he sets himself up as some class of God-fearing paragon. What do you call the fellows who believe that judgement is at hand and we must all keep our bibs clean?'

Paraic O'Donnell

'Millennialists, sir. One of my masters at Selwyn College was of that persuasion, though he had introduced some eschatological features that many would—'

'I have the gist of it, Bliss. Now, Massey has other high notions too. He has convinced himself that he is near to anointed as the next commissioner, though it is far from a foregone conclusion. You see, Massey must account to the chief, whereas Assistant-Commissioner Flood – our own guardian angel, as you might say – answers directly to the Home Secretary. It is a thing that Massey resents mightily. He would never cross Flood openly, but he would crawl into a sewer if he thought there was filth in it that might stick to us. So, if he is not digging graves, he is at least digging for treasure. Which means we must what?'

Gideon hesitated. 'Exercise caution, sir?'

'We must do more than that. We must hide the shovels and burn the fucking map. So, I will be saying as little as possible and you will be saying precisely nothing. Understood?'

'Understood, sir.'

'Good. Now give those shoes one last going over. They pillaged half of India to furnish this place, and even the doormat is probably priceless.'

Avoiding conversation with Sir Alastair Massey presented no great difficulty, at least to begin with. Having been admitted without incident to the East India Club, Gideon and the Inspector were shown to a dining room and seated opposite a compact but rotund gentleman with a roseate complexion and a plume of white hair that quivered above his scalp in the manner of a hackle on a regimental helmet.

When the attendant had pulled out their chairs and announced their names – he rendered Gideon's as 'Sergeant Whist' – Sir Alastair gave them a glassy look. He issued a brief rumble that might have

156

been a greeting or an admonishment, then gestured abruptly with his fork to indicate that he was presently occupied with his dinner. The dinner in question was a pie of no mean proportions, and for the next fifteen minutes Gideon and the Inspector sat in silence while with dogged resolve, if not with evident relish, Sir Alastair consumed every morsel.

When he had finished at last, he marked the achievement by hammering three times on the table with the handle of his fork. He then reached for a decanter and filled his wine glass to within a finger's breadth of the brim before adding perhaps a teaspoonful of water. Having gulped down at least half of this mixture he sat back and rested his fists on the tablecloth.

'Partridge,' he said finally, indicating his empty plate with a fingertip. 'Game birds I will have, since they are provenance of God's own greenwood, and killed clean too. It is no hardship to spit out a pellet or two. But beasts of the field, those I will not countenance. Were there cowsheds in the first garden, eh? Were there milking parlours?' He raised a finger in vindication. 'There is your answer.'

Sir Alastair looked to each of them in turn, perhaps anticipating some contrary argument. Gideon, being well acquainted with the scriptures, might have submitted that Abel made an offering to the Lord of a firstling lamb, and that Abraham himself offered veal to his guests, but he responded with the most tentative of nods.

'And my wine – ' Sir Alastair refreshed himself with another mouthful, all but draining the glass. 'Adulterated, as you saw. And what else did our Saviour partake of, when he broke bread with his brothers? What did he bid us do in his memory? For are we not gathered here in his name? Well, Cutter, are we not?'

The Inspector arranged his face. 'We're gathered here, sir, because you asked us to come.'

'Well, precisely.' Sir Alastair spread his hands, as if this amounted to much the same thing. He touched the neck of the decanter. 'You distrust yourself, as I recall, so I will not offend. What about your sergeant? Will he raise a cup with me?'

Cutter answered in a measured voice. 'I have never touched liquor, sir, so I have no reason to distrust myself. In any case, we are both on duty.'

'Of course, of course.' The Assistant-Commissioner caressed his belly. 'The redoubtable Inspector Cutter is always on duty, so they say. Sleeps in his boots when he sleeps at all. And you have had little rest of late, by all accounts. You have been applying yourself – what shall we say now? – applying yourself most diligently, is that not so?'

Under the table, the Inspector clamped his hands about his thighs. 'I don't often find myself idle, sir.'

'Oh, no doubt.' Sir Alastair refilled his glass, supped at it and set it down with a little gasp of satisfaction. 'No one would accuse you of idleness, I'm sure. Not that. But you have been making your presence felt, have you not?'

'I've been busy, yes. And when I leave here, I'll be busy again. Was there something in particular you wanted to discuss with me, sir?'

'Ah, very good.' Sir Alastair made what might have been a mirthful noise. 'That is the Cutter of whom I have heard so much. A stallion who can scarcely be dragged from the gallops, so they say. Though of course, police business is not all thundering over the turf. And in the hunt, some might say, it is not the proud horses who run the quarry to ground – it is the hounds, eh? The tireless hounds who will not be kept from the deepest ditch or the thorniest thicket.'

'I wouldn't know, sir. I am not a sporting gentleman, or a gentleman of any sort.'

'No,' Sir Alastair thumbed the border of his silk waistcoat. 'One must be born to such things, I suppose. Yet what of your sergeant here? Couldn't make do with a plain bread-and-butter sort, eh? Got yourself a young man of refinement, so they tell me. A Cambridge man, no less. Bliss, isn't it?' The Assistant-Commissioner licked his lips as he turned to Gideon. 'Well, Bliss? I'd have thought a scholar like yourself would find this an ugly business.'

Gideon glanced at the Inspector. 'I'm afraid I did little good as a scholar, sir. And now I have a chance to be of service.'

'Of service? To Cutter here? A severe sort of taskmaster for a tender youth like yourself.'

'It is the public we serve, sir. And the truth, when we may.'

Sir Alastair gathered his fingers in a show of relish. 'The *truth*, is it? Now there's a notion. And have you come across it in these last days, tell me? Did you find the truth under the skirts of one of those pansies in the Strand? Or was it something else that leapt out at you?'

The Inspector laid his palms on the table. 'Sir,' he said, 'if you have an interest in some case of mine, I'd be obliged if you would state it.'

'Some case of *yours*,' Sir Alastair replied. 'Is that what you call it? Have you such a wide domain, Cutter? For you have been sticking your beak into more than just knocking shops for arse jockeys, haven't you? You have been making free in high places too. And you have not always been welcome, have you?'

The Inspector's weathered face was often ominously expressive, but now it seemed as opaque as a slab of oak. 'I go where my duty takes me,' he said. 'And I will answer for my conduct if I am called to. You know who I answer to, I believe.'

'Oh, that I do. And I know who he answers to, when he answers at all. All very cosy, that arrangement. I'm sure it suits you very nicely. Lets you get up to all sorts, I daresay. But I'll let you into a little secret, Cutter. There are higher powers than that bag of bones Flood, or the Home Secretary, come to that. There are other great offices in this land, you know.'

The Inspector picked up a salt cellar, a heavy item of solid silver. He examined it idly. 'That is no secret, Sir Alastair. There are flags on the buildings.'

Sir Alastair hunched over the table. 'And that is all the likes of you will ever see of them. But some of us have business in such places. Oh, yes. The Branch is no longer out of favour, though we do not shout it from the rooftops. It suits us well enough to let people think they have our measure. Oh, the Branch, yes, the fellows you send out to break a strike or crack the heads of a few rowdy Fenians. But that is not all we are, my boy. We are defenders of the realm, and of those who rule over it. And think on this, Cutter. To protect those in high office, we must be often at their sides. We must have their confidence.'

Cutter nodded. 'I'm sure you have their great admiration, sir. Perhaps you will remember me to Her Majesty when you see her next.'

Sir Alastair leered at this. 'Are you making free with *me* now, Cutter? Do you think yourself such a bruiser that no one can correct your manners?'

The Inspector looked away for a moment, his fingertips spread across his brow. 'I do not doubt your influence, sir, but I'm sorry to say that even you might be hard put to improve my manners. However, I would not have you endure my company for longer than you must. If there's nothing else, the Sergeant and I will leave you to finish your dinner in peace. Bliss?'

As Cutter moved to rise, Massey seemed to struggle with himself. 'Come now,' he said, raising his palms. 'A few hard words, and hardly more than needed saying. Surely it takes more than that to send Henry Cutter running.'

'I'm not running anywhere, sir. I'm going back to work.'

'Of course you are, and your dedication does you credit. But I would not have you leave with a mistaken impression of me. Spare me a few more minutes, Cutter, and I will show you that I am not all harsh talk. I can be a sweet-natured fellow, too. Sit down, do.'

The Inspector sat grudgingly, keeping to the edge of his chair.

'That's better,' said Sir Alastair. 'Now, let's start afresh, shall we? I didn't bring you here for a dressing down, far from it. I brought you here because I heard of your difficulties, and because I saw that I might aid a brother officer in need.'

Cutter settled back in his chair, the better to meet Massey's stare, but he kept his face empty. 'My difficulties, sir?'

'Now, Henry, you know I mean no slight, for there is no disgrace in it whatsoever. You are an able sort of fellow, no doubt about it, but this present case . . .' Sir Alastair shook his jowls in commiseration. 'A prickly sort of business, and no mistake.'

'Which case are you speaking of, sir? I am looking into more than one.'

'Which case, he says. Come now, you need not play coy with me. I mean these murders of yours, as you very well know. And don't bother telling me they are separate matters either, not when the dogs in the street could tell me otherwise.'

'The dogs in the street will tell you whatever pleases you, sir. They are your dogs.'

Massey crimped his lips in irritation, then seemed to master himself once more. 'Very good, Cutter. My dogs, indeed. I do not like the term, but I can take a ribbing like the next man. All the same, you must be straight with me. Why, your own reports tie the two matters together.'

'You found time to look into my reports, sir? I'm honoured to hear it. But I'm afraid I must correct you again. The file on the most recent murder refers only to "certain other matters".'

'Ach, enough of this tomfoolery, Cutter. You know damned well—' Sir Alastair checked himself again. 'Look here, I'm not trying to trip you up, man. I'm trying to do you an honest turn. Naturally, you observed the niceties for the official record, but we have both been long enough in harness to speak frankly. Two gentlemen of that stripe, butchered within a week of each other? And both clever-looking jobs too? Do you mean to tell me that was no more than a nasty run of luck?'

Cutter lifted a hand from the arm of his chair. 'None of the particulars escaped me, sir. I'm examining many possibilities.'

'Yes, yes, and that is all fine and proper. But while you are examining your possibilities, some of us must think along more practical lines.'

The Inspector raised his chin by a fraction. 'You will have to explain what you mean, sir.'

Massey looked about him with a show of caution. 'We must think of what is next. We must think—' He leaned across the table. '—of who is next. It has occurred to you, surely? And you will recall what I said about the work of the Branch. It falls to us to protect certain people. Those people are well informed, as I need hardly tell you. And when they hear of a case like this, one that might touch them close to home? Well, they do not take it kindly, do they? They look for assurances, and who do you think they look to? Do you see? I will not be found wanting, Cutter. I mean to take measures. Do you take my meaning? Do you see now how our interests lie close together?'

Inspector Cutter's face clouded as if in puzzlement. 'Well, sir, I cannot say that I follow you exactly. The victims in my cases – they were men of station, certainly, but it had been some years since either one held any high office. I lack your connections, so perhaps I speak in ignorance, but it seems to me that there must be thousands

162

of men still living who answer to that description. I do not doubt your determination, sir, but even you can hardly protect all of them.'

Instead of flaring again into indignation, Sir Alastair responded with a contented smirk. 'You are right there. Her Majesty's treasury is not bottomless, and I have no great horde of men under my command, whatever you might have heard. No, you are quite right there. I cannot protect all of them. But if need be, I can protect some.'

Gideon had sat through the greater part of this interview in an attitude of rigid propriety, concerned with letting nothing show in his face or posture that might give offence. Yet as he absorbed what the Assistant Commissioner had just said, he could not help stirring uneasily in his seat. Glancing at the Inspector, he saw that he too had grasped the implication. Neither Massey nor his associates could protect anyone from the murderer unless they knew something of the murderer's motives.

To anyone else, Cutter's expression might have appeared grimly amused, but Gideon knew better. It was a look that put him in mind of some coiled and ancient basilisk.

'If need be,' he repeated, stroking his chin. 'And what need might that be, sir? I would have an easy time of it if murderers put notices in the paper a week before time, but that is not yet the common practice. If there are men with something to fear, I cannot tell you their names.'

Massey took up his glass with a satisfied air and slurped at its contents. 'Can you not? After all your labours? But you see, Cutter, that is just where I can help you.'

Nine

'*That cozening little* prick,' Cutter spat under his breath before they had even left the East India Club. 'That preening Calvinist goblin, with his "high places" and his "great offices". Does he take me for some green-eared Harry with a fortnight's service? That is just where I can help you, indeed. Help me, my hairy arse. He wouldn't piss on me if I was on fire, the conniving, skew-faced little gnome.'

Gideon merely agreed that Sir Alastair seemed a disagreeable sort of officer, and it was some hours later before he ventured to ask how Cutter meant to proceed. By then they had made their way to the Yard, where the Inspector left terse instructions with the desk sergeant. If a cat so much as pounced on a mouse anywhere between Hounslow and Barking, he said, he was to hear of it before the little fucker squeaked.

Afterwards, they went upstairs, to the neglected rooms on the second floor that served as the notional headquarters of their half-acknowledged division of the Metropolitan Police. In the rear-most of these, overlooking the Met's stable yard and, beyond it, a much-trafficked pair of public urinals on Parliament Street, Gideon kept a tidy desk at which he composed official reports. He had lately secured a typewriting machine of his own and was growing quite proficient in its use. For his part, the Inspector rarely seated himself at all while at the office, having little use for any of its appurtenances other than the coat stand.

This evening, however, he settled behind the table nearest the window, swung his feet onto the still and for three-quarters of an hour, he stared out in silence at the mottled and coky dusk.

'Might there not be something in it, sir?' Gideon asked at last.

Cutter scratched at his ear and shifted slightly in his chair, but he did not look around. 'Something in what, Bliss? The Ark of the Covenant?'

'In the Assistant-Commissioner's offer, sir. I'm sure you are right to view it with a degree of suspicion, but might he not have information of real value, even if he is not altogether transparent in his motives? A man in his position would not perpetrate an outright deception against a fellow officer, surely?'

The Inspector scraped with a whittled matchstick at the underside of his thumbnail. 'He is the head of the Special Branch, Bliss. Perpetrating deceptions is his job.'

'Yes, sir. But even so, it is one thing to conduct covert operations against enemies of the realm but another thing entirely to pass off a fabrication to an officer he knows to be astute and experienced. Think of the consequences if you were to expose him in such a falsehood.'

Cutter snorted. 'If I were to expose him in a falsehood? Where do you think we are, at the court of King Arthur? This is Scotland Yard, Bliss, where London's dirty work is done. And as for London itself, it's the belly of a beast that has flung its claws too wide. Its treasures are heaped on a midden, where bodies with hatchets in their backs have been piling up for a thousand years. There's no honour in this place, and there never was.'

'Then what was the point of it all, sir? Why would Sir Alastair take all that trouble if he had no hope of gaining your confidence?'

Cutter shook his head and scowled. 'Have you not learned yet, Bliss? You must listen to what a man is doing, not to what he is ing. Massey isn't half as sharp as he thinks he is, but he isn't stupid. He knows full well that I will doubt every word he tells me, but he also knows that I'm at a disadvantage. He doesn't know the whole of it, thank Christ – he doesn't know that I haven't two hard facts to rub together – but he knows I have three murders on my plate, the last of them the nastiest anyone can remember, and I'm nowhere near to bringing someone in. He knows I am in no position to be passing up chances.'

Gideon considered this for a time in silence. It was not an admission of defeat, but it was as frank an accounting as the Inspector had ever given. If nothing else, it explained why they were here. For as long as Gideon had known him, Cutter had seemed constitutionally incapable of sitting still, yet he was slumped now in a draughty corner of this forgotten annex and he had no apparent object in mind other than waiting for something to happen.

Gideon uncapped a pen and reached for his blotter. He scrawled idly, ornamenting the empty page with flourishes and curlicues. He scratched through them, conscious of an unaccustomed irritability, and he pushed the blotter away. 'Do you not think, sir,' he said at last, 'that Massey is at a disadvantage himself?'

Cutter half turned at this, cocking his jaw in intrigue or amusement. 'You'll have to explain that, Bliss.'

'Well, in the first place,' Gideon said, 'he does not know what you know. You said as much yourself. He can make certain inferences, but he cannot be sure that you are not on the point of hauling a man before the magistrate.'

'A man, is it?' said Cutter. 'Go on.'

'And then there is the matter of the unnamed person.' Here Gideon was using Sir Alastair's own description. 'If we wish to avail of his offer, he said, he will arrange for us to meet with this unknown person at six o'clock tomorrow evening. He was precise about the

66

time, but he would not give the location. That will be revealed "in due course", he said. Did that not strike you as an oddity?'

'That's the Branch for you, Bliss. They would take you to a secret location just to give you a tip on a horse. It's all show.'

'Sir Alastair did seem to relish the air of mystery, sir. However, I did wonder whether the arrangements were all of his own choosing. In fact, I wondered whether he himself knows who the unnamed person is. If you recall, sir, he spoke of "a person of influence and position, such as I often encounter in my line of work". He was making much of his connections, as he is fond of doing, but he did not say outright that he and this person are directly acquainted.'

The Inspector turned in his chair and eyed Gideon narrowly. 'That would make it a chancy business for him. He would be throwing his lot in with someone he cannot answer for – someone who might have designs of their own. I wouldn't put it past him, mind you. He'd befriend a scorpion if it had a cousin on the right committee.'

'Exactly so, sir. And he may have less choice in the matter than he would have us believe. No doubt you know more of the man than I do, but Special Branch or no, he can hardly be on truly intimate terms with anyone of real substance. We have both had our share of dealings with such people, sir, and you have said it yourself – to them a policeman is little different from a rat-catcher. No doubt he is useful to some, given the resources he commands; useful enough, perhaps, that they flatter his vanity in small ways, but is he any more than that?'

'If anything, he is less,' Cutter answered sourly. 'I told you, we're all doing someone's dirty work, but he's doing the dirty work of the shit-shovellers. He's the one who must wipe the tools clean and hose out the workshop. And he thinks he has a seat in the Lords waiting for him. A deep ditch on a dark night, more like.'

'All the more reason, then, to suppose that he is doing someone else's bidding. This unnamed person would not have it otherwise, surely? Not if it is someone who really does have knowledge of this affair.'

Again, the Inspector's look was keen and intent. 'And what affair might that be? You talk as if you know a good deal about it, Bliss. You talk as if you know more than I do.'

Gideon looked down at his lap. He scratched at a spot of grease above the knee of his trousers. 'If I may, sir, I believe you are not being candid with me. No doubt you have your reasons, but nevertheless, you have not told me all you know or suspect.'

'Have I not? And yet here you are making pronouncements about the nature of this affair as if you know it inside and out. If I have not been candid, as you put it, then it hasn't hindered you much. Or have you some other source of intelligence?'

Gideon looked up, conscious of a flaring about his cheeks. 'You know I do not, sir. You know I have nothing but the facts of the case.'

'Is that right?' said Cutter, leaning back in his chair. 'Only the facts of the case. So, you spent hours on end in registry offices and inns of court, copying down names and dates and deeds of title and you made nothing of it whatsoever? You watched Milo play out the last moments of Considine's life down to the eighth of an inch, so that you might as well have been standing at the murderer's shoulder, and you never gave it a second thought? You heard me say all manner of peculiar things – you entered some of them into the official record, come to that – and you saw me pocket some poor child's fingerbone, knowing full well that it belonged in evidence. You paid no mind to any of that – is that what you're telling me?'

'Sir, I . . .' Gideon struggled to assemble his recollections. 'Sir, I simply trusted that you would make your reasons plain in due course, that you would . . . that when the time came, you would explain everything.'

'That I would *explain everything*?' Cutter grimaced and shook his head. 'Do I look like one of your doddering professors, Bliss? When have I ever *explained everything*?'

'I don't . . . I'm not sure I . . .'

'Tell me something, Bliss. What did you tell Miss Hillingdon, when I sent you to ask for her – well, when I sent you to talk to her? Did you give her any notion of what to look for, or did you send her off to dig through the whole of recorded history? Is she starting with the Domesday Book and working her way to the present day?'

'Well, sir, I—'

'And this afternoon,' the Inspector went on, 'when the esteemed Assistant-Commissioner was speechifying about great affairs of state, you had no notion of what affairs he meant? How could you, when I have kept you in the dark, eh? When I have not *explained everything*?'

Gideon fell silent for a time as he tried to piece together all he had seen and heard since – since when? Since that morning in Josiah Pruitt's reeking yard? Since the arrival of the letter with the black seal, weeks before that? It was like trying to tease together fragments of paper scattered on water. 'I suppose . . .' He halted and began again. 'I suppose you may have made certain intimations.'

Cutter made a coarse sound. 'Certain intimations, my arse. What did you tell Octavia?'

'I told her about Considine, sir, just as you instructed. I said that there was reason to believe that the case had its roots in some past wrongdoing.'

'The past is a big place. A big place with no shortage of wrong-doing. She'd still have her work cut out. Did you say nothing about when?'

'I mentioned when Sir Aneurin received his honour, just as you suggested. But that is an example of what I mean, sir. You made no mention of that date when we began trawling through all those reams of archives. You set me to work with no notion of what I was looking for or why. I spoke in earnest when I said that you have taught me a great deal by example, but surely on some rare occasions you might contemplate simply speaking your mind.'

Cutter swung his boot heels from the sill and slammed his fist against the table. 'I will ask you once more, Bliss. What did you tell Miss Hillingdon?'

Gideon straightened his blotter. He took up an ink bottle and tightened its cap. He set it down again. 'I told her that I was certain of nothing, sir, and that I was constrained in what I could say. However, I suggested to her – that is, I may have intimated that crimes might at one point have been committed against children.'

The Inspector leaned back in his chair. He loosened his shoulders and folded his arms behind his head. 'May you, indeed? Well, there's a puzzle for you. You know next to nothing, by your account, yet there you were, intimating away to your heart's content. Where did you come by these intimations, I wonder? Did you come across a burning bush up on Hampstead Heath? Did a little bird tell you?'

Gideon picked up the ink bottle again. He worried with his thumbnail at a wrinkle in its label. 'I suppose, sir, that I have seen and heard things in recent days that led me to make certain inferences.'

Cutter raised his eyebrows. He nodded slowly, as if marvelling over some prodigious invention. 'Inferences, is it? And from things you saw and heard? Lord above, it's like hearing one of those talks at the Royal Society.'

Gideon shifted in his seat. He brought up his hand to cover what was not quite a cough.

The Inspector, meanwhile, had settled into a more natural posture. He thumbed the underside of his lip as he considered his final words on the matter. 'Don't mistake my meaning, Bliss, when I talk of doing dirty work. We were born into a filthy world, so we have little choice in the matter. Our first steps were dirty work, and our last breath will be no different. We cannot hope for honour, in this life, so we must make do with what we have. I've been knocking about this place a good while, but I'm no nearer to understanding its workings. I'll show you as much as you have the stomach for, Bliss, but don't hold your breath waiting for me to explain things. I have no explanations to offer you.'

He turned to the window again, where a gaunt crow had settled to contemplate the dusty jade of evening. Cutter lifted his boot heels cautiously, seeming reluctant to disturb it.

'Now, then,' he said, when he made himself comfortable. 'You were holding forth on the life and opinions of an unnamed person, I believe. Have you more to say on that subject?'

Gideon cleared his throat. Cutter's last remarks had made a considerable impression, and he lacked the Inspector's gift for conducting three or four conversations at once. 'You mean the unnamed person that Massey spoke of? Yes, sir, though on that point I am still at a loss. If our murderer is avenging some past wrong, then those in danger must be people with something to hide.'

'And?' said Cutter.

'Well, that is the part that gives me difficulty. It would certainly help us to know of such people, since we are no nearer to finding the murderer. But why would the unnamed person identify these potential victims? They are not so desperate for our protection, surely, that they are willing to admit involvement in some past wrongdoing? And why come to us at all, if they already have Massey at their beck and call? He commands the Special Branch, as he was at pains to remind us. Surely he can provide all the protection they might wish for.'

Cutter gave a terse snuffle. 'You'd think so, wouldn't you? So, how do you account for it all?'

'Account for it? I can't, sir. Or not in any satisfactory way. I wondered if Massey's unnamed person might not also have something to hide – and something to fear. Maybe he means to cast himself upon our mercy, and to offer up the other conspirators? We have encountered such informants before, have we not?'

Cutter tapped idly at the glass with his shoe. The crow eyed him for a moment with bleak disparagement, then returned to its ruminations. 'We have, Bliss, yes. We've encountered them among the halfwits who plot the murders of postmistresses in gin shops, or schemes to tunnel into the Bank of England. We are not dealing with such people now. We're dealing with powerful people who wouldn't give us the time of day, never mind a confession. Not that there is anything to confess to, since we have no proof yet of any conspiracy.'

Gideon pondered this. 'What are we to make of it all, then? Must we simply go along with Massey's proposal, whatever our doubts?'

Cutter's expression soured. 'You needn't think I like the idea. Assistant Commissioner Flood gives me a good deal of leeway, but he had a dyspeptic look the last time I was in to see him. The newspapers are fairly shrieking after that bit of business in the Damask, and I can't be seen to turn away offers of aid. That is what galls me about Massey's infernal bit of chicanery. It's an offer I can't refuse, though I know in my bones that it will do me no good. I must trot along to meet this unnamed associate, and in the meantime I can apply myself to nothing else in earnest. I must sit here like a beached sea captain, praying that some other dotard will have the goodness to get himself knifed in the brain.'

'I confess that I do not understand that part, sir. Why must you wait here? If our murderer were to strike again, God forbid, word might be sent to you anywhere. You have contrived such things before.'

'Why should God forbid it? He never bestirs himself for the innocent, never mind anyone else. I have contrived such things before, yes, but matters stood differently then. Our murderer wasn't the talk of the town, and I didn't have to wonder about half the men in the Yard. If you want your enemies to show themselves, Bliss, then you must put yourself in plain sight. And where better to—'

The Inspector broke off abruptly and whipped a finger to his lips. A moment later he had surged to his feet and was edging soundlessly towards the door. Gideon noticed too that Cutter's right hand had crept inside his coat. By rights his own revolver ought to have been concealed in the same fashion. Cutter himself had overseen the fitting of his holster, on the morning after the murders in St James's, but after unslinging it that night Gideon had wrapped the gun in an old nightshirt and hidden it under his bed. He had not thought of it again until this moment.

The Inspector paused at the door jamb, his entire frame tensed and still, then he lunged for the handle. In the next moment, following a sequence of thuds and a brief, throttled shriek, an indistinct figure had been flung bodily against the opposite wall. It now lay twitching beneath a roll of confiscated carpet.

When Cutter had manoeuvred the carpet aside, Gideon saw a young man of about his own build. His complexion was unwholesome, but he was outfitted – as Gideon was himself – in dark fustian of approximately matching shades. 'Leave off, sir!' the young man squawked. 'Leave off, will you. It ain't but me, Eccles!'

'It's who?' demanded Cutter, who had planted a boot heel in the small of the young man's back. 'I know no Eccles and I was expecting no Eccles. Why didn't you knock and call out like any man on honest business? What were you doing skulking and shuffling with your lug to my door, you creeping streak of nursling's shite? Who sent you, eh?'

'Sir, Meacham sent me. Sergeant Meacham from down the front desk. Which I'm Constable Eccles, sir. I weren't doing nothing but fetching up a message, only I were . . .' Here Eccles faltered in his account. He lapsed into plaintive wheezing.

'Only you were what?' demanded Cutter.

'Only I were trying to work up the bottle, sir, on account of it was yourself. Begging your pardon and that, but I've heard stories.'

'Stories, is it?' Cutter's tone was still fearsome, but he adjusted the set of his right leg so that the young man could at least breathe freely. 'They'll be telling a new story this time tomorrow if you can't give me a straight answer. It'll be the tale of young Jack, who climbed up the beanstalk and got a kick in the magic beans from the giant. Now, what message? Who's it from?'

'Pair of young ladies, sir. Proper posh, or one of them was. I could tell, on account of she was covered in dog hairs and dressed like she was off to shoot something. Anyhow, the other one said she had an urgent message. Had to be delivered by hand. If I could just . . . if you could just let me up, sir, I'll fetch it out.'

Eccles was allowed to stagger to his feet, and following an interval of anxious fumbling he produced a plain brown envelope.

'Well?' said Cutter. 'What are you waiting for, a bugle blast? Give it here.'

Eccles's mouth worked vacantly for a time. 'Which it ain't . . . Begging your pardon, sir, but the letter ain't for you. It's for the Sergeant there.'

The Inspector appeared to struggle with this proposition. 'For the Sergeant? What sergeant?'

Gideon coughed. 'I believe I may be the party in question, sir.'

Cutter looked on in frank amazement as Gideon retrieved the envelope. He collected himself somewhat when he found that Eccles was still present. 'What are you gawking at, you drooling simpleton?' he said, shoving the constable out the door. 'Get on with yourself, before I do you a proper injury.'

When he had scuttled away, Inspector Cutter assumed an air of solemnity. 'Well, now,' he said, folding his arms. 'An item of private correspondence, is it? Will the young master be withdrawing to his study?'

Gideon had not yet stirred from where he stood. He thumbed the edges of the envelope, which bore Octavia's handwriting. 'It is from Miss Hillingdon, sir.'

'Is it now? How nice. Be sure to give her my regards.'

'Yes, sir.' Gideon still held the packet stiffly, making no move to open it. 'Perhaps I ought to . . .'

'Not for me to say,' said Cutter. 'A gentleman's private affairs. I wouldn't dream of intruding.'

'Yes, sir.' Gideon fidgeted with the seal. 'And Eccles gave us to understand that there was a degree of urgency.'

He considered taking the letter to his desk, but that might have been too pointed a gesture. Instead he inched his way to a table near the middle of the room. 'Shall I just . . .'

'Oh, don't mind me,' said the Inspector, averting his eyes.

The envelope contained a single sheet of what might have been butcher's paper, folded carefully in four. Gideon was puzzled at first by its crumpled appearance, and by the traces of charcoal dust. Then he spread it flat on the table.

He put his hand to his mouth. Something lurched softly beneath his ribs. 'Oh,' he said. 'Oh, my.'

'Glad news, is it?' Cutter was studying his cuffs. 'Is sir off to a wedding? Or a reading party in Eastbourne?'

'It's a rubbing, sir.'

The Inspector looked up. 'What?'

'A rubbing, sir. One uses a piece of charcoal to—'

'I know what a rubbing is, you dazed cockatoo. A rubbing of *what*?'

'Of a memorial plaque, sir, commemorating a fire at an orphans' asylum. On the night of—' But Cutter had already crossed the room, shunting Gideon aside as he stooped over the table.

'The 20th of January, 1872,' the Inspector murmured. 'That would be near enough to the mark.'

Gideon did not ask what mark he had in mind. He looked over the children's small and ordinary names. He counted thirty-six of them. 'Remembered by the Governor and Trustees of the Salus House Asylum for Orphaned Children,' he read aloud. 'Salus House. Is that not a name we have encountered, sir?'

But Cutter had risen from the table. He settled again by the window, where he began scrutinising some official memorandum plucked from a notice board. 'Look at that now,' he said, seemingly engrossed. 'We are to be allowed a shilling a head for "upkeep of apparel". A shilling a head, eh? A fellow could save up for a new pair of bootlaces.'

Gideon let this pass. 'And Miss Hillingdon's note, sir. What do you make of it?'

'Was there a note, Bliss? I must have overlooked it, not wishing to pry.'

This did not seem likely, but Gideon persevered. 'Yes, sir. She has added a note in the margin. She gives the whereabouts of this asylum. I am to meet her there first thing tomorrow. I am not to come alone, she says. That part is underlined.'

'Making up a foursome, is it? Lord, for the life of a leisured gentleman.'

Gideon strove to keep a civil tone. 'If I may, sir, your point has been made. This discovery of Miss Hillingdon's might be significant, surely?'

Cutter studied his memorandum for a moment longer, but presently he seemed to relent. 'She is not one for wasting time, I'll give her that much. And she took some trouble over that rubbing. I suppose we must give her a hearing. If there is anything in it, we'll know it soon enough.'

'Indeed, sir,' Gideon agreed. 'Miss Hillingdon may have more to tell us.'

The Inspector looked out into the encroaching darkness. Above the pediments of the Home Office, some noble figure – Britannia herself, perhaps – clutched her stony robes against the sullied violet of the evening.

'So she may,' he said after a time. 'But that's not what I meant. We are hunting great beasts, Bliss, and we may be coming within scent of them. I'm sure of very little, Christ knows, but this much I can tell you. When we do get close, we will know it.'

Ten

The *Salus House* Asylum had once been a grand institution, but the memorial to the lost children was small and plain. At the foot of one northern wing, a simple slab of granite, perhaps three feet by two, had been set into the gable wall. The stone had weathered, with the passing of twenty-odd years, leaving little to mark it out.

Octavia led Gideon to it in silence, with Cutter and Milo following at a slight remove. They had not lingered long before she led them away again, refusing to say any more until they had gathered in a nearby tool shed.

'Well,' said Cutter, shaking the drizzle from his hat, 'someone spared no expense.'

'Six pounds, eight shillings and ten pence,' said Octavia. 'About the price of a half-decent suit. The local paper sent someone on the day the memorial was unveiled.'

'And by the looks of it,' said the Inspector, 'that was the last time anyone came to see it. The place is deserted, as far as I can see. So, what are we doing standing around in this shed?'

'It's not deserted,' Octavia said. 'Not entirely, anyway. I'll come back to that soon enough. You saw the repairs?'

'What little there was to see,' said Cutter. 'I had visions of some great conflagration, but I saw no sign of that.'

'I'm sorry to disappoint you,' Octavia answered. 'The fire didn't spread beyond that wing. As far as I can tell, it didn't spread beyond the second floor.'

Cutter showed a flicker of interest. 'What stopped it, I wonder? Did the children line up with buckets?'

'I can't say.' Octavia's tone was even. 'There's quite a lot I can't say, since the records aren't nearly complete. It could have been much worse, certainly. At that time, there were almost six hundred children here. Only thirty-six died.'

The Inspector heaved a sigh. 'As you say, it might have been worse. Now then, Miss Hillingdon, I like a bit of sightseeing as much as the next man, but I've had little in the way of leisure lately. Would you be good enough to tell me why you have dragged me all the way out here to Epping Forest?'

Octavia flicked something from her skirts. She was dressed today in fine town clothes. 'I think you'll find, Inspector, that it was Gideon I invited.'

Inspector Cutter had been examining a rusty hacksaw. He tossed it aside with a look of grim amusement. 'That's how it is, is it? Bliss, you might ask Miss Hillingdon why she dragged you all the way out here.'

'Ah,' said Gideon, who was poking at a cache of desiccated rags. 'I'm sure, sir, that Miss Hillingdon is coming to the, er . . .'

Above them the tin roof shuddered and fretted in the wind. Roused dust uncoiled itself in a spar of sunlight. 'I'd be delighted,' said Octavia smoothly. 'Do you remember, Gideon, what I said about finding traces of a particular kind?'

Gideon lurched away from the workbench, having disturbed a spider of unsettling proportions. 'Traces, yes. I remember it distinctly.'

'Well, sometimes it isn't what you find that matters. It's what you don't find. A fire broke out at this asylum in January of 1872. People notice fires, as a rule. People can see them, sometimes from miles away. And afterwards, there are the dead, the damage, the inquests, the insurance claims. All written down and filed away. This fire was unusual, though. I only came across it because your friend Sir Aneurin was one of the trustees here. I might have missed even that detail if you hadn't mentioned the orchids.'

For a moment Gideon was at a loss. 'The orchids?'

'He built a conservatory here, during the spring of 1870. For the educational improvement of the children, according to him. We know about that because there was a garden party when it was opened. The *Wanstead Examiner* carried that story too, accompanied by a good deal of editorial guff about Salus House and the betterment of the helpless. The Asylum was a prominent local employer, so that's the sort of thing you expect. That might be why the *Examiner* showed such a light touch when they came to report on the fire. *The Governor noted that more grievous losses were prevented by the Asylum's insistence on stringent standards in the construction of its facilities,* and so on.

'What's odd is that the paper didn't print another word about the fire until the unveiling of the memorial almost a year later. What's odder still is that the *Examiner* didn't so much as mention the Asylum again until it closed in 1877, at which point the original trust was dissolved and its records were deposited with the local library. That caught my attention, as you might imagine, so I paid a visit to the library in question. What do you imagine I discovered?'

Octavia had addressed herself to Gideon, but at this the Inspector put aside the hand drill he had been tinkering with. 'All right, Miss Hillingdon,' he said. 'You may save yourself any further theatrics. I see what is wanted.'

He crossed to the centre of the shed's creaking floor, where a void in the rusting roof admitted a rift of greyish light. He stood scratching at his jaw for a moment, then he grimaced as if swallowing a knot of gristle. 'Miss Hillingdon,' he said, 'I have been remiss. I ask your pardon for it.'

Gideon stared as if at an apparition.

The Inspector frowned and checked himself. He lifted one bulky shoulder and kneaded it distractedly. 'Miss Hillingdon, Octavia. I haven't asked for your help, and no doubt you remarked upon the fact to Bliss here. I didn't ask for your help, just as no one asked for mine. I cannot even tell you what help is needed, yet here we all stand. I cannot tell you all I know yet, and you may make of that what you will, but I will say this much. Men are being killed over some wrong that was done long ago. It was a wrong that cannot be righted, and a wrong that cannot be forgotten. Someone remembers. Someone does little else. I'm not asking anything of you, but something is being asked of all of us. Will that do?'

'Well,' said Octavia, when he had returned to his place. 'That was certainly something to see. And you used the word *help*, which counts for something. Some practical matters, then. I was followed home last night, after stopping at Scotland Yard. Does that surprise you?'

'I can't say that it does,' said Cutter. 'People are watching my doings. Some that I know of, and likely more some that I don't. No one followed us here, as far I can tell, so you needn't have kennelled us up in this shed.'

'I'm glad to hear it,' said Octavia, 'but that's not why I was being cautious. This man you've brought with you . . . Forgive me, sir, but I must be direct – this man Milo. I don't want to know the details, but I imagine he's dangerous, yes?'

Milo stirred from his own shadowy corner and took a step forward. His suit today was sombre, and as beautifully cut as ever. He took off his hat and caressed its brim with a thoughtful look. 'I keep a cat,' he said, and when the others looked at him in puzzlement, he added: 'With my cat, I am very gentle. I give it nice fishes, the cream from the milk. But if the *mademoiselle* wishes it, then yes, I can do certain things. I can be dangerous.'

'I see,' said Octavia. 'Well, thank you. It may very well come in useful. And you, Gideon. You're already clever and polite, but have you ever played at dressing up?'

Gideon's mouth worked vacantly for a time. 'At . . . dressing up?'

'No? Well, never mind. I've brought things for you to wear. I've always wanted to see you with spectacles. Don't worry, you'll be marvellous. Now, then. Here's what we're going to do.'

Gideon and Octavia left their improvised hideout by a circuitous path. Threading their way past the brooding marches of Epping Forest, they kept out of sight when they could, but they were near enough now that the Asylum was always at the edges of their vision, a greying mass that had held too many souls to ever be truly abandoned.

It had been known to some as Salus House, Octavia said, though properly it had been the Salus Hospital for Orphaned Children. In Latin, *salus* meant 'health', though the word had other uses. Sometimes it meant 'salvation'. To the children, it would only ever have been 'the Asylum'. For them, there would have been nothing else.

It possessed a forbidding sort of grandeur still. Its many wings seemed to spread over acres, and above them rose turrets and cupolas that once must have gleamed white and magisterial over orderly lawns. The grounds were untended now, and shabby ponies grazed among the briars and thorn bushes. The flags were long gone from the soaring finials, leaving only scabbed needles of ironwork.

'The same architect as St Pancras,' said Octavia. They were skirting the northern limits of the grounds now, close enough to glimpse the faded interiors of the upper rooms. They spoke quietly, and not only out of caution. Some other instinct moved them. 'And the Home Office, come to that. They began with grand notions.'

Gideon watched a crow settle above a weathered chapel. In the high windows of the chancel, the stained-glass windows showed signs of damage. Children had been throwing stones, perhaps. A warrior saint was draped in half an azure cloak, raising a lance to the broken heavens. A haloed infant whispered benedictions into its own shattered hands.

'What do you think happened here?' he said. 'I mean, the fire must have been awful, in its way, but fires happen.'

'There are things you should know,' Octavia murmured. 'But not yet, not here. Shall we go? It isn't much further.'

She set off again, seeming anxious to put the Asylum behind them. They skirted the edge of a wide pond, under a procession of high beeches that might once have marked a boundary. Beyond the water was a wilder patch of woodland, and Octavia quickened her step as they drew near it, seeming unhindered by her fine clothes.

She didn't speak again until they were some way into the wood, but when she did, her mood had lightened. Clambering over a fallen holly tree, she turned and made a brisk gesture. 'Pick up my hem, will you. Oh, go on. They're just ankles, they're not going to bite you. So, this place – you can let go now, by the way.'

'Hmm? Oh, yes.' Gideon rose abruptly and plunged his hands into his pockets, but Octavia was already pressing on.

'I don't know that anything happened here,' she said, glancing back. 'What I do know is that someone reclaimed those archives I mentioned, and quite recently too. That's an unusual occurrence, and most libraries wouldn't stand for it, but who knows what sort of pressure might have been brought to bear. And the library in Wanstead kept an index, so at least we know what's missing. There were lists of admissions, reports of sanitary inspections, the gazettes they used to send to the patrons, all sorts of things. If something was covered up, then someone wasn't taking any chances.'

Gideon considered this. 'Or someone didn't know. What they were covering up, I mean.'

She glanced back at him. 'Very good, Gideon. We'll make an archivist of you yet. Now, we ought to be approaching the—' Octavia came to a halt and held out an arm. The trees had thinned out and before them stood an old lychgate with sagging roof timbers. 'There, that's Wanstead High Street. Suki will be waiting with the carriage, so I'll have to look presentable. She only pretends to be improper, you know. Check my clothes at the back, will you. Pick off any twigs and burrs and things.'

'Ah,' said Gideon. 'Right you are.' He edged around her at a decorous distance, and after some hesitation he plucked a single catkin from near her elbow.

'Oh, for heaven's sake, Gideon. You can *touch* me, you know. You can't even feel a girl properly through this get-up, take it from me.'

When he had done as good a job as he could decently manage, Gideon straightened to find Octavia studying him. Her expression was fond, but there was something else in it too.

'You are a pet,' she said after a moment. 'Has there been anyone lately? A girl, I mean? It is very much girls with you, isn't it?'

'Is what girls? Oh, I see. Mmm. Well, I suppose so, yes. But has there – gosh. Well, no, not since—' He couldn't say her name, even now. 'Not since, you know.'

'Yes, I know. I do. But she wasn't ever— No, never mind. Just try to remember that we're real, won't you?'

'That you're . . . I'm sorry, I don't . . .'

'That we're real, women and girls. Not apparitions, not ethereal beings. That we ache and sweat and want things. Want things very much, sometimes.'

'Mmm.' He drew a careful breath and scratched an eyelid. 'No, yes. Yes, of course.'

'It might make things easier, that's all. Harder, too. But in a good way.' She turned and ducked under the lychgate, checking for passers-by before crossing into the street. Gideon hurried to follow, though he did his best to make it look like energetic strolling. 'Anyway, look, I'll have to tell you the rest later. Your name's going to be Edwin, by the way. Did I mention that.'

'Edwin? Really? *Edwin*?'

Octavia grinned back at him. 'What? You could be an Edwin. And the part called for an Edwin, I thought. Your real name is Gideon, for heaven's sake. How difficult could it be?'

All told, it took less than a quarter of an hour for Gideon to be outfitted in the guise of the Reverend Edwin Sturridge, brother to the likewise imaginary Lucinda Sturridge and newly installed vicar at St Ranulph's Parish in Wisborough Green, Sussex. Miss Bryant had stationed her carriage at the top of Wanstead High Street, and whatever her attachment to propriety, she proved a formidably capable accomplice in this fraudulent scheme.

She first addressed the faults in Miss Hillingdon's own costume, having greeted her in what seemed their accustomed fashion. 'Octavia, you contemptible trollop. Look at your boots. Oh, get in, get in. Thank goodness I brought rags and polish.'

With that she produced a heaving travelling bag and tumbled out a great quantity of gentlemen's clothing, including at least five black suits and several fistfuls of white neckwear.

'What's his parish like?' she demanded, heaping the clothes in her lap and rifling through them with a critical eye.

'His what?' said Octavia, who had set about her shoes with a polishing cloth.

'His parish, the living you picked for him. Is it rich?'

'No idea,' Octavia answered, only half attending. 'I know the old vicar is dead, if that's of any use. I found the place in the death notices.'

'Oh, for pity's sake,' said Suki, holding up two competing suits and squinting at each in turn. 'He has to dress for his parish. It's what they do. Where is it, East or West Sussex? I know families in the east. It's bursting with money.'

'Suki, everyone you know is bursting with money. It's a village on the Downs. I doubt anyone's ever been there. Can we please get on? The others will have taken up their positions by now.'

Miss Bryant was unpersuaded, and she remained so a short time later when Gideon stepped down from the carriage in the person of a young clergyman of indeterminate means. The ladies had dismounted some minutes earlier, so that he might shift his clothes in something near to dignity, and both now turned to appraise him. Octavia suppressed a smile, but Miss Bryant's look was pained.

'Oh, no,' she said. 'Oh, dear me, no.'

Gideon looked down at himself, dislodging the unaccustomed pair of spectacles. Their bridge gripped his nose fiercely, though not in the right place, and their curls of brass wire made only approximate circuits of his ears, terminating in spiteful points that jabbed against the soft portions of his neck.

'Oh, no,' Miss Bryant was saying again. 'Why are the cuffs like that? Why don't your arms hang correctly? And what *have* you done with the cravat? It looks like you're hiding a stolen napkin.'

'*Suki*,' said Octavia, nudging her sharply. 'That will do. I'll tuck him in a bit, but a certain awkwardness is part of the desired effect. It's important that we not appear intimidating.'

'Well, really,' answered Miss Bryant. 'Unintimidating is one thing, but unkempt is quite another. And what about you? *You* don't look a fright. You couldn't.'

'You said I looked a fright only moments ago, you viper. And no, I don't. I'm a girl, so I'm not allowed to. I'm going to be unimposing in my manner instead.'

Miss Bryant made a scornful sound. 'I dread to think,' she said. 'In any case, I wash my hands of it all. Though you'll be requiring my services again later, I imagine.'

'Quite possibly,' said Octavia. 'You can't wait because it would look odd, so you'll have to come back. Shall we say four o'clock? You won't forget?'

'You're certain that's all?' Miss Bryant said. 'You won't be wanting sandwiches this time, or a team of hounds?'

'You're a perfect darling,' said Octavia, kissing her cheek fleetingly. 'Now we really must go.'

But Miss Bryant latched onto her forearm. 'I'm being peevish because I'm worried,' she said. 'You haven't told me everything, but I'm not a simpleton. I'm not easily frightened either, but I prefer the sort of danger I can look in the eye. And this business isn't like that, is it?'

Octavia freed herself gently. 'I certainly hope not,' she said. 'It would mean we'd gone to all this trouble for nothing.'

The gate lodge where Mr Silas Abelard had taken residence was not a commodious dwelling, but it was, Mr Abelard assured his visitors, much more comfortable than might be supposed. Gideon and Octavia also learned, within moments of being shown in, that this living arrangement was strictly temporary in nature and was not to be construed as a hardship. Though not yet a partner in his firm, Mr Abelard was so near to attaining that office that the distinction all but vanished. He had only to bring this present affair to a neat end before the matter was made final.

'For you are to understand, sir,' he said, addressing Gideon. 'You are to understand that— Your pardon, but I have forgotten your name.'

'My name, yes.' Gideon had been made to repeat it over a dozen times, but he now found himself at a loss. 'My name is—'

'Oh, Edwin,' said Octavia, intervening. 'My brother is unused to his new station, Mr Abelard. At home he was always Little Ned, being the youngest, but he has lately become the Reverend Edwin Sturridge. I am Lucinda Sturridge, of course, and alas, I remain a Miss.'

Mr Abelard caressed his silk tie as he absorbed this. He was not an imposing young man, but he had dressed with small touches of ostentation. 'I believe I understand,' he said. 'Well, you are to understand, Reverend—'

'Oh, just Ned,' said Octavia. 'Do just call him Ned, he prefers it. And I shall be plain Lucinda. You'll find it odd, I'm sure, being such an accomplished gentleman, but it's how we were raised. My late father, you see – the Mr Sturridge who sat on the board here – my late father always insisted upon it, even in his own case. He valued humility above all virtues, didn't he, Neddy? One would never have guessed at his wealth.'

'His wealth, you say.' Mr Abelard's chin twitched minutely. 'And your business is connected with his . . . Well, we shall come to that, I imagine. Well, then, as you wish, I suppose. What was it I was saying?'

'That Ned was to understand something, I believe. That we were both to understand it, perhaps, since I was also within hearing.'

'Eh? Oh, yes. Do take a . . .' He began clearing detritus from a cramped sofa, pausing to puzzle over an ancient embroidery box.

'Do make yourselves . . . yes. That is, you are to understand, both of you, that though I occupy the gate lodge, it is solely out of prudence. The firm, you see, and there I must declare a proprietorial interest, being so very nearly in a position of equity. My cousin – quite a close cousin, you know – having reached an age where he no longer keeps a hand in . . . well, it is spoken of as being expected in the ordinary course, though naturally—' He had been lowering himself with some deliberation into a narrow armchair, but he stood again as some urgent consideration struck him. 'In the most respectful terms, you are to understand. These discussions of my expectations are couched in the most respectful terms, vis-à-vis my cousin, whom I naturally hold in esteem, yes?'

'Naturally,' said Octavia sweetly.

'Indeed, yes,' Gideon offered. 'Your esteem is plainly evident.'

'Oh, the utmost,' said Mr Abelard, cautiously seating himself again. 'In terms of the utmost esteem, and without any suggestion of vulgarity. But all the same, a thing can be made plain, between gentlemen, and so it is in this case. And what I meant to say, in the matter of the gate lodge, was that it is out of an excess of zeal, as it were, for the interests of the trust – for we act in that capacity, you know. The governor of the, er, of the institution, was provided with quite handsome apartments, but if I were to reside in the principal buildings, I could hardly exercise the proper vigilance. Why, anyone might wander in, do you see.'

'Oh, we can quite imagine,' said Octavia. 'We noted the extent of the grounds, didn't we, Edwin? It seems a great acreage, and with a good many outbuildings and what-have-you, where unwanted persons might secrete themselves.'

Mr Abelard's expansive gesture was partly thwarted by the confines of his armchair. 'Oh, immense, immense. Naturally, however, I need not concern myself with common trespassers. We have engaged a very able man – that is to say, a very able man has been made available to us by a certain party. A Mr Blakelock, by name, whom I despatched not half an hour since to roam the perimeter. Oh, a very able man. Very . . .' He puffed out his cheeks and splayed his arms to suggest a more robust frame than his own.

'Very imposing?' Octavia ventured.

'Oh, very, very. With the manners one expects in such a person, I'm afraid, but that is a reassurance in itself. He would give a good account of himself, I am sure, if any unpleasantness were ever to . . . but my point was, you see, that this is a considerable situation. Oh, quite considerable. And naturally a woman comes in from the town to see about the house. It isn't her day today, or I should not have come to the door myself, but really it is preferable – for a young gentleman, you know – to make do in the mornings. And after three o'clock, when she is gone, well, I have my papers to attend to. Goodness, yes, such a wealth of matters to . . . all awaiting my . . .'

'I wonder,' Octavia put in, 'if we might turn to the purpose of our visit. You won't think me forward, I hope. Only you do seem such a busy man, and we are terribly mindful that we mustn't abuse your patience. Aren't we, Neddy?'

'Oh, terribly,' agreed Gideon, feeling himself prodded sharply. 'Distinctly mindful.'

'The purpose of . . . ah, indeed.' Mr Abelard fondled the hem of his waistcoat. 'The purpose, yes. I believe I have your letter near to hand, in which you . . . pardon me a moment while I . . .'

'Oh, you really needn't trouble,' said Octavia. 'It was dashed off, I'm afraid, though Neddy was good enough to look it over. Still, I'm sure we muddled all our legal terms. The matter is near to our hearts, but perhaps above our understanding.'

'That may very well be,' said Mr Abelard. 'You are to understand, however, that the will has been duly proved at probate, and that in acting for the trustees we can do no more than serve their wishes and those of the testator. It is all in train, do you see, notwithstanding the passing of the years and the various proceedings by the several parties, and if you should have formed an impression to the contrary – and I must caution you against misconstruing any proceedings now in Chancery, which perhaps you mistake for more than small questions of promissory estoppel – or if you – that is to say, if any person representing to hold an overlooked claim should at this juncture . . . should at this late hour seek . . .'

'If I may,' said Octavia. 'We are not claimants, Mr Abelard. We represent my father's estate. We are executors too, in our small way.'

'Not claimants?' said Mr Abelard. 'What is it, then, that you . . . that is, how might I . . .'

'Our father was a friend of the late Mr Bartram. He served on the board of the Asylum for a time and he remained devoted to the cause. He provided for us, of course, though our needs are modest, but most of what he left – and it seems quite a sum to us, though no doubt you are accustomed to great legacies – most of what he left is to go to the trust.'

'To the trust?'

'To the trust for which you act, Mr Abelard. I understand that it's called the Salus House Trust. In any case, my father saw it as the natural successor to the Asylum itself. He had faith, you see, that these matters before the courts would be resolved—'

'Oh, most assuredly,' said Mr Abelard. 'Mere quibbles over mortmain, which we have all but disposed of, and as to the notion of escheatment in the present case, well, I shall not tax you, but it is all very much . . .'

'In train?' Octavia suggested. 'We are relieved to hear it, aren't we, Neddy? Just as Father would have been. For surely that means that the trust will soon be free to re-establish the hospital here on these very grounds, and that its work can begin again.'

'Oh, surely,' said Mr Abelard, rubbing with some passion at his tie. 'Altogether surely.'

'How joyous to hear you say it. If only Father had lived to see this moment. I suppose that only leaves the question of the – what are they called, Neddy?'

Gideon sat up abruptly. 'The codicils,' he said. 'Our father attached certain codicils, requiring us to satisfy ourselves on certain points. On the question of record-keeping, for instance.'

'Oh, but that makes it sound terribly burdensome,' Octavia objected. 'Father wanted us to look over the records, that's all, to ensure that they're safe and in good order. He wasn't just concerned with the future of the asylum, you see. He wanted to preserve its past, its proud achievements.'

'I see,' said Mr Abelard. 'Yes, I do see. And by records, I imagine you mean ... that is, what exactly might be encompassed by such a ...'

'Which records?' said Octavia brightly. 'Oh, they'd be quite dull and ordinary. Enrolment lists, academic reports, infirmary charts, that sort of thing.'

'Oh, those,' Mr Abelard dabbed at his cuffs. 'Good Lord, for a moment I thought you meant the proceedings of the trust, which naturally would be subject to ... and quite out of the ... but yes, I do see. Well, those are here.'

'Here?' Octavia straightened. 'Here at the gate lodge.'

'Hmm? Oh, yes. We had to fetch them here from the main building. The damp, you see. The roof has held up quite well, but naturally the whole of such a structure cannot be heated, as it were, in perpetuity. The funds, you are to understand, would have to be authorised by the—'

'Yes, of course.' Octavia clasped her hands in her lap. 'But the records you brought here – might we look at them? Today?'

Mr Abelard adjusted the set of his chin. 'Today? Goodness me. How very precipitate. In the usual course, one might receive an application and, following due consideration one might conceivably—'

'We quite understand,' said Octavia. 'And I suppose we can begin a formal application, the next time we're both in town. Only, it is rather seldom, isn't it, Neddy?'

'Quite seldom,' Gideon agreed. 'My new parish, you see. There are certain expectations.'

'But perhaps by next spring we could begin the proper process,' Octavia said. 'Father did value correctness in all dealings. Of course, that would mean delaying the bequest, too. But I'm sure that's a small consideration, given the grand affairs you have in your charge.'

Mr Abelard probed delicately at the arms of his chair. 'The bequest being . . . ah, being the sum to be assigned to the trust?'

'Why, yes. Just as Father wished it. And that day will come soon enough, I suppose, even if it does seem a terribly long way off.' Octavia gave him a rueful smile then dipped her head. 'Well, that rather settles the matter for now, doesn't it? Come, Neddy, we must take up no more of the gentleman's time.'

Gideon hesitated. He lacked Miss Hillingdon's gift for artifice, and he could not tell whether she was improvising or accepting defeat. 'Ah, indeed. We really ought to . . .'

He left off gratefully, seeing that Mr Abelard had himself risen from his place. He was patting at his sleeves now with an air of gathering purpose. 'I rather think,' Mr Abelard said, 'that is to say, on reflection, it seems to me that in the circumstances, a more expeditious . . . Yes, I am quite settled in my view of the matter.'

He coughed and brought his hands together with a flourish, as if concluding some resounding argument before the bench.

'I shall put the case more simply,' he said, though he seemed to find the notion distasteful. 'I would be delighted to furnish the documents you require. Perhaps you would be so good as to follow me.'

Leading them to the rear of the house, he ushered them into a disorderly sitting room. He indicated a door at the end of a short passage. 'Now, then,' he said, producing a long brass key. 'A temporary arrangement, I assure you, on account of the . . . There was the question of the damp, you see, and until more suitable . . .' He worked the key into the lock with an air of hectic determination. 'Used to be a larder, is the fact of it, but a larder has the virtue at least of – damnably awkward, this mechanism – has the virtue of being dark and dry, which is of paramount—'

He stumbled out of sight for a moment, having set his shoulder to the door just as it yielded, then reappeared with a look of modest triumph. 'There we are,' he said, patting his cravat. 'The lock is admirably sound, as you see . . .'

'I'm sure it's more than satisfactory,' said Octavia. 'But perhaps we might step in now and make a start on our inspection. The sooner we begin, the sooner we can leave you in peace.'

'Your inspection, yes. By all means. I ought to warn you, however, that you may find the files rather out of order, owing to certain exigencies of circumstance. A wheelbarrow was obliged to be employed, of all things, though it was perfectly sturdy and—'

'I'm sure we'll manage.'

'Very well, then,' said Mr Abelard, shuffling aside. 'You'll find a lamp on a hook just inside the door to your right, and there are matches just to hand on a shelf. Naturally, I must ask that you exercise the utmost—'

'Caution, yes. I'm quite at home in libraries and archives, Mr Abelard. Your records will be perfectly safe.'

'Indeed, indeed. I suppose that will be—' Mr Abelard broke off. 'Ah, it's you. I hadn't expected you until . . . well, never mind. Allow me to . . .'

Gideon turned. In the sitting room they had just come from, a man slouched by the chimney breast. He had come in without a sound, perhaps by some unseen kitchen door. He held himself loosely, a crumpled raincoat slung from one arm, but his gaze was intent. He lifted an eyebrow when Octavia came into view, tweaking the match that he held in his teeth, but he remained silent.

'Yes, well.' Mr Abelard clapped his palms together without conviction. 'Here you are, at any rate. This is Mr Blakelock, whom I spoke of earlier in connection with . . . as you will doubtless recall. Mr Blakelock, allow me to introduce our visitors. This is, I believe, the Reverend—'

'No, it ain't.' Blakelock's voice was low and blunt.

Mr Abelard fussed with his cuffs. 'Perhaps there is some . . . that is, unless I am . . . you see, I had not yet mentioned the gentleman's—'

'Don't matter.' Pushing himself upright, Blakelock tossed aside his damp raincoat. 'Whatever names they gave you, they ain't real. Ain't that right, miss?'

Glancing at Octavia, Gideon saw that she had already made her calculations. There would be no more swift improvisations. There was nothing in her face now but wariness. He inched aside, meaning to put himself nearer the stranger. Blakelock noted every movement, his face creased now with amused interest.

'You geeing up to go at it, boy?' He shifted his matchstick, showing a nap of greyish tongue. 'Be something to see, that. A delicate flower like you.'

Abelard pivoted between them in dim consternation. 'Now look here,' he began, faltering at a glance from Blakelock. 'I fail to see, Mr Blakelock, what concern it might be of—'

Blakelock took a pace forward. He splayed his furred knuckles over the back of a chair. Without looking away, he spat his matchstick into the grate. 'Course you fail to see,' he said idly. 'Weren't supposed to. You ain't got but one little job here. It ain't this, though.'

The solicitor managed a last show of watery dignity. 'You rather forget yourself, Mr Blakelock. I am the agent of the, ah, of the parties having proprietary interest . . . and whatever your suspicions, this is hardly a seemly manner in which to . . .'

'Shut your fucking yap now, boy.' Blakelock kicked the chair towards him. 'Shut your yap and sit yourself down. What you're here for, in case you forgot, is to make it look proper. Lob out a few fancy words if anyone comes scratching about. Then sling the visitors out, but polite like. That was their thinking. Except you couldn't even manage that, could you?'

Abelard had slunk to the chair. He crouched on it now like a disgraced schoolboy. 'I assure you, Mr Blakelock, that I subjected these, ah, visitors to the most rigorous—'

Almost indifferently, Blakelock hurled the back of his hand at Abelard's face. It was a loose-knuckled blow, but it was enough to draw a trickle of blood from the corner of his mouth. He shrieked and shuffled back in the chair, not daring to look up.

'I *told* you,' said Blakelock, shaking his head wearily, 'to shut your fucking yap. This is what it comes to, see. When you don't do your little job, it means I've got to do *my* job. Means I can't be nice and polite no more. Not for you, and not for these two neither.'

His gaze settled on Gideon. 'So, boy. Playing dress-up, was it? Her ladyship there ain't stretching it too far. Wears that get-up like she's used it. State of you, though. Mind you, I reckon you was born awkward. I reckon after your old bird squeezed you out, she took one look and said, what the fuck is this supposed to be? So, what *are* you supposed to be, eh?'

Gideon took care to keep his voice steady. 'I might ask the same of you, sir. We know your name but nothing else.'

Blakelock leered in amusement. 'Will you listen to that. The choirboy here's got a mouth on him. What about you then, miss. You was all meek and mild when I was listening in, but look at you now, staring daggers. You got real daggers under all them velvets? You going to give me a bit of sport when I go looking for them?'

'Ask the last man who threatened me,' said Octavia. 'I can give you directions to the churchyard.'

Blakelock gave a harsh, clotted laugh. 'A bit of spirit, that's what I like. Brightens up my day, it does. Now, I'll tell you what I'll do. I'll play fair with you and maybe you'll play fair with me. How's that sound, eh?'

He approached a cluttered table set against one wall. Scratching his jowls, he surveyed the soiled crockery that littered it, the parched inkstands and ancient orange rinds. With a heavy sigh he swept all of it to the floor. Abelard jerked at the noise, but he did not look around. 'That's better,' Blakelock said, contemplating the bared oilcloth. 'Lives like a pig, this fucker does. We've had words about it before.'

He reached for his satchel, and from it he produced a coil of greasy rope. Tossing it onto the table, he rooted in the bag again and paused for a moment in deliberation. He drew out a hunting knife, its handle bound with fraying leather, and a pair of iron tongs. They were of the kind a dentist might use, or an animal surgeon. Next, he laid out a length of coarse wire strung between two knurled pegs. A garrotte.

Gideon clutched at his cuffs. He pressed himself to speak. 'You should know—'

'I already know,' said Blakelock. He was arranging his implements neatly, as if setting out a shop window. 'Like I said, cards on the table. I know you're a copper, leastwise. Supposed to be two of you,

though. Queer-looking little sprat and a big fellow, bit of danger
about him. Sound familiar, does he? And here you are turning up
with a lady friend, who I ain't been told about. Fellow sees that
sort of thing, he gets to wondering. He says to himself, who's this
sprightly-looking lass, then? He says, I might be trying my luck
there, if she weren't looking at me like she wants my eyes out.'

'I wouldn't start with your eyes,' said Octavia without hesitation.
'I'd want you to see.'

Blakelock gave another throaty laugh. 'That's it, girl. Keep it up
while you can. But I'll tell you what I'm curious about, will I? And it
ain't just me, I don't mind saying. It's them that pays me. I'm curious
about what you was looking for. We knew some coppers was sniffing about. Been keeping an eye on them for a while now, Sergeant
Lilywhite here and his boss. Only there weren't much to find, my lot
said. Even less now, with certain distinguished gents getting sent off
in style. Been a new one today, by the by.'

Gideon tried to keep his face empty, but Blakelock's glance was
carefully timed.

'Yeah, reckoned you wouldn't have heard. Never mind, eh? Maybe
your guvnor has. Maybe that's why he ain't here to protect you. But
listen to me, rabbiting on. Ain't me who should be doing all this
talking, is it? But before we get to that, I got something I want you to
see. You ever been to one of them magic shows?'

Blakelock turned and stooped over a nearby sideboard, whistling
thinly as he rummaged among its drawers. At length he produced a
linen napkin, and with oddly fastidious movements he shook it flat
and refolded it by careful quarters.

'What's the magician up to, eh?' Sidling to the middle of the room,
he approached the back of Abelard's chair. The solicitor had been
hunched in chastened silence, but now he stirred again, whipping
his head around and fidgeting in alarm.

'Now, look here ... I really must insist, Blakelock, that you ... that whatever your concerns regarding our mutual—'

'Hush now, lad.' Freeing a hand, he patted Abelard's cheek. Then he pinched the napkin at its centre and twirled it gaily before the seated man's eyes. 'Just showing our friends here a little trick, see? And your great magician's got to have an assistant, ain't he? Don't worry, though, you ain't got to do nothing yet. You just sit back and take your ease. Won't take but a minute.'

Abelard settled himself with a queasy look, his fingertips flitting about his person. Blakelock made soothing noises as he spread the napkin flat again. He held it up by its corners, displaying it to Octavia and Gideon in turn.

'Now, then, ladies and gents,' said Blakelock. 'I can see you're getting restless, so I'll get on. This here is just a plain white cloth, as you can see. Ain't hidden nothing in it, have I? Right, then.'

Withdrawing the napkin, he quartered it again and smoothed it out on his right palm. Then he crooked his right arm in front of Abelard's face. 'Be a gent, Mr Abelard, and have a poke up my sleeve. Make sure I ain't hiding anything up there.'

Abelard complied with jerky trepidation, straining again to look about him before dabbling a fingertip in Blakelock's sleeve.

'Eyes front, if you please,' said Blakelock. 'Have a good root around up there, boy. Got to show these fine folk they ain't being deceived. You find anything?'

When Abelard shook his head, the groundskeeper transferred the napkin to his left hand. 'Very good. Now check up my left sleeve. Has to be done right, this sort of thing.'

Abelard did as he was bid, as if hopeful that his good behaviour might be rewarded. When Blakelock asked no more of him, he made to settle back, then righted himself as if remembering something. He brought himself as near to stillness as he could, knotting his hands in his lap. He murmured something soundless, and for a moment he closed his eyes.

'So, ladies and gents,' said Blakelock, balling up the napkin and enclosing it in his fist, 'what comes next, eh? You seen with your own eyes that I ain't up to no trickery, so what am I about to show you?'

Keeping himself pressed close to Abelard's back, he passed the balled napkin from hand to hand. He did this deftly enough, but he made no particular effort to keep the cloth from showing. And as he watched them register this, his tongue oozed between his teeth. His face was creased with manic glee, but his eyes were intent.

Octavia had edged nearer. 'Gideon,' she said, a quiet urgency in her voice.

Gideon sensed it too. The shape of the danger, almost but not quite distinct. He had watched Abelard searching Blakelock's person, and he had thought inevitably of his new pistol. *You never know who you will come up against,* Cutter had said. Would it have made any difference, Gideon wondered, if he had thought to strap on the gun this morning? But even as the thought occurred to him, he found that he stepped forward. 'I am giving you warning, Blakelock.' He hardly knew his own voice. 'I am a sergeant of the Metropolitan Police, and I am not here alone. Stop this now, whatever it is.'

Still unseen by Abelard, Blakelock bared his teeth in warning, though he kept up his ragged efforts at showmanship. 'Must ask that the patrons keep their places, sir.'

He was still passing the napkin from hand to hand, but carelessly now, spilling loose furls of linen that Abelard followed with sickly bemusement. Keeping his eyes fixed on Gideon, Blakelock bent lower.

'Back away now, sir. Wouldn't want any rowdiness breaking out, would you? Spoil the show, that would.'

Gideon pressed on, though his legs felt slack and nerveless beneath him. Somewhere to his right, Octavia slid noiselessly out of view. 'Step back from him,' he called out, his own voice still unrecognisable. 'I will not say it again.'

Again Blakelock stooped lower at Abelard's back, as if enfolding him in a protective embrace. But he had twisted himself curiously, dropping his right elbow under the seated man's chin, and the napkin now flitted lazily between hands that had drifted apart.

'Always one awkward punter, ain't there. Still, the show must go on, eh?'

Abelard gave a pouting frown at this, and for a moment he seemed about to venture a final complaint. Then his face slackened with approaching recognition.

Blakelock's next movements were scorpion-quick. He stamped his foot, then with his left hand flung the napkin aloft. Gideon knew he had moved too late. He saw that Abelard had been fooled, saw the moment of infant distraction as he looked up, baring the sheeny flesh of his throat.

His neck was clamped in Blakelock's arm then, his head braced as it twisted through an impossible arc. Gideon heard the sound it made, the bright ratcheting crunch. Abelard's legs spasmed twice, undirected, then his body slumped in Blakelock's arms.

Blakelock let his body spill to the floor, shunting it aside with a boot heel. 'Good lad,' he murmured. 'Had to be done, eh?'

Gideon was lunging at him, but Blakelock was ready. Swiping aside his outstretched arms, he jabbed his bunched fingertips into Gideon's kidneys. The pain was sudden and monstrous, sending him heaving to his knees. He retched, but he shuffled closer. Wrapping himself around Blakelock's legs, he clawed at his belt buckle, at his shirt buttons. Finding a swell of matted flesh, he tore at it with his fingernails.

Something slammed into the back of his head – a fist, a boot, he couldn't tell – and his vision whitened. The moments that followed were distended and clamouring. He was absent, touching his own blood, then he was somehow halfway upright, holding fast to Blakelock's collar, clambering onto his back.

Then he became aware of Octavia, or of the raging shape that had her voice. It was a rust-coloured whirl somewhere near him, and it was swinging something. It was lunging, cursing, striking. He recognised the nightmarish *thuck* of iron on bone only when Blakelock jerked backwards against him, howling obscenities.

'*Bitch!* I'll fucking *gut* you, you bitch!'

As Blakelock staggered, Gideon managed to lock an elbow about his throat, levering himself out from behind him before he crashed into a dresser. Though still unsteady, he was at least on his feet and his vision had cleared a little. Seeing Blakelock reeling, he made ready to land a blow before he realised his own intention.

Keep out of the way, Cutter often told him. *You are not built for brawling, so keep out of the way when it happens.*

But Cutter was seldom content with issuing a single piece of advice, and he knew better than anyone that violence cannot always be avoided. *If it comes to it,* he would say, *then for the love of Christ do not try thumping the fellow. You haven't the weight for it, and you will only get his blood up. Curl up and mind your head, but if you see your moment, if he shows you—*

His throat. When Octavia hit him – with a poker, Gideon had since realised – Blakelock had rocked back against the dresser, spreading one hand out behind him for balance and clamping the other to his skull. In doing so, he had tipped back his head and bared his throat. Gideon took an instant to memorise the target, the knot of gristle bobbing in its nest of shadowed jowls.

Then he dipped one shoulder, twisted away and with all the force he could summon, he drove the spike of his elbow into Blakelock's larynx.

If Cutter had been there, he might have conceded that the attempt was no disgrace. The blow connected solidly enough, sending a fizz of shock up Gideon's arm, and it did some damage, to be sure. He felt the stout well of cartilage fold grotesquely on itself. But it did not rupture, and Gideon had given no thought to how he might follow through.

He danced away, now off balance and crazily contorted, and above him Blakelock loomed like some cackling ogre. 'That it, you puddle of puke? You finished now?' He raised one fist and clubbed Gideon savagely in the side of the head. ''Cos I ain't even fucking *started* yet.'

Swaying on his hands and knees, Gideon had time to vomit thinly before the next blow came. He thought of crawling away, of curling up as Cutter had advised, with his elbows wrapped tightly about his head. Then it came to him that he was already sightless and unmoving, and that even these last thoughts were fading as they formed.

He couldn't hold. The remnants slipped from him, grey and sundered. He sank deeper, under himself, down into the blood-black quiet.

'Gideon?' The voice was somewhere in the dark that was not dark, in the swim of murk and aching colour. He tried, but he couldn't find it. Couldn't move or turn in all these fathoms of hurt. His head weighed too much, and his guts were full of—oh christ, oh christ. He couldn't, and his hands couldn't. Were held and hurt.

'*Gideon!*' Octavia's voice. That was nice. She was here. But he still couldn't move. Because of the— Jesus, oh god. His head, brimming with pain. But Octavia. So good of her to come.

'Gideon, squeeze your eyes a bit before you try to open them. They're crusted over.'

He tried to speak. A sound came, but it was clotted and senseless.

Squeeze your. He didn't understand, but it seemed important to try. He found parts of himself, of his face. Felt answering twitches. He strained, pressed hard. He tried again, loosening a fierce rivulet of pain. Now he was crying, or could feel tears. That was good. *Your eyes.* That was promising.

'That's it.' Octavia's voice again. So kind. She had hit someone, had done it very hard. So thoughtful. 'Now give it a minute, but keep trying. I don't think there's much time.'

Yes, try. There was something important. Something they were meant to do. He moved his head, meaning yes, but too much. New pain now, molten and consuming. He whimpered, and that was good. That was a sound. He had made it.

'Gideon? Do try, please. He won't be gone for long.'

He. Oh, yes. That *he.* That pain. Important, yes. Urgent. He, the man who. Was he – and were they still . . .

His eyes, at last. Peeled half open, but spilling something. Gritty and viscous. The darkness a dusky gauze now. Dark at the edges. Scaly and hot. In his mouth too. Something ferrous. He lifted his head. Careful this time. He found her. The shape where the voice was.

'There you are,' she said. 'I was worried. You're a bit of a fright, I'm afraid, but you'll be all right. Now, listen. We have to—'

'Ottay . . . Ock—' Gideon gave a juddering cough. Something in her voice, slow and lopsided. He squeezed his eyes shut again, impatient now. Wanting to see. 'Octavia, your face. What did he—'

'Gideon, stop jerking about, you'll hurt yourself. You're tied to a chair. We both are. And never mind what he did. What matters is what he does next. What *we* do next. Are you listening?'

Prising his eyelids apart again, striving to fix on her. His field of vision was hemmed in, furred red at the margins. But her face, Octavia's face. Stripes of blood, from her temple, down her neck. And her lips, smeared on one side. A slick envelope of bruising.

'He . . . he hurt you. That filthy dog, he *hurt* you.'

'Yes, but I hurt him first. Now, listen. He's gone to get rid of Abelard's body. He won't risk leaving us for long. That man, Milo – do you trust him?'

Gideon worked at the words, at the sense of them. 'Wait. Milo, yes. The Inspector, he trusts him. For some things. For bad things.'

'Mmm.' Octavia glanced away. 'Well, good. You remember what he said, Blakelock? There's been another murder, so Cutter might have been called away. Milo should still be keeping watch, though, and he ought to make an appearance soon. If he's as dangerous as he says he is, this would be a good time to prove it.'

'Do you think he'll—' He stopped himself. His thoughts were clearing now. 'Yes, of course he will.'

'Probably, yes. But he has to answer to them, whoever they are. They'll want to know what we knew. We have to tell him something, something he'll believe.'

'But we can't. If he . . . if the worst happens, if he . . . if we're gone, they'll destroy everything, every trace. No one will ever know.'

'No, of course we can't. I said something he'll believe, not the *truth*. He already knows who you are, and knowing Scotland Yard, he's probably well enough informed. You said someone approached you and the Inspector, someone from Special Branch?'

This took a moment. 'Special Branch? Yes. *Yes*. The East India Club. Manning, was it? No, Massey. Said we could help each other. Said the murderer is a threat to the realm.'

Octavia managed a bitter smile. 'Yes, I'm sure. Someone's realm, anyway. Tell Blakelock that, then. That you've taken the hint from

Special Branch, and you're working to protect the realm. Not too readily, but tell him. And I'll tell him just enough of the truth. I'm an archivist, so I'm helping you. But all I know is that I'm helping you to find someone dangerous. It's not perfect, but it might hold up for a while.' She glanced again towards the back of the house. 'I think that's him. Close your eyes again. Pretend you haven't come around yet.'

Gideon shook his head, provoking another vivid bloom of pain. 'No, I want him to start with me. You needn't . . . He knows who I am, and you needn't . . .We shouldn't have brought you here, and I don't want to see you—'

'Gideon, shush. That's sweet, but I'm the one who brought us here and I don't have any use for gallantry just now. Quickly, or he'll know we've been talking. Do it now.'

It wasn't a relief, closing his eyes. It felt shameful, and in the dark there was nothing but the pain, nothing but the helplessness. Letting himself slump in the chair, he found there was nothing to relieve the strain of his bonds. His ankles were hooked around the chair legs and lashed from above, so that the ropes bit deeper as his weight settled, and the chafing had already broken the skin. His wrists were cinched together somewhere below the small of his back. They had been tied with his palms facing outwards, no doubt to worsen the discomfort. Those cords had rasped against the tender skin of his wrists. He felt blood beading and slinking among the fissures of his palms, finding the easiest course.

He heard something in the next room. It was a kitchen, maybe, with a door to the garden. Something was set down. He heard the ponderous scrape of iron against stone, a vacant clang. Then Gideon understood. A wheelbarrow. The body.

Blakelock busied himself a little longer. His boot heels knocked and scuffed. A washbowl was filled and sloshed, some bottle or jar unstopped. He took a noisy draught of something, water or ale, and afterwards he gave a sated gasp. He fell silent, and Gideon understood then these were sounds he expected them to hear. Was he scratching himself idly now, as he contemplated what was next? Was he fingering one of his coarse implements?

And would he even bother to interrogate them? Was there anything more that he and his masters truly needed to know? Perhaps it made no difference. Gideon would do his part, if he could, and maybe Milo really was somewhere close by. Either way, there would be more pain. Either way, it might come to the same thing. He would not hear the scrape of the barrow then. There would be no more pretending.

The sound was forced out of him – an unshaped noise, not even a scream – by the suddenness of it. He was in darkness, slumped and unready, then he was shoved and spilled into emptiness. His eyes opened just soon enough to make sense of it – the walls tipping, the shearing light – then he was slammed against the floor.

He had registered Blakelock's proximity at the last instant – a peripheral reek, an indrawn breath, a heel squeak – but there had been no time. He made sense of it as Blakelock hauled him upright, pain spearing from his shoulder, and he cursed himself. Blakelock had found him helpless and unseeing. He had tipped his chair over. It was simple and brutal, as everything would be from this moment on. Their daydream of a plan would do no good, and he had done no good in his daydream of a life. It was simple and brutal, and this was how it would end.

'Wakey, wakey, Sergeant Limp.' Blakelock was bent low to Gideon's face, still gripping the arms of his chair. His breath had a riverine dankness. His clothes smelled of burning, and of something like tallow. 'Not that you was really out, mind you. I weren't born yesterday, boy. I been doing this a good long while.'

He turned to Octavia. 'Been scheming while I was away, princess? Eh? Course you have. Tell him this, tell him that. Horrible coarse sort like that, he won't know no better. That's what you said, ain't it? Don't worry, my feelings ain't hurt.'

Drawing back, he stood with his feet planted apart and his thumbs hooked in a belt of rough twine. He let his gaze drift between them, his expression at once wistful and hungry. 'I'm a bit cross, though, I don't mind saying. You spoiled my little show good and proper, didn't you. Here I was making an effort, putting a bit of style into it, and what do I get? I get a lump took out of me with a poker. I get clawed up and smashed in the voice box. Weren't nice at all. Weren't what you'd call *genteel*. Course, you both got taught. Showed you what happens, didn't I, when you carry on like that?'

'We were afraid,' said Octavia. She spoke more gently than before, as if chastened. She was still trying, still clinging to the daydream. 'Afraid for our lives, which I suppose is what you wanted. What did you expect?'

'Listen to her,' said Blakelock, his lip twisting sourly. 'All meek and mild now, the same one that came howling at me like a savage. You playing a little game, princess? You reckon I won't catch on? And you ain't got that quite right neither. Course you were afraid, and you were right to be, but that weren't the point. The point was, that was one of ours whose neck I broke. A useful idiot, they used to call him, though I never could work out how he was useful. He was one of ours, but he shit where he ate his dinners, didn't he? All he had to do was mind his little shop. All he had to do was spout off some of his law book talk if anyone came sniffing about, give them chapter and verse about binding codicils or whatever the fuck. Do his *ah*-ing and his *that-is-to-say*-ing until they went on their way, which they always did, 'cos how long could anyone sit and listen to that twitchy, stammering cunt?

'And what does he up and do, the first time a bird turns up who's got soft manners and fills out her velvet in the right places? He takes her straight to the crown fucking jewels, that's what he does. I'll be straight with you. I ain't looking forward to telling them about it, them as I work for. They ain't the sort for making allowances. You know what they'll say to me, soon as they're finished tearing strips off me? They'll say, Blakelock, my lad, this ain't a happy story. Here we was passing the port around, eyeing up this nice bit of cheese, and you come and tell us a story like that. It's taken the shine right off our evening, they'll say, and you're going to have to do your best to cheer us up. And you know what I'll say?'

Blakelock had returned to the table where his tools were laid out. He picked up the blackened pair of tongs. 'I'll say, you're right, gents. It ain't a happy story at all, and it pains me to have to tell it. But never mind about that cheese course, sirs. You can get cracking on your nuts with a glad heart.' He snapped the tongs shut. The sound they made was bluntly distinct. It was simple. 'You know why? Because this might have been a sad story, but your boy Blakelock made sure it had a happy fucking ending.'

He put down the tongs and took up the garrotte, turning to the window as he drew it taut. Against the light, scabs of dark matter showed on the coarse wire. 'You getting the idea now?' he said. 'The point ain't getting lost, is it? Whoever got to them old boys in town knew what they were about, 'cos they weren't exactly easy pickings. But they weren't the worst of the bunch, let me tell you. And the ones I answer to – well, maybe the less said the better. But you poked your little stick in the wrong nest, my friends. You stirred up some wasps that ain't shy about stinging.'

'It won't make any difference,' Gideon said. The words were slurred but vehement.

Blakelock circled the table and took a pace towards him. 'What's that, vicar? Clearing your throat, were you?'

'I said, it won't make any difference.' He spoke more forcefully this time. This wasn't the daydream. It was all he was sure of. It was simple. 'I saw what was done to them, the men you're talking about. And the others, the ones you work for – it won't matter how powerful or well protected they are, not to the one we're looking for.'

Reaching Gideon's side, Blakelock dropped to his haunches. He gave a low, seething whistle. 'Well, there's talk. That supposed to put the fear of God in me, is it? Listen, boy. I told you about the sort of company I keep. We ain't quivering in our beds at the thought of your bogeyman. It's us who'll be coming for *him*.'

Gideon said nothing, but something flickered in the murk of his thoughts. *For him.*

What he was sure of, without ever knowing how.

Did a little bird tell you?

He felt Blakelock's breath on his face as he bent nearer. 'You didn't think you were the only ones out looking, did you? Except unlike you and your gaffer, we've got some idea who we're looking for.'

Simple. The simplest thing.

In the shadowy deeps, the bright trinket stirred and shivered free – the looks and answers Cutter had given him, testing him, urging him towards the fault in his thinking. He had not grasped it then, but now he saw.

This is how we made you, little bird.

He looked Blakelock in the eye. 'No, you don't. Whatever you think you know, it's wrong.'

Blakelock stared for a moment, his face distended with contempt. Then he spat abruptly and seized Gideon's left hand, splaying it flat beneath his own. 'Right,' he said. 'I was going to start with the princess there, but seeing as you like working your gob . . .'

He pivoted to get a better hold and Gideon did not struggle for long. He let his gaze drift as his smallest finger was prised apart and pinned. He studied the milky light beyond the net curtains, the sifted bodies of the trees. He saw something else. A quick and purposeful shadow. He lost it again.

Blakelock grunted and altered his stance, pressing his bulk close to Gideon's face. Gideon twisted away to escape his odour. Then the tongs bit, capturing the frayed rim of his fingernail. He waited for the pain, letting himself weep silently.

The shape again, somewhere beyond Blakelock's back. A dark glyph in the dissolving welter, but resolving itself. Becoming something.

'You ready, lad?' Blakelock meant to keep up his foul patter, even at this monstrous moment. 'Took a bit of fiddling, what with you being a filthy little nail-biter, but it's always worth starting with the little 'un. Makes them think, fuck me, how much worse is the next one going to be? Now, then, let's see about you.'

Gideon snuffled twice then went still. A precise snick, a preliminary tearing. Then from its tiny perch the pain leapt screaming and clawing.

For a moment he could not see or hear. He felt himself sobbing, writhing against his bonds. It cost him effort, and it made the pain worse.

He was gone. He thought he had been gone a long while, but that didn't make sense. He wasn't sure anymore. Something hurt his head again, when the chair fell. And the bright new pain, scraping the rust from the other hurts. He wasn't sure, but he saw it again, drifting up through the stained and brackish shallows. Something happening. Slow but not slow.

Milo. The shape was Milo, surging across an interval of daylight like ink spilled over porcelain. A gesture – a finger tensed for silence

– then the shape, then Milo. Blakelock was enfolded, something urging and twisting him. It was silky and fierce. It was like ballet.

Gideon stirred and strained, wanting to see.

Milo must have broken Blakelock's hand first, after wresting it away. Blakelock was clutching it and roaring, but Milo spun briskly on one heel and smashed the other into Blakelock's kneecap. It buckled back, and Blakelock staggered and sank, but Milo was not waiting. He was everywhere, dipping and coiling. A slender knife flickered, and Blakelock was bleeding from the gut, from a slash above his eyes. He lashed out again, and still Milo swerved and considered, inflicting wounds like brushstrokes, like variations on a theme. The blade arced out from a sidestep, severing the tendons of Blakelock's forearm.

He collapsed at last, barely struggling now, but Milo persisted calmly. Stooping, he clamped the bigger man's hips under his shin and drove his blade into each of his haunches in turn. He watched impassively as Blakelock's legs jerked and settled into stillness.

He rose and wiped his knife, but he shifted the flat of one foot to Blakelock's neck, applying a carefully calibrated pressure.

'You can breathe but not speak, yes?' said Milo. He hardly seemed out of breath. When Blakelock wheezed in response, he nodded his approval. 'Good. You talk very much, you know this? It is not professional, your manner. Now you must be quiet.'

Milo examined his own light wounds, then with a terse sigh he glanced over his shoulder. 'I make my apologies. I would have come sooner, but I met others like this one. They detained me a little. You are not too much harmed?'

'We're perfectly fine,' Octavia answered.

Gideon wanted to say it too, wanted to be glad and alive, but he was slipping again. It had taken effort, just watching. He was slow with pain still and he didn't understand. Only the one thing. The simple thing.

'Very good,' said Milo. 'Now, forgive me. I must finish with this one before I release you. Is there anything you need from him?'

Gideon was lapsing now, swooning into a pinkish numbness. He hoped it would last. He couldn't see, couldn't hear much. But he thought he understood.

Octavia was calling him, saying something about names. *Know their names. Gideon, listen.*

'Won't matter,' he said, or thought he said. It was all right. The pain was everywhere and the world was fallen. It was all right. 'Their names won't matter to her. Their names or their ancient houses. Like dust. She will pass through them like dust.'

Somewhere near him, Milo spoke calmly. Some great beast snorted and raged. Hearing his confession maybe. Administering the last rites. *Mea culpa. Tibi omnes angeli.*

'Their names,' he said, or some other voice said. It didn't matter. 'They made her perfect, and she is coming. All the angels. Speak their names.'

III

THE KNIFE AND THE WOUND

April, 1894

Eleven

'Well,' said Inspector Cutter. He had been pacing for some time about the parlour at Leggett's, and now he halted before the hearth. He bent to poke at the coals then rose again, scrubbing at his jaw with his knuckles. 'Well,' he said again.

He seemed ill at ease, and it was not a condition for which he was naturally equipped. It was uncomfortable to contemplate.

'Sir,' said Gideon, moving to get up. 'Will you not take your seat?'

At Cutter's insistence, Gideon occupied not his own customary armchair but the Inspector's, Miss Hillingdon being seated in his usual place. This too was a thing without precedent, and although the two armchairs were alike, Gideon might just as well have been commanded to rest on an Alpine precipice.

The Inspector ignored him. Returning his attention to the fire, he glared in dissatisfaction at the coals. 'Look at this worthless dirt,' he grumbled. 'A shovelful of gravel would be better. Do you feel that chill, Miss Hillingdon?'

Octavia appeared perfectly at home in the opposite armchair, her legs curled up beneath her as she sifted through a sheaf of yellowed papers. Gideon noticed, too, that her face now seemed all but unmarked. A scabbed fissure still showed where her lip had been split, and a bruised patch that was turning from violet to ochre, but there were no other signs of what she had endured. 'It's quite comfortable,' she said, not looking up. 'You're fussing, Inspector.'

'Fussing, my arse.' Cutter strode to the doorway. 'When have you known me to fuss? I want my money's worth, that's all. Barney! Barney, there! Fetch in some decent coal, you little mongrel! And more of that – what is that tea called, Miss Hillingdon?'

'Chamomile,' said Octavia. 'But there's really no need. I've hardly touched this cup.'

'It will be stone cold, then,' the Inspector answered. 'How could it be otherwise in this accursed morgue? Another cup of that chamomile tea, boy, before the lady perishes from the frost!'

He paced the floor again, then he fixed Gideon with a rigorous look. 'What about you, Bliss? Will you not take a small brandy? I will allow it under the . . .' He swept out his hand, indicating a swathe of contingencies. 'Well, matters being as they are.'

'He has already had a small brandy,' said Octavia, answering on Gideon's behalf. 'You insisted on it, though it was "very much at odds with your way of thinking". He's fine, aren't you, Gideon? We're both fine.'

'Oh, yes,' said Gideon, tucking his bandaged fingers under his haunches. It had been two days, and he could now flex them without much discomfort. His face was still puffed up and discoloured on one side, and Dr Carmody had advised that the stub of his missing tooth be drawn out to prevent 'the incitement of abscesses and other sequelae'. His injuries had otherwise troubled him remarkably little. It was the sleeplessness that disquieted him, and the episodes – he had so far kept them hidden – of cold and implacable rage. 'We're quite recovered, on the whole.'

The Inspector grunted. 'I will have Carmody look at you again. You have a twitch I do not like the look of, and taking knocks to the head like that . . . I knew a fellow once, a fine stout Cornishman who was stablemaster over at the Yard. He was kicked by a horse, near enough between his eyes, but he declared he was right as rain. Went about the place singing "Hail to the Homeland" for a week and a half, then one morning he was filling the manger, and what happened? He dropped down dead, with blood fairly spurting from his—'

'Inspector,' said Octavia firmly.

'Yes, well. It was an uncommon case, no doubt. But if I'm to pass you fit for duty, I must do it in good conscience. We have a good deal of work before us.'

'Dr Carmody has already done so, sir. I am to make no close arrests, since he suspects a fine fracture of the mandible, but he has no other reservations.'

'No close arrests, indeed. Does he think we stuff featherbeds for a living? It was making a close arrest that got you clobbered in the first place.'

Gideon looked away. 'No, sir, the fault was my own, sir. I ought to have . . .' But he ought to have what? Been carrying his gun? But what difference would that have made, when the moment came?

The Inspector made no reply. He addressed himself instead to Barney, who was tending to the fire. 'Bank that up properly, you misshapen pygmy. You are not scraping lard over a slice of bread. And where is this lady's tea?'

'You asked for the coal first, sir,' said the boy. 'And I ain't got but one pair of hands.'

'Never mind about the tea,' said Octavia, looking up at last. She rooted in her purse and fished out what looked like a sixpence. 'Here. Take this and make sure we're not disturbed.'

'Miss,' said Barney, touching his pallid little brow. 'What about that foreign gent? Chap always wears them flash rags? Ain't you expecting him?'

She looked at Cutter, who lifted his chin by a fraction. 'I suppose we are. But no one else, all right?'

Cutter was still staring at her when Barney slipped out. In the usual course, giving instructions to the menials of the establishment was his sole prerogative. 'Did you tip that child *sixpence*,' he said, confining his objections to a narrower subject. 'He will never be seen again.'

'Never mind that,' said Octavia, unfolding her legs and brushing herself down. She marked her place carefully before squaring up her pages. 'I've found something more, in the papers from the gate lodge. But tell me about this new murder first. I've only heard the barest details.'

Since Cutter would not entrust the matter to anyone from the Yard, Milo's taciturn driver had been employed to haul away the archives from the Wanstead gatehouse. Octavia had sequestered herself with this trove of documents for most of the last two days, and Gideon doubted whether she had eaten or slept. Since reappearing, she had made it plain that she was now attaching herself to the investigation and expected to be made privy to its every detail. Cutter could hardly refuse her, since she had led them near to the heart of the conspiracy, but nor had he managed to mask his reservations.

Tucking a thumb under his collar, he worked energetically at the sinews of his neck. 'Two new murders,' he said at length. 'I've had cause to revise my count.'

Gideon edged forward in his chair. This development was new to him too. 'Sir?' he said.

'I was coming to it, Bliss. I had to send a fellow down to Hounslow for the details, and he only got back an hour ago. Hounslow, mark you, not Mayfair or Belgravia. It was for that reason that it nearly passed me by. It was a fellow by the name of Hilliard, who was something in the army years ago. Not commissioned, and no sign of money or connections. He was living in poor digs, certainly, and doing nothing much beyond soaking himself in gin shops, so little was made of it when he turned up dead behind his landlady's henhouse. I only heard of it in the first place because two fellows from that division were nattering about it at the Yard.'

'And what was it that struck you?' Octavia said.

'The neatness of the work, for one thing. He was killed with a shovel, which is a common enough occurrence. Two workmen go at it over a few shillings' worth of split winnings, and one batters the other to death. Leaves him looking like the scrapings from a butcher's block, as often as not.'

'I'm sure,' said Octavia. 'And this man Hilliard?'

'Decapitated,' said Cutter, chewing at his lip. 'A single stroke, one of the local lads said. Not the word of the police surgeon, granted, but it was enough to make me stop and sniff the air. I asked him if anything else looked out of the ordinary. Well, he says, there was a grave dug that the dead man weren't put in. Shallow grave, mind, but neat as you like. That queer enough for you?'

'Yes,' said Gideon, seeing it in his mind. Since the violence at Salus House, the ordinary business of the world had seemed muted and remote. But she was surely something other than ordinary, this resurrected orphan. Gideon felt near to her, though he had never so much as glimpsed her. The traces she left shimmered cold and distinct, like rime on dead grass. 'That was enough.'

'It might have been nothing,' said Cutter brusquely. 'Some workaday killer who was disturbed before tidying up. But yes, it was worth a look. I would have gone myself, not being inclined to leave crumbs about the place, but I was short-handed and I had a murder scene of my own to visit. Hounslow is under T division, which is Inspector Buckley's patch. Solid man, and slow in the right way. A fellow who would spend three days examining a burned-down privy. I asked him to look over this grave, and to take care over it.'

'And?' said Octavia.

But Gideon already knew. 'Bones,' he said. 'The bones of a child.'

'Aye,' said Cutter. 'Or more than one. But making up a goodly part of a whole one, whatever the case. I am having them sent up to Golden Lane for inspection, since I cannot very well stuff a whole skeleton into my pockets.'

Octavia put aside her papers. 'Since you cannot *what*?'

'You will have to catch up as we go, Miss Hillingdon. I cannot jot it all on the back of an envelope. There were markings in blood, too, on the side of the henhouse. Another message. Buckley reckoned he was lucky to find it after the showers we have had.'

Gideon waited, but Octavia was less patient. 'Oh, for goodness' sake. It's like getting laudanum drops from the chemist. Are you going to tell us or not?'

Cutter stared at her, his jaw thrust askew. '"They will be raised". Happy now?'

Octavia reached for a clean leaf and made a note. 'That's not the word I'd use, no. It's interesting, though. There have been other bones, I gather.' She paused, giving the Inspector an astringent look. 'So, haven't they been raised already?'

Gideon's injured fingers flexed minutely. He pressed them flat with his good hand. 'Figures. She speaks in figures.'

At the word *she*, Cutter's face hardened, but he let it pass without comment.

'Well, naturally,' Octavia said. 'But bones don't. They have to be unearthed and carted about, for something like this. They have to be stored. There's something in this, something we need to think about. What about the other murder, Cutter? The one Blakelock mentioned. What was his name, Wesley?'

Cutter bridled at her brisk manner, but again he held himself in check. 'Thomas Wesley, yes. Something high up at the Admiralty Office. Oversaw the Standards and Measures Board, so they tell me, which sounds dull enough to mean something secret and dirty. If that's the case, then he died as he lived. He was found at the bath house in Bishopsgate. Must have gone there after hours, seeing as he was discovered first thing. What was left of him, anyway. In one of the hot chambers, on a bed of open coals. Someone from the Admiralty had to come and identify his bits and pieces. A watch, and a fancy signet ring of some sort. Ceremonial, so they tell me. Otherwise, not a trace I wasn't meant to find, same as before.'

'And the traces you did find?' said Octavia. 'Or are you saving those for a special occasion?'

The Inspector worked a kink from his neck. 'I'm making allowances, Miss Hillingdon, on account of I'm tending to the wounded, but it seems to me that you're making a remarkable recovery.'

'I'm being brave, in spite of my horrible disfigurement. What did you find?'

'A skull,' said Cutter with a scowl. 'High up on a ledge. Looking down on him, you might say. I couldn't very well pocket that either. And before you ask, the message was different. "They will be seen."'

'Curious,' said Octavia. 'It sounds like quite the vivid tableau. Bathing. Someone looking on. I think I can imagine. It wasn't a rare occurrence in those places. God, men are wretched creatures.'

Cutter gave her a slantwise look. 'I cannot argue that point. All the same, though, this kind of talk is too near to embroidery for my liking. I'm a detective, not an archaeologist, and here I am with a great pile of artefacts and not a scrap of evidence. I'm weary of it, I don't mind telling you.'

Gideon shifted in his seat. His aches had lessened, but sometimes they pieced themselves together. 'Sir,' he said. 'If I may, you are not . . . you are not listening to her.'

'Ach, don't start that—' Cutter broke off as he turned to face him. 'Are you having a turn, Bliss? This is just what I was warning of.'

'I am all right, sir. Maybe it is the wrong way to put it, but who were they left for, if not for us? All these signs, these emblems? Is she not speaking to us?'

Cutter's face grew congested. 'In the first place, Bliss, I don't know who you're referring to. But leaving that aside, if someone is speaking to us, then I must be going deaf. And what is a bone an emblem of, whatever that might mean? A fingerbone, say?'

'Accusation,' said Gideon quietly. 'Or the beginning of a count. I cannot say for certain. I only meant that we should pay attention.'

'Mother of God,' said Cutter. He seldom welcomed Gideon's intuitions, but he seemed especially impatient with this line of thought. 'You'll have us reading tea leaves next.'

'Wait,' Octavia said. 'What if it's both? What if the murderer, this person, is leaving messages *and* evidence?'

The Inspector touched his brow gently, as if it were a fragile vessel. 'Miss Hillingdon,' he said, 'I don't pretend to be all-seeing and all-knowing, but I have spent a good many years poking around under the sideboards of the dead. I searched every inch of those places. There was nothing else to be found.'

'That's not what I meant, Inspector. What if the bones *are* evidence?'

He cast his eyes imploringly to the ceiling. 'Evidence of *what*, for the love of Christ? These men did not choke to death sucking on legs of chicken. In case you're in doubt, when I talk of evidence, I mean something I can show before a jury box when I am explaining who did a thing and how. I don't mean relics, whatever they might signify.'

'I meant evidence of other crimes. Against the children. Signs of injury. That happens, too.'

Cutter hesitated before answering, a flicker of something beneath his impatience. 'I'm not investigating those crimes. I couldn't, even if I had a mind to. If they happened at all, it was twenty-odd years ago.'

'Something happened,' said Octavia evenly. 'Not just a fire, something more. You already know that much, don't you? And by rights you ought to be desperate to find out what it was. This murderer is practically a ghost, by all accounts, so you're not going to find him or her in the usual way. You have to find the men who are being hunted, if there are any left. You have to reach them first.'

'So everyone keeps telling me,' said Cutter. 'Massey gave me much the same advice, though I wonder if he ever had any names to give me. It's not as if the thought had never occurred to me. But where would I start, eh? Should I be banging on doors up and down Whitehall, twisting the arms of permanent secretaries? What am I to say to them? You got any old boys knocking about the place who might have dirtied their bibs back in Disraeli's time? Have a look into your files, there's an obliging fellow.'

Octavia fingered the rim of her teacup. 'Have you finished? Good. This may still astonish you, Inspector, but I'm not unfamiliar with how the world works. Take these files, for instance. Do you think I've been poring over them looking for the agenda of the Conspiracy Committee? For expenditures related to arson? I've been looking for gaps in the right places, of which there are quite a few, and for the very faint traces people leave when they're trying to hide something dreadful. Some of the traces aren't even faint. These archives were taken from the library for a reason. They were *guarded* for a reason.

'There are thirty-six names on that memorial. None of the children on that floor survived the fire. That number struck me as odd from the start. I know places like that. I *came* from a place like that. I've been the lady at the garden party, marvelling at how fine the children's manners are. And I've been the little girl in a starched pinafore, trembling at the thought of getting her curtsey wrong. I know how these places work.

'Let's start with those thirty-six children. Thirty-six. Why so few? In the other dormitory wings, there were almost eighty children on each floor. On the second floor of the north-west wing, there were only thirty-six. New dormitories had been built the year before, in May of 1871, at a cost of over £320. That was quite the expense, in case it isn't obvious, and it was approved by a committee of some sort called the Modern Accommodations Board. As you'll have gathered, the people who ran this place kept admirably detailed records most of the time. That makes it easier to spot the missing pieces.

'Once the works were complete, that floor became known as the Hawthorn Wing, and it seems to have been reserved for children of special merit. The Hawthorn Wing was segregated, and not just from the rest of the Asylum. There were three dormitories, each accommodating six boys and six girls. The dormitories were separated from each other, and not just by a nurse's station. They installed steel doors, at a cost of eight pounds and six shillings each.

'Then there were the tests. The score sheets must have been kept in Hawthorn Wing itself, because those that survived are badly charred. The children were tested every week, and they were shuffled back and forth between dormitories as their scores increased or dropped. Would you like to know what they measured, these tests? They measured fitness, strength, agility, ingenuity, obedience, self-preservation, concern for others and tolerance of discomfort. Some of the tests took the form of special activities, though I can't tell what those involved. "The Bead Game", one was called. Then there was "the Splinter Trial", "Method No. 8", and so on.

'The children's scores eventually settled, and those who performed best ended up in Hawthorn No. 1. The middling ones were moved to Hawthorn No. 2. Hawthorn No. 3 was for the hopeless cases. The last of the score sheets is dated the 10th of January, 1872, ten days before the fire. It records scores for thirty-six children, just as before.

'The infirmary kept records of its own, just as you'd expect. Eleven deaths were recorded during 1871, which isn't out of the ordinary. There was an outbreak of measles, cases of scarlet fever and diphtheria. One little girl had a tumour of the brain. The journal for 1872 begins like all the rest. Each day's admissions and discharges were noted by the infirmary's clerk. The first three weeks of January were quiet. On the day before the fire, the infirmary recorded it admitted no patients at all.

'The next day was rather different. The fire must have started in the small hours, and by three in the morning they'd begun bringing the bodies down. By eight, fifteen children were listed as deceased upon admission. Seven of those children were unnamed, which I take to mean that the bodies were unrecognisable. By the third day, they had recovered twenty-five of the dead. One was an adult woman, one of the matrons. Most of the others had names by then too, though I'd imagine there was some guesswork involved. A footnote was added two days later, indicating that the physician in charge had certified those deaths.

'After that, nothing much seems to have happened for eight entire days. That's not terribly odd in itself. The infirmary was probably serving as a morgue, and burials might have been delayed by the cold. What is odd is that on the 28th of January, over a week after the fire, twelve more names appear in the infirmary journal. Those children aren't listed as "deceased upon arrival"; they're simply declared dead. No footnote, and certainly no mention of death certificates.'

The Inspector had been attending closely to all of this, though his expression remained unintelligible. 'I've known it to happen,' he said. 'It's a god-awful slog, bringing the dead out after a fire. It is a job just to reach them sometimes, never mind carry them out in one piece.'

'No doubt,' said Octavia. 'That was something I wondered about. Hawthorn No. 3 might have been harder to reach, since it was furthest from the main building, but these last twelve children weren't all from the same dormitory. Seven were from No. 1 and four from No. 2. One of them, a girl, was from No. 3. And in this case, there's no sign that more bodies were recovered. Just more names.'

Cutter gave an equivocal sort of grunt. 'They had their hands full. They might have let matters slip when it came to record-keeping.'

'The staff of the infirmary had nothing to do for a week. And I told you, their record-keeping was exemplary, when they kept records at all. Besides, these aren't the sort of records you can be lax about. The fire was a matter of public record. Coroners don't usually bestir themselves in such cases, but there's no guarantee. The rest of the death certificates were noted because they were duly issued by the physician in charge. They're here in the archive. He didn't sign any for the last twelve because he didn't have any bodies. He didn't sign them because those children were never found.'

'Christ,' said Cutter.

'Quite. And that isn't all. Someone scoured these records, but they can't have had an easy time of it. The Asylum had a lot of committees, and they kept extraordinarily detailed minutes. Take the Visits and Inspections Committee, for instance. They convened five times over the course of that December and January. It's pretty tedious stuff, for the most part. "Refreshments for the party of Lady Stafford, distinguished benefactress" and "works pursuant to inspection by District Supt. of Sanitation", that sort of thing. But one entry did catch my eye. On the 19th of January, a "Capt. Phillips, ASC" was lodged in the visitors' quarters and stabling was provided for his two wagons and their teams. By the morning of the 20th, Captain Phillips and his wagons had departed for points unknown. The itemised costs included £3 8s 6d for board, accommodations and ostlery. They also include £5 10s for transportation. That struck me as curious. What do you suppose they were transporting, on the morning after the fire?'

'Well, now,' said Cutter. He had propped himself against a door jamb and was working a stone from his boot heel with a pocket knife. 'Credit where it is due, you went at those boxes of papers like a ferret in a rats' nest. And some of the particulars you gave us, well . . . I won't say they didn't raise my hackles. If it was twenty-two years ago and I was working that beat, I'd be making myself a most unwelcome visitor. But what am I meant to do with any of it now? I only heard one name mentioned, and that was an army man. The army does its own policing, and it doesn't extend many courtesies to the likes of me. Even if this Phillips is still alive, he's probably a Brigadier-General by now, and I doubt he'll put himself at my disposal to talk about who paid for his bed and board one night in 1872.'

'That's not what I was suggesting,' said Octavia. 'I'm aware of how things work in the services – my brother was in the Navy, remember. And "ASC" means Army Service Corps, which means this Captain Phillips probably spent half of his life hauling wagons filled with men and ordnance and heaven knows what else. If he gave his name, then he almost certainly had no idea what he was going to be carrying away. No doubt he found out soon enough, but what if he did? It wasn't in his orders to be curious. I'm curious, though. I'm curious about where he was taking this unusual load. Aren't you?'

The Inspector said nothing.

'Are you going to make me say it?' Octavia demanded. 'Because I've been watching your face, and I can tell you've reached the obvious conclusion. They were transporting children, though I can't imagine where they were taking them or why. It was clever of them, using army transports. Less likelihood of unwanted interest. Still, though, they were carrying away a dozen children. Frightened and subdued children, to begin with, but they were going to attract notice sooner or later. So, where were they taking them? It couldn't have been that far, and it had to be the right sort of place. A place where there would be no one to ask awkward questions.'

Cutter's look was impatient, but something in his manner was unsettled. 'If I were obliged to go along with your little story, I might point out that there must a thousand such places within the bounds of Middlesex. Ten thousand that are within a night's drive. If it was men of means who set all this in motion, no doubt they had lands and houses aplenty. Some abbey set aside for an unwed son. A hunting lodge, even.'

'A place like that might do, for a time. But only for a time. They had plans for these children, surely, or they would not have gone to such trouble. They needed to settle them somewhere. And we know now that they had friends in the army. Who better to provide accommodations of that kind?'

'You think they lodged them at a *barracks*? To mess with a company of artillerymen? And how long would that secret be kept?'

'Not an ordinary barracks, no. Let's not pretend any longer, Inspector. These weren't just any men of means. They were particular men with particular connections. Think about the ones who've already turned up dead, who were something at the War Office, or the Home Office. And this latest fellow from the Admiralty – you said yourself that he was no petty bookkeeper. And you know as well as I do that the army traffics in secrets as well as shells.'

'That much I will grant you,' said Cutter. 'Half the brass at the Yard seem to be old army spies. But even so, it's one thing to know that the army has dirty dealings. It is quite another to suppose they had a hand in this. Indeed, it strikes me that you're doing a great deal of supposing on the strength of one captain's name in a visitors' book.'

Octavia nodded, as if conceding the point. 'I thought so too. And then you mentioned the old drunkard in Hounslow. The man who was killed with a shovel. He was in the army, too. Something lowly, you said, and yet your murderer had reason enough to seek him out. When I said you might both be right, this is what I meant. The shovel, the grave, the bones, the words. Those are messages, but they are evidence too. They are testimony.'

The Inspector was toying with his pocket knife. He rested it across two braced fingers, seeking the point of perfect balance. 'Do you think so? And what is being said, in this testimony?'

'Sir,' said Gideon, who found that he could no longer keep silent. 'I wonder if you are truly asking in earnest.'

Cutter set his head on one side, not looking up from his knife. 'You seem to have lost some of your gentle manners, Bliss, since taking that blow to the head. I hope you have not lost your wits into the bargain. Are you accusing me of some deception?'

Gideon faltered at this. 'I did not mean that, sir. I am sorry if I . . . Since the events at the gate lodge there have been moments when – I am not unwell, it is not that – but sometimes a feeling takes hold of me, a feeling of certainty. I find I cannot keep myself in check.'

The Inspector studied him for a moment, then his face softened and he folded away his knife. 'If that is all it is, you needn't trouble yourself. I go about the place in a perpetual rage because I am nearly certain of something that is nearly clear. No doubt I will keel over from it all one day, but so be it. We must all die of something. And as to the question I believe you were asking, I will remind you again – I will remind you both – that I am a police inspector and not a town crier. If I do not announce every thought that enters my head, it is not out of spite or perversity. As for your line of thinking, Miss Hillingdon, I will admit that we are not quite at odds.'

'So, you will look into it further?' Octavia said. 'The part that this man Hilliard might have played?'

'I have already taken certain steps. I have asked Buckley to find out where Hilliard served, if he can. I may not have an aptitude for secret signs, like Bliss here, but even I can tell what a shovel and an open grave might mean. Maybe Hilliard buried children and maybe he didn't, but children were buried somewhere. Whatever these unfortunates were wanted for, it was not to lead long and contented lives. They would have been buried somewhere safe, or somewhere that seemed safe at the time, though it seems plain enough that our murderer knew where to find them.

'Again, this is all supposing for now, but if we are to do that kind of supposing, we might as well see it through. My money says it was the same place from the start, and a place that met many needs. The children were raised there, after some fashion, and they were kept out of sight until they could be put to use. And they were buried there, once they had served their purpose. It is true, Miss Hillingdon – not many places would have fit the bill. I have spoken to Flood about it, my boss at the Yard. He is an old spy, too, though he is a man I trust as well as any. I hope to hear from him before the day is out.'

'Really, Inspector,' said Octavia. 'You're quite impossible. You poured scorn on practically every word I uttered, yet you were of the same mind all along.'

'It's called the Socratic method, or so Bliss tells me. And look at you, there's a bit of colour in your cheeks again. It did you a power of good.'

Octavia was on the point of responding when Milo appeared in the doorway. As always, he had made his entrance noiselessly and, noting that he appeared to be interrupting, he reached back to tap gently at the door frame.

'Forgive me,' he said. 'Perhaps my moment is bad, but I could not choose it exactly. I met with some small problems, and for this reason my appearance is not satisfactory.' He indicated his fine woollen suit and immaculately polished shoes.

'What problems?' said Cutter.

'These other policemen who have been watching you, from what is it – the Special Stick?'

'Special Branch. Though your name might be nearer the mark.'

'Special Branch, yes, though I cannot see what is special about them. Men with pig faces who are too heavy on their feet. And they think they are being secret? But there were more today than usual – four, I counted, within five hundred metres. One of them, I had to hurt him gently.'

Octavia had uncurled herself and was gathering up her papers. She paused. 'How does one hurt a man *gently*?'

'Miss Hillingdon,' said Milo, dipping his head. 'I am glad to see you well. Perhaps it is the wrong word. I meant that I injured him quietly and not forever. So that I would not be seen, you understand. And this reminds me, Henri – the business tonight, with your little appointment. Your friend Massey had a hand in that, if am I not wrong. Did he not promise that he would order his pigs away?'

Cutter drew out his watch and huffed at its face. Having polished it, he noted the time with a sour look. 'He's no friend of mine, Milo, and I put no stock in his promises. If anything, he will be doling out overtime for the occasion. He will have his trolls propped up against every second lamp post. It will do him no good, however, since the other party seems to have dispensed with his services.'

'Wait a moment,' said Gideon, getting to his feet. 'The meeting that Massey brokered, sir – was it not to take place two nights ago? After the incident at . . . while I was . . ?'

'Yes, Bliss, while your lights were out. And more to the point, while I was twenty feet below ground in Bishopsgate, poking at the Sunday roast that used to be Thomas Wesley. I sent word to Massey before I left – Inspector Cutter regrets and what have you – but I daresay he knew my business as soon as I did, and no doubt he was haring off to smooth things over before I'd even left the Yard. Someone certainly knew it, because no sooner had I packed Wesley's remains off to Golden Lane than a boy came out of nowhere and poked a card into my pocket. Here, have a look for yourself and pass it to Miss Hillingdon. I have enough to think about without wondering who's sulking over feeling left out. Besides, you're both mentioned.'

Gideon swept up the card. It was of fine stock, creamy white with a decorous black border. The hand was a faultless copperplate and the message was curt.

We are advised of your pressing engagement. It has been quite the season for us all. Since bones are so much in fashion, we propose a visit to the museum at South Kensington. Friday, a minute before midnight.

Bring your companions, if they are not tied up. The young ought to glimpse the marvels of the past.

P.S. Note that we have dispensed with our uncouth intermediary.

'Tied up.' He passed the card to Octavia. 'They know about what happened. They're taunting us.'

'Of course they know.' Octavia returned the card to Cutter with a look of disdain. 'They had other employees at Salus House, remember. Blakelock was bragging about it. Did you see others, Milo, aside from the ones you, well, dealt with?'

Milo formed a complicated gesture, meaning to indicate some fine nuance. 'I deal with the ones who try to deal with me. But if I see a man who is simply sweeping leaves? I am not a plague from the scriptures.'

'No one is faulting your workmanship,' said Cutter. 'They would have heard about it one way or the other, since the Yard is overrun with rats. Not that we can be sure it's the same *they*, mind you. Maybe our conspirators are turning on each other – what's left of them, anyway – or maybe some other interested parties have decided the shop needs tidying up. There is nothing our betters enjoy more than knifing each other, unless it's shooting at flightless birds in the drizzle. Whatever the case, it's a safe bet that we will be putting ourselves in harm's way. Bliss, have you your Webley about you or is it still at the bottom of your sewing basket?'

Gideon touched the bulge in his coat. He was troubled obscurely by its presence – its poised heft, its implacable hardness – but he could no longer sustain his moral equivocations. He had been hurt, and Miss Hillingdon had been hurt. Things had become simpler. This morning, at no one's urging, he had gone alone to a quiet place out beyond the Vauxhall pier. He had put in an hour of practice.

'I have it,' he said. 'But this meeting, with this unknown party. Is it not an unconscionable risk, sir? What can we hope to gain by it?'

'It's madness,' said Octavia firmly. 'Outright madness, and I cannot believe we're entertaining the idea. However—'

The Inspector interrupted her. 'Who is this *we*, Miss Hillingdon?'

'*However*, it's an opportunity to at least glimpse these people, or someone close to them. They will reveal something of themselves, whether they mean to or not. They have already revealed something, even if it is only that they are in fear of their lives. And given that we're no nearer to finding the one hunting them, I don't see how we can do otherwise.'

Cutter nodded grudgingly. 'It seems there is something else we agree on. Talk about signs and wonders. But you needn't think I've forgotten the first part. There is no *we*, Miss Hillingdon. Not when it comes to going out on a job. And certainly not when it comes to a job like this. I'm only taking Bliss along because I can answer for my conduct if he gets a bullet in the puss. He's a police constable, and he's equipped with a sidearm, though he hardly knows which end of it to squeeze. Whereas you, Miss Hillingdon, are a civilian. More than that – though you will not thank me for pointing it out – you are a lady. Worse still, you are a society lady, even if you're only pretending. You have shared boxes with dukes, and Christ knows who else. Have you any notion what would be said of me if any harm were to come to you? It is out of the question.'

Octavia rose smoothly and crossed the floor. Standing squarely before the Inspector, she jabbed him with carefully measured force in the sternum. He regarded her finger with doubting astonishment, as if it belonged to a phantom.

'In the first place,' she said, 'I have already come to harm. I'm quite upset about it, in point of fact. And when I'm upset, I have to *do* things.'

'That was entirely different. You instigated that little wheeze out in Wanstead, and I was not even present at the time. It was certainly not official police business.'

'Oh, and this is? What will you put in your report? "I was examining dinosaur bones at the British Museum pursuant to a secret communication from an urchin"? Almost nothing about this investigation has been official, as far as I can tell. In the second place, you'd have barely anything to investigate if you hadn't had my help. If you'd like to continue to benefit from my archival expertise – which is quite unrivalled, by the way – this is my price. You include me. In everything.'

'Miss Hillingdon,' said Cutter, still staring at her fingertip, 'I will thank you to—'

'I already know you're going to agree.' She tipped her head to one side. 'Shall I tell you how I know?'

He gave her a baleful look. 'Miss Hillingdon, I—'

'It's because you're worried that they'll let something slip and you'll miss it. You're a clever man, Cutter, but you're clever enough to know what you don't know. It will be almost nothing – a name, a date, a turn of phrase, some scrap, some fragment that almost no one else would recognise. But I would. I'll have read it somewhere, or heard it somewhere, in certain company. I won't miss it. It's what I do. But you –' She raised her finger to his tie knot and tapped it lightly. '– just might.'

He looked away, passing a hand over his face. For a long moment, he stood in silence.

'Fine,' he said at last. 'But I might as well warn you now. We'll be travelling by unusual means, and those nice clothes of yours are going to get dirty.'

Twelve

L eggett's *Fine Wines* and Viands offered a variety of unadvertised amenities that reflected the peculiar vocational demands of its clientele. It employed upwards of a dozen youngsters who served as lookouts; for example, occupying rotating posts on surrounding street corners or rooftops and providing timely intelligence when persons of general or specific interest entered the vicinity.

Also provided free of charge – and in the interests of preserving order – was a strongbox for the safekeeping of surrendered weapons and a variety of scales and standard weights to facilitate the uncontentious exchange of certain precious commodities.

Naturally, however, some services commanded a premium.

In certain pressing contingencies, for instance, the patrons of Leggett's might wish to evade the scrutiny of their fellows, or of the general body of the public. When such a need arose – as in cases of imminent arrest, or where some bodily hazard was threatened that could not be averted by traditional means – such customers might avail themselves of the Night Laundry.

The mechanics of this service were not complicated or esoteric. London's many hotels and boarding houses generated a great quantity of soiled linen in the course of their daily business, and many engaged contracted parties to carry it away and return it at convenient hours. As a result, a great many commercial laundries operated at night, and it was common on otherwise deserted streets to see their broad carts labouring along, burdened either with forlorn heaps of tangled cloth or with papered stacks of freshly pressed bedsheets.

It was so common, indeed, that the drays of the night laundries went all but unseen about London's slumbering thoroughfares. They did not go unnoticed, however, by the proprietors of Leggett's. To the customers whose needs they served, a vehicle that traversed the metropolis unremarked during the hours of darkness was not merely a curiosity of modern life; it was a ready-made business proposition.

Being persons of acumen and resolve, the proprietors had therefore annexed a yard and a cluster of outbuildings at a neighbouring premises. There they had equipped a modest stable and stationed a suitable cart bearing the livery of Peplow & Sons, a real and thriving concern with its headquarters at Shepherd's Bush. Travelling by the Night Laundry required an hour or two of notice, since the driver had to be alerted and the cart given a suitable appearance, and passage aboard was not cheap. Such a service could operate only infrequently, for fear of betraying its covert nature, and the price of passage was calibrated accordingly.

But tonight, since it was the Inspector who found himself in need, the fare was waived. At the appointed hour, young Barney appeared once more in the doorway of the parlour. Cutter was conferring privately with Milo, whose expression appeared gently sceptical, but at the end of the exchange Milo gave a curt nod and slipped wordlessly from the room. Whatever part he was to play in the night's events, he would be making the journey by other means.

'Here, guvnor,' said the pot boy, once Milo had departed. 'Jasper says that's all laid on for you. Says you ain't to trouble over the five pound.'

'Very good, Barney,' answered Cutter, who was easing a compact package into his coat pocket. 'We'll be with you presently.'

'Didn't say you couldn't sling me a bob,' said Barney, flashing out a filthy palm.

'You were given sixpence already, you grubby little savage. Wait outside the door, if you please, and pretend you know your place. Miss Hillingdon, are you ready?'

Octavia was deftly folding a tablecloth, which she now slung over one shoulder. 'A little trick I've learned,' she said, in answer to his enquiring look. 'I've done my share of tramping through muck to get to places. I'm ready, yes, but I'm a little worried about those papers. Where did you say they were putting them?'

'The takings room,' said Cutter. 'We could have another Great Fire and they would come to no harm. What about you, Bliss? You have the look of one of those fellows in the sanatorium who must be kept away from the scalpels. Are you sure you're up to this?'

Gideon had been clutching his bruised jaw. It was conceivable that he had fallen to brooding for just a moment. 'I am quite well, sir. Shall we go, then?'

The Inspector scrutinised him for a moment longer, then he squared his coat about his shoulders and righted his hat brim. 'Right, then,' he said. 'Let's go and have a look at these ancient fucking reptiles.'

The Night Laundry delivered them to a quiet yard within the precincts of the museum. The journey had taken them hardly more than a quarter of an hour, and Gideon had spent it in what struck him as passable comfort. At the stable they had been directed to 'curl up good and low' in the bed of the broad cart, whereupon a false bottom of slatted planks had been fitted in place above them. This in turn had been thickly laden with oddments of bed linen and clothing before the tailboard was at last lifted and bolted home.

Naturally, these conditions had proved somewhat cramped, but having endured days on end of strain and nervous extremity, Gideon had found it oddly relieving to lie hidden away in a rattling cocoon of darkness. He had thought of nothing, for the first time in what seemed an age, and he had welcomed it.

Inspector Cutter, however, had found the experience less congenial.

'Suffering Christ,' he said, when he had extricated himself from the cart. 'It's like being buried alive in a dotard's dirty drawers.'

'Didn't you enjoy it, then?' said Octavia. Having been allowed to dismount first, she was calmly unpinning the tablecloth she had wrapped herself in. 'I seem to recall that it was your idea.'

'It was an unfortunate necessity,' said Cutter sourly, smacking dust and lint from about his person. 'Like bringing you along.'

'Oh, look, you've got—' Approaching him solicitously, Octavia plucked a scrap of filmy cloth from his shoulder. 'Gosh, it's a chemise. Have you seen one of those before?'

Cutter snatched it from her with a dour look and hurled it onto the mounded cart. He rapped on the tailboard, giving the driver leave to depart, then looked about him to get his bearings. 'We came in by way of Princes Gate, I believe, so we're well enough placed. I mean to go in from the rear, as I need hardly tell you. Somewhere high up, too, if that can be managed. No doubt we're walking into a trap, so we'll get a look at it first if we can. This way, look, and keep your voices down from now on.'

Gideon could walk well enough, but it cost him more effort than usual to keep up. Octavia was keeping a gentler pace near his side, seeming untroubled by her own injuries. She glanced at him, and her fingertips grazed his forearm. 'Are you managing? I've been worrying.'

'What? Oh, yes. And please don't – I mean, if anyone has a right to . . . well, it was so much worse for you. I'm so sorry.'

'Gideon.' Grasping his wrist, she brought them both to a halt. 'No, it wasn't.'

He gestured ahead. 'We should probably—'

'We'll catch up. I don't think you remember it all clearly, but take my word for it – it wasn't worse for me. And whatever you think you failed to do, you didn't. That's not what you are, and it's certainly not what I am. Do you understand?'

He cast his eyes down, tugging his cuffs lower on his wrists. The rope marks had not quite faded. He nodded.

'Good,' she said. 'Come on, we'd better get moving.'

When they caught up with Cutter, he was crossing the gardens to the east of the museum itself. No windows were lit at the rear, which loomed vast and blank in the night air, but lamplight spilled from the steps facing the Cromwell Road. Perhaps the façade was always illuminated at night, though Gideon suspected that special arrangements had been made. That was what they did, people like these. They ordered the world to their own liking. They made special arrangements.

'Suki did this once,' Octavia whispered. 'Invited guests to a museum, I mean.' They were skirting the verge of a wide lawn bordered with cherry trees. The cherries were not in leaf yet, but above them among the vague branches were traces of ghostly blossom. It was a moment before Gideon recalled who Suki was.

'Oh,' he said, unsure what to make of this. 'Did she really?'

'Don't worry, Suki's not one of them, though I'm sure her family is moderately evil. All that money had to come from somewhere. It's one of the reasons I had to – no, never mind. This isn't the time. It was a smaller museum. She did it for someone's birthday.'

'It sounds lovely,' said Gideon. He could not remember celebrating his birthday. He had been very small when he was left alone.

He remembered a school, somewhere in the north. A wash bowl, feathered with ice. A pin cushion he had hidden and clutched.

He stopped for a moment, feeling something flex and tighten within him. He took hold of a nearby bough.

'Gideon?'

A spasm, and it was passing, but something was lodged in him that could not be expelled. Hard and bitter, like a swallowed seed. When he let out his breath, it seethed hot and sour against his teeth.

'Gideon?'

'I'm fine.' He shook himself and pressed on. 'I was just . . . sorry, it was nothing.'

She frowned at him for a moment, then peered ahead again. They were perhaps fifty feet from the back of the museum now, where a low annex enclosed a courtyard. All of it lay in deep shadow, and Gideon could not imagine how they might find a way inside. More pressingly, he could see no sign of the Inspector.

'He dashed off that way,' said Octavia, pointing towards the near corner of the annex. Beyond it, at the darkened margins of the parkland, was a cluster of outbuildings. 'He made one of his abrupt policeman gestures first. I think he wants us to wait.'

'Yes, that sounds right,' said Gideon. 'You'll find he gestures a lot, when he can't bellow at people in the usual way. Wait, is that him?'

A figure had appeared at the edge of the courtyard, obscured by some indecipherable shape. Then the shape swung about, revealing a distinctive geometry. The figure raised an arm. It gestured impatiently.

'Yes, it's him. He seems to have found a ladder.'

'I'd gathered that, yes.' Octavia shook her head in irritation. 'I think he wants us to come over there, though I've a good mind to just wave back. *Such* an irksome man. Shall we, then?'

They fell into step again, keeping to the verge of the grass while they could. As they neared the main building, Gideon surveyed it in snatched glances. He saw hulking turrets, glimpsed vast and lightless galleries. He knew that anyone might be watching, might be waiting. But he was not following blindly, not this time. He understood.

If he was walking into a trap, it would be a trap that the surviving conspirators had set. He would lay eyes on them at last, those malignant princelings, those careless and cosseted monsters. Whatever their plans, they would come to nothing. All this – this high-handed intriguing, this flourishing of residual power – all of it would fall away. They were doing all this not because they were untouchable but because they were not. *She* had found the others. She would find them soon enough.

He recalled himself and looked up. Up ahead, Cutter was hefting his ladder and gesturing again in agitation.

'He knows something,' Octavia murmured as they drew near. 'He always knows something, blast him, but I mean about tonight. He knows something, or he thinks he knows.'

'You think so?' In his distracted state, Gideon had devoted less attention than usual to divining the Inspector's moods and intentions. It was a peculiar sensation, and not altogether unwelcome.

'And whatever it is he knows, I don't think he's terribly pleased about it.'

'Look at the pair of you,' Cutter hissed, as they came within range of him. 'Sauntering along like a pair of lovers in a meadow. Shift your arses, will you.'

'I see you've found a ladder, sir,' said Gideon mildly. 'That was a stroke of luck.'

'Yes, Bliss, I found a ladder in a museum full of high ceilings and giant skeletons. I was astonished myself. Now, take hold of one end of it. I want to get it through the courtyard without waving it like a flag. We'll have to carry it slung low and keep to the edges.'

Gideon moved into place and took hold of a rung with his good hand, leaving Cutter free to shift his own grip. When they had settled the ladder's weight between them, the Inspector nodded and made to move off. 'Remember, down low and in by the walls. And try not to put any windows out.'

They set out in silence, keeping to the deeper shadows beneath the great thrusting eaves. Gargoyles noted their passing, crouched on pedestals high above them, and living creatures stirred too. A fox sidled to within touching distance, then slid away into some unseen recess, and twice Gideon glimpsed what must have been a hawk. The first time it was by chance, as he searched the windows of a vacant gallery. He saw it idling, where the darkness was city-tinged and sulphurous. It vanished then, until he caught it settling on a parapet. It folded itself away, black brushstrokes against a black ground. He felt it watching still, unslaked and infinitely attentive.

'Here, Bliss,' said Cutter. They had come to a corner where the shoulder of the museum's east wing joined the central edifice. 'Let your end down, nice and easy.'

When Gideon had stepped clear, the Inspector shuffled his grip back along the ladder's length. He swung it about in careful increments, mindful of the skirling breezes, and began the painstaking business of edging it upright. As he nudged the top into place against some scarcely perceptible lintel, Gideon felt a tremor of something. Exultation, maybe, or terror. In his altered state he was less susceptible to his habitual anxieties, but he was not heedless. The ladder was a fine stout article, and it had a reach of twenty-five feet or so, yet set against this titanic structure it looked a toy fashioned from matchwood. It scarcely cleared the lowermost tier of arches, and it came nowhere near to touching the roofline.

If Cutter had spied a way in, it was somewhere high above the top of the ladder.

'Well,' said Octavia, who had appeared without a sound by his right shoulder. 'That looks promising.'

Gideon searched her face. Miss Hillingdon had made a profession of stealing unseen into inaccessible places. Perhaps the prospect did not trouble her. After a moment she relented with a smirk. He gave a forlorn laugh of his own. 'Have we gone quite mad, do you think? I can't even see what's up there.'

'Oh, I don't know.' With a gloved fingertip, Octavia flicked a scrap of lint from her collar. 'It's difficult to tell. All of this descended into madness days ago. I do know that it's horribly cold, and that if it were up to me I'd have mesmerised some nightwatchman twenty minutes ago and we'd be inside by now. Then again, he clearly knows something we don't, and since he's insisted on taking charge, I'm forced to assume that he has something resembling a plan. You do, Inspector, don't you?'

'What's that now?' said Cutter. He turned from the foot of the ladder, where he had been squinting up into the darkness with a pencil braced inexplicably against his thumb. Perhaps it had something to do with trigonometry, or with astrology.

'I said, we're assuming you know what you're doing. What is it we're trying to reach, exactly? Because it looks like we've brought a footstool to the Matterhorn. Why aren't we trying those lower galleries? We can reach those, surely, and the windows are enormous.'

'And they'd make an enormous racket if we broke them, which is what we'd have to do. They're fine big windows, right enough, but they don't open, except for those little vents near the top. You might get a spaniel through, at a stretch, but we find ourselves without one. No, the only windows that are any good to us are up in the attics. Even a place as grand as this needs its slates patched and its gutters cleared, and you can't throw up a scaffold every time there's a bit of nasty weather. See up there, beyond that pediment? There's a valley where the roof line joins the east wing, and there's some class of work going on the next valley over. I saw tools left out, which means someone is coming back for them in the morning. And that means they're within easy reach of a window. Does that meet your standards, in the matter of planning?'

'You saw tools?' Octavia said, with no trace of scorn. 'All the way up there?'

'I have a creditable pair of eyes, so they say. And a bossing mallet has a distinctive look to it, in fairness. All the more so when it is left hooked in a roofing ladder, though I doubt I would have caught it by day. Moonlight can work in your favour. In any event, that's where I'm aiming for. The ladder will take us to that lintel up yonder, and from there I'll get to the roof by way of that downspout. Those stone courses are hardly twenty years old, so there'll be decent enough handholds.'

Gideon grasped his chin as he peered up into the unfathomable darkness. He persuaded himself that he could discern the glint of a drainpipe, but the rest he was obliged to take on faith. 'Yes,' he said. 'Yes, that sounds . . . it sounds eminently achievable.'

The Inspector regarded him with frank pity. 'You will not be going up the same way, you mithering twit. I'm not spending the night scraping your brains off these cobbles. The window above the lintel does open. I will make my way down and let you in there.'

Gideon nodded, accepting the wisdom of this. 'Very good, sir. You will be vigilant, won't you? We cannot tell what awaits us.'

Cutter cast his eyes up. 'I have some notion,' he said. 'And as for me, I'm not a pleasant thing to encounter in a dark passageway. I will try my luck. Right, that's enough discoursing. Stay out of sight once I'm gone, but keep a hand to that ladder against the wind.

And don't stir from the ground until I am at the window, do you hear me?'

He turned to scour the face of the building one last time, then with a grimace of resignation he launched himself up the ladder. Cutter did nothing at a leisurely pace, but it was disconcerting all the same, seeing him surge skywards like some deckhand about his ordinary business. In moments he had reached the lintel high above them, and he hardly seemed to pause before hoisting himself over it and beginning the next stage of his ascent.

After that he was lost to sight. Gideon tried counting off the minutes in the silence that followed, but he found that he kept losing his place. Octavia touched his sleeve. 'Gideon. He'll be fine.'

But in the same moment, noises tore from the darkness above them: an urgent oath, a resonant clang, then the deep judder of shearing metal.

'Oh, God.' Gideon's whisper was disbelieving. 'Octavia. Oh, God.'

'Just wait.'

'But the Inspector, he . . .' Gideon couldn't articulate it, the blank impossibility. 'What could have—'

'Gideon. We have to wait.'

He kept looking for a time, kept staring up into the answering darkness, but presently he bowed his head. It would be midnight soon, and all about them church bells would sound unheeded. The appointed time would have come and gone, but that would not matter. It would all be over.

Octavia was reaching for his arm when she stopped short, suddenly attentive. Gideon heard it too. From somewhere above them, a faint and laboured scraping.

They looked up just as a head appeared, craning from side to side with familiar impatience. Then his voice reached them, a whisper whose ill-tempered force could be felt even five fathoms below.

'What are you waiting for, you pair of mantel ornaments? A winged fucking chariot?'

Octavia had gone up first, and she made light work of the climb. When Gideon's turn came, he refrained from looking up, but by the time Cutter hauled him through the window, Octavia was rummaging idly amongst a stack of crates.

Gideon righted himself – he had been propelled inwards with enough force to make him stumble – and took a moment to settle his breathing, steadying himself discreetly against a bench.

'I must own,' he said, having weathered a fierce squall of nausea, 'that I should quite like to leave by a door.'

'We'll be doing well if we're not carried out in boxes,' said the Inspector, who remained hunched in the narrow casement, straining with effort at something down below. With a vociferous oath, he abandoned his efforts and withdrew from the window, setting aside a coil of rope fastened to some elaborate contrivance of brass. He bore a nasty graze on his cheek, Gideon noticed, and his knuckles were darkened and torn. 'I had hopes of hauling up that ladder, for the wind will surely upset it before long and it'll go down with an ungodly clatter.'

'Perhaps, sir,' said Gideon, who still felt notably light-headed, 'it will fall in the manner of one of Bishop Berkeley's trees. No one will be nearby to hear it, and therefore the ladder's very existence will be susceptible to dispute.'

Cutter drew down the window sash with quiet emphasis. He let out a heavy breath. 'Is that philosophy, Bliss?'

'Yes, sir. It is from a treatise on the metaphysics of knowledge.'

Cutter stared for a time, then he pointed at the peculiar brass implement. 'Do you see that chandelier hook? No one will see it if I stick it up your arse. I'll warrant it will still exist, though.'

'Stop it, Cutter,' said Octavia, looking up from her crates. 'He's babbling because he's been under strain, and because he thought you were dead. We both did.'

'Dead? What gave you that notion?'

'Well, sir,' said Gideon, 'we did suffer a moment or two of misgiving, but—'

'We heard something give way, as you very well know, and we heard you struggling. Then you just disappeared. And look at you – you've clearly been injured, yet God forbid you should admit to the slightest vulnerability or allow it in anyone else. Least of all in someone who cares for you, however inexplicable that may be.'

Cutter stared, as if perplexed by a riddle, then something shifted in his face. He lifted his bloodied hand, letting his eyes flicker over it, then dropped it again. He shook his head slowly. 'All right,' he said, in a tone that seemed oddly weightless. 'All right, yes. It was a lightning rod, not a gutter. My own fault, no doubt. They're not made to take any weight. But that is by the by, I suppose.'

He stopped and looked away, out into the night. 'Look, I know my own ways, for who better? My own faults. Hard words, to be sure, but there are worse failings than hard words. Much worse. Christ, listen to me wandering. You would think a man in my game would know his way to a confession, yet when it comes to it . . .'

He shook his head again.

'Listen, we haven't the time for this now, but if I'm right, we'll have it soon enough. I have been trying to tell you both, after my own fashion. I've been trying to warn you, but it'll be out of my hands soon enough. I slipped, yes, and I came damn near to falling. And do you know what I said to myself, in that moment? I said, not yet, you black-hearted bastard, and not like that. You'll not get out of it that easily. So, if anyone was minded to mourn me, all I can say is that he should give it another hour or two. He might find he has cause to reconsider. Now, before someone starts lighting candles and singing hymns, might I remind you that we have work to do. And the first order of business, I believe, is to find out where we are.'

'Mineralogy,' said Octavia, lifting something heavy and obscurely lucent from a crate. 'This is chrysoberyl, according to the tag. Apparently, it exhibits something called "chatoyancy", though it doesn't seem to exhibit anything much in the dark. Stop looking at me like that, Cutter, there is a point to this. My grandfather used to bring me here when I was younger. I had to look at everything, no matter how dull, because it was edifying. If the layout of these storage rooms corresponds to the halls down below, then we must be somewhere above mineralogy. That's towards the back, as I recall. Where do you expect to find our new friends?'

'You saw their invitation, Miss Hillingdon. They gave us very little in the way of particulars, but that's not to say they took no trouble over them. No doubt they mean to make an occasion of it, one way or another. Tell me this, since no one ever thought to edify me as a youngster – where are the grandest rooms in this place? Where do they show off the bigger articles, the great man-eating elephants and such like?'

Gideon did not venture a correction, as he might once have done. He recognised for once that he was being teased, even if he did not feel moved to share the joke. He wondered how much he had misunderstood, for all this time, how much he had failed to see.

Octavia considered the question. 'Well,' she said, 'it would have to be one of the main galleries. You come to those first, from the public entrance, and the dinosaurs and things were in the hall on the right. But why would they choose a place like that, a vast room where everything is on display – where *they'd* be on display. Aren't they supposed to be shadowy conspirators?'

'That I can't say,' said Cutter. 'But when I'm faced with a puzzle of that kind, I'm inclined to suspect that the answer will be one I don't like.'

'Mmm,' said Octavia, stowing away her mineral sample. 'I'd had a similar thought. It occurred to me, for instance, that they might have chosen the place because they want *us* to be on display. Because they want *us* to be seen.'

Gideon grasped his left arm discreetly. He had been troubled by peculiar spasms, rippling upwards from the injured hand. The sensation in his forearm was one of sinuous constriction, as if it were wound about by a snake. 'Or perhaps,' he said quietly, 'they were not the ones who chose the place.'

Cutter gave him an oblique look, his chin thrust aside. He shook his head and moved to the door, where he conducted a hasty inventory of his pockets. Gideon glimpsed a package, narrow and tapering, wrapped closely in brown paper, which he recognised but could not place.

'I fear we are worrying the point to death,' said Cutter. 'It's a long time since I was in the way of stepping out with ladies, but I recall it as a simple enough business. If she named a railway station you would find her near the doors or the ticket office, not crouching in an engine boiler. We'll make our way to these main galleries, and we'll make as little racket as we can help. Creeping up on people is not a complicated undertaking either.'

Gideon took his place by the door, reaching beneath his coat as he did so. The revolver felt cold to the touch always, though it was next to his body. This time he did not draw his hand back at once. He skimmed its contours for a moment, letting his fingertips memorise them. 'I'm sure you are right, sir,' he said, though he had not been attending. 'I'm sure it will be all right.'

Octavia turned at this, her fingers slowing as she pinned up her hair. He offered her a placid smile.

'Yes,' she said. 'Yes, all right, Gideon. Cutter, what's the time?'

'Eighteen minutes to midnight. Have you any recollection of the distance?'

'I was a bored child, Inspector, not a surveyor. But I suppose it's three hundred yards or so, from this side to the public entrance. I don't think the exact distance matters, though. We're not an army marching over open country. We shall be sneaking along unlit passageways, coming upon locked doors and blind turns. I wouldn't hold out much hope of timing our arrival to the minute.'

'Well, so be it,' answered Cutter. 'I doubt it makes any odds, a minute before midnight or five minutes after. All I want is to be there a minute before they know it. If we find they have watchers and hatchet men crouching behind every glass case, that will be another matter. I doubt they went to such lengths, however. This is a delicate bit of business, and they'll want to keep it close. I am counting on another point, too, though I will say no more about it for now. In any case, I have something near enough to a plan, but it's not without its faults. For one thing, it will mean that I must go most of the way without a hand on my gun.'

He stooped to attend to something in the darkness. A dim scuffling followed.

Octavia spoke with icy forbearance. 'I don't suppose you'd care to explain any further, Inspector? Why won't you have your hands free? And what on earth are you *doing*?'

'I'm taking off my boots, Miss Hillingdon. You might make a start on your own, since you have a good deal more unlacing to do. I did tell you it was a straightforward business. We won't have our hands free because we'll be carrying our shoes.'

*

They kept to the attics at first, to make what ground they could out of anyone's hearing, but in this place even the attics were a labyrinth of cloaked treasures. Even in the dark, they sensed the close press of accreted mysteries, of the blind eyes and arrested wings that were massed all about them, waiting to be named. What little they could feel or see they did not recognise. Gideon would put a hand out – an awkward business, with his shoes in his hands – and his fingertips would graze illegible fissures, arid spines or papery husks. Even when some meagre light reached them, from a slatted window or a hidden skylight, it hardly helped. It showed them crouched beasts riven with pins or plumbed to flasks of bitter-smelling fluids. It showed them tablets of scabbed slate, inscribed with indecipherable lobes and incomplete symmetries. It showed them ranks of great jars, gravid with undersea murk and the stilled forms – fat coils, tender membranes, pallid vanes – of things that must once have lived and were now forbidden to perish.

At any other time, Gideon might have been moved to awe. What surrounded him, he supposed, were the spoils of unresting schol-arship and no doubt such labours were to be honoured. All he felt, though, was a brooding indignation. All these specimens, all these relics, all these bones. They could not leave the world untouched, these people, or even the worlds beneath it. They could not be content with dominion over the living. They wanted it even over the dead.

No doubt he was not quite himself. He certainly felt irritable. He had been ordered to bring up the rear, since only he and Cutter were armed, but that was surely a laughable notion. Octavia had proved more than once that she was no defenceless ingenue, and Gideon was hardly a dependable marksman at the best of times, never mind while he was tiptoeing through a darkened maze with a damp and decrepit shoe in each hand.

Octavia must have sensed his impatience. When they came at length to the head of a narrow staircase, she called to him in a whisper. She had seemed at ease with this undertaking from the start, tugging her high boots off without ceremony and knotting their laces together so that she could carry them slung about her shoulders. She had, as she reminded Cutter, done this sort of thing before. In any case, when Gideon drew near enough to make it out, he saw that her expression was composed.

She studied him for a moment. 'Are you all right, do you think?'

'Yes, I'm— What? Why are you looking at me that way?'

'You've been muttering to yourself. It isn't like you.'

'What? Don't be—' Gideon hesitated. 'Really? Are you sure?'

'Well, muttering to someone. It was almost as if— Oh, it doesn't matter. I just wanted you to know that we're getting quite close now. These stairs ought to lead us down to the middle galleries, giving onto the central hall. I've sent Cutter down to check – well, I prompted him to think of it, which comes to the same thing. The central hall will take us to the main galleries. Gideon, are you following all this?'

He had been staring down into the shadows below the steeply raked staircase. And he had heard something, he was almost sure. A solemn tapping that faded when he tried to fix upon it. 'Sorry, yes.' He made a show of attentiveness. 'Nearly there. To the central galleries.'

She pressed her lips together. 'Look, just stay close behind me. And try to remember— Oh, hang on, he's back. Well, was I right?'

'Near enough,' said Cutter, emerging from the gloom beneath them. 'These take us to the upper tier of the fish gallery, but there's a long corridor beyond that. We'll have to follow that to get to the central hall. That part I'm not fond of, since it's a corridor lined with doors and little else. Nothing to duck behind if someone pokes a head in.'

'You went that far ahead?' said Octavia.

'Without you to look out for me, you mean? I didn't, no. They put floor plans up, for the visitors. All labelled, as neat as you like. Oh, and that's the other thing. There's lights down there.'

'What, everywhere? Was it them?'

'No way to be sure,' said Cutter. 'I doubt it, though. Would have taken them an age, a place this size. And it's lit for night duty, not for visitors. Just one lamp in every five, and burning fairly low. It's what nightwatchmen do when they start a shift. Otherwise, they would burn twice their wages in kerosene. And it's all they had to do tonight, I'll be bound, before someone let them out on unexpected leave.'

Octavia tutted lightly. 'Well, I don't suppose it matters much. We would have come upon lighted rooms eventually, and now we'll make quicker progress.'

'Quicker, yes, but not too quick. Do you hear, Bliss? I see you perking up and taking notice, which is a small relief to me, but remember you will be crossing marble floors in your stockinged feet. If you set off at a gallop, you will end up clattering into a stuffed dragon and waking the whole house.'

Gideon gave Cutter a look that he hoped would go undetected in the dark. He was indeed paying closer attention now, and his thoughts no longer felt quite so disordered. But he felt something else, too, now that they had drawn near to what awaited them. It flickered at odd moments at the periphery of his awareness, and it made him think of a showman's fingertips grazing the surface of a bulb; of empty air crazed blue by a pulse of summoned charge. He was growing frankly deranged, no doubt, but he found he did not mind it. 'I will take care, sir,' he said, 'not to upset any dragons.'

*

The lamps in the fish gallery burned low, just as Cutter had described, but he insisted all the same that they take a moment to let their eyes adjust. 'We have spent the last age straining after gleams in pitch-black rooms,' he said. He had braced both his shoes together in his left hand and was swinging them cautiously to test the new arrangement. 'And from now on, our lives might depend on catching a stray shadow. We can afford to lose half a minute.'

Gideon surveyed the gallery below them, a grand barrel-vaulted hall where a shark was suspended above a staid arrangement of glass cases, unseeing and vastly inert. There was light enough to pick out the ancient nicks and slash marks on its dull flank, the serried trap of teeth in its hungerless mouth. There were deep shadows, certainly, between the display cases and amongst the regimented cabinets that lined the walls, but it seemed impossible that even a moth's wings could stir unnoticed in this muted sepulchre of a place.

He could not tell if this made the Inspector right or wrong, but he chafed nonetheless at his sudden show of caution. 'But, sir,' he began, 'surely it is—'

Gideon broke off. He had heard it again, rising and fading at the limits of his hearing. A ticking, not quite precise. Like a failing metronome, set to *andante*. The others gave no sign that they had heard, though Octavia seemed as alert as ever and Cutter, at most times, seemed to possess the hearing of a famished watchdog.

'Surely it's what, Bliss?'

Octavia, who had been adjusting the arrangement of her boots, cast her eyes up in exasperation. 'I don't mean to be unkind, Inspector, but your voice wasn't made for whispering. It sounds like a gramophone recording of thunder. Perhaps you could give hand signals from now on.'

Cutter passed a hand over his mouth. 'Should I answer you with a hand signal, Miss Hillingdon. Because I have one in mind.' He rooted for his watch. 'It's time. Stay close behind me from now on and watch what I do, hand signals or no. And one last thing. I said that certain truths might come out here, but that doesn't mean you should trust all you hear and see. You'll have time enough for doubting me if I'm still standing tomorrow, but for tonight you must mind what I say. Understood?'

'Fine,' said Octavia. Gideon gave only a brief nod, when he saw that Cutter was waiting for his response. His attention had been elsewhere.

'Right,' said Cutter. 'Whoever these bastards are, let's have a look at them.'

They made their way in silence through the fish gallery, scarcely glancing at the creatures they passed. In his state of peculiar fixation, Gideon could summon little curiosity for the exhibits, and he looked aside only when some quirk of the light caught his attention, silvering the belly of a listless carp or the gelid coin of a turbot's eye.

He was grateful when they reached the corridor beyond, though Cutter took on a grim look when he paused to check that the way was clear. It offered little in the way of concealment, it was true, beyond its slender ornamental pillars and a procession of dour busts, and even the rationed lamplight would be enough to betray them at once. Gideon was mindful of all this, and with some effort he kept to their careful and steady pace, his eyes flickering from Cutter's back to the shadowed doorways up ahead. He was conscious of an obscure elation, though, now that the way ahead lay straight and unobstructed. He had even recognised the source of that strange ticking, now that they were drawing near to it. Footsteps. It was the sound of footsteps.

Cutter put out a hand when he came to the last door, but Gideon and Octavia had already slowed and halted. After all the bickering

and shambling progress of the last hour, they had fallen into formation now, each of them attentive to every gesture and hesitation, all
of them moving with measured purpose.

Only once, when they had crossed into the vast and pristine central hall, was this pattern disturbed. The concourse had widened as it
approached a soaring atrium, and Cutter was skirting the pediment
of a column so as to keep to the scalloped margins of the mouth of
the passage. He froze, one stockinged foot flexed above the gleaming
flags, and he canted his head aside by a cautious fraction. Octavia
and Gideon each skidded minutely as they noted this, then waited
anxiously for some further sign.

Cutter glanced back, then raised a scooped hand to his ear. A
hand signal. When he lowered it and looked back again, his expression was difficult to interpret. There was wariness in it, but there was
a trace of bemusement too. He made another pantomime gesture,
scissoring his fingers over empty air.

Footsteps, he meant.

Gideon gave a terse nod. *Well, yes*, he wanted to say. *This is hardly
a recent development.*

Cutter gestured again, holding up a single finger. He had counted
only one set of footsteps, though he seemed to doubt his own conclusion. He shook his head in dissatisfaction, then flicked his free
hand to lead them on. In the next moment he had slipped out of
sight behind the towering column.

Octavia moved to follow him at once, and Gideon ought to have
done the same. They were moving in closer formation now, striving
to remain within sight of one another. Beyond the atrium were the
main galleries. Soon they would gather in the shadows to confer in
silence on what little they had learned. They would stoop awkwardly
in the dark to lace their shoes, intent and wary of fumbling. They
would get ready for what came next.

Paraic O'Donnell

Yet Gideon hesitated, troubled by some unnameable doubt. His entire being seemed to thrum now with alertness. His senses were impossibly distended, their surfaces stretched so taut that the flicker of an eyelash might disturb them, or the tiny kiss of a mote of dust.

And he had sensed something. Something vanishingly gentle, like a down feather settling on water.

What happened next had the fluid senselessness of a dream. Gideon felt himself lifted and gathered backwards into the dark. Limbs whipped about him, spider-quick and fiercely precise, and by the time he had formed his first conscious thought, he had been dragged into some unseen alcove, fully eight or nine feet from where he had been standing, a hand clamped to his mouth and his right arm wrested behind his back, held at the brink of un-bearable pain.

They were hard and narrow, the limbs that held him fast, but otherwise the body pressed close to his own betrayed nothing of itself. It waited, wanting to be sure of something, and while it waited it was soundless, unbreathing and ferociously still.

Then it spoke. It was a woman's voice, but it revealed nothing else. It was a voice among many, chosen for this moment. 'You're the innocent, aren't you? I know you a little. I've been watching. We must be quick.'

It was her, of course. It was always going to be her.

He let out an assenting breath, since he could not even nod. *The innocent.* Perhaps he ought to have felt indignant, but what differ-ence could it possibly make? He imagined he knew her a little too. What she had been, and what she must have become. To her, anyone might seem an innocent. Or no one.

She shifted her grip. Keeping his mouth covered, she scrawled a fingertip over his cheek. 'You were hurt here, weren't you?'

260

He was strangely unafraid – or perhaps he was terrified beyond all sense – but he felt a moment's reluctance. Then he saw that his embarrassment was useless. Anything he might feel or do would be useless. He let out another breath.

'Pity,' said the voice. Her breath was scentless, but it was warm. It was human. 'That's not what you're for, hurting. I won't hurt you, unless I have to. And I won't have to, will I?'

Gideon withheld his breath, since it was the only other sign he could give.

She waited, perhaps considering this. 'No, of course not. But I'm less sure about our friend the Inspector. I know him a little, too, but I'm no longer certain of what he wants. I'm beginning to think that *he* is not certain.'

Gideon exhaled again, this time without hesitating. This insight into the Inspector's nature had only just come to him, but he felt oddly certain of it.

The voice made a sound that might have been sorrowful. It might just as easily have been a promise of death. 'He hasn't changed, then. I suppose we'll see. That's what you want, isn't it? To see, to understand?'

A quick breath, then another.

'Listen to me, then. You will understand a little, after tonight, but not everything. The people waiting in there – one will be just what he seems, though he will lie about that. Not the other. You will recognise her, but you do not know her. She's a liar too, but she has a gift for it. She's very dangerous, but she's also frightened. Do you know what she's frightened of?'

She loosened her grip by a fraction, then something cold touched his cheek. The flat of a blade. After an instant of liquefying fear, he realised that she was simply explaining.

He breathed out, in relief as much as affirmation.

'Good,' said the voice. 'Now, listen. The Inspector's coming this way. Do you hear?'

Gideon waited and listened, but there was nothing. His heightened senses had deserted him, or they had been overwhelmed. He held his breath as well as he could manage.

'Perhaps you wouldn't. He's looking for you. He's trying to be quiet. He's good at it, for a big man. In a moment I will let you go, but before I do there is something else you must know. They want it to end here, these people. They fear for their lives, but that's not the only reason. They want me dead, and they want Cutter dead. They think it's the only way to be sure. You're a clever boy, aren't you? Do you see how they might achieve that?'

Gideon did see. He could not say when the realisation had come to him, but perhaps he had known it from the beginning, from the night they found the first body. Cutter was a man of fearsome capabilities, and Gideon had seen him subdue adversaries who might have shambled out of his own nightmares. But the one he was presently hunting – the one who had snatched Gideon into the shadows not ten paces behind Cutter's back; who was speaking to him now in that borrowed and colourless voice; who had stroked his cheek with the fleeting curiosity of an angel of death – if such a creature had ever been within the reach of Cutter's power, she was surely not now. If he were to try to overpower her, she would slaughter him without flinching.

He let out a slow breath.

'Yes,' she said. 'Yes. But that's not what I want. Do what you must, if you care for him. Now go, and don't look back. You'll see me soon enough. You'll see everything.'

Gideon tumbled into the open, only just managing to keep his feet. He could not tell how much noise he had made and for a moment he did not care. He had turned already, heedless of the danger, to search the darkness where she had been. He saw only the shadowed folds of some robed stone figure, its hands raised in imprecation to the empty air.

When the Inspector came upon him, he had straightened and all but recovered his wits. He gave a haphazard shrug, and Cutter spared him only a flickering scowl before urging him onwards. But before he turned back towards the atrium, something altered in the Inspector's expression. His narrow look slid past Gideon and ranged for a moment over the empty hall beyond. Then he shook his head, his face revealing nothing that Gideon recognised, and stalked away in resolute silence.

Hardly another sign passed between them when they gathered at last to put on their shoes and make what final preparations they could. It was an awkward and delicate business, all of them crowded into a narrow gap behind some looming memorial, and each of them crouching and fussing with agonising caution over a task that would never otherwise cost them a thought. And afterwards, when they had laced their boots tight and worked the kinks from their limbs; when they had done all the patting and probing about their persons that could usefully be done; and when Cutter had lifted and turned the face of his watch in the scarce light – it was two minutes from midnight – there seemed very little left to be said.

It was time. They had arrived, though by extraordinary means and not without incident, and they had arrived at very near to the appointed hour. Close by now, somewhere beyond the far end of the atrium, those footsteps ticked on, patient and unvarying. Waiting.

Octavia looked to Cutter, and in the shifting darkness her pale face formed a question. It was a moment before Gideon understood her meaning. The Inspector had spoken of a plan, of something he would be depending on when this moment arrived.

Cutter gave a nod of acknowledgement, but for now he showed no further reaction. He leaned back in the narrow recess, supporting himself against the plinth of the monument. Casting his eyes down, he lifted one foot and examined it idly. He straightened the hem of his waistcoat and raised a hand to cover a silent but protracted yawn.

Gideon looked to Octavia, who only flicked up her eyes. Had Cutter abandoned his plan? Had something made him wary? He had expected to find only a few people here, and it seemed he had been proven right. They had only heard the footsteps of a single person, though *she* had spoken of two, the one who had held him in the shadows. Others might well be waiting for them in silence; Gideon could not tell how that might change Cutter's calculations, and he could think of nothing else that—

But no, whatever his altered state, he could not shy away from what was plain. *She* was here, and that would surely change Cutter's thinking if he knew of it. Gideon flinched in the darkness and turned his face away. He could find a way to tell him, even now, if he were truly determined. But he knew that he would not. He would not have told him even if he had been free to speak when Cutter found him, and not only because he might not have been believed. He would not tell him, and more than that, he felt certain that he *should* not.

Do what you must.

He had accepted the necessity of that, but why? Who was she, that he should place such trust in her? And what was it that he *must* do, other than his plain duty? Yet what *was* that duty, truly? What course was open to him now that would not amount to a betrayal of someone?

He stirred and looked to the Inspector. There was still time, if he was quick. He was wearing shoes now, and the need for silence was more pressing than ever, but it was only a matter of a few paces.

How could they hear anything in any case, over those incessant and unnatural bloody footsteps?

But even as he levered himself sideways, raising an arm to catch Cutter's eye, the Inspector was drawing himself upright and reaching casually into his coat. Octavia was looking on intently, and her gaze shifted for only an instant at Gideon's tentative movement.

Gideon faltered, then drew back. He might have slumped in self-reproach, but now he too was transfixed. There was a finely judged purpose to the Inspector's movements – he had seen it often in such moments – and though he could not tell what was about to happen, it seemed safe to assume that a great many other things would happen soon afterwards.

Cutter had eased himself into position behind a pillar. He had found a handhold that allowed him to swing his upper body out into the open, and he had drawn back his free arm with the jaunty resolve of a bowler on a gentle May morning.

He glanced back at them, one eyebrow cocked, then he steadied himself. He hefted something that Gideon barely glimpsed, then he gathered back his throwing arm and swept it with furious precision through an immense arc of air.

It was not one sound that reached them an instant later but two, a clipped percussion followed by a crisply tinkling detonation. Gideon wasn't sure what he had been anticipating – it would not have been beyond Cutter to toss a grenade – but he realised now what the Inspector had intended.

It was the sound that a fragile object might make if it were knocked from its place and sent crashing to a floor of polished stone. And it had come from the opposite side of the gallery. It was not an uncommonly sophisticated ruse, perhaps, but it might just prove effective.

Gideon listened closely as he watched Cutter's next movements. Out in the gallery, the footsteps had finally halted. He heard a faint exchange of voices – at least two, then – but it was cut short by some terse but indistinct command. The voice that gave it was icy and exact.

You will recognise her.

Cutter remained poised behind his pillar, his palm raised to delay any movement. Whatever he might have been waiting for, it had not happened yet.

Then the voice from the gallery called out. It was a woman's voice, crisp and disdainful. 'Goodness, how clever. But there really wasn't any need. No one's going to leap out at you, no matter which way you come in. It isn't that sort of evening.'

Cutter dropped his hand and gave a weary sigh. He did not bother to whisper when he spoke. 'Christ,' he said. 'That woman.'

'What woman?' said Octavia.

'So much for that plan,' said Cutter in disgust. 'And it wasn't the easiest of shots, mark you. Near enough to eighty feet, and an awkward item to put a spin on, I can tell you.'

'What did you throw, sir?' said Gideon. It was not what he ought to have said, now that they were free to speak again, but he was genuinely curious.

'Damned if I know,' said Cutter with a loose shrug. 'Some wicked-looking fellow with a dozen claws on him. He was encased in good thick crystal, is all I know, so he served the purpose. Or he might have.'

'It might have been priceless, sir.'

The Inspector scratched his ear. 'So it might. It isn't now.'

'Oh, for heaven's sake,' said Octavia. 'What woman?'

Cutter shook his head again and cast his eyes up. 'You'll see. She will introduce herself, no doubt. Right, let's get along to this little show. And pay no mind to what you just heard. Whatever kind of evening she is planning, I don't expect to enjoy it much.'

*

They found Mrs Lytton in the gallery of birds. She had resumed her pacing as she waited, and as they descended the steps to the cavernous entrance hall, the source of the sound became unmistakeable. It came from the arched entranceway to their right, flanked by a pair of raptors whose wings flared in stilled menace almost to the bounds of their cases.

Gideon's eye was drawn, too, to the opposite wall, where a great tableau of bones hung in an alcove. It was a plaster cast, he supposed, of remains that had been hopelessly sundered before their entombment. He glimpsed the segments of a colossal spine and the lipped plate of a shattered pelvis, but he could make nothing of the remaining shards. Nor could he decipher much, at this distance, of the gilt lettering on the frame. Somewhere in what was now Sussex, he gathered, a creature beyond his conception had once lived and died.

Perhaps it was no great loss. Creatures beyond his conception seemed to be living and dying all about him.

Cutter kept a step or two in front as he led them into the gallery, directing Gideon to follow on his left side. 'In case there is shooting,' he murmured. 'It will be right-handed shooting, most likely. As I said, I can answer for you, but not for Miss Temerity Gallivant here.'

Octavia gave him a scornful look. 'I can tell you're pleased with that. Did you think of it just now?'

They carried on at a measured pace. Cutter was no doubt mindful that their approach would be clearly heard. He would not want to appear timid, but he would be mindful too that Mrs Lytton might have placed hirelings anywhere about them. This grand gallery was not a single hall like the others they had seen but an arrangement of annexes about a broad central aisle. The rooms they passed were hushed. They glimpsed sullen corvids, attentive owls, swifts poised like brushed glyphs against a pallid backcloth. Nothing stirred in the shadows.

In the last hall, at the end of the gallery, all the lamps were lit. They saw the scaffold first, hung with great dust cloths. They saw the foot of a ladder, slack folds of rope, the scuffed ribbon of a measuring tape. Mrs Lytton was on the platform of the scaffold, still tirelessly pacing. They saw the drifting hem of her ivory gown first, and the immaculate matching shoes.

She greeted them before they were fully in sight. 'So good of you to come,' she called out. Her stride did not falter in the least. 'And only a little late. You could have avoided that, if not for your diversionary antics. Honestly, what did you imagine I'd do? Send someone dashing out to the right, while you swooped in from the left? What was the point?'

Cutter gave no answer until they had passed under the archway and stood in full sight before the scaffold. His sour glance slid past her, taking the measure of the scene. The structure dominated the gallery, rising to fifteen feet or so at its uppermost railings. The exhibits at its base had been shunted aside to leave a clear aisle, so that those approaching the platform did so in the manner of supplicants admitted to a throne room. No doubt that was the intended effect.

The man behind Mrs Lytton was elderly, though his lean frame and hawkish features must once have lent him a commanding presence. His glare was arresting even now, but it was not what Gideon had noticed first. What he had noticed first was that the elderly man was sitting in the wheeled chair of an invalid, and that he was bound to it at his ankles and wrists.

'The point of it,' said Cutter, 'was to make you reveal something of yourself, which you duly did. We've had a similar conversation once before, if I'm not mistaken.'

Mrs Lytton came to halt at last. Resting her hands lightly on the platform's makeshift railing, she turned to look down at them. 'Ah,' she said, fluttering her fingertips. 'I see you've noticed my guest. Don't worry, I shall introduce you in due course. I didn't reveal *that*, did I? And that was the only surprise I had prepared for you. No lurking mob, no deadly trap, no knives in the dark. Are you terribly disappointed?'

Gideon had let his gaze slip aside at the mention of knives in the dark. He resolved to be more careful. No doubt there was much he did not know about Mrs Lytton, but their first meeting had left him with certain clear impressions. She was not, he felt sure, a person given to overlooking small details.

Cutter held her gaze for a moment, then turned away to survey the rest of the room. 'Am I disappointed?' he said. He was noting the obscure spaces between the display cabinets, and among the cornices and buttresses overhead. He was puzzling out the contours of the deep arches set into the opposite wall, though these were partly hidden by the drapes that hung from the scaffold. 'I was born disappointed, Mrs Lytton, so you had little work to do there. You're making an effort, all the same. I've gone to a deal of trouble tonight, having been in two minds about setting out in the first place. And what do I find at the finish of it all? I find you got up like Juliet on her balcony, all set for a night of preening and purring, and I find some elder statesman tied to a wheelchair.'

He covered a gaping yawn.

'That is false imprisonment, madam. I do not get worked up over petty torts, most days, but in your case I might bestir myself. I must ask that you release that fellow before I climb up and do it myself. After that I might hear you out, if you can keep your crowing and cackling to a minimum.'

'Oh, Inspector,' said Mrs Lytton, spreading her fingers in luxuriation. 'I'd forgotten how splendidly diverting you are. Do feel free to try climbing up here. But a chair with *wheels*? On a platform this high? One need hardly strain to imagine it. And besides, you'd have quite wasted your journey. I brought you here to make certain revelations that will interest you. You don't mean to squander that chance, surely? Shall I make those introductions, then?'

She turned briefly to the man in the wheelchair, whose lip curled in disgust, then her gaze alighted on Gideon. He held himself rigidly and strove to keep a neutral countenance. She smiled sweetly at this. 'Sergeant Bliss, yes? I fear you've suffered a misadventure since our last meeting, yet here you are looking every inch the dauntless foot soldier. Aren't you precious. Tell me, did you bring your little notebook?'

Gideon felt a surge of loathing rise in him, and for once he was not compelled to babble a response. He swallowed once and fixed his gaze on the base of the scaffold.

'Oh, dear,' said Mrs Lytton mildly. 'I've hurt someone's feelings. It's a habit of mine, I confess. Now, this rather tousled-looking young lady in barely acceptable clothing. It's Miss Hillingdon, isn't it, who plies a trade in newspapers, of all things. Which is odd, because I feel sure I've seen you in tolerably good company. And in better clothes, come to that.'

'You have,' said Octavia curtly, at which Gideon registered a momentary surprise. 'I remember you, Mrs Lytton, or I remember not liking you. And I feel sure you've enquired more closely than that.'

'Oh, don't be unsporting,' said Mrs Lytton. 'You'd have done the same, I'm sure. That *is* what you do, isn't it? And I discovered that we share – how can I put it – a sort of kinship, I suppose. Isn't that startling?'

Gideon ventured a glance in Octavia's direction. He noticed a stripe of something tarry on her cheek – she must have handled something as they passed through the attics – and it adumbrated her look of fierceness. 'We share nothing,' she said with cold emphasis. 'Why don't you get on with your little performance? I imagine you'll prove my point.'

'Ah, perfect.' Mrs Lytton affected a shiver of delight. 'How perfectly you're all delivering your lines. It's so much as I hoped it would be. Oh, but wait. I've overlooked someone. Where's that trusted associate of yours, that winsome colonial with the good tailor? What was his name?'

'You know his name, madam, and I'll warrant you know he is not a colonial but a Frenchman. In any case, you didn't invite him.'

'Ah, yes, a Frenchman, but *un Français par le sang versé*, is that not so? Your very own legionary, Inspector, who once spilled blood for the Third Republic. And now he spills it for you? You must feel quite the potentate. And no, I didn't invite him, since it hardly seemed necessary. One doesn't invite the reaper. One simply accepts that he will make an appearance. But never mind, I suppose I must get on. Without further ceremony, then, I am pleased to present Sir Austin Gault, formerly of – well, where should I begin, when he has held so many offices? Which should I pick, Sir Austin? Oh, and don't be boorish. Say how-do-you-do to our visitors.'

Sir Austin made a seething sound, and for a moment Gideon thought he meant to spit at Mrs Lytton's feet. 'I told him,' he said. His voice was coldly forceful, whatever his infirmities. 'I told that fool you were a mistake. Never listened. And never whipped you when it might have made a difference.'

Mrs Lytton wore a necklace whose principal stone was a marquise-cut sapphire of arresting brilliance. She caressed it lightly. 'He spoiled me, you mean? Oh, but he didn't. I wasn't his favourite, remember. It's just that his methods were more refined than yours. And we'll come to the question of whipping during your testimony, so do be patient. Well, now that we've dispensed with the formalities—'

'We haven't,' said Cutter.

Mrs Lytton tilted her head by a small increment. 'Haven't we, Inspector? You puzzle me.'

'You haven't introduced yourself.'

'Again, you mystify me. I introduced myself at our first meeting, which was a passably memorable occasion. My elderly uncle had been skewered in the neck. Do you recall it? But since you appear to be insisting, I am Mrs Sylvia Lytton, widow of Mr Nathaniel Lytton, whose merchant bank still bears that name, and niece of the late Aneurin Considine, Commander of the Most Excellent Order of the British Empire. Are you satisfied now? Have I been sufficiently heralded?'

'You were not Considine's niece, madam. He had no brothers or sisters. And you'd been married to your banker for all of four months when he was trampled to death under his own town coach. You came away from that with a name, and no doubt a good deal besides, but you still lacked a few necessary items. A registered birth, for one.'

Gideon risked a glance in Cutter's direction, since this had taken him by surprise. The Inspector had not strained himself unduly during their many visits to registry offices, and he had certainly not revealed any discoveries of his own.

Mrs Lytton remained silent for a moment, but if she was unsettled she gave no sign of it. 'Is that it? Is that your great coup? Honestly, Inspector, you're betraying your ignorance again. Assuming identities is only disgraceful if you're ordinary. For us, for people of consequence, it's positively encouraged. It's only the rabble who think pedigree matters, you know. Oh, it's talked about, but only out of desperation. The dukes who have to borrow from me to heat their houses, they prate on about lines going back to Agincourt, but the people who *matter*, who are depended upon? We have our places because we whored out the right daughter, or we lay still under the right dotard, or we paid for the right war. All it means is that you've done what you must, and in this country there is nothing, *nothing*, that matters more than doing what must be done. That's why we're here, as a matter of fact.'

She paced a little way along the platform, gazing about the grand chamber with an air of proprietorial satisfaction. Finding another vantage point that pleased her, she came to a halt and spread her hands. 'So, then. Some preliminaries. No doubt you've been wondering about my chosen venue. Why the South Kensington Museum? Why the bird gallery, for goodness' sake? The reasons are mostly dull and pragmatic, I'm afraid, though I confess the birds are of some small private significance. I wanted a setting that would confer a certain solemnity, you see. I also wanted a raised platform of robust construction – you'll see why in just a bit – and, well, this place naturally suggested itself. I'm on a lot of Boards, as you might imagine, so there were no formidable obstacles. And as luck would have it, they're installing a new exhibit here – suspending a giant albatross from the ceiling, would you believe. Evidently they're not at all superstitious.

'As to the nature of these proceedings, well, consider them a sort of tribunal. I won't rehearse what you already know beyond the bare essentials. There have been other murders since my uncle's, and it won't have escaped your attention that the victims were all men of considerable standing. You've formed certain impressions, I'm sure, and of course you'll have gathered items of evidence. I don't have all the details, you'll be heartened to hear, but I gather that it was all rather lurid. Messages daubed in blood, and so on. Melodrama remains alluring, I suppose, to the untutored mind.

'Again, you'll have formed certain impressions. And meanwhile, the doughty Miss Hillingdon has been rootling about in cupboards and uncovering what she imagines are secrets. And they are secrets, I suppose, to people like you. To some of us, though, they're just souvenirs.'

'There,' said Octavia quietly. 'I did say you'd prove it.'

'Hmm?' Mrs Lytton paused, stroking her clavicle with a white-gloved fingertip. 'Oh, yes. My irredeemable wickedness. The great moral gulf that separates us. But that was nothing, my dear. Just wait. You began, as I was saying, to suspect that you'd stumbled upon an old conspiracy, and that the murders you were investigating were acts of retribution, deeds borne of *sæva indignatio* – of savage indignation – and meant to exact atonement for unspeakable offences against innocents. That was the general flavour of it, yes?

'Well, let's get that much out of the way, then. There *was* a conspiracy, though I don't like using such a grubby term in this instance. Yes, these men performed duties that necessitated a degree of secrecy, but so do many of the Crown's loyal servants. Would you have us advertise all our methods? And if we did, how long do you suppose we'd keep our position in the world?

'However, I will allow that these particular servants of the Crown were granted broader latitude than is common, and that they may have misused that latitude on occasion. Their little experiment did yield some notable successes, but it seems there were quite a few mishaps along the way. I say *seems* because I'd never much looked into it until recently. I wasn't terribly curious, to be truthful. But this recent unpleasantness hasn't left me with much choice.'

'What concern was it of yours?' said the Inspector. 'We've established that you were nothing to Considine, so you had no dog in the race.'

'I assure you, Inspector, that I was many things to Sir Aneurin. Some of them would shock you. And now I'm many things to many other people. The world has changed since these old men were given their medals and put out to pasture, but our institutions endure. I have many dogs in many races, to put it in your own coarse terms, and among them is the preservation of those institutions. And that, I confess, is why you found me less than hospitable during your visit to Carlton House Gardens. And it didn't end there, I'm afraid.'

'I had little hope that it would,' Cutter answered. 'It was you who set Massey on me, I suppose, to croon to me about empire and glory while his lackeys were crawling halfway up my arse.'

'I took certain steps, yes. And with Massey, it's all so convenient. That imbecile has soiled himself so thoroughly that it doesn't even cost anything. But compromised halfwits don't make for dependable allies, so I never had terribly high hopes. And besides, I soon had a change of heart.'

'Your tender nature got the better of you, did it?'

'I revised my calculations. It wasn't terribly complicated. The more the bodies piled up, the less concerned I became with defending the old guard. And I don't mean that in the way you might imagine. It wasn't a matter of loyalty, much less of personal affection. It was a matter of keeping the doors locked and the house tidy. But there are only so many mutilated bodies one can make excuses for. It was growing rather tedious. People were paying attention, as you know, and disturbing rumours were getting about. And perhaps it was misguided of me, hoping that you'd get on with your job and put an end to it all. I'm sure you're a perfectly adequate policeman, for all your unpleasantness of demeanour, but I ought to have known better. After all, I knew what none of the victims knew, or not until their last moments. I knew what you were up against.'

The Inspector had begun wandering about the gallery. He paused now before a display case and spoke without turning his head. 'I might surprise you there, Mrs Lytton.'

'You mistake my meaning, Inspector. I am referring to the murderer. To the murderer's particular nature and abilities.'

'I understood your meaning. And I said I might surprise you.'

'Well, I'm sure that demonstrates admirable resolve, but the point may soon be moot. You may not be able to help me in the way I once imagined, but we can still bring these matters to a satisfactory conclusion. We can still come to an agreement.'

'Can we now?' Cutter was examining what might have been an ostrich egg. 'Mrs Lytton, I believe I have spoken plainly through all our dealings. I wouldn't get into a lifeboat with you, never mind an agreement.'

'Wouldn't you, though?' Mrs Lytton said. 'Not even if I could grant your wishes? *All* your wishes?'

'I wish you would shut your squawk hole and climb down from there so that I can get home to my bed. Will you grant that one?'

'Don't be tiresome, Inspector. You aren't nearly as inscrutable as you think, you know. You want to solve these murders because you can't bear the thought of failing, but your heart isn't in it. You want to know what these men did, all those years ago, but it isn't so that you can choose the lesser evil. Your duty wouldn't allow that, would it? It's so that you'll know what you must live with.'

Cutter turned slowly to face her. His expression was empty. He said nothing.

Mrs Lytton regarded him placidly. 'It needn't end that way, Inspector. There's still time, you see. Your murderer hasn't finished yet. One name has yet to be stricken out.'

'And what name might that be?'

She gave a brisk sigh. 'Haven't you been following? Sir Austin Gault is the last surviving conspirator.'

'Is he, indeed? If he is, he was once known by another name. I daresay it's the name he would be remembered by.'

Mrs Lytton studied him. 'How curious,' she said. 'Is that a supposition of your own, or was it one of Miss Hillingdon's discoveries? He was known as the Dean, since you mention it. He held a position of authority. He presided over an institution called the Chapel. And that, one imagines, is why he's last on the list.'

Cutter scratched his cheek. His expression was bland. 'The man in charge, eh?'

She stared at him a moment longer. 'Just so. The man in charge. May I continue? Finding himself in this invidious position, Sir Austin grew anxious for his safety. Certain friends of mine were moved by his plight, and I was prevailed upon to bring him under my protection. Naturally, my friends and I imposed certain conditions. We demanded a full accounting of past misdeeds, duly signed and witnessed. Sir Austin was good enough to agree, on the understanding that his testimony would be seen by no one beyond our little circle of friends. And that was just what I intended, at the time. Forgive me, Inspector, am I boring you?'

When Gideon glanced across the hall, he saw that Cutter had wandered to another display case and was bent over it as if absorbed. He leaned over further, making a close study of some diminutive nesting bird, and rested his hands on the back of the cabinet. Gideon might easily have missed what happened next. The Inspector had his broad back to the room, and he appeared to be doing no more than tutting in fascination over one particular specimen. Then he altered his position by a fraction, and as he did so the fingers of his left hand twitched almost imperceptibly.

Gideon turned away, fearful of drawing Mrs Lytton's notice, and it took him some moments to make sense of what he had seen. Cutter had slipped something into the shadows behind the cabinet. It was the slender package wrapped in dun-coloured paper and this time Gideon remembered where he had seen it before. It had been at Leggett's, on the day of their visit to Pruitt's yard. It was the package he had with him when he spoke of fearing for his life.

'I'm listening,' said the Inspector, not hurrying to rise and turn around. 'It was just what you intended, but then you had your little change of heart.'

'I reflected on the matter, yes.' Mrs Lytton's tone was chilly, but Gideon could not tell if there was suspicion in it. Like the woman whose voice he had heard earlier, Mrs Lytton seemed to consider her every inflection. 'I told you that my first concern was to keep our house tidy, but as I digested Sir Austin's little memoir, I came to see that we'd gone beyond that point. Sometimes the house can no longer be cleaned, Inspector. Sometimes it must be burned down.'

Cutter turned from the cabinet with a show of weariness, swiping his hand over his face to cover another yawn. 'Tell me if I have this right, Mrs Lytton. You brought me here to hand over some pensioner you have trussed up, and you have it in your head that I am going to wheel him off to the Yard on the strength of a confession that was made – by your own account, mind – under duress and false pretences. For someone who makes so much of being well informed, you have a poor grasp of our criminal laws.'

'The confession will stand, Inspector. You'll find it tallies closely with evidence already in your possession – Miss Hillingdon, I imagine, will find it especially fascinating – but what matters more is that Sir Austin will not contest a word of it. Why do you think he has so little to say for himself, though he has sat here through all of this? It's because he has nowhere else to go but the dank cell that awaits him. There's nowhere else he will be safe.'

Cutter chafed at his jaw with the back of his hand. 'You have me at a loss, madam. You said I would have all my heart's desires. You said you would make revelations, and you have gone one better. You have served me up a head on a platter. I am moved nearly to tears by it all. But you said I would have my murderer too, so that my cup would fairly— wait now, I told you I was wanting in education. Am I mixing up my proverbs, Bliss?'

Gideon was mildly startled. 'Sir? Oh, I see. The head on the platter is from the Gospel of Mark, if that is what you mean, whereas the cup that runneth over is from *Psalms*, but perhaps . . .' Gideon had glanced again at the recess behind the cabinet. The package was gone. He struggled to find the thread of his thought, but the Inspector relieved him of the need.

'Right you are, Bliss. Chapter and verse, as ever. My sergeant is a learned fellow, Mrs Lytton, and I am often struck by his uncanny insights. Only tonight he said a most peculiar thing about— no, but never mind that now. You promised me my murderer, much to my amazement, but there's something I can't puzzle out. If I had the murderer in irons, then Gault here would be out of harm's way and he would have no use for my jail cell. Do you see why I am in difficulty?'

Mrs Lytton tugged a wrinkle from one of her spotless gloves. 'I see that you're putting on a performance of your own, Inspector. You will have your butcher once this particular lamb has put himself beyond reach. In the meantime, those long knives must be left to glitter in the darkness. You must be patient. I have proven myself capable, and when the time comes, I will prove it again.'

The Inspector drew in a long breath. He shook his head slowly, and his manner became almost sorrowful. 'Do you know, Mrs

Lytton, you have raised yourself a little in my estimation. You put on a poor show the last time I saw you, but tonight you outdid yourself. I had to take hold of myself once or twice, since I was coming near to believing you. You have a gift, no doubt about it, and someone took trouble over your training. It's no wonder you have clawed your way to such high places. It does you credit, I suppose, for you had a long way to climb.'

Mrs Lytton lifted her chin, her fingertips poised beneath her sapphire. 'Are you testing your wiles against mine, Inspector? You know nothing about me beyond what I have chosen to reveal, and I have chosen very carefully.'

Cutter shook his head again. 'Not carefully enough, Mrs Lytton. You told me very little about the man you called your uncle, but you thought to mention that he had an orchid named for him. I have very little schooling, as you know, but I have enough to make use of a library. Librarians are helpful and obliging souls, I have often found. With their help, I discovered that Sir Aneurin had named a good many orchids, though most of those names were great clumps of Latin that I could make nothing of. One librarian was good enough to puzzle over them with me, and I learned that he had given himself a whole species, and from another he had bred two crosses – cultivars, I believe they are called. When that is done, it seems, an ordinary English name can be put at the end of all the Latin. The names he put were Cora and Lydia.'

Mrs Lytton made no answer to this, but her eyes never once left his face.

'It's a common practice, I'm told, and it's often done to honour a loved one. A wife or a sister. A daughter, commonly. But Sir Aneurin never married, and we know he had no sister. He had no daughters either, or none that he ever acknowledged. Were you ever shown those orchids, Mrs Lytton? Did they look like – what was it now? – like "dishevelled slippers"? Or were they prettier things than that?'

When Mrs Lytton spoke at last, her voiced had hardened. 'The offer I made can be withdrawn, Inspector. I have made provisions for an unhappy outcome. Is that the outcome you want?'

'Oh, you made provisions, right enough. I counted four of your men as I came through the grounds, though it seems they were told not to trouble me on the way in. Did you tell them not to trouble Milo either, or should I offer up a little prayer for them?'

Mrs Lytton's gaze flickered away for an instant. 'Inspector, I will state my position only once more. I have taken a great deal of trouble, to say nothing of considerable risks—'

'Oh, you've taken risks, all right. I doubt you have any notion. How many did you have guarding that man on the way here? Half a dozen? You took no chances, anyway, since you knew how closely you would be watched. And you did not want the bait taken before it was time. By the by, Sir Austin there seems to lack your discipline. He is trying to slip his knots already. Either he has forgotten that he is playing the part of a prisoner, or something has made him nervous. I wonder what it could be.'

Gideon had missed this, being so much taken up with the Inspector's stream of talk, but Sir Austin was indeed struggling against his bonds. His eyes were scouring the far reaches of the gallery. He snarled in rage at Mrs Lytton. 'I warned you, you vain, witless *bitch*! Cut me loose, damn you! Cut me loose while there's still time!'

She did not so much as glance at him, only fluttering her fingers in dismissal. 'Oh, be quiet. I made those knots tight for a reason. Now, Inspector, let us be candid with one another at last. If there is indeed a ghost at this feast, our positions are not altered. I'm standing twenty feet above the floor, and I have you and your sergeant for sentries. You *will* do your duty, if it comes to it. You'll take no joy in it, I'm sure, but you can hardly do otherwise. You're an officer of some standing, and you could not very well creep unseen into a prominent public building in South Kensington.'

'Funny you should mention it, Mrs Lytton. All I will say is that you're not the only one who plans ahead. As for doing my duty, well, there's time enough for that. It wouldn't be doing my duty, anyway. Not here, not tonight. It would be doing your bidding. I've made my share of mistakes, God knows, but I will not make that one.'

Mrs Lytton averted her face for a moment. Her fingers traced the taut contours of her neck. 'It's your only chance,' she said quietly. 'He is the last. After that, she will disappear.'

She. Mrs Lytton had not used the word until now. She had danced around it with curious artfulness, just as the Inspector had for so long. Gideon watched for his response.

'Enough, Mrs Lytton.' Cutter bent his head for a moment, scratching absently at his nape. 'Enough,' he said again. 'I'm going to tell a little story, if I still have time. When I was an eager young sergeant, I was out on my beat one night. It was a balmy evening in May, and I had just turned out of Drury Lane to cross the court towards the opera house. Likely I had it in my mind that there would be young ladies climbing the steps in their summer silks. I was a younger man then, as I say, and still inclined to scent promise in a gentle breeze.

'If I hadn't been in such a daze, I might've been quicker in my wits. There was a crowd in front of the opera house, right enough, but they were all huddled about some commotion on the steps. The only ladies I saw were the ones shrieking about the blood and the wickedness of it, about the poor young gentleman, so soft in his manners and hardly more than a babe. Some said the poor young prince, but that proved to be high of the mark. It makes no difference who he was, if I'm to be truthful.

'It was no more than luck that I saw what followed after. If I had come upon the scene by another way, I would have gone straight up the steps and ended up doing little good beyond roaring for order and jotting down nonsense. But I had turned that corner for good or ill, and do you know, it was not even her that I saw first. It was the man pelting after her with his hat gone and the rest of his opera finery hanging half in tatters. I thought to myself, there's some upstanding fellow meaning to do half my job for me, but when he caught sight of me he gave me reason to wonder. There I was, a copper plain as day in a fresh-pressed uniform, but did he point and sing out, *look there, constable* or *stop that blackguard*? He did nothing like it. His face soured and closed up when he saw me, and he tucked in his chin to hide what he could of it. But by God, he was keeping up the chase as if his life depended on it.

'By the time I thought to turn and look for his villain, he was near to passing me by and I hadn't shaken my blundering stupor. It was a whole second before I saw her, and to this day I cannot tell if it was my own blind dithering or her gift for going unseen. But see her I did, in the next instant, and I can see her in that moment even now.

'I caught a flicker of pale silk, something between blue and grey. I wonder still if she didn't choose that fine gown for that reason alone. It was fit for the opera, no doubt, but it was also a very near match to the air of a May evening. In any event, I caught that flicker because she'd been running like a stone skimming a pond, but when she came to the corner – the same corner I'd just turned – well, I won't say she came to a halt, for she never did that entirely, but she seemed to fling herself into the air and pivot like a vane in a storm.

'When she touched the ground again, she was stretched out like a drawn bow, one knee thrust out in front of her and the other leg stretched back like no leg was ever meant to do. She had one arm gathered back, too, though I made that out too late. I had only half a heartbeat to take it all in – that she was barefoot under that gown, that she was hardly more than a child, for Christ's sake – and by then she was fixed on him. I saw her spread a hand low for balance, and I saw something glint above her shoulder, then her arm was flung out and already she was launching herself away again. The sound came a fraction later. A neat little sound, like someone halving an apple on a folded cloth.

'He was only two paces past me when it struck him, and the next I knew of it was that the upright young man was upright no longer. He was on the cobbles with his arms and legs all askew, and it was plain enough that nothing could be done for him. By rights I should have touched nothing, but I had myself half fooled already. I would be preserving evidence, or some such notion. There was not much thought in it, if I am honest.

'I had never seen a throwing knife before, so I was struck by how dainty the little handle looked. Hardly the size of my thumb – the weight is all in the blade, you see – and traced all about with little patterns of white gold. I whipped out a handkerchief, and I'm afraid I was none too delicate about wrenching it free. It was near enough buried in his right eye, is the fact of it, and there was no nice way of going about it.

'In the next moment, needless to say, I was whipping back around the corner of Drury Lane and I'll spare you most of the chase that followed. I will say that I found sense enough to grow puzzled after the first minute or so. I was a young man, to be sure, but I was galloping fit to burst my heart and I was barely keeping her in sight. And all the while I knew that she need only jink aside once to lose me, for it is all a maze of lanes and alleys between there and the river.

'Whatever her reasons, I stayed in the hunt for half a mile or more, but I believed by then – and I believe it still – that I stayed in it only for as long as she chose. And when she tripped – we were halfway over Waterloo Bridge by then – I was more than half in doubt about my turn of luck. Remember, I was a keen young copper, and I was not so filled with marvel at this creature that I could not see the glory in catching her. Narrow young lass or no, she had just put knives in two men, and one of them was something near to a prince. I doubted my luck, but I was not about to put it to waste.

'She was hardly stirring by the time I took hold of her, but there was not a mark on her and she sprang up in my grip like a willow sapling out of a bank. She seemed barely strained, though I was all in a lather and wheezing like a racehorse. For a while, I was fool enough to think I had collared the most docile little bird that was ever hauled into the nick. "It's only eighty-five yards to that police station," she said, meaning the Thames station, which stands just in the lee of that bridge. Eighty-five, mind you, not just shy of a hundred or anything that might have come out of a squint and a guess. "You can take me there, if you want. But first there are things I must tell you."

'I won't share the whole of her tale. Not all of it matters just now, and more to the point, not all of you deserve to hear it. But I will tell you what you should hear – you, Mrs Lytton, because you were something else before you were a heart of marble hung about with sapphires and ivory; and you, Gault, because for all your whips and your torments, it wasn't you who made her what she is.

'She told me they were taken, though I couldn't tell exactly what she meant. We were taken, she said, and we were remade. She told me that she didn't know her age then and could only guess at it now. Seventeen, she made it, and no doubt she was as exact in that as she could be. Eighty-five yards, remember. She told me how she learned what she was being fitted for, and of the children who were found to be unfit. Remember now that she had only the space of a short walk;

she must have known how small a hope she had of being believed. This tale of hers might have come out of some ancient storybook full of wicked witches and dark forests, but you cannot grasp what it was like without hearing her tell it. She talked like no young girl I ever encountered, and like no lunatic either. She had a voice like cold water, and though she was obliged to be quick, she never faltered once or uttered a single word that didn't fit into its place like a bead on a bracelet.

'For years afterwards, I doubted the account I just gave you. I told myself I had been lulled like a country simpleton, that I'd witnessed two murders and failed in the plainest of my duties only because the demon I hunted down wore torn silks and had the face of a tranquil child.

'I asked her about the man with the knife in his eye. He was there to watch over her, she said, and to see that the job got done. Because she had run, his last duty was to cut her throat and leave her in a gutter. I would find a knife and a pistol on him, she said, but I would find nothing else that might put a name to him. That much turned out to be true, by the by.

'By this time we had come a little over half the distance, and either I was not watchful or she gave no sign of her intention. The river was high after a spring flood, and I did take note of the quickness of the water. There were scraps of blossom scattered amongst all the wrack and the rubbish, and the water carried them like embers from a bellows. I think I was still set in my purpose when the moment came. I had her right arm braced hard to her shoulder blade and my left hand clamped tight over her shoulder, but maybe I knew in my heart that I might as well have my hands in a basket of eels.

'Whatever the case, what she said last was meant to give me a choice, I think, or the look of one. She said that dying was the only course left to her, though what she meant by dying I couldn't exactly tell. Maybe all she wanted was to disappear. Maybe she was just weary of it all. She said the boy on the steps was younger than she was – the boy she was sent to kill – and that she would've disobeyed if the soldier had not been so close. Then she said this. They wounded me to make me a knife, she said, meaning they raised her up to kill. They wounded me to make me a knife, but that is not how knives are made. I was always a knife and always a wound. I was never theirs to use. I want to lay myself down.

'So, that was my failing, whether I failed knowingly or not. She slipped from my grasp, or I let her slip. It makes no difference. She leapt from that bridge like a blue-grey knife into the blue-grey water, and she was beyond seeing before she ever broke the surface. She laid herself down, and for sixteen years I hoped she was at rest, one way or the other.'

'Inspector,' said Gideon, taking a pace towards him. He hardly knew what he meant to say. He had not made sense of it all yet. All he knew was that it was a secret that might just as easily have been his own, for he would surely have done just the same.

But Cutter only shook his head. *Not now.* Octavia, who was standing nearer, stretched out a hand and laid it for a moment upon the Inspector's arm. That arm was shaking slightly, a thing Gideon had never witnessed, and the Inspector's chest was settling as if after some great exertion.

'Well,' said Mrs Lytton. She had resumed her pacing during the Inspector's story, though Gideon had been only faintly aware of it. Sir Austin, too, had begun writhing again, his wheelchair rattling forlornly against the scaffold boards, or perhaps he had never left off. 'That was a pretty version of the tale, I'm sure, and you yourself seem moved even if no one else is.'

Cutter said nothing. His gaze had settled somewhere in the empty air.

'I'm not sure that you've achieved anything, though,' Mrs Lytton continued. 'Well, beyond unburdening yourself. Your information comes from an untrustworthy source. You may feel that you know this deranged person, but you're surely not depending on her to save the hour. Even with all I know, I can only predict so much. And if she does come, so be it. I'm still standing out of reach, and at a moment's notice I can deprive her of her final prize.' She paused by Sir Austin's chair and tapped at its frame with the toe of her finely sculpted shoe. 'Isn't that right, Dean?'

Gideon started forward again. '*Inspector*,' he said, making no effort to keep the urgency from his voice. He could not tell what Cutter might know, but he could surely keep it to himself no longer. 'Inspector, she is—'

The Inspector lifted a hand to silence him, but he met Gideon's look with the briefest of skimming nods. When he addressed Mrs Lytton, he didn't bother to look up. 'You are right, madam. I don't know where she is at this very moment, but I do know where she was eight minutes ago. Not ten minutes, mark you. Eight. And I know where she was nineteen minutes before that. Is that good enough for you? Oh, and one other thing. You may be out of my reach, but I'll warrant you're not out of hers. You're not the only one who keeps souvenirs. I held onto that throwing knife, the one I retrieved from the scene at the opera house. I kept it locked away for years, having little inclination to reminisce over it. Just lately, however, I discovered that it was one of a matched pair. Its twin was left on my doorstep the day before Sir Aneurin's death. By way of a calling card, I suppose, though I mistook its meaning at the time. In any case, I haven't much call for such items, even as keepsakes. I have returned them to their rightful owner. I'm sure she'll find a use for them.'

Mrs Lytton must have made sense of this a moment too late. She had paused again behind the railing, and at first she appeared only faintly quizzical, but in the next moment her gloved fingers tightened about the iron strut and she lifted her face to search the darkness.

The knife was soundless almost until the last instant, when it lodged itself with a terse whisper in the flawless stem of her throat. She raised her fingers to it with a look of slanted curiosity, then she made a harsh retching noise and guided herself to her knees. The blood had soaked her white glove and was spilling freely from the crook of her wavering arm.

They surged forward at almost the same moment. Octavia was quickest to rouse herself, but Cutter swept past her and turned with his arms spread. '*No!*' His face was hard and earnest. 'No. You can't put yourselves in her way, not now. I will . . . leave it to me. I will try, for all the good it will do.'

He was skittering backwards as he spoke, and with a final upward glance he turned and broke for the ladder.

The shape appeared – *she* appeared – before he had taken a full stride, unfurling herself impossibly from behind an immense buttress and flinging herself sidelong through a great chasm of vacant air. She alighted on a slender brink of cornice-work, and Gideon glimpsed a head shorn to an intimate stubble. He saw dark and restive eyes, their hollows deepened by ashy smudges.

She stirred again, unfolding the black cipher of her body. She was clothed for the shadows, but for ease of movement above all else. She wore close-fitting hose and a vest of the same dark and sturdy cloth. Her lean upper arms were bare, but they were smeared and streaked with inky grease. Her forearms were wrapped to the wrists with what might have been blackened bandages. Her knives too were strapped close – across her back, along her calf, at her hips.

Crouching to meet the curve of the ceiling, she scissored across a ribbon of stone fully twenty-five feet above the floor. Then she ducked beneath another soaring buttress, made the briefest of inward calculations and reached up to brace the great beam of stone between her hands. If Gideon had known what she meant to do, he might have looked away in horror, but she had swung herself outwards before he had time to puzzle out her movements. Perhaps she had a surer grip than he could make out from so far below, her fingertips driven into fine furrows of stonework, but he was by no means sure of it. As nearly as he could tell, she hung for an instant with her whole weight supported by nothing more than the fierce pressure between her flattened hands.

As she swung backwards, she tucked her feet up, making a pendulum of her body, and in a half-breath she had catapulted outwards, her shape flickering into the empty darkness. She came down on the edge of the platform before Cutter got above the third rung of the ladder, shuddering only slightly as her splayed limbs dispersed the shock. Then she straightened with quiet decorum and approached the head of the ladder. 'Don't,' she said simply, looking down at him. For a moment her still face took on a curious innocence. 'Please,' she added.

The Inspector looked briefly irresolute, then he let his shoulders slump and lowered himself to the ground. 'You know I can't,' he said, but already he had drawn back by a pace. 'I can't look away again, not this time.'

She seemed to consider this, though not for long. 'Wait,' she said. 'I have to look first.'

Without explaining further, she crossed the platform and crouched over Mrs Lytton's still form. 'Lydia,' she said. There was no regret in her voice. There was nothing Gideon recognised. 'I would not have looked for you, even knowing what you became. You should not have chosen this.'

She rose and moved on to Gault. He wore a look of dogged contempt, but he would not meet her eyes. She stooped to test his bonds. 'Are you afraid?' she said quietly.

His lip curled, and beneath it a pallid tongue slid and darted. 'Afraid of *what?*' His voice was still strident, but something congealed rattled at its edges. 'Of a crazed runt come to bite the hand that fed her? I should have done it when I had the chance. I should have tossed you in a pit like the worthless mongrel you were.'

For a moment she seemed not to have heard him, then she drew her arm back and her knuckles whipped like a gate chain across his cheek. When he hauled himself straight in his chair, his face was pale beneath the bright lacerations.

'Are you afraid?' she said again.

His mouth twitched once, but he did not speak again.

'Good,' she said. 'You must know how it will be, with you. You must remember.'

She returned to Cutter's side of the platform without the slightest sign of agitation. 'I know what you think you must do,' she said. 'And you know I can't permit that, not yet. I listened to all you said. This will not end here, but it will end soon. I will tell you where and when. The last of them will be gone by then, so you need not see. You need not make a choice like this again, but I will give you an easier way. It will be over for me, and I will lay myself down again. I will not care then, if you decide that you must take me. But nothing is ever over. Everything is always happening again.'

'Christ,' said Cutter. 'I must be out of my mind.'

'You can go now,' she said. 'You can find them afterwards, like with the others. Her men, too, but I did not take all of those. Your friend in the fine clothes, he is skilled with his hands.'

The Inspector gave a weary grunt. 'He speaks highly of you too. What should we call you now? You told me the name they gave you, last time, but no doubt you rid yourself of all you were given.'

She reflected on this, and for the first time her smirched and unflinching face seemed to soften. 'Not all. I have another name now, but it is a name I might need. You can use it for now, the one from before.'

Cutter nodded. He studied her for a moment longer, seeming at once solemn and bewildered, then he turned away from the platform.

She came to the railing to watch them go, but neither Octavia nor Gideon had stirred yet. Her gaze settled on Miss Hillingdon first. 'You find out what is true, is that right? So that you can write it down for others to know?'

Octavia seemed mildly startled. 'Yes. I suppose so, yes.'

'Good. I shall send for you, too. You must write down what you see.'

She turned to Gideon. 'And you, the innocent. But you are no longer that, are you?'

Gideon had waited a long time to see her face, but studying it now was no easy matter. Her gaze was everywhere and nowhere. 'I am not . . . I am not sure that I know, miss.'

'Then come and see,' she said. 'All three of you. I will take you there. I will tell you the story of innocence. It's the first story they tell you, the first lie. You were born into a fragrant garden, they say, where the blossoms never fade. You can return to it, one day, if you repent your sins. Or if you commit the sins we want. It's a pretty story, a pretty lie. But I will show you the garden we were born into.' She glanced behind her. 'I will show you the garden, and the beasts that dwell there. You should go now. We will see each other again.'

Gideon coughed and shuffled, conscious of a ludicrous urge to bow before turning away. But she was already busying herself when he glanced upwards again, and he heard the scrape and clink of implements being readied. Yes. Yes, he should go now.

Octavia too was hesitating when he turned, seeming reluctant to let this go unwitnessed, but when she caught his eye, she gave a small, sad nod of acquiescence. Cutter was already waiting under the arch of the central aisle, his back to the gallery. Whatever he felt, he had squared his shoulders and made his choice. He set out down the hallway the moment he heard their footsteps behind him.

She must have waited, after seeing them go, to spare them what she could of what followed. But she did not wait long. Gideon heard the first lash of the whip before they had gone a third of the way, and the first of the screams was desolate but still defiant. Those that followed were not.

He did not hear her voice raised until they had reached the great central hall where the fragments of the ancient monster hung in their grotto, broken and unintelligible.

It was more forceful now, that voice, but still as precise and deliberate as calligraphy.

'What is my name?' it was saying, with rising insistence. '*What is my name?*'

Thirteen

T*he place that* had once been the Chapel was not yet a ruin, but it was plainly long abandoned. It stood in a fold of low and listless hills, among fields poor enough to look poisoned. It was cloistered by shattered outhouses and yards choked with ragwort and dock. Its turreted core might have been some ancient remnant, but its jutting brick wings could never have risen to anything like grandeur. They might have housed a school of middling ambitions – Gideon had known such places – or the pensioners of some disbanded guild. Even its trees were unremarkable; a scattering of field maples, common alder and ash, stirring late into leaf.

Only a venturesome wild cherry showed any life or colour. An overlooked trespasser, it had spread within touching distance of the broadest wing, and it was alight now with pale coral blossom. One of the upper windows was vacant and staring, perhaps smashed by a wind-tossed bough. The rest were boarded or glaucous with dust, blinded or near to unseeing.

The Chapel was isolated and dismal, and it was enclosed in part by high walls, but so were many buildings of no special importance. It resembled no prison or barracks that Gideon had ever seen, though it had no doubt been chosen for that very reason. It lay somewhere between Guildford and Aldershot, thirty-odd miles southwest of London, and was reached by farm tracks that wound through spireless and undistinguished country. They came to the gates having walked the last two miles and changed at the last village from a coach to a cart. If anything had been altered in Cutter by the events of the last days, it was not his habit of wariness.

'That chain looks new,' said the Inspector, rattling it with a dour look. He had not spoken much during the journey, and his humour had been unassailably sombre. 'Maybe the place is to be put on the market.'

Gideon surveyed the rutted track beyond the gate. A cart with a split axle was slumped amongst the weeds, as was the sunken carcass of its pony. 'I wonder if that is likely, sir.'

Cutter lifted his hat and gently thumbed his temple. 'No, Bliss. It's not likely.'

Gideon dabbled with the toe of his boot at a slate-dark puddle. Octavia had made him a present of a stout new pair and their imperviousness still enthralled him. 'Might I trouble you to check your—'

'We have not come too early, Bliss, or too late. It is two minutes before noon, and no doubt she will be punctual. She leaves very little to chance, as far as I can tell.'

They fell silent again, though Octavia's pencil was already flickering swiftly over the pages of a fresh notebook. Gideon wondered how she would describe the scene, and which details she would seize upon that he himself had missed. The Inspector turned, roused from his ruminations, and spent a moment studying the pitted lane behind them.

'This friend of yours, Miss Hillingdon, and his equipment – is it a great load to haul, would you say? These roads are hardly better than rat runs, and no doubt there are all manner of delicate parts. What about all those bottles of chemicals? Are they liable to explode if they're jiggled about?'

Octavia paused in dissatisfaction, then struck something out. 'What?' she said, looking up. 'Oh, that. It's just a box on a tripod, for heaven's sake. I had one fastened to my bicycle once. Don't you have cameras at Scotland Yard?'

'We have one that I know of, and an ill-tempered Frenchman who will let no one near it. I can't say I blame him either. There are fellows in the Yard who would find a way to break a crowbar. In any case, we might find nothing worth taking pictures of.'

'Is that really what you are expecting?'

Cutter's lip curled. 'No,' he said. 'I am expecting things that no one should ever set eyes on.'

'All the more reason, then,' said Octavia, returning to her notes. 'That's what photographs are for.'

She appeared silently, the woman who had called them here, and she appeared *otherwise*. Gideon turned his head, his eye drawn by a startled blackbird, and found her standing behind them as if waiting to be summoned. It was a moment he would later tease apart, uncertain whether he had indeed recognised her or merely seized upon the only possibility that made sense.

Her eyes seemed unmistakeable, in the next moment, as did the unearthly stillness of her face, but he wondered if those eyes were truly and knowably hers, or if her still face – like her distant and affectless voice – was simply what remained when she subtracted all the others. At any other time, he felt sure, she might have approached him in any guise she chose, speaking with a voice he had never heard and showing a face that could be seen only once.

'Miss Nightingale,' Gideon said, inclining his head. He felt reluctant to use her name, having learned it in the hours after they first met, but politeness seemed to require it. It surely required a *Miss*, too, as did her manner of dress. Gideon remained almost entirely unschooled in ladies' fashions, but the grey woollen skirts she wore beneath a matching jacket struck him as quietly elegant, the sort of thing an established countrywoman might wear while touring her own gardens. Her hair was drawn up neatly beneath a simple dark-ribboned bonnet, and was remarkable – was unnerving – only insofar as it seemed wholly and natively her own.

Cutter and Octavia had turned at his greeting, though Nightingale herself chose to ignore it for now. Her eyes flitted over them briefly. 'I've changed,' she said, not quite neutrally. Then, sensing their misunderstanding: 'Not my clothes. Those are a practical necessity, though they help in other ways. I mean that I might speak differently. Sometimes that's a practical necessity too. Today it's because of the things I must say. It's something I do.'

'Fair enough,' said Cutter, having weighed this. 'I'm afraid I'm stuck with the one voice, myself.'

She adjusted her lips, to show that she recognised the joke. 'All right. It's this way.'

She set off smoothly, then paused after only a few paces. 'Just Nightingale,' she said, without turning. 'Not Miss. I didn't keep that part. Only the things I wanted.'

Nightingale moved as carefully as she spoke, not slowly but seeming always to follow a cautiously chosen path. Crossing an untended field, she would weave aside at times, as if deferring to unseen presences. Coming to a gate left slightly ajar, she would slide through whatever gap remained, or widen it no more than she needed to.

She kept them at a small distance, too, as she led them through the grounds, so that Gideon had time to study her habits. Perhaps she had no habits left that were natural and unconscious, yet he could not help imagining her as a wary and silent child, threading her way with equal distrust among dangers and curiosities. He wondered if she had ever felt entirely happy or entirely sad, or if those ideas had held any meaning for her. He wondered, too, when she had come to recognise her own aptitude for ferocity. But perhaps that too had gone unquestioned.

I was always a knife.

He did not know what to feel about such a person. Nothing had prepared him for it, though he had once been a student of divinity. He had given much contemplation to sin and redemption, to the fallibility and imperfection of our natures, but nothing he remembered seemed adequate or apt. Those doctrines were rearing monoliths that could only ever be approached. They could not be carried out into the world and put to use, even in ordinary cases.

He had learned a little of the law too, now that he was charged with enforcing it, but the law was of less help still. In law this woman was plainly guilty of grave crimes, but in law, guilt was nothing more than a determination, a mark set against a name. The men she had murdered were guilty too, dyed to their deepest fibres by the harms they had done, but no mark would ever be set against their names. In law, guilt was only ever an ending, never a story, whereas innocence—

It is the first story they tell you, the first lie.

Yes, perhaps she was right. It was the story he had been told, certainly, and the story that had been carried forward with only fine adjustments since the time of Tertullian. We are made in God's image, but we are born far from the grace that He designed for us. We are stained from the first, and our native state is not innocence but adulteration. We are stained, too, to the very last, since mere righteousness cannot correct the fault in our nature. We may strive for redemption, but salvation must wait. We can be perfect only in death.

It was a story he had repeated to himself many times, without ever quite believing it. It was a story that shimmered and sang, but with the radiance of untouchable spheres and the voices of unearthly choirs. It was a story we could take no part in, which did not even concern us, much less belong to us. But if there were a truer one he could not imagine it, not even how it might begin.

Nightingale led them through an overgrown coach yard and halted before a doorway. They stood now almost at the junction of the principal wing and whatever tower or keep it had been built to adjoin.

'I have his keys now,' she said, 'so this will be easier.'

She saw that her meaning was not clear.

'He was called the Chancellor, the man I left for last. He never came here, not then, but he did afterwards. He was here yesterday.' She turned to Cutter. 'I'll take you to him when we've finished, so that you can do what you must. There isn't much to see. He was old, and it was quick. He never showed himself, so I didn't either.'

Here she paused, and for a moment her face became curiously lifeless. Then it changed.

'I want you to understand certain things, before we go inside.' Her voice was another instrument now, restrung and newly tempered. 'I'll show you a little of what we saw, but I haven't brought you here to excuse or explain myself. I wouldn't want to do that, even if I knew how. And you, all of you – you're not here to stand in judgement, or to weep in pity. You didn't live this, but you've lived. You're not apart from it. Do you understand? This is what we are, and it is what we do. All I did was make it complete.'

She seemed to rest for a time. Her show of feeling effaced itself as if from a slate.

'All right,' Nightingale said. 'Are you ready?'

She showed them through the Chapel's dank halls as if conducting a tour that had long since come to bore her, fixing only at odd moments on details that might be worthy of closer inspection. The dormitories were only dormitories, she said. Her fingers strayed to the rusted hasp of a lock. The bolt was two fingers thick.

She could not point out where her cot had been because the floor on that side had fallen through. At this time of year, she said, she had sometimes watched the moon rise above the other wing. She had dreamed of the fire, as they all did, but sometimes she had the dreams that any child might have. She dreamed of strange animals and distant lands. She dreamed that a deadly snake lived entwined about her arm, but it had not been a nightmare. The snake's head was joined to her own hand. It could not bite her even if it meant to.

At the infirmary she waited outside, since it was so narrow and cramped that they were obliged to enter one by one. She pointed to the collapsed shelves where the medicines had been kept. There were white pills that made them ravenous and sleepless, but those were given out only on the days when they were made to fight in the side yard. The honey-coloured draught made them sleepy and blissful, but the nurse kept it locked away unless someone had been wounded.

'What became of that nurse?' said Cutter. 'Or am I going to be sorry I asked?'

Nightingale's eyes slid away. 'Natural causes. Eight years ago. A pity.'

She shook her head, recovering the thread of her recollections. The girl called Robin, she said, was given the honey-coloured draught on the night she died. Robin had been troubled almost from the start, and by then – she might have been fourteen or so – nothing they did made any impression. She would lie curled up in the passageways, stirring cobwebs with her breath. She would lurch from her seat during lessons to shriek out filthy words or the names of saints. Something had broken in her that could not be mended.

One morning, Nightingale said, the master known as the Proctor had led her from the classroom and explained that she was to be taken for 'a day's work'. Not even the dull children had believed that. They knew what doing a day's work meant. It meant showing that you could follow someone unseen, or that you could pass for a well-bred boy in a smithy and come out with a fine new hunting knife. Later, to the last of the children, it would mean other things. Worse things.

'What worse things?' said Cutter, but Nightingale went on as if she had not heard. Perhaps she was coming to the answer.

That evening after supper, some of the others had drawn the story from Robin and repeated it afterwards in envy and amazement. The Proctor had taken her to some little town, she said, and he had brought her to a tea shop. She had licked the jam and cream from a bun, and afterwards she had gone to a park and fed the leftovers to the ducks. Wasn't that the proper treat, they said, and what did that mad little tramp ever do to deserve it?

But Nightingale had understood, she said. She knew what it meant, this seeming kindness, and she ought to have known what would come next. But Robin had gone to see the nurse before bed, and in the morning Nightingale had been woken by screaming, and she had gone to stand with the others over Robin's bed. The girl lay on her back, her face white and rippled blue where her veins had distended. Her limbs were stretched and taut, and the vomit had spilled over her cheek to soak the sheet. It was thin stuff, mostly whey-coloured, but there were shreds of pulp that still gleamed pink. Strawberry. The jam had been strawberry.

'Which one was he?' said Cutter, having left a small silence. 'This Proctor?'

'Not yet,' said Nightingale. 'There's something else you should see first. Veins aren't really blue. They're almost colourless, and of course the blood is red. The blue is the light that can't enter us, the light that returns.'

Cutter took this in without comment, but Octavia made a note. 'You learned many things,' she said, taking care with her tone. 'Did you learn them here?'

'They taught us things, yes.' Nightingale was leading them away already. 'But learning is something you must do for yourself.'

She showed them the schoolroom, where they had been instructed in Latin declensions and lines of succession, where a dancing master had shown them the quadrille and an armourer had instructed them in the use of a sabre. In a hall where a portrait of the sovereign still listed above an archway, she showed them where they had lined up to receive their new names.

'That was the Chaplain,' she said. 'That was Aspell, the man you found in the brothel. He whipped some of us, that first day, but most of the whipping came later. He took us to his study sometimes, but he wasn't fastidious in that way. In the schoolroom sometimes, or kneeling over our beds. Here, often enough, under this portrait. He had a rostrum that he would drag out.'

Her eyes flickered to Her Majesty's cracked likeness. She hesitated, then her voice changed again. 'He favoured boys, or they were nearer to his liking. He would strap them to his rostrum and strip their backs, or strip them entirely. It lasted for hours, sometimes, and there was often blood. Afterwards he would pleasure himself over them. Or in them. He made me watch, more than once. *Are you watching, little bird?*'

She turned away, tracing a figure along her left forearm with her forefinger. 'And I was. I was always watching.'

Nightingale wandered a little way down the hall and paused before a smeared window. Without any apparent forethought, she made a blade of her fingers and stabbed at the glass in a way that seemed precisely calibrated. The pane exploded outwards as if struck by a brick. She picked the remaining shards free and arranged them neatly on the sill. 'Sorry,' she said, noting their expressions. 'Some fresh air.'

They waited at a respectful distance, and presently she spoke again, this time in the voice that Gideon had come to think of as her own. 'I suppose I'm tired of it all now. You can look about afterwards, if you like, but I don't think there's much more I want to show you. Considine, the one I began with, his name here was the Surgeon. He had many interests. I suppose you've discovered that he was something in the Royal Society. He taught us botany at first. Sepals and calyxes. Inflorescences. I used to like the words. Later he showed us how to make poisons. Then there were the anatomy lessons. He would pierce our ears and explain why it didn't hurt. Later it was other places, so that he could explain why it did. Median, ulnar, radial. The names and the mechanisms. How we live and breathe. How we suffer.'

She waited, as still as waxwork.

'Once, after a boy called Rook died, he made us watch while he dissected the corpse. *Now, ladies and gentlemen, pay close attention please.* And I did. I paid close attention. I showed him how close, when I came for him. I gave him a lesson.

'The one in the bathhouse was called the Choirmaster. We could never really tell what he was supposed to be teaching us. I suppose it was a sort of doctrine, except that there was no God. There was Empire, sometimes, or there was duty. Mostly there was the Chapel. It was never really a place. It was a failed idea, like honour or innocence. Like England.

'Almost every sin was permissible in his theology. He showed us many examples. He would make us sit naked through lessons, and if a boy became hard he would make him stand. That delighted him particularly. He didn't touch us, though, so I didn't touch him.

I watched, like he used to watch. And the Dean, the man you saw in the museum – but no, there's no need. He kept records you can see. And I think that's almost enough.'

She led them last into the tower, having provided the Inspector with a lamp. 'The steps are old and uneven,' she said. 'You have to know them by heart.'

The darkness was enveloping, even with a lamp, and Gideon was obliged to keep a hand pressed to the wall. The stone was cold and damp to the touch. It felt crudely hewn about the edges.

He ventured a question, in part because the silence was so profound. 'A Norman keep, perhaps?'

'I don't know.' Nightingale's voice was remote. She was descending already into the dark. 'They never mentioned it. They only ever passed through here, to reach their own quarters. Or to reach the other place.'

When they reached the bottom of the tower, her manner became hushed and ceremonial. Taking Cutter's elbow, she led him slowly towards the centre of the floor. 'You'll come to stone that's raised an inch above the others. It's to mark the place in the dark. Keep behind it, there's a drop. Now raise your lamp.'

When he lifted it, Gideon saw that they were gathered on the brink of a pit that might have been six feet deep. At the bottom of the pit was a hatch of some kind, its thick staves bound and braced with tongues of beaten iron.

Once she was satisfied with their positions, Nightingale leapt down into the pit, alighting with practised ease by the lip of the hatch. She stooped and drew back a bolt, then after a moment's consideration she raised the hatch.

They could see nothing. The hatch was no more than two feet square, and the darkness beneath was perfect and unknowable. Gideon felt a coldness feathering his spine.

'The oubliette,' said Nightingale without emphasis. 'Pass me the lamp. Please.'

When Cutter had handed it down, she lowered the light carefully into the void. Gideon had been expecting some immeasurable abyss, but what he glimpsed was worse. The rough flags of the oubliette's floor were hardly four feet below the hatch. He saw vague, spreading stains. A tracery of scratch marks. Husks and needles of bone.

Having given them time to look, she climbed without any sign of trepidation into this deeper pit. Then, setting the lamp down, she folded herself neatly into the only seated position her confines allowed. Only by tucking her head between her knees could she keep it beneath the level of the opening.

'It's almost a perfect cube,' she remarked. 'Four feet on every side. It was easier when we were small, but only a little. The bones are just rats, by the way. They completed the effect, I suppose. Some of the others used them for scratching.'

'Oh, no.' It was Octavia's whisper. 'No.'

'This was the Proctor's favourite. The darkness, the silence, the cold. And the hours. The hours.'

Gideon could not see Cutter now, but he heard him shift his footing and take a considering breath. 'Will you tell us who he is now, this Proctor? He is not yet accounted for.'

'No.' Nightingale took the lamp between her hands and set it down on the floor beyond the hatch, so that only her face showed. 'I took care over all I did. I joined each end to its beginning. But him, this. You might think it was no worse than all the rest, but you didn't endure it. I was brought here more often than anyone. I spent more hours here than anyone. More days.'

She went quiet. The lamp's flame dipped and quickened. In its pool of restless shadows, her face was a still mask.

'I was locked inside myself. I am still. There is no end to that beginning. I will not tell you his name because he has none now. He has nothing but the hours. You will not find him. No one will ever find him.'

Nightingale said nothing else as she climbed from the oubliette and closed the hatch. She passed the lamp back to Cutter without a word, only lifting her chin to indicate that he should lead the way back up. It was not until she had locked the tower behind them that she spoke again.

'Where to now?' said the Inspector, when he judged that he had shown enough deference.

'You know where.' When she said it, Gideon wondered if she had chosen another voice. Perhaps some words could only be spoken softly. 'To the boneyard.'

It was a scrap of rough ground outlying what might once have been a kitchen garden, enclosed on two sides by walls of cut stone and hidden on their approach by a squalid shed. The shed's tin roof had split and folded upon itself. It had rained while they were indoors, and dregs of rainwater dripped between the sundered halves. Nightingale did not alter her pace as she drew closer, and nor did Octavia or the Inspector. Gideon let himself fall a little way behind.

When he took his place at Cutter's side, he saw that a broad tarpaulin had been stretched and pegged over the opened ground, pitched so that water was carried off to an improvised gutter. A robin was busying itself at the far edge of the cloth, and presently it fetched up a shorn worm. Nightingale gave no sign that she minded.

'I took as much care as I could,' she said. 'I read books on archaeological methods. I was patient, or I tried to be. When it rained, I stopped and covered everything. But still, I couldn't always be sure. I remembered all of it, when each of them went, but that wasn't enough. It was just a pit that they closed and reopened. They were sloppy in their work. The children were piled up, pressed close. They were damaged, by shovel blades or carelessness. They were broken.'

Cutter cleared his throat, making an effort to do it softly. 'The old soldier, in Hounslow. He buried them?'

Her gaze ranged over the covered plot. 'Three that I'm certain of. Probably more. They had another dogsbody, too. A man called Rickard. He died years ago, after a brawl. It might have been much worse for him. I didn't like that, taking one of the children whole, leaving her like that. It was the same with the boy I laid out in the brothel, or what I could find of him. I don't know about dignity. There are things I never learned to say right, or to feel right. But I know about living and dying. I know what is sacred, and what should never be touched. Was it less dignified than this, than here?'

No one offered an answer. Perhaps she did not want one.

'And I wanted them to know, the masters who were left. I wanted to lay it all bare. What was done, and what was coming.' Pointing to one corner of the tarpaulin, she tipped her head back to address the Inspector. 'Can you help with that side?'

Cutter shifted his weight and thumbed the edge of his collar, but he started forward without a word. He took his place opposite Nightingale and watched for her movements, waiting before lifting each peg and taking care to match his folds with hers. Near the top of the incline, they drew the folds taut and weighted the ends with stones she had piled up for this purpose.

Gideon observed all this without letting his eyes stray from the edges of the pit. Octavia waited with her head bowed. Neither of them looked until Cutter returned to stand next to them and Nightingale took up her own position, standing in silence a small distance apart.

No one spoke after that. The rainwater still dripped, each pulse thrumming lightly against the folds of tin. The robin lingered for a time, stitching wayward patterns above the turned earth, but when Gideon next looked up it was gone.

When she had shown them all she meant to, Nightingale led them to a scrubby field beyond the walls. At its western edge was a wiry stand of thorn trees, all thickly powdered with white blossom. She gave them a moment's consideration before seating herself on a broad hummock of stone.

'I found this place when I first came back,' she said, when they had gathered about her. 'I like it because it's out of sight of the windows. And because of this rock.' She skimmed her fingers over it. 'They would've had to plough around it. Too heavy to be moved. And why should it be moved? It's been here longer than the field. Longer than anything. We should leave things untouched, when we can.'

The Inspector chafed at his chin, no doubt anxious to begin a more practical conversation. Octavia turned to appraise the view, if only absently. She had been silent since leaving the boneyard, though she had not faltered for a moment in her notetaking.

'And the blossoms,' Gideon brought himself to say. 'Those blossoms are really quite . . .'

He abandoned the effort. It was an inane observation, and he could not seize upon an adjective that might redeem it.

'Yes,' said Nightingale. 'Those are *Prunus spinosa*. Blackthorns.'

'Ah,' said Gideon. 'Ah, indeed. Your botany lessons.'

'I learned that later,' she said, without evident displeasure. 'And these aren't poisonous. The fruit, the sloes – people put them in gin.'

'Of course, of course.' Gideon could not tell why he was persisting with this prattle. It had undone him, that open pit. That unconfrontable sorrow. Yet this was what now spilled from him. If he was returning to his former self, he hoped that the process could somehow be arrested. 'Sloe gin, yes. I have heard of it. Most restorative, they say.'

'All right, Bliss,' Cutter said. 'You might do well to take a breath of air. Well, miss – pardon me, not miss. Nightingale, then. Don't think I am carrying around a heart of stone, but we still have a few small matters to discuss.'

'Yes,' she said. 'It's why I brought you here last. And a heart of stone is what you need now. I told you, I didn't show you all this to move you to pity or tears. I did it because it's my last duty, because that end – the one you just saw – that must be joined to its beginning too. And that duty won't be mine. It can't be mine. Because by the time we leave here, I will be one of two things. I will be a murderess, a reviled beast, an abomination, or I will be a girl who is now long dead. I will still be the girl who jumped from Waterloo Bridge sixteen years ago, and whose drowned body was pulled from the water three days later. I will be long gone.'

Gideon had been observing in dutiful silence, but at this he looked up. Octavia turned too, showing no further interest in the view.

'Wait, now,' said Cutter, raising a hand. 'That part of it is neither here nor there. We have said all that needs to be—'

'I see,' said Nightingale. 'You didn't mention it at the museum because you didn't intend to mention it at all.'

'Wait,' said Cutter again, but his outstretched arm had slackened. 'Ah, Christ. *Christ.*'

'But why does it matter, that detail?' Nightingale persisted. 'After all you said, what difference does it make?'

The Inspector shook his head. 'I mean no slight in asking this – you're no fool, whatever you may be – but have you any notion how many girls are pulled from the Thames every week?'

Her eyes flicked away for a moment, then she nodded slowly. 'Of course. I never really lived there, but that is something I should have seen. A city of so many souls. And so many cruelties.'

'That it is,' said Cutter. 'And most of those who are pulled out are known to no one. The girl who was pulled out three days after you jumped would have been known to no one, but since I had reported our little encounter, I was obliged to go and look at her. Her and two others from the day before.'

'You identified her,' Octavia said. It was not an accusation. She seemed bemused, nothing more. 'You named her as your fugitive.'

'I did more than that.' Cutter swabbed a hand over his face. 'I put a blue silk gown on her. A gown I had bought myself on a sergeant's wage, and that I had steeped in river muck to make it look the part. The drowned girl looked no more like you in it, to tell you the truth, so I had foolishness on my conscience on top of desecrating some unfortunate's remains. But my head was full of your stories still, your talk of wicked masters with powerful friends, so I did what I could. Mad ravings, for all I knew, but if there was any truth in it, well – if you're going to do it, I thought to myself, you'd better make damned sure you do it right. Because such people would be inclined to make enquiries.'

'They did,' said Nightingale. 'I knew they would, when the body was found. It's why I ran. I ran, and I didn't come back. Not for a long time. I knew they would send someone, and then they would know. I had scars, from the fire.'

She held up her left hand. The marks were faint, just silvered swathes where the grain of the skin seemed altered. Perhaps they had once been more pronounced.

'Nothing like that would show,' said Cutter. 'Not after three days in the water. A fresh wound might, or a tattoo, but you had none that I could see. And she was a reasonable match, the girl I found. Our own police surgeon might have been hard-pressed.'

Nightingale considered this. 'You did a great deal for me.'

The Inspector shifted awkwardly and looked about him. He had met no one's eyes since beginning his account.

She straightened and settled her hands in her lap. 'It's easier to say things when you become someone else, but it's not really saying things. You become who you must, to achieve a particular thing, and you say what you must. It's just another instrument, another kind of knife. But when I am myself . . .'

Gideon studied her carefully. He had not heard her make this distinction before. Nor had he known her to hesitate.

'There was a boy here.' She tipped her head back minutely, in-dicating the buildings beyond the walls. 'With him, sometimes, I could speak in ordinary ways. He tried to show me, to teach me. He would laugh, sometimes, when I tried, but not always. He was the only one who got away from this place. He wanted me to come too, but I wouldn't go. I believed that I had to – well, it doesn't matter what I believed. I miss him. I would like to see him again. There are things I want to learn, if I can.'

A look passed between Gideon and Octavia, but no one spoke.

'And if I can't . . .' Again Nightingale hesitated. Her gaze was fixed before her and her fingers had tensed slightly in her lap. 'I have lived, after all. The fire was long ago, and the blossoms have come again. They are beautiful. It is beautiful, even here. I am grateful.'

'Well, that is something,' said Cutter after a time. 'I disgraced myself and made a lie of all I have done in the years since, but at least someone is grateful.'

Nightingale gave what might have been a faint sigh.

'There's nothing to regret,' she said. 'Nothing you did made any difference in the end. I would have run, and no one would have found me. No one ever did, not for all those years. Not until I made myself seen.'

'And why did you?' Octavia said. 'Why did you come back, after all that time?'

For a moment, Nightingale did not seem to hear or understand. She lowered her head, covering her left hand with her right. 'I tried not to. I tried for a long time. To touch nothing, and to keep myself untouched. But I knew I would come back one day. I knew because of my sin. My first sin. My seed.'

Gideon looked to Octavia, who only shook her head.

'Do you know about our rooms at the Asylum, at Salus House?'

Again, Octavia answered carefully. 'We know a little.'

'I was younger then. I was still learning how to watch, how to listen. I must have believed them, about the tests and the iron doors. We were special, and we were being kept safe.'

She paused, enclosing her left hand more tightly.

'I didn't understand, though. The door at the end of the wing might have kept us safe. The other children in the hospital weren't special, so they might want to get in. But why were there iron doors between the rooms? Weren't we all special? And they weren't even closed, most of the time. We knew which rooms we belonged in, and the matrons went back and forth all the time, making sure we were safe.

'Then the night of the fire came. There were twelve of us in Hawthorn No. 3, six boys and six girls. It happened very quickly. I remember girls sitting on their beds rubbing at their eyes and wondering about the strange smell. Then all we knew was that the doors were locked and the matrons wouldn't come. The fire was behind us, very close. The only way out was towards the end of the wing, towards Hawthorn No. 1. The screaming, at that door, and the banging. The black air, the heat. They were piling up already. Clawing at each other, trampling over each other.

'Then the hatch opened, in the door. With squares of wire, a grill. I didn't know that word then. The words for this are the words I had. Her face was in the wires, the matron's, and it was talking as if we were misbehaving at supper time. *Just wait quietly, children.* To the screaming children and the dying children. Her big pink-white face. She knew. She was wiping with her handkerchief, wiping the smut and the sweat, and she knew. When her teeth showed, and when she said the word *children. Children, please wait your turn.* She knew.

'I had to crawl on my belly, back through the dormitory. Had to crawl under the fire, to get to the windows. I only knew where because of the glass, because the glass showed dark still, in all that heat. I was high up when I squeezed out, so I didn't look down. First all I saw was the ladder. Against the wall, near the end of the wing. That was Hawthorn No. 1, which was for the most deserving children. One ladder only, for all of us. Only not for all of us. *Wait your turn.*

'I don't remember how I did it, that clinging and crossing between. I was still learning, about paying attention, and I could only think of one thing. There was only one thing left in the world.

'I came to the window where she was, on the other side of the iron door. The matron's station, between No. 3 and No. 2. She had a ring of keys in her hands and she was running back and forth between the two iron doors. The wire hatch in our door was shut again, but the other one was open, and I thought maybe she really did mean it. We were the least deserving, the children in Hawthorn No. 3, but maybe she was only waiting until it was safe.

'But she stopped then, stopped running between. After that, her big pink face shut and she wouldn't look anymore at the screaming door and the turning black walls. She turned away, just turned away.

'I had to smash the glass to reach the word I didn't know. The hasp to free it and pull it up. I used my wrapped black hand, in my black nightgown that tore when the glass, and I strained up hard and it gave. Then I was a black thing sliding under out of the night, I was black on the floor and I was crawling to get to her. The pink mouth and the showing teeth just stared first, but then she saw what I only was and she stood wide with her black keys in her white clutch, saying I was a selfish and disobedient wretch and I would go back in there this minute; I would wait my turn in an orderly fashion, wait my turn back in there, and she wouldn't stop and I wouldn't stop, wouldn't ever stop wanting us to breathe and live.

'I had glass taken in my hand, broken from the window. I had my torn sleeve and I wrapped it around the shining broken in my black hand. I got up on my burning feet and came very near her, because now I was truly slow and truly listening for the first time. Now I knew about small careful words. I knew about silence.

'I said, *unlock it* and that was all. She knew which door. She understood.

'But still she said more, she said about my *outrageous* and my *impudent* and who would *hear of this*, but I made her see my silence and my simple meaning and my cold edge in my black hand. Because the children, the children were barely even thumping anymore and maybe not breathing.

'I said *now, unlock it now*, but only once more because the wrong things were in her big pink sweating face and she was turning to the wrong door and the wrong end. She should have known. I could not allow that, not ever. Not ever.

'I pushed the bright glass into her, in her side where she was soft. I kept hold tight to get it back out, because I didn't know yet how much or how many places. Maybe twice, maybe five times, before she let go of the keys. Maybe I did it as many times as it wanted, because it was wound close, the black nightgown, it was a snake coiled tight and it was fierce and it was gentle and it knew. It knew the beginnings and the ends of everything. It knew the ways.

'It knew to be quick when it was done, and to slip-stumble quick through the blood black to the burned black door, and to quick-try every shivering black key until it turned, until the iron gave and opened. And I tried as hard as I could when I saw; I pulled and I grasped and I tried, but I didn't know the air I gave it, the air it feeds on. It was hell bright now, and it was feasting. It was shrieking out over the spill of them, and it was long ago and now. It was too late, and still and now it is always too late for all of them, for the deep of them, the dust of them. All twisted and stretched and open their mouths, and only the teeth white now, and so long, they are still and gone for so long and it's too late for so long, and not even breathing anymore, not even crying.'

No one moved or made a sound, when this spill of talk came to an end. The Inspector stood with his head bowed. Octavia had folded up her notebook and held it clutched at her side.

'I suppose that sounded strange,' said Nightingale at length. 'It did to me, too. I've never said all that before, not out loud. And when I began, those were the only words I could find. The words from then.'

Gently, she freed her left hand from her right. She let her breathing settle.

'That's how I burned my hand, holding that door open. I can't tell for how long. Then I had to let go. I'd let the fire in, and I didn't have long. It was too far to the ladder, when I got back outside, so I just jumped. I crashed through the roof of a glasshouse that was filled with strange plants. The Surgeon had been keeping them, I found out later. Considine, I mean. Perhaps they saved me, but I didn't feel saved. I was burned. I had new cuts, deep cuts. It was hard to breathe. I lay still. I lay down in the dark.

'But I woke up, or I was woken. Two young girls were standing over me, girls my age. But they spoke differently, like young ladies. One said, "She's awake, Lydia."

'The other said, "Well, she oughtn't to be. She crashed through Father's orchid house and it's ruined."

'Then the first girl said, "We ought to tell Father she's here. He's saving other children. He might want to save this one."

'And Lydia said, "Don't be ridiculous, Cora. Why should he want to save this creature? She's filthy, and she can't even talk. I expect she's one of the imbeciles."

'But Cora had run off already, to tell Father. I don't remember anything more, until we were on the wagon. You remember those names, I suppose?'

'Mrs Lytton and her sister,' said Cutter.

'They weren't sisters,' Nightingale said. 'And they weren't Considine's, as you already know. I don't know where he came by them. The Asylum, probably. But I had never seen them before. He must have taken them when they were infants. They had never known that place. I could tell.

'You asked why I came back. I stayed away for years, but I watched for any news. Maybe I wanted a reason. Maybe I was hoping for one. I read that the Asylum had closed years before, that it was locked up and abandoned. I wanted to see it again. It was different from this place. It was mine, what happened there. I knew there was a plaque, a little memorial. I wanted to see it. Maybe I wanted to destroy it. I was the memorial.

'I started coming once a year. The anniversary of the fire. It was dangerous, but only a little. I had ways. I dressed in mourning, with a veil. I might have been anyone. I saw no one else, anyway, not until my last visit.'

'When you met another lady in mourning,' said the Inspector.

She looked up.

'Finish your story first,' said Cutter. 'We've had a good many diversions.'

'I never stayed long. A few minutes, no more. She must have been waiting. I showed nothing, but I made myself ready. She stood near me for a little while, then she raised her veil and turned to me. It was Lydia. Older, but not changed. Perhaps more than ever what she was. "Forgive my intrusion," she said.'

She used Mrs Lytton's voice as if she had taken possession of her body. It was unearthly, this facility of hers, but she seemed to think nothing of it.

'"I only wanted to say that you have my deepest sympathy, since you are grieving someone who perished here. I am Mrs Sylvia Lytton. I oversee the trust charged with renewing the mission of this institution. We intend to begin its work again, though of course we will be mindful of the dreadful mistakes that were made. Knowing that, I hope, will be of some small comfort to you."'

Cutter worked his jaw from side to side as he took this in. 'She said no more than that?'

'She didn't need to. She didn't even need to be sure of who I was. But if she was right in her suspicions, it was more than enough. She was the inheritor of all they had done, and I wasn't just the ingrate runaway who had endangered everything. I was the filthy creature who had destroyed her father's orchid house. I was the serpent she should have crushed under her heel. And there I was, almost close enough to touch. Now, how did you know she was there?'

'What?' said Cutter. 'Oh, I didn't until just that moment. As you were talking, I hit upon the answer to a riddle that has been galling me like a bad tooth. I received a letter some weeks ago, done out in fine copperplate on handsome paper with a black border. Very much like a funeral invitation, in fact, and no doubt that was not by chance. It wasn't signed, this letter, but it was from someone who knew far more about my business than I liked. It needled me for a time, I must say. Even Sergeant Bliss took note of it, as I recall.'

Gideon answered as temperately as he could, being mindful of the more weighty matters under discussion. 'If I may, sir, I did not merely take note of it. I became gravely concerned about it, and I feel sure that I mentioned it. You were not inclined to take me into your confidence, however. Indeed, while I am glad that you have returned to the subject, I feel obliged to point out that, *sensu stricto*, you have still not done so. I would take it as great kindness, therefore, if you were to impart even the general sense of—*damn it, sir, will you for the love of God tell us what the letter said?*'

'There, you see,' said Cutter. 'Even Bliss was a bit curious. Now, as to the message, I don't have it off by heart, but it began along these lines. "I write to say that today I have cast off my mourning after many trying years." In other words, it was written in as grating a way as Mrs Lytton used to talk. It went on to say that the "beloved daughter of our house" who was "thought lost to the cruel deeps" – and she gave the exact date, in case I was in any doubt – was *something, something* "returned among us" and was sure to set about displaying the gifts that she was known for. She had to tie herself in knots then, making sure that she worked a clear threat in amongst all the flowery nonsense. I would no doubt wish to correct the official records, the letter said, since alas – I'm nearly sure she put an *alas* – this returning vision of prodigious youth cannot but remind us of our own frailty and of the *something, something* of our own mortal hour.'

'Hmm,' said Octavia. 'You did have it almost by heart.'

Gideon deliberated for a time before making any remark of his own. 'Well, sir,' he said, 'I suppose I am glad to know the substance of it, at last, but I am not sure I have grasped its intent. If Miss— that is, if Nightingale had returned, why would she mean to harm you? And why use that threat to force you to acknowledge your . . . well, your momentary lapses?'

'There was no *she* at that point. As far as I was concerned, there was only a *they*. And my guess was that they had no interest in seeing me confess my sins. They wanted me to know that they knew of them, that's all, so that I would sit up and take notice. As for the threat, I had no reason then to feel sure of myself. I knew very little about them, though I knew more than they liked, no doubt. I had let Nightingale go, sure enough, but I had also seen her land a knife in some fellow's eye at twenty paces, and before her change of heart, she had – pardon me for talking freely of you in your company – she had put a knife in some half-pint little earl. She was doing their bidding before she ran, and for all I knew she might be doing their bidding again. And then I found her knife on my doorstep, which gave me very little in the way of comfort. It wasn't until we found Coulton and Considine that I began to breathe easy again. Whatever the case, it seemed a safe enough bet that she had come back to stick something in someone, so I was inclined to keep an eye to my back.'

He turned again to Nightingale, who had shown only the faintest interest in Mrs Lytton's letter-writing and intriguing. 'Well,' he said, 'we have come near to the end of your tale, I believe.'

'Of Nightingale's tale,' she said. 'Yes, we have come to the end of that.'

The Inspector gave her a measuring look. 'In any case, I find myself in a peculiar position. First, I am obliged to thank you. You gave your word and you kept it. And all you've shown us here today, all you've told us – I won't say I'm glad to know any of it, but I'm glad it has come out. It was necessary, and even for a person as – well, I haven't yet hit on the right words – but even for you, I doubt it was easy. You did a duty today, and I am not usually a man for such high talk, but I honour you for it.

'Now, before my head starts spinning over what I have just said to a wanted murderer, I must add something else. You gave your word on another matter, too, and it is still before us. You got off to a promising start when you told us about Mrs Lytton taking over the family concern, but that's all you told us. And as I need hardly remind you, Mrs Lytton is no longer available to answer any questions. So, no more talk about joining up circles. I'm already fit to string myself up over what I *have* done, never mind what I might do next, so please, give me something I can go out and put my hands on. Tell me what you think is happening.'

Nightingale rose from her stone seat and looked about her. 'I am not going to tell you anything more,' she said placidly.

The Inspector let out a weary breath and thumbed the seams of his brow, but before he could answer she spoke again.

'I'm going to give you something,' she said. She paused, then reached beneath her neatly tailored jacket as if the thought had just come to her. She might have been concealing anything, Gideon reflected – a rare dagger, a vial of hemlock, a dripping scalp – but what she produced was an ordinary envelope. She passed it to Cutter, who accepted it with a strained look.

'And this is?'

'A deed of title, to a property that was recently purchased in Chelsea. It used to be a lying-in hospital. It will be again, in a way. The deed is in the names of the trustees of Salus House. The new trustees, not the ones from before. They're all living, except for Mrs Sylvia Lytton.'

The Inspector handled the envelope carefully. Noting a bulge, he held it up and shook it gently.

'Mrs Lytton's key,' said Nightingale. 'You should pay a visit. It's empty still, but it won't be for long. They have initials and dates, for the new arrivals. They have initials next to the deposits, too. The gentlemen paying, I expect. Inconveniences arise, even in the best of families. And newborns won't be nearly as troublesome.'

Cutter scratched at his cheek. 'Newborns?' he said. 'They'll have their work cut out. And for what? Assassins aren't that hard to come by, take it from me.'

'No memories,' said Nightingale simply. 'No awkward questions. But it's true. There are easier ways to have people killed. It's something I have wondered about. But who would they have been masters of then? It always comes down to mastery, with men of that kind. Orchids and children. Specimens to be ordered, to be named. Nothing ever left untouched.'

'If you say so,' said Cutter. 'But even so, I cannot arrest someone for bookkeeping, never mind for adopting a babe-in-arms. It is a kindly thing to do, in the general opinion.'

'You couldn't have arrested the ones who brought us here, after the fire. And you wouldn't have, not then. But you know what you know. You have time.'

At this, Cutter's lip curled and he looked away. 'I might have less time than you think.'

But Nightingale had nothing more to say. Now she was simply waiting.

It was some time before the Inspector spoke again, and when he did, it was not Nightingale he addressed. 'Bliss, Miss Hillingdon, you have both been obliged to stand for a long while with nothing much to occupy you. You would be glad to stretch your legs, I'm sure. Have a little wander, the pair of you. I will meet you at the gate.'

Gideon stared at him for a moment in bemusement, but he found he had no reasonable objection at the ready. He looked to Octavia for support, since she was seldom reluctant to speak her mind. He saw at once that there were many things she wanted to say, but she was not looking at Cutter. She was looking at Nightingale. In the end she said nothing.

Gideon understood. When Octavia had turned and walked away, he did as she had done. He looked at Nightingale, searching that illegible face for all he had hoped to understand. He could not tell who it was that looked back at him. An orphan once, maybe, and something near to kindred. An orphan twice resurrected now. Beyond that he could give only a faltering testimony. A loveless child, maybe, waking to endless dreams of fire. A creature that scales city walls to whisper last words to the merciless. An angel of death. Now and always the wound, or now and always the knife. An end joined forever to its beginning. He could not tell, and perhaps it no longer mattered.

Whoever she was, she offered him the faintest intimation of a smile. Gideon smiled back, though he was by no means sure what he felt. Maybe it was awe. Or maybe it was only sadness.

He turned and set off after Octavia, and soon he found he was walking at a steady clip. His injuries were hardly troubling him anymore, and the surrounding country no longer seemed so dour. Perhaps the Inspector had been right, after all. Perhaps he had been in need of some fresh air.

Inspector Cutter did not keep them waiting for long. Gideon and Octavia had come back to the chained gate by a meandering route, in part because they were not sure of the way and in part because they had fallen into easy conversation, never once touching on the day's events and revelations. They kept up their light talk as they waited, and even when Octavia confided that she and Suki were no longer on intimate terms, their shared levity was hardly altered.

'I thought I'd be an operatic ruin,' she said, 'but honestly, all I feel is relief. I said it was because she didn't come to see me when I was injured, and it was, in a way. I mean, how utterly disgraceful of her, though of course, I'd have been horrified if she had. With my face like that, can you imagine? I'm not terribly vain, I don't think, but I draw the line at being kissed by someone who's visibly flinching. And anyway, she was just too irredeemably rich. I thought – oh, I don't know – I suppose I thought I could alter something without altering someone, which is always misguided. She was sweet and devoted, in her way, but it's just astonishing how *impervious* the wealthy are. I did love parts of her, I suppose, but then I discovered all the parts that were three hundred years old and wanted everything just as it was.'

'Mmm,' said Gideon. 'I can see how it would be upsetting, suddenly uncovering someone's unexpected parts.'

'Gideon Bliss! Are you being wicked? I'd never have thought it— Oh, look, is that him? He seems to be alone, doesn't he?'

'He does,' Gideon said. 'But I'm sure he'll be happy to explain.'

'Oh, eager to explain,' Octavia agreed. 'Look at him, he's practically bursting with news. He can hardly contain himself. Should we show him where that gap in the hedge is? It was quite tricky to find.'

Gideon glanced through the bars of the gate, but Cutter had already stalked out of view. 'Too late, I'm afraid. But I'm sure there's no need. We were distracted, whereas the Inspector is a man of single-minded resolve. I'm sure he'll emerge any moment now.'

It was several minutes, however, before Cutter made an appearance in the lane, and when he did, he was not serene in his demeanour. 'One cursed thicket after another!' he bellowed. 'And what are you waiting over there for?'

Gideon might have reminded him of his own instructions, but he found he lacked the inclination. Instead, he simply raised a placatory hand. 'Well,' he said, 'I suppose we'd better hurry over there.'

'Oh, at once,' said Octavia. 'In fact, we really ought to race each other. He'd appreciate that.'

When she raised a hand to cover her giggle, Gideon had to turn away so that Cutter wouldn't see why he was bent double. Octavia was still dabbing at her eyes when he managed at last to compose himself.

'Oh, dear,' she said. 'I don't know what's got into me, do you? I feel as if it's the last day of term.'

'I do too,' said Gideon. 'I mean, I was always going somewhere just as bleak on the last day of term, but still. It's very strange.'

'And after all that,' said Octavia. 'After all we—'

'I know. I know what you mean.'

'Is it dreadful of us, do you think? Are we monsters?'

'I don't know,' said Gideon. He wiped the last wet traces from his own cheek. He hadn't ever cried with laughter before, he was almost sure. 'I just don't know anymore.'

'Well,' said Cutter, as they came within scowling distance. 'You made the most of your leisure time, I see.'

For once, Gideon felt no obligation to answer. 'And you, sir?'

'Right,' said the Inspector, as if he had not heard. He lifted a hand and squinted against the late sun. 'We had better be off.'

'Sir,' said Gideon. 'She is not with you. Does that mean you decided—'

'Nothing is decided,' said Cutter, settling his coat about his shoulders. 'I told her I must reflect on the matter. I told her I would go for a walk and turn it over in my mind, as I often do in such cases.'

'And?' said Gideon. He looked to Octavia, who only shrugged.

'And I am going for a walk.' Cutter righted his hat, and without further ceremony he set off at an energetic pace towards the next bend in the lane. That way would lead them at length to the road for Guildford, where coaches could be boarded that would take them to the London train.

Gideon looked to Octavia again, but this time there was no unspoken question. He could not read her face, but then he could hardly make sense of his own thoughts. They stood for a moment, allowing Cutter to gain a little distance, then they fell in behind him without a word.

'I've just remembered,' said Gideon, after they had gone a little way in silence. 'There was something else I meant to ask him. He talked about not having much time.'

Octavia didn't answer at once. There was a chill in the air now, but the day had brightened a little as it drew to a close. The bird-song was softening among the dogwoods and the elders, and the light was growing dissolute with colour. Madder and sienna. Fading cadmium.

'Yes, I heard. And I saw your face. He's written a letter of resignation, I think.'

Gideon fell silent. He had come upon a supple wand of willow and he was trailing it lightly over tender drifts of early nettles. He ought to feel stricken, perhaps. But there were many things he ought to feel.

'I don't think he's submitted it,' Octavia said. 'Or that he's made up his mind. He seems rather uncertain lately.'

'Mmm,' said Gideon. They had rounded a bend, and before them the lane ribboned westwards. Cutter could be seen off in the distance, upright and unflagging amid the shorn fields and the deepening folds of shadow. 'Though you wouldn't think it to look at him now. He's ravenous, I expect, and hell-bent on reaching Leggett's before the kitchens close.'

'What about you?' Octavia said. 'Will you be joining him?'

Gideon's gaze had drifted out to the furthest fields. The dusk was deeper there, and the ground was glazed with colours he couldn't name. Foxglove, maybe, and something like amethyst. He thought about it, but he hadn't yet made up his mind. That was all right. It would be all right. There was still time.

About the Author

Paraic O'Donnell is a writer of fiction, poetry and criticism. His first novel, *The Maker of Swans*, was named the Amazon Rising Stars Debut of the Month for February 2016 and was shortlisted for the Bord Gáis Energy Irish Book Awards in the Newcomer of the Year category. His second novel, *The House on Vesper Sands*, was a *Guardian* and *Observer* Book of the Year, and an Oprah Daily and CrimeReads Best Historical Novel of 2021. He lives in Wicklow, Ireland with his wife and two children.

http://vspr.st | @paraicodonnell